**THE SEAFORT SAGA**

"A ripping good read – the sort of thing that attracted us all to SF in the first place"
*S. M. Stirling*

"Something special indeed . . . Feintuch has at last captured for the science fiction community the quintessential spirits of greats such as C. S. Forester and F. Van Wyck Mason" *Bill Baldwin*

"An excellent entertainment" *Analog*

"Feintuch has constructed a fascinating story . . . You'll find his adventures highly entertaining"
*Science Fiction Chronicle*

"An excellent job of transferring Hornblower to interstellar space. A thoroughly enjoyable read"
*David Drake*

D1419884

*By David Feintuch:*

**The Seafort Saga**

# Midshipman's HOPE

## DAVID FEINTUCH

ORBIT

An *Orbit* Book

First published in Great Britain by Orbit 1996
Reprinted 1997 (twice), 1998, 1999

This edition published by arrangement with Warner Books, Inc., New York

A CIP catalogue record for this book
is available from the British Library.

ISBN 1 85723 434 0

Printed and bound in Great Britain by Clays Ltd, St Ives plc

Orbit
A Division of
Little, Brown and Company (UK)
Brettenham House
Lancaster Place
London WC2E 7EN

*To Ragtime Rick of Toledo, and Ardath Mayhar,*
*who made it possible,*
*and to Jettie,*
*who makes it worthwhile.*

# MIDSHIPMAN'S HOPE

*Being the first voyage
of Nicholas Seafort, U.N.N.S.,
in the year of our Lord 2194*

# PART I

October 12, in the year
of our Lord 2194

# 1

"Stand to!" I roared, but I was too late; even as Alexi and Sandy snapped to attention, *Hibernia*'s two senior lieutenants strolled around the corridor bend.

We froze in stunned tableau: I, the senior midshipman, red with rage; a portly passenger, Mrs. Donhauser, jaw agape at the blob of shaving cream on her tunic; my two middies stiffened against the bulkhead, eyes locked front, towels and canisters still clutched in their hands; Lieutenants Cousins and Dagalow, dumbfounded that middies could be caught cavorting in the corridors of a U.N.N.S. starship, even one still moored at Ganymede Orbiting Station.

If only I'd come down from the bridge a few seconds sooner I'd have been in time, but I'd been helping Ms. Dagalow enter the last of our new stores into the puter's manifests.

Lieutenant Cousins was curt. "You too, Mr. Seafort. Against the bulkhead."

"Aye aye, sir." I stiffened to attention, eyes front, furious at my betrayal by a friend whose sense I'd thought I could trust.

Alexi Tamarov, the sweating middy at my side, was sixteen and third in seniority. When I'd first reported aboard, he'd considered challenging me but hadn't, and we'd since become comrades. Now his antics with Sandy had gotten us all in hot water.

Across the gleaming corridor Ms. Dagalow's eye betrayed a glint of humor as she pried the canister of shaving cream from Sandy Wilsky's reluctant fingers. She passed it to Lieutenant Cousins. Once again, I wished she were the senior lieutenant; Mr. Cousins seemed to take undue pleasure in the ship's discipline he dispensed.

Lieutenant Cousins snapped, "Yours, middy? Are you old enough to use it?" From close observation during the five weeks since I'd joined *Hibernia* at Earthport Station, I knew that at fourteen Sandy had not yet made the acquaintance of a razor. That meant he had, um, borrowed it. From me, perhaps. At seventeen, I was known to shave, if rarely.

"No, sir." Sandy had no choice but to answer. "It's Mr. Holser's." I bit my lip. Lord God, that was all this fiasco needed: trouble with Midshipman Vax Holser.

Vax, almost nineteen, resented me and didn't care if it showed, for he'd missed being first middy by only a few weeks. He was full-grown, shaved daily, and worked out with weights. His surly manner and ominous strength encouraged us all to give him a wide berth.

Lieutenant Cousins nodded to Mrs. Donhauser, whose outrage had subsided into wry amusement. "Madam, my sincere apologies. I assure you these children"—he spat out the word with venom—"will not trouble you again." His look of suppressed fury did not bode well.

"No harm done," Mrs. Donhauser said peaceably. "They were just playing—"

"Is that what you call it?" Mr. Cousins's grip tightened on the canister. "Officers in a Naval starship, chasing each other with shaving soap!"

Mrs. Donhauser was unfazed. "I won't tell you your duty, Lieutenant. But I will make it clear that I was not harmed and have no grievance. Good day." With that she turned on her heel toward the passenger cabins, presumably to change her tunic.

For a moment Lieutenant Cousins was speechless. Then he rounded on us. "You're the sorriest joeys I've ever seen! A seventeen-month cruise to Hope Nation, and I have to sail with *you!*"

I took a deep breath. "I'm sorry, sir. It's my responsibility."

"At least you know that much." Cousins's tone was acid. "Is this how you run your wardroom, Mr. Seafort?"

"No, sir." I wasn't sure it was the right response. Perhaps

my amiable manner encouraged Sandy and Alexi to step out of line. Certainly they would never have done so under Vax Holser's tutelage.

"I expect stupidity from these young dolts, but it's your job to control them! What if the Captain had come along?"

Lord God forbid. If they'd squirted Captain Haag rather than Mrs. Donhauser, Alexi and Sandy would see the barrel, if not the brig. For good measure, the Captain might break me all the way down to ship's boy. Mr. Cousins was right. I could think of no way to placate him, so I said nothing.

It was a mistake. "Answer me, you insolent pup!"

To my surprise, Lieutenant Dagalow intervened. "Mr. Cousins, Nick was on watch. He couldn't have known—"

"It's his job to keep his juniors in line!"

I did, when I was present. What more could I do?

For some reason Ms. Dagalow persisted. "But they're young, we're moored to Ganymede Station, they were just letting off steam . . ."

"Lisa, take your nose out of the puter long enough to remember the rest of your job. We have to teach them to act like adults!" From another officer it might have been a blistering rebuke, but Mr. Cousins's acid manner was well known to all, and she took no notice.

"They'll learn."

"When our shaving cream runs out?" Cousins glared at us with withering contempt before turning back to Ms. Dagalow. "Consider that by the end of the cruise at least some of them should be fit to be officers. I grant you, it's unlikely any of these fools will ever make lieutenant. But what if one of us is transferred out at Hope Nation? Do you want silly boys standing watch, fresh from shaving cream fights?"

"We've time to teach them. Nick will issue ample demerits." I certainly would. Each demerit would have to be worked off by two hours of hard calisthenics. They'd keep Alexi and Sandy out of trouble for a while.

Lieutenant Cousins's voice grew cold. "Will he?" A chill of foreboding crept down my rigid spine. "Nicky should never have been senior, we all know that." Even Lieutenant Dagalow frowned at the blatant undercutting of my authority, but Mr. Cousins was oblivious. "He'll wag his finger at them, as always." That wasn't fair; I'd kept wardroom matters from the attention of the other officers, as was expected. Except this once.

"Will you cane the two of them, then? After all, it's a wardroom affair."

"No, I'll let Nicky handle them." From the corner of my eye I saw Alexi's shoulders slump with relief. Then Mr. Cousins added sweetly, "But perhaps I can teach Mr. Seafort more diligence." He sauntered toward his cabin. "Come along, middy."

A half hour later I stood outside our wardroom, jaw aching from my failed effort not to cry out, eyes burning from the stinging pain and mortifying humiliation Mr. Cousins had inflicted across the hated barrel.

I slapped open the hatch. Inside the cramped compartment Sandy and Alexi, on their beds, dared say nothing. I crossed slowly to my bunk, stripped off my jacket and laid it on the chair. With care, I eased myself onto my bed.

After a time Alexi said quietly, "Mr. Seafort, I'm sorry. Truly." As was the custom, Alexi called me by my surname even within our wardroom. After all, I was senior middy. Only Vax Holser had the resources to ignore that tradition and get away with it.

I fought down a smoldering rage; it should have been Alexi who was caned, not I. "Thank you." My thighs smarted with exquisite agony. "You should have known better, both of you."

"I know, Mr. Seafort."

I closed my eyes, trying to will away the pain. At Academy, sometimes, it worked. "Who started it?"

"I did," they said in unison.

My fingers throttled the pillow. "Sandy, you first."

"We were in the head, washing up. Alexi splashed me. I splashed back." He glanced up, saw my face, gulped.

Skylarking, like cadets at Academy. "Go on."

"After he flicked me with a towel I grabbed the shaving cream. He chased me so I ran outside, and I was squirting him when Mrs. Donhauser came out of the lounge." I said nothing. After a moment he blurted, "Mr. Seafort, I'm sorry I got you into troub—"

"I'll make you sorrier!" I sat up, thought better of it, eased myself back on my bunk. "No officer would look into the middy's head to see how you behave. But running out into the corridor . . . Mr. Cousins is right; you *are* dolts."

Alexi flushed; Sandy studied his fingernails.

Angry as I was, I wasn't surprised that they'd frolicked like the boys they were. What else could be expected, even on a starship? One had to go to space young to spend life as a sailor, else the risk of melanoma T was too great. Unfortunately, aboard such an immense and valuable vessel as *Hibernia*, there was no room for youngsters' folly.

I growled, "Four demerits apiece, for letting your foolishness get out of hand." Severe, but Mr. Cousins would have given much worse, and my buttocks stung like fire. "I'll write it as improper hygiene. Alexi, two extra for you."

"But I started it!" Sandy's protest was from the heart.

"You ran into the corridor, which should have ended it. Mr. Tamarov chose to follow. Alexi, how many does that give you?"

"Nine, Mr. Seafort." He was pale.

I growled, "Work them off fast, because I'm in no mood to overlook any offense." Ten would earn him a caning, like I'd just been given; Alexi would have to be vigilant while he worked down his demerits. "Start now; you have two hours before lunch."

"Aye aye, Mr. Seafort." They scrambled out of their bunks. In a moment they'd slipped on shoes and jackets and departed for the exercise room, leaving me the solitude I'd sought. I rolled onto my stomach and surrendered to my misery.

"It's time, Mr. Seafort." Alexi Tamarov jolted me from my fretful dream, from Father's bleak kitchen, the creaky chair, the physics text I'd struggled to master under Father's watchful eye.

I shoved away Alexi's persistent hand. "We don't cast off 'til midwatch." Groggy, I blinked myself awake.

From the hatchway, Vax Holser watched with a sardonic grin. "Let him sleep, Tamarov. Lieutenant Malstrom won't mind if he's late."

I surged out of my bunk in dizzy confusion. Reporting late to duty station would be a matter for Mr. Cousins, and after the incident two days prior, Lord God help me if I called his attention anew. I glanced at my watch. I'd slept six hours!

In frantic haste I snatched my blue jacket from the chair, thrust my arms into my sleeves as I polished the tip of a shoe against the back of my trouser leg.

"Why do we bother waking you?" Vax sounded disgusted. I didn't answer; he left for his duty station in the comm room, Sandy Wilsky tagging behind him.

"Thanks, Alexi," I muttered, and nearly collided with him in the hatchway. I scrambled into the circumference corridor and ran past the east ladder, smoothing my hair and tugging at my tie as I rounded the bend to the airlock. I'd barely reached my station when Captain Haag's voice echoed through the speaker.

"Uncouple mooring lines!"

Lieutenant Malstrom returned my salute in offhand fashion, his eye on the suited sailor untying our forward safety line from the shoreside stanchion.

"Line secured, sir," the seaman said, and by the book I repeated it to Mr. Malstrom as if he hadn't heard. The lieutenant waved me permission to proceed.

"Close inner lock, Mr. Howard. Prepare for breakaway." I tried for the tone of authority that came so naturally to *Hibernia*'s lieutenants.

"Aye aye, sir." Seaman Howard keyed the control; the thick transplex hatches slid shut smoothly, joining in the center to form a tight seal.

Lieutenant Malstrom opened a compartment, slid a lever downward. From within the airlock, a brief hum, and a click. He signaled the bridge. "Forward inner lock sealed, sir. Capture latches disengaged."

"Very well, Mr. Malstrom." Captain Haag's normally gruff voice sounded detached through the caller. The ship's whistle blew three short blasts. After a moment the Captain's remote voice sounded again. "Cast off!"

Our duties performed, Lieutenant Malstrom and I had little to do but watch while our side thrusters alternately released tiny jets of propellant in quick spurts, rocking us gently. Our airlock suckers parted reluctantly from their counterparts on the station lock. U.N.S. *Hibernia* slowly drifted free of Ganymede Station. When we were clear by about ten meters I glanced up at Lieutenant Malstrom. "Shall we secure, sir?" He nodded.

I gave the order. The alumalloy outer hatches slid shut, barring our view of the receding station. Lieutenant Malstrom keyed our caller. "Forward hatch secured, sir."

"Secured; very well." The Captain seemed preoccupied, as well he might. On the bridge he and the Pilot would be readying *Hibernia* for Fusion. I felt a bit queasy as our weight diminished. We were slowly losing the benefits of the station's gravitrons, and the Captain hadn't yet brought our own on-line.

We waited in silence, each lost in his own thoughts. "Say good-bye, Nicky." Lieutenant Malstrom's tone was soft.

"I already did, sir, back in Lunapolis." I would miss Cardiff, of course, and aloft, the familiar warrens of Lunapolis. I would even miss Farside Academy, where I'd trained as a cadet three years ago. But Ganymede Station was another matter. It had been over a month since I'd cried out my regrets in an unnoticed corner of a service bar in down-under Lunapolis, and by now I was long ready.

The fusion drive kicked in. In the rounded porthole the stars shifted red, then blue. As the drive reached full strength they slowly faded to black.

We were Fused.

External sensors blind, *Hibernia* hurtled out of the Solar System on the crest of the N-wave generated by our drive.

"All hands, stand down from launch stations." The Captain's voice seemed husky.

I locked Seaman Howard's transmitter in the airlock safe.

"Chess, Nick?" Lieutenant Malstrom asked when the sailor had departed.

"Sure, sir." We headed up-corridor to officers' country. In the lieutenant's bleak cabin, a windowless gray cubicle four meters square and two and a half meters high, Mr. Malstrom tossed the chessboard onto his bunk. I sat on the gray navy blanket at the foot of the bed; he settled by the starched white pillow at the head.

"I'm going to learn to beat you," he said, setting up the pieces. "Something I can concentrate on besides ship's routine." I smiled politely. I had no intention of letting him win; chess was one of my few accomplishments. At home in

Cardiff I had been semifinalist in my age group, before Father brought me to Academy at thirteen.

We played the half-minute rule, loosely enforced. In the weeks since *Hibernia* had left Earthport Station I'd won twenty-three times, he had won twice. This time it took me twenty-five moves. As was our habit we shook hands gravely after the game.

"When we get back from Hope Nation I'll be thirty-five." He sighed, perhaps a trifle morosely. "You'll be twenty."

"Yes, sir." I waited.

"What do you regret more?" he asked abruptly. "The years you'll lose, or being cooped in the ship so long?"

"I don't see them as lost years, sir. When I get back I'll have enough ship's time to make lieutenant, if I pass the boards. I wouldn't even be close if I stayed home." I didn't dare tell him how strongly the ambition burned within me.

He said nothing, and I reflected a moment. "Thirty-four months, round-trip. I don't know, sir. I tested low for claustrophobia, like all of us." I risked a grin. "It depends whether it's three years playing chess with you or being reamed out by Lieutenant Cousins." For a moment I thought I'd overstepped myself, but it was all right.

Lieutenant Malstrom let out a long, slow breath. "I won't criticize a brother officer, especially to one of junior rank like yourself. I merely wonder aloud how he ever got into Academy."

Or out of it, I added silently. If only Mr. Malstrom had been the one assigned to teach us navigation. But his primary duties were ship security and passenger liaison. Judiciously, I said nothing.

I wandered back to the wardroom. Inside, Sandy Wilsky sat attentively on the deck, legs crossed. From his bed, Vax Holser scowled. "Well?"

With a shrug of despair Sandy blurted, "I don't know, Mr. Holser."

Vax's eyes narrowed. "You're not by some chance still a cadet? Have we a genuine middy who can't find the munitions locker?"

I crossed to my bunk, ignoring the boy's hopeful look. Vax was entitled to haze him a bit. We all were; Sandy was junior and just out of Academy.

"I'm sorry." Sandy glanced to me as if for succor, but I offered none. A middy should know such things. I kicked off my shoes, flopped on my bed.

Vax demanded, "What's the Naval Mission?"

Sandy took a hopeful breath. "The mission of the United Nations Naval Service is to preserve the United Nations Government of and under Lord God, and to protect colonies and outposts of human habitation wherever established. The Naval Service is to defend the United Nations and its—its . . ." He faltered.

Vax glared, and finished for him. "—and its territories from all enemies, internal or foreign, to transport all interstellar cargoes and goods, to convey such persons to and from the colonies who may have lawful business among them, and to carry out such lawful orders as Admiralty may from time to time issue. Section 1, Article 5 of the regs."

"Yes, Mr. Holser."

Vax said, "It's worth a demerit or two, Nicky."

I made no answer. If Vax had his way, the juniors would spend their lives in the exercise room. Within the wardroom, only I could issue demerits, though Vax could make the middies' lives miserable in other ways.

"Laser controls?"

"In the gun—I mean, the comm room." The youngster wrinkled his brow. "No, it must be . . . I mean . . ."

Vax scowled. "How many push-ups would it take—"

A few push-ups wouldn't hurt Sandy—we'd all been subjected to worse hazing—but Vax got on my nerves. He even had the boy calling him "Mr. Holser," which I resented. By tradition, only the senior middy was addressed as "Mr." by the juniors.

I snapped, "Laser controls are in the comm room. You should know that—were you asleep during gunnery practice?"

"No, Mr. Seafort." A faint sheen of perspiration; now he had us both annoyed at him.

I made my tone less grating. "On some ships the lasers are in a separate compartment called the gunroom, which is also what old-fashioned ships call their middy's berth."

"Thank you." Sandy sounded appropriately humble.

Vax growled, "He should have known it."

"You're right. Not knowing your way around the ship is a disgrace, Sandy. Give me twenty push-ups." It was a kindness. Vax would have made it fifty.

Dinner, as usual, was in the ship's dining hall rather than the officers' mess. I sat at my place sipping ice water, waiting for the clink of the glass. When it came I stood with the rest of the officers and passengers, my head bowed. Captain Haag, stocky, graying, and distinguished, began the nightly ritual.

"Lord God, today is October 19, 2194, on the U.N.S. *Hibernia*. We ask you to bless us, to bless our voyage, and to bring health and well-being to all aboard."

"Amen." Chairs scraped as we sat. The Ship's Prayer has been said at evening in every United Nations vessel to sail the void for one hundred sixty-seven years, and always by the Captain, as representative of the government, and therefore of the Reunified Church. Like crewmen everywhere, our sailors considered shipping with a parson to be unlucky, and any minister who sailed in *Hibernia* did so in his private capacity. Few ships had it otherwise.

"Good evening, Mr. Seafort."

"Good evening, ma'am." Mrs. Donhauser, imposing in her elegant yet practical satin jumpsuit, was the Anabaptist envoy to our Hope Nation colony. "Did yoga go well today?"

She smiled her appreciation of my offering. Mrs. Donhauser believed that daily yoga would get her to Hope Nation sane and healthy. Her stated mission was to convert every last one of the two hundred thousand residents to her creed. Knowing her, I had no reason to disbelieve it was possible.

Our state religion was the amalgam of Protestant and Catholic ritual that had been hammered out in the Great Yahwehist Reunification after the Armies of Lord God repressed the Pentecostal heresy. Nonetheless, the U.N. Government tolerated splinter sects such as Mrs. Donhauser's. Still, I wondered how the Governor of Hope Nation would react if she succeeded too well in her mission. Like Captain Haag, the Governor was ex-officio a representative of the true Church.

*Hibernia* carried eleven officers on her long interstellar voyage: four middies, three lieutenants, Chief Engineer, Pilot, Ship's Doctor, and the Captain. We all took our breakfast and lunch in the spartan and simple officers' mess, but we sat with our passengers for the evening meal.

Our hundred thirty passengers, bound for the thriving Hope Nation colony or continuing on to Detour, our second stop, had their informal breakfast and lunch in the passengers' mess.

Belowdecks, our crew of seventy—engine room hands, comm specialists, recycler's mates, hydroponicists, the ship's boy, and the less skilled crewmen who toiled in the galley or in the purser's compartments caring for our many passengers—took all their meals in the seamen's mess below.

Places at dinner were assigned monthly by the purser, except at the Captain's table, where seating was by Captain Haag's invitation only. This month I was assigned to Table 7. In my regulation blues—navy-blue pants, white shirt, black tie, spit-polished black shoes, blue jacket with insignia and medals, and ribbed cap—I always felt stiff and uncomfortable at dinner. I wished again I could wear the uniform with Vax Holser's confident style.

At his neighboring table Chief Engineer McAndrews chatted easily with a passenger. Grizzled and stolid, the Chief ran his engine room with unpretentious efficiency. To me he was friendly but reserved, as he seemed to be with all the officers.

The stewards brought each table its tureen of thick hot mushroom soup. We dished it out ourselves. Ayah Dinh, the Pakistani merchant directly across from me, sucked his soup greedily. Everyone else affected not to notice. Mr. Barstow, a florid sixty-year-old, glared as if daring me to speak to him. I chose not to. Randy Carr, immaculate and athletic, wearing an expensive pastel jumpsuit, smiled politely but looked through me as if I were nonexistent. His aristocratic son Derek strongly resembled him in appearance, and copied his manner. Sixteen and haughty, he did not deign to smile at crew; what courtesy he had was reserved for passengers.

"I started a diary, Nicky." Amanda Frowel favored me with a welcome smile. Our civilian education director was twenty, I'd learned. I'd thought her smile was for me alone, until I'd seen her offer it to all the other midshipmen and two of the lieutenants. Ah, well.

I focused on her comment. "What did you write in it?"

"The start of my new life," she said simply. "The end of my old." Amanda was en route to Hope Nation to teach natural science. It was common practice to have a passenger fill the post of education director.

"Are you sure you mean that?" I asked. "Doesn't your new life really start when you arrive, not when you leave?" I took a bite of salad.

Theodore Hansen cut in before she could answer. "Exactly so. The boy is correct." A soy merchant, he was investing three years of his life to found new soy plantations with the hybrid seed in our holds. If all went well he'd be a millionaire many times over, instead of the few times he already was.

"No, Mr. Hansen." Her tone was calm. "That would only be true if the voyage is a hiatus in life, just a waiting period before I get to Hope Nation and resume living."

Young Derek Carr snorted with disdain. "What else could it be? Is this"—he waved a hand airily—"what you call living?"

His tone offended me but I had no standing to object. Miss Frowel, though, seemed not to notice. "Yes, I call this living," she told him. "I have a comfortable berth, lectures to arrange, a trunkful of holovid chips to read, enjoyable dining, and pleasant company to share the voyage."

Randy Carr poked his son ungently in the ribs. The boy glared at him; he glowered back. Some signal passed between them. After a moment Derek said coolly, "Forgive me if I was rude, Miss Frowel," not sounding greatly concerned.

She smiled and the conversation turned elsewhere. As I finished my baked chicken I closed my ears and imagined the two of us alone in her cabin. Well, it would be a long voyage. We'd see.

"So you finally got something right, Mr. Seafort!" Lieutenant Cousins examined my solution on the plotting screen, rubbing his balding head. "But Lord God, can't Mr. Tamarov even learn the basics? If he's ever let loose on a bridge he'll destroy his vessel!"

Mr. Cousins had us calculating when to Defuse to locate the derelict U.N.S. *Celestina*, lost a hundred twelve years ago with all hands. I checked Alexi's solution out of the corner of my eye. He'd made a math error matching stellar velocities. Basically correct, except for the one lapse, but his omission could have been catastrophic. Perhaps *Celestina* had foundered because of some careless navigation error. No one knew.

"I'm very sorry, sir," Alexi said meekly.

"You're very sorry indeed, Mr. Tamarov," the lieutenant echoed. "Of all the middies in the Navy, I get you! Perhaps Mr. Seafort and Mr. Holser will inspire you to study your Nav text. If they don't, I will."

Not good; it was an open invitation to Vax Holser to redouble his hazing, and there was already bad blood between the two.

I had nothing against hazing; we all had to go through it and it strengthens character, or so they say, but Vax took a sadistic pleasure in it that disturbed me. Naturally, as first middy, I'd hazed Alexi and Sandy myself. From time to time I'd had one or the other of them stand on a chair in the wardroom in his shorts for a couple of hours, reciting ship's regs, or given extra mop-up duty for minuscule infractions. As low men, they had to expect that sort of thing, and did. I decided to keep an eye open. I couldn't wholly protect Alexi from Vax, who was second in seniority, but I could try to keep the brooding middy from going too far.

"Back to work." With an irritable swipe, Mr. Cousins cleared Alexi's screen and brought up another plot.

Of course, our calculations were only simulated, with the help of Darla, the ship's puter. In reality *Hibernia* was Fused and all our outer sensors were blind.

Our first stop was to be at *Celestina*, if we could find her without too much delay. She was but a small object, and deep in interstellar space. Then, after many months, we would drop off supplies at Miningcamp, sixty-three light-years distant, before completing our run to Hope Nation. But simulation or no, Lieutenant Cousins expected perfection, and rightly so.

While the fusion drive made interstellar travel practical, the drive was inherently inaccurate by up to six percent of the distance traveled in Fusion. So, we aimed for a point at least six percent of our journey from our target system, stopped, recalculated, and Fused again, as a safeguard against blindly Fusing into a sun, which had happened at least once in the early days. During Fusion our external instruments were useless; we couldn't determine our position until we actually turned off the drive.

I tapped at the keys. So many variables. Our N-waves traversed the galaxy faster than any known form of communication. Though the Navy talked of sending out messenger drones equipped with fusion drive, in practice it didn't work well. The drones frequently disappeared, and no one knew just why. You'd think a puter could handle a ship as well as a mere human, but—

"Pay attention, Seafort!"

"Aye aye, sir!" I squinted at the screen, corrected my error.

Anyway, engineering a fusion drive was so expensive, it made more sense for the Navy to surround it with a manned ship, to ferry passengers and supplies to our colonies as well as mere messages.

Perhaps someday, if the drones were perfected, our profession would be obsolete. It would be a shame. Ours was a glamorous career, despite the slight risk of developing melanoma T, the vicious carcinoma triggered by long exposure to fusion fields.

Fortunately, humans whose cells were exposed to N-waves within five years of puberty seemed almost immune, though there were exceptions. Even for adults going interstellar for the first time, the risks weren't excessive, but they grew with each successive voyage. So, officers were started young, and crew men and women were recruited for short—

"Daydreaming again, Mr. Seafort? If it's about a young lady, you could go to your wardroom for privacy."

"No, sir. Sorry, sir." Blushing, I bent over the console, my fingers flying.

One way to determine our location was to plot our position relative to three known stars and consult the star charts in the ship's puter. We could also calculate the energy variations recorded during Fusion and estimate the percentage of error that would result. This method gave us a sphere of error; we could be at any point in the sphere. Then we merely had to calculate what our target would look like and see if we observed anything that matched.

I don't care what the textbooks say. Navigation is more art than science.

When nav drill was over at last, I chewed out Alexi and sent him to the wardroom with a chip of Lambert and Greeley's *Elements of Astronavigation* for his holovid.

# 2

The clock ticked against me. Blindfolded, I felt for the bulkheads, hoping not to trip over an unexpected obstacle. I groped my way to a hatch. Lockable from the inside, full-size handle. That meant I was in a passenger's cabin. I felt my way out to the corridor. I turned left, arbitrarily, and walked slowly, my arm scraping along the corridor bulkhead. I sensed I was moving upward, almost imperceptibly. It meant I was coming to a ladder.

One of our training exercises was to figure out where we were, without sight. We'd be given a Dozeoff and would wake some minutes later, Lord God knew where. If we took too long to orient ourselves, we were demerited. I suppose, if a ship's power backups and all our emergency lighting failed at once, the drill could be useful. But I couldn't imagine a situation that would cause that to happen.

I bumped into the ladder railing. It extended both up and down; that meant I was on Level 2, in passenger country. Amanda's cabin was somewhere near; as our friendship had progressed I'd finally been invited inside it.

Where was I, east or west? If east, there'd be an exercise room about twenty steps past the railing. I couldn't remember what was west, except that it wasn't the exercise room. Throwing caution aside to improve my time I staggered down the passage. If Mr. Cousins had put a chair in the corridor I was done for.

No exercise room. "Passenger quarters, second level west, about fifteen meters west of the ladder, sir."

"Very good, Nicky." Lieutenant Malstrom's voice. I took off the blindfold and blinked in the light. I grinned, and he smiled back. I could imagine how our first lieutenant would have said the same thing.

Cut out three foam rubber disks an inch thick, set them one on top of another, and stick a short pencil through the center. Now stand the pencil on end. You'd have a rough model of our ship. The engine room was within the pencil underneath the disks; below that sat the drive itself, flaring into the wave emission chamber at the stubby end of the pencil.

We, crew and passengers, lived and worked in the three disks. The portion of the pencil above the disks would be our cargo holds, full of equipment and supplies for the colony on Hope Nation and for Miningcamp.

A circular passage called the circumference corridor ran around each disk, dividing it into inner and outer segments. To either side, hatches opened onto the disk's cabins and compartments. At intervals along the corridor, airtight hatches were poised to slam shut in case of decompression; they'd seal off each section from the rest.

Two ladders—stairwells, in civilian terms—ascended from the east and west sections of Level 3 to the lofty precincts of Level 1. The bridge was on the uppermost level, along with the officers' cabins and the Captain's sacrosanct quarters I'd never been allowed to view.

Level 2 was passenger country, holding most of the passenger staterooms. A few passengers were lodged above on Level 1, and the remainder had cabins below on Level 3, where the crew was housed.

Passenger cabins were about twice the size of those given the lieutenants. Below, the Level 3 crew berths made even our crowded middy wardroom seem luxurious. Naval policy was to crowd us for sleeping but allow us ample play room. The crew had a gymnasium, theater, rec room, privacy rooms, and its own mess.

The exercise over, Mr. Malstrom and I climbed up to Level 1.

I had just time enough to get ready for my docking drill on the bridge. I showered carefully before reporting to Captain

Haag. I still only shaved about once a week, so I had no problem there.

I dressed, tension beginning to knot my stomach. Though I was a long way from making lieutenant, I had no hope of eventual promotion until I could demonstrate to the Captain some basic skill at pilotage.

I gave my uniform a last tuck, took a deep breath, and knocked firmly on the bridge hatch. "Permission to enter bridge, sir."

"Granted." The Captain, standing by the Nav console, didn't bother to turn around. He'd sent for me, and he knew my voice.

I stepped inside. Lieutenant Lisa Dagalow, on watch with Captain Haag, nodded civilly. Though she'd never gone out of her way to help me, neither did she lash out like First Lieutenant Cousins.

I couldn't help being overawed by the bridge. The huge simulscreen on the curved front bulkhead gave a breathtaking view from the nose of the ship—when we weren't Fused, of course. Now, the other smaller screens to either side were also blank. These screens, under our puter Darla's control, could simulate any conditions known to her memory banks.

The Captain's black leather armchair was bolted to the deck behind the left console. The watch officer's chair I'd occupy was to its right. No one else ever sat in the Captain's chair, even for a drill.

"Midshipman Seafort reporting, sir." Of course Captain Haag knew me. A Captain who didn't recognize his own middies in a crew of eleven officers had problems. But regs were regs.

"Take your seat, Mr. Seafort." Unnecessarily, Captain Haag indicated the watch officer's chair. "I'll call up a simulation of Hope Nation system. You will maneuver the ship for docking at Orbit Station."

"Aye aye, sir." It was the only permissible response to an order from the Captain. Cadets or green middies fresh from Academy were sometimes confused by the difference between "Yes, sir," and "Aye aye, sir." It was simple. Asked a question to which the answer was affirmative, you said "Yes, sir." Given an order, you said "Aye aye, sir." It didn't take many trips to the first lieutenant's barrel to get it right.

Captain Haag touched his screen. "But first, you have to get to Hope Nation." My heart sank. "We'll begin at the wreck of *Celestina*, Mr. Seafort. Proceed." He tilted back in his armchair.

I picked up the caller. "Bridge to engine room, prepare to Defuse." My voice squeaked, and I blushed.

"Prepare to Defuse, aye aye, sir." Chief McAndrews's crusty voice, from the engine room below. "Control passed to bridge." Naturally, the console's indicators from the engine room were simulations; Captain Haag wasn't about to Defuse for a mere middy drill.

"Passed to bridge, aye aye." I put my index finger to the top of the drive screen and traced a line from "Full" to "Off". The simulscreens came alive with a blaze of lights, and I gasped though I'd known to expect it. Stars burned everywhere, in vastly greater numbers than could be imagined groundside.

"Confirm clear of encroachments, Lieutenant. Please," I added. After the drill she'd still be my superior officer. Lieutenant Dagalow bent to her console.

Our first priority in emerging from Fusion was to make sure there were no planetary bodies or vessels about. The chance was one in billions, but not one we took lightly. Darla always ran a sensor check, but despite the triple redundancy built into each of her systems, we didn't rely on her sensors. Navigation was based on an overriding principle: don't trust machinery. Everything was rechecked by hand.

"Clear of encroachments, Mr. Seafort." Technically Ms. Dagalow should have called me "sir" during the drill, while I acted as Captain, but I wasn't about to remind her of that.

"Plot position, please, ma'am. I mean, Lieutenant."

Lieutenant Dagalow set the puter to plot our position on her star charts. The screen filled with numbers as a cheerful feminine voice announced, "Position is plotted, Mr. Seafort."

"Thank you, Darla." The puter dimmed her screens slightly in response. I'm not going to get into the age-old question: was she really alive? That one caused more barroom fights than everything else put together. My personal opinion was—well, never mind, it doesn't matter. Ship's custom was to respond to the puter as a person. All the correct responses to polite phrases and banter were built into her. At Academy, they'd told us crewmen found it easier to relate to a puter with human mannerisms.

"Calculate the new coordinates, please," I said. Lieutenant Dagalow leaned forward to comply.

Captain Haag intervened. "The Lieutenant is ill. You'll have to plot them yourself."

"Aye aye, sir." It took twenty-five minutes, and by the time I was done I'd broken out in a sweat. I was fairly sure I was right, but fairly sure isn't good enough when the Captain is watching from the next seat. I punched in the new Fusion coordinates for the short jump that would carry us to Hope Nation.

"Coordinates received and understood, Mr. Seafort." Darla.

"Chief Engineer, Fuse, please."

"Aye aye, sir. Fusion drive is . . . on." The screens abruptly went blank as Darla simulated reentry into Fusion.

"Very well, Mr. Seafort," the Captain said smoothly. "How long did you estimate second Fusion?"

"Eighty-two days, sir."

"Eighty-two days have passed." He typed a sequence into his console. "Proceed."

Again I brought the ship out of Fusion. After screening out the overpowering presence of the G-type Hope Nation sun, we could detect Orbit Station circling the planet. Lieutenant Dagalow confirmed that we were clear of encroachments. Then she became ill again and, increasingly edgy, I had to plot manual approach myself.

"Auxiliary engine power, Chief." My tone was a bark; my grip on the caller made my wrist ache.

"Aye aye, sir. Power up." Mr. McAndrews must have been waiting for the signal. Of course he would be; Lord God knows how many midshipmen he'd put through nav drill over the years.

"Steer oh three five degrees, ahead two-thirds."

"Two-thirds, aye aye, sir." The console showed our engine power increasing. Nervously I reminded myself that *Hibernia* was still cruising in Fusion, that all this was but a drill.

I glanced at the simulscreen. "Declination ten degrees."

"Ten degrees, aye aye, sir."

I approached Orbit Station with caution. Easily visible in the screens, it grew steadily larger. I braked the ship for final approach.

"Steer oh four oh, Lieutenant."

"Aye aye, sir."

"Sir, Orbit Station reports locks ready and waiting."

"Confirm ready and waiting, understood," I repeated, trying to absorb the flood of information from our instruments.

Dagalow said, "Relative speed two hundred kilometers per hour, Mr. Seafort."

"Two hundred, understood. Maneuvering jets, brake fifteen." Propellant squirted from the jets to brake the ship's forward motion.

"Relative speed one hundred fifteen kilometers, distance twenty-one kilometers."

Still too fast. "Brake jets, eighteen." We slowed further, but the braking threw off our approach. I adjusted by tapping the side maneuvering jets.

Our conventional engines burned $LH_2$ and LOX as propellant; water was cheap and *Hibernia*'s fusion engines provided ample energy to convert it, but there was a limit to how much we could carry. To go faster we would spend more water. We'd spend an equal amount slowing down; nothing was free. Theoretically we could sail to Hope Nation on a few spoonfuls of $LH_2$ and LOX, but not in our lifetimes. How much time was worth how much loss of propellant? That depended on how much maneuvering lay ahead. A nice logistics problem with many variables.

Mine was not a smooth approach. I backed and filled, wasting precious propellant as I tried to align the ship to the two waiting airlocks. Captain Haag said nothing. Finally I was in position, our airlocks two hundred meters apart, our velocity zero relative to Orbit Station.

"Steer two seven oh, two spurts." That would move our pencil to the left, still parallel with the nearby station. It did, far too fast. I had forgotten how little fuel is needed for a correction at close quarters. *Hibernia*'s nose swung perilously close to the station's waiting airlock.

I panicked. "Brake ninety, one spurt!"

Lieutenant Dagalow entered the command, her face impassive.

Lord God in heaven! I'd compounded my error by pulling away the tail of the ship, instead of the nose. "Brake two seven oh, all jets!"

The screen darkened as Orbit Station loomed into our shadow.

Alarm bells shrilled. The screen suddenly jerked askew. My hand flew to the console to brace myself for a jolt that never came.

Darla's shrill voice overrode the screaming alarms. "Loss of seal, forward cargo compartment!"

Ms. Dagalow shouted, "Shear damage amidships!"

The main screen lurched. Darla's voice was urgent. "*EMERGENCY!* The disk has struck! Decompression in Level 2!" I was sick with horror.

Captain Haag pushed his master switch. The alarms quieted to blessed silence. "You've killed half the passengers," he said heavily. "Over a third of your crew is in the decompression zone and is most likely dead. Your ship is out of control. The rupture in the hull is bigger than the forward airlock."

I'd done more damage to my ship than even *Celestina* had sustained. I closed my eyes, unable to speak.

"Stand, Mr. Seafort."

I stumbled to my feet, managed to come to attention.

"You didn't do all that badly until the docking," the Captain said, not unkindly. "You were slow, but you got the ship into correct position. You failed to anticipate decisions, and so you had too much to do in a short time. As a result you lost your ship."

"Yes, sir." I'd lost my ship, all right. And with it any chance of making lieutenant before home port.

He surprised me. "Review the manual again, Seafort. As many times as it takes. By next drill I'll expect you to have it right."

"Aye aye, sir."

"Dismissed." I slunk out.

It was the worst day of my life.

"I don't want to talk about it, Amanda." She was perched on her bed in her ample cabin on Level 1, while I sat on the deck nearby.

I was off duty, and ship's regs permitted officers to socialize with passengers. Sensibly enough, the Naval powers had decided to endorse what they could not prevent.

"Nicky, everyone makes mistakes. Don't punish yourself, just do better next time."

My tone was bitter. "Vax and Alexi dock the ship and come out alive. I'm the senior midshipman and I can't."

"You will," she soothed. "Study and you will."

I didn't tell her how Lieutenant Cousins would have to coach me all over again to prepare for the drill. When he was done I'd be lucky if I could remember how to dress myself. I writhed in disgust. I didn't normally panic; I handled some problems reasonably well or I wouldn't have made it through Academy. But knowing everyone's life depended on me was too much. I knew I'd never be able to cope.

Morose, I settled into a chair. "I'm sorry I bothered you with this, Amanda."

"Oh, Nicky, don't be silly. We're friends, aren't we?" Yes, but that's all we were. I'd have liked to be more, but there were three long years between us and she didn't seem interested. "Why do they torture midshipmen with those drills, anyway? That's what the Pilot is for."

"The Captain is in charge of the ship," I said patiently. "Always. Pilot Haynes, like the Chief Engineer and the Doctor, is staff, not a line officer."

"What's that supposed to mean?"

"It means he's not in the chain of command. If the Captain fell ill, the first lieutenant would command, then Ms. Dagalow, then Lieutenant Malstrom."

"But you'd still have the Pilot to dock the ship. Everybody can't be sick or gone."

"But the Pilot wouldn't be ultimately responsible. It's not his ship."

"Still, it's silly to expect boys just out of cadet academy to know how to fly the ship."

"Sail. Sail the ship."

"What's the difference? You know what I mean."

I tried to explain. "Amanda, we're here to learn what the lieutenants and the Captain do. That's what the drills are for."

"I still think it's silly," Amanda said stubbornly. "And cruel." I let it be.

# 3

"Turn that thing down, Alexi." I got myself ready for bed. It had been a bad day all around and I was cross.

"Sorry, Mr. Seafort." Quickly he lowered the volume of his holovid. Just a year younger than I, Alexi Tamarov was everything I wanted to be: slim, graceful, good-natured, and competent. But he was addicted to his slap music, while my own taste ran to classical composers: Lennon, Jackson, and Biederbeck.

I regretted my temper, but still, I thanked Lord God I was senior and had the right to order the music turned low. I'd have managed somehow even if I weren't in charge, but life had enough trials without that. As senior, I had my choice of bunks and got first serving at morning and afternoon mess, and I supposedly controlled the wardroom, though I was aware my authority was precarious at best.

In a Naval vessel, midshipmen were thrown together with little forethought. Fresh from Academy or with years of service, we were expected to live and work together smoothly. By ship's regs it was the senior middy's duty to run the wardroom, but tradition gave any middy the right to challenge him. In that case the two would fight it out. Because conflicts were inevitable and their resolution necessary, officers turned a blind eye to the scrapes, black eyes, or bruises a midshipman might develop from interacting with his fellows.

Vax Holser and I had an unspoken understanding; he bullied the other middies, and we left each other alone. We both knew that if I pulled rank on him I'd have to back it up. I ignored his calling me "Nicky" with barely concealed contempt; beyond that, we both avoided the test.

Vax stirred, opened one eye to glare at Alexi. I hoped he wouldn't start anything, but he growled, "You're an asshole."

Alexi made no reply.

"Did you hear me?"

"I heard you." Alexi knew he couldn't tangle with Vax.

"Tell me you're an asshole." The trouble with Vax was that once he started he wouldn't let up.

Alexi glanced at me. I was noncommittal.

"I don't feel like getting up, Tamarov. Tell me."

"I'm an asshole!" Alexi snapped off the holovid and threw himself on his bed, facing the partition. His back was tight.

"I already knew that." Vax sounded annoyed.

In the unpleasant silence I glumly recalled my arrival a few weeks before. Lugging my gear, I'd reported to *Hibernia* at Earthport Station, the huge concourse orbiting above Lunapolis City. Preoccupied with loading the incoming stores, Lieutenant Cousins glanced at my sheaf of papers and sent me to find the wardroom on my own.

As I bent awkwardly to open the wardroom hatch a figure cannoned outward through the hatchway, propelling me across the corridor, duffel underfoot, papers flying. I fetched up against the far bulkhead in disarray. My shoulder felt broken.

"Wilsky, get your ass in here!" The bellow came from within.

The young middy froze in horror as I swiped helplessly at a cascade of papers. He darted forward and bent to help me pick up my documents. "You're Wilsky?" was all I could think to say.

"Yes, uh, sir," he said, glancing at my length of service pins, knowing instantly that I was his senior.

"Who's that?" I beckoned to the closed hatch.

"That's Mr. Holser, sir. He's in charge. He was going—" Wilsky grimaced as the hatch sprang open. A huge form loomed over us.

"What the devil do you think—" The muscular midshipman frowned down at me as I crouched in the corridor stuffing papers back into their folders. "Are you the new middy?"

"Yes." I stood. Automatically I checked his length of service pins. When I got my orders I was told I'd be first middy, but mistakes happen.

"You can put your—" His face went white. "What the

bloody hell!'' With dismay, I realized that no one had told him. He'd thought he was going to be senior.

Remembering, I sighed. Our first month had not been easy, and I had seventeen more to endure before landfall. I couldn't physically overpower Vax Holser. Unfortunately, I didn't know how I could tolerate him either.

"It is precisely because of that, Mrs. Donhauser, because the distances are so great and the voyages so long, that authority is made so rigid and discipline so harsh."

Mrs. Donhauser listened closely to Khali Ibn Saud, our amateur sociologist and, by profession, an interplanetary banker.

It was a quiet afternoon some two months into the voyage, and I was sitting in the Level 2 passengers' lounge.

"I'd think distance would have the opposite effect," she countered. "As people got farther from central government, bonds of authority would be loosened."

"Yes!" His tone was excited, as if Mrs. Donhauser had proven his point. "They certainly would, if all were left alone. But central authority, our government, reacts, you see? To maintain control it provides rules and standards and insists we adhere to them regardless of circumstances. And our government is willing to invest time and effort in enforcing them."

The lounge was decorated in pale green, said to be a calming color. From the look of Mr. Barstow, sound asleep in a recliner, the decor was effective. The size of two passenger staterooms, the lounge could seat at least fifteen passengers comfortably. It was furnished with upholstered chairs, recliners, a bench, two game tables, and an intelligent coffee/softie dispenser.

I was only half interested in the debate. Mr. Ibn Saud's theory was not new. In fact, they had presented it better at Academy.

Mrs. Donhauser appealed to me. "Tell him, young man. Isn't it true that the Captain is his own authority here in midspace? That he answers to no one?"

"That's two questions," I answered. "Yes, and no. The Captain is the ultimate authority on a vessel under weigh. He answers to no one aboard ship. But his conduct is prescribed by the regs. If he deviates from them, on his return he will be removed, or worse."

"So you see," Ibn Saud said triumphantly, "central authority is maintained even in the depths of space."

"Foo!" she threw at him. "The Captain can sail slower, faster, even take a detour if he wishes. Central government has nothing to say about it."

He shrugged, looking at me as if to ask, "What's the use?"

"Mrs. Donhauser," I offered, "I think you make a mistake trying to contrast the Captain's powers with United Nations authority. The Captain isn't opposed to central authority. He IS that authority. Legally he can marry people, divorce them, even try and execute them. He has absolute and undiluted control of the vessel." That last was a quote from an official commentary on the regs; I threw it in because it sounded good. "There was a ship. *Cleopatra*. Have you heard of it?"

"No. Should I?"

"It was about fifty years ago. The Captain, I don't remember his name—"

"Jennings," put in Ibn Saud, his head bobbing in anticipation of my point.

"Captain Jennings acted quite strangely. The officers conferred with the Doctor and relieved him of command on grounds of mental illness. They confined him to quarters and sailed the ship directly to Earthport Station." I paused for effect.

"So?"

"They were hanged, every one of them. A court-martial found them mistaken in believing the Captain unfit for command. Even though they acted in good faith, they were all hanged." A silence grew. "You see, the government is absolutely determined to maintain authority, even in space," I said. "The Captain is the representative of the government, as well as the Church, and he must not be overturned."

"It's a bizarre case!"

"It could happen today, Mrs. Donhauser."

"And besides, that must have been a Naval vessel," she said. "Not a passenger ship."

That was too much for me. You'd think people would know what they were getting themselves into. "Ma'am, you may be confused because *Hibernia* has a Naval crew, carries a full complement of civilian passengers, and has a hold full of private cargo. What counts is that the Captain and every member of the crew are Naval officers and seamen. *Hibernia* is a commissioned Naval vessel. By law the Navy carries all cargo bound for the colonies, but legally that cargo is no more than ballast. And the passengers, technically, are just extra cargo. You have no rights aboard this ship and no say whatsoever in what happens on board." I spoke courteously, of course. A midshipman overheard insulting a passenger was not likely to do so again.

"Oh, really?" She was unfazed. I decided she would make a formidable missionary. "Well, it just so happens we vote on our menus, we have committees to run social functions, we elect the Passengers' Council, we even voted on whether to stop at the *Celestina* wreck next week. So where's your dictatorship now?"

"Window dressing," I said. "Look. You have to be a VIP to afford an interstellar voyage, right? The Navy doesn't go out of its way to alienate important people. All of us, officers and crew, are required to be polite to passengers and to assent to your wishes wherever possible. Because you're valuable you get the best accommodations, the best food, our best service. But that changes nothing. The Captain can override any of your votes anytime he has a mind to." I wondered if I'd gone too far.

The feisty old battle-ax put me at ease. "You argue well, young man. I'll think it over. Next time I see you I'll tell you why you're wrong."

I grinned. "I look forward to the lesson, ma'am."

I stretched, excused myself, and went back to Level 1 and the wardroom. Whatever arguments Mrs. Donhauser marshaled wouldn't change a thing. The U.N. knew our world had had enough of anarchy. Central control was not imposed by the government on an unwilling populace. Rather, it was appreciated and respected by the vast mass of citizens. Brushfire wars and chaotic revolutions had finally ceased; our resulting prosperity had powered our explosion into space and the colonization of planets such as Hope Nation and Detour. The Navy, the senior U.N. military service, was the U.N.'s bulwark against the forces of diffusion inherent in a colonial system.

I stripped off my uniform and crawled into my bunk, trying not to wake Alexi. Lieutenant Cousins had set him over the barrel yesterday. Now Alexi had to eat standing, and he wasn't sleeping well. One learned to live with canings, but I knew Alexi too well to believe he'd been insolent and insubordinate as the lieutenant had alleged. Cousins was having a bad day, or was looking for an excuse to assert his authority.

According to regs any middy could be caned, but tradition held there was a dividing line. Alexi, at sixteen, should have been over the line except for a grievous offense. By statute Lieutenant Cousins was within his rights, but not by custom. Alexi was miserable but hadn't complained, which was right and proper.

I slept.

# 4

Two weeks later they gave me another docking drill. It took me forever to plot our course. I labored an hour just to calculate our position, until even the Captain was fidgeting with annoyance. By the time I came off the bridge I was wringing wet, but I hadn't wrecked the ship, though I'd bumped the airlocks together fairly hard.

I went looking for Amanda to tell her of my accomplishment. I found her in the passengers' lounge watching a holovid epic. She turned it off and listened instead to my excited replay of my maneuvers.

Though I no longer sat at her table in the dining hall, Amanda and were becoming good friends. We took long walks together around the circumference corridor. We read together in her cabin. She told me about her father's textile concern, and I told her stories of Academy days. Our only physical contact was to hold hands. I could have slept with her; it wasn't against regs, and I lined up with the other middies for my sterility shot from Doc Uburu every month. But she didn't invite me and I couldn't push, not with a passenger.

A few days after my success on the bridge I relaxed on my bunk, watching Sandy tease Ricky Fuentes, our ship's boy.

"C'n I try it? Please, sir? Please?" The ship's boy reached for the orchestron Sandy held over his head, grinning. We all liked Ricky, a happy twelve-year-old. Even Vax was congenial to him. The youngster's trusting good nature encouraged it.

The ship's boy roamed crew quarters, officers' country, and passenger lounges with impunity. It was all part of his job as ship's gofer. Ricky took messages, retrieved gear that crewmen or officers forgot, generally made himself useful. Every capital ship had a ship's boy, usually an orphan of a career sailor. Traditionally, he graduated to seaman first class and usually made petty officer before he was twenty.

Sandy gave him his orchestron. The boy selected harpsichord, French horn, and tuba, set down a bongo beat, and tapped out a simple melody on the tiny keyboard. He set it to repeat. Then he set up a counterpoint, using different instruments.

Ricky listened to the orchestron develop the theme he had created. "Zarky! Real zarky!" I think that meant he liked it. I was only five years older than he, but joespeak changes fast. The machine burbled to a stop. "Thanks, Sandy, I gotta run. I'm helping in the kitchen tonight. I mean the galley. Bye, sir!" He ran off.

At Ricky's age, I was chopping wood for Father. I wasn't outgoing and sociable, as he was. I never would be. At home Father and I didn't talk often, and we certainly didn't laugh.

Sandy left, and I dozed.

Sometime later Vax came and slapped the light on, waking me from a pleasant dream.

I muttered, "Turn it off, will you?"

He ignored me, undressing slowly.

"Vax, turn off the bloody light!"

"Sure, Nicky." He slapped it off, managing to express contempt with the gesture.

Perhaps it was the heavy dinner, or the lack of exercise. Drugged and lethargic, I fell instantly back to sleep.

Sometime later I was aware of a complaining voice. "It's cold. Turn the heat up, Wilsky." I heard the rustle of sheets as Sandy dragged himself out of bed to dial up the heat.

A few minutes later Vax started again. "Sandy, it's too hot. Turn it down." Once again the boy got up and turned off the heat. This time it took me longer to get back to my dream.

"Turn the heat up, Wilsky!"

I snapped awake, inwardly raging. Alexi groaned. Sandy, who must have been asleep, did not answer.

"Wilsky, you damned asshole, get up and give us some heat!" Now Vax was adding blasphemy to his boorishness. I heard the rustle of sheets as Sandy climbed out of his bunk and adjusted the temperature.

I lay awake, debating. I wouldn't protect Sandy from all Vax's hazing, but there came a point when Sandy had enough. More would cause him emotional problems. For that matter, more would cause ME emotional problems. Where should I draw the line? And how could I do it without getting my head knocked off by the muscular gorilla in the next bunk, and permanently losing control of the wardroom?

"Now turn it down."

"It's fine in here," I heard myself say.

"It's hot. That jerkoff doesn't know how to adjust it properly."

"Get up and do it yourself, Vax."

He ignored me. "Wilsky, put your pretty little ass on the deck and fix the heat!"

I'd had enough. "Stay put, Sandy. That's an order."

"Aye aye, Mr. Seafort." His tone was grateful.

"What in hell are you pulling, Nicky?"

I tried to sound authoritative. "Enough, Vax."

"The hell you say!" So much for my sounding authoritative.

"Vax, turn the light on." I waited, but he did nothing, forcing the issue. From the silent breathing I knew we were all awake. "Alexi, get up. Turn on the light."

"Aye aye, Mr. Seafort." Alexi slapped the light switch, his eyes bleary, hair tousled. Quickly he sank back into bed, out of harm's way. Vax sat up, glaring.

I lay back in my bunk, arm behind my head. "Vax, please give me twenty push-ups." I was in big trouble.

"Prong yourself, Nicky."

I heard Alexi's sharp intake of breath.

"Vax, twenty push-ups. That's an order."

"Don't be more of an ass than you can help." Vax's challenge was now in the open. Give me orders? Enforce them—if you can. He had the right, according to custom. But a first middy wasn't entirely without resources.

"This is a direct order, Vax. Twenty push-ups, on the deck."

"No. You're not man enough to give orders. Not inside the wardroom." A wise distinction. His challenge was to my authority in the wardroom, not to ship's authority in general.

"Mr. Holser, put yourself on report at once." That meant, go knock on the first lieutenant's hatch and tell him I had written you up for insubordination. It would most likely cause him to be put over the barrel, even at his age.

"You've got to be kidding. You know what that'll do to you."

I knew. "Mr. Holser, go to the duty officer, forthwith, and place yourself on report."

"I will not." Vax was taking a chance, but not a big one. He knew as well as I that a middy who called on an officer for help to run his wardroom was finished in the service.

"Alexi."

"Yes, Mr. Seafort?"

"Put your pants on, go to the duty officer, and tell him the senior midshipman reports a mutiny in the wardroom. Mr. Holser is written up but refuses to obey a direct order to place himself on report. I request a court-martial to determine the validity of my allegations."

"Aye aye, sir." Alexi threw aside the covers and reached for his trousers.

"Belay that, Alexi. You can't do it, Nick." Vax's tone was urgent. "It'll ruin you too. You'll never get command if you can't even hold a wardroom. You won't even get another posting!"

"That's no longer your concern, Mr. Holser." I remained icily formal; it was my only chance. "Mr. Wilsky."

"Yes, sir?"

"Dress yourself. Go to crew quarters. Wake the master-at-arms. Have him bring an escort to the wardroom, flank. As for you, Vax, you are under arrest."

"Aye aye, sir." Sandy was so nervous his voice soared into the upper registers. Frantically, he began throwing on his clothes.

Alexi, dressed, headed for the hatch. Vax grabbed his arm in a huge hand. "Nick, call it off. This is a wardroom matter. Settle it here, among us!"

I had him.

"It's too late, Vax. You ignored my order. Let go of Alexi." I lay motionless, under my covers.

"Hold off, Nick. Talk it through." He hesitated. "Please." Vax knew that I'd throw away my career if the two junior middies went on their errands. He also knew that he himself now faced court-martial and almost certain imprisonment in the brig, if not summary dismissal from the Navy.

I made my tone reluctant. "Alexi, Sandy, sit down." I turned to Vax. "I'll turn the clock back, Mr. Holser. Twenty push-ups."

He stared, trying to read me. I looked away. I didn't care what he thought he saw in my face. Apparently my indifference convinced him; he got down on the deck. "We'll settle this later, Nick." It was a growl.

"Yes, we will." I spoke with confidence I didn't feel.

He gave me twenty push-ups. Good ones, like the Academy taught in basic. At the end he got up on one knee.

"Now twenty more." This time I stared him straight in the eye.

Having given in the first time he had little choice. Rigid with fury, he did twenty more push-ups.

"Thank you." I looked at the two junior middies. "Back to bed, you two."

Neither dared say a word. Vax was still a potent force in their lives. He stood up and yanked on his clothes. "It's a good time for a walk, Nicky," he spat. "Care to join me?"

At that moment I regretted not letting him order Sandy in and out of bed all night, if he wished. Vax was twenty kilos heavier, a head taller, and a lot stronger than I was. And two years older, as well. I was about to get the tar beaten out of me, and I had no choice but to go through with it. I got out of bed and put on my pants, socks, and shoes. I didn't put anything over my undershirt; no point in ruining a dress shirt or jacket.

We strode in silence to the passenger exercise room on Level 2. At that hour, past midnight, it was deserted. He went in first.

I knew the best thing was to circle while he stalked me, and try to avoid his lunges. He knew I knew that. So the moment I was through the hatchway I hurled myself straight at him, fists flailing at his face. I got in a few good licks before he got his cover up and held me off. I backed away.

He came at me, livid with anger. I backed away again. He drove at me faster, and again I went right at him, hammering. He caught me a good one on the side of the head that made me dizzy, but momentum carried me past his guard and I was all over him, pounding at his stomach, chest, jaw. Then I unexpectedly dropped down and rolled away.

He was disconcerted, as I wanted him to be. My only chance was to do what he least expected. He came at me warily this time, guard up. I went into karate position. He did the same. We both feinted. I fended him off, but he steadily advanced, pushing me toward the corner. I had no choice but to retreat.

The next few minutes were bad. He got in a lot of blows, knocking me down, slapping my head back and forth, slamming me into the partition, raining punches on my chest and arms. I wasn't strong enough to hold him off so I concentrated on convincing him he was hurting me more than he really was. It wasn't easy, because he hurt me plenty.

I staggered, apparently semiconscious, blood flowing freely from my nose and mouth. My legs buckled. He grabbed under my arms with both hands, holding me as I sagged. It was what I'd waited for. I drove my fist into his crotch with all the strength I could muster.

Vax bent over in reflex, let go to clutch himself. I backed away, wiping blood off my face. Damn, he could hit. Vax leaned against the bulkhead, his eyes half shut, face white.

My arms ached from the pounding they had taken. I didn't have strength left to hit hard. So, clasping my hands together, I bent and, like a battering ram, ran straight at him. My shoulder smashed into his side. He went down. So did I. He was a rock.

Vax scrambled to his feet, a murderous look in his eye, fists clenched. I got up, put my head down, and rammed him again. This time he bounced off a bulkhead. My shoulder was numb. We both staggered to our feet. His nose bled from his impact with the bulkhead. I lunged again. He had both hands out, and fended me off. I put my shoulder down and dug in, straining to ram him.

"Wait!" His breath came hard.

I backed off. "Prong yourself, joey." I lowered my head and charged. He tried to knee my face, but was too slow. I butted him in the stomach and he toppled over. I wondered if I had broken my neck. After a moment I managed to get up. So did he.

"Enough!" Vax covered his stomach with both hands.

I leaned against the partition, trying not to black out.

"Truce." He held up his hand as if pushing me off. I waited, trying to catch my breath enough to answer. "I can't take you, Nick. And you can't take me. Truce."

"No." I drove at him again. I didn't have much left but he was too busy clutching his aching ribs to fight back. He slid down to the slippery deck, then pulled himself back up.

"For God's sake, Nicky, enough! Neither of us wins."

I nodded. "Lay off Sandy," I gasped. "You're hazing too hard."

"Hazing's part of it."

"Not that much. Haze him some, but lay off when I say."

He nodded reluctantly. "All right. Deal."

"I'll leave you alone," I said. "And you don't look for trouble with me."

"Deal." He swallowed. Cautiously, he tried letting go of his stomach.

"And you don't call me Nick in the wardroom." If I didn't get it this time, I'd never have another chance.

"No." He looked stubborn. "Not that."

I launched myself at him. He put out both arms to block me but my charge knocked him into the bulkhead. Instead of backing off I rammed him with my shoulder again and again, thumping his ribs and back. I wasn't doing much damage but he was too exhausted to deck me.

My vision went red. I heard grunting, his or mine, as I felt myself slip into total exhaustion. Then I became aware that he held both my arms in his big hands, holding me at arm's length away from his body. I was braced against the deck, straining to get at him.

"Truce," Vax said again. "Truce—Mr. Seafort."

I slumped back. "Name?" I managed.

"Your name is Mr. Seafort." He didn't look at me with fondness, but his expression held a wary respect I hadn't seen before.

"Truce," I agreed.

We staggered out of the room and back up to Level 1, neither saying a word. I went directly to the shower. I stood under the warm spray, watching my blood swirl down the drain to the recycler in the fusion drive chamber below. I didn't pretend I was victorious.

I had survived. It was enough.

# 5

To my surprise, the greatest change in the wardroom wasn't how Vax acted toward the other middies. He remained surly to them, and they were still cautious in his presence. It was not in how Vax acted toward me. He spoke to me as seldom as possible and rarely used my name, but when he did, it was Seafort and not Nicky.

No, the biggest difference was in how the other juniors acted toward me. Because I'd stood up to Vax and survived I was unquestionably in charge as far as they were concerned, and they were eager to win my approval.

Alexi in particular seemed to undergo a case of hero worship. He and Sandy straightened my bunk, crease-ironed my pants along with their own, and showed me unexpected deference. Though I tried hard not to let it show, I loved it.

Vax, for his part, eased off on his hazing. One day I came

upon him forcing Alexi to stand naked in an ice-cold shower. When I ordered him to lay off, he did, without argument. Alexi stumbled quickly out of the shower room, blue with cold and trembling from humiliation. Perhaps Vax felt that having given his word he had to keep it, but my interference didn't make him any more friendly.

I reported for watch each day, sometimes with Mr. Cousins, occasionally with Ms. Dagalow. With Lieutenant Cousins I sat stiffly, hoping to stay out of trouble. Ms. Dagalow, though no Dosman, chatted about puters, as she often did. Though I didn't share her interest, I enjoyed her company and did my best to please her by learning what I could.

The next week I was transferred to engine room watch. There Chief McAndrews tried to teach me the intricacies of the fusion drive. I discovered that I had little aptitude for it. By now I'd shown myself impossibly slow at astronavigation, thoroughly muddled as a pilot, and hopelessly inept as a drive technician. Vax was older, bigger, and stronger. Both Vax and Alexi were better able to handle the crew. I was proving incompetent at navigation, pilotage, engineering, and leadership. An ideal midshipman.

Except for chess. I could concentrate on that; I didn't feel our thirty-second limit as pressure. I always looked forward to my afternoon game with Lieutenant Malstrom. But one day when we set up the board his manner was subdued. I led with queen's pawn, and before I knew it I had trapped him in a fool's mate in five moves. He was not a good player, overall, but he was far better than that.

We started to put away the pieces. "What's wrong, sir?" I had known and liked this man for months now, but nonetheless I'd taken a daring step. A middy does not ask a personal question of a lieutenant. It is not done.

Lieutenant Malstrom looked at me without speaking. He began unbuttoning his shirt. He pulled it out of his pants, rolled it up from his waist. He turned, showing me his side. Just above his hip was an ugly blue-gray lump.

I met his eye. "What is it, Mr. Malstrom?" By not using his rank I was getting as close to him as I could. We were friends.

He said the words so quietly I could barely hear him. "Malignant melanoma."

"Melanoma T?"

"Doc thinks it might be."

My breath hissed. The disease was an occupational hazard. In Fusion, it was impossible to shield ourselves from the N-waves that drove the ship, and over time N-waves transmuted ordinary carcinoma to the virulent T form that grew with astonishing speed.

Like all of us, Mr. Malstrom had shipped interstellar as an adolescent, and should have been nearly immune.

"At least they're not sure, sir." I tried to look on the hopeful side. Most forms of cancer were easily cured nowadays, hardly worse than a bad cold. But the new strain of melanoma didn't respond well to drugs. The treatment of choice was still amputation of the affected part, where possible.

I asked, "Have you been treated?"

"Tomorrow morning. Radiation and anticar drugs. They caught it early; Doc Uburu says I have a good chance."

"I'm very sorry, sir."

"Harv." He caught my look. "Here in my quarters. My name is Harv." He must really have been shaken. I forced myself to say his unfamiliar name.

"I'm sorry, Harv. You'll be all right. I know you will."

"I hope so, Nicky." He tucked in his shirt. "Don't mention it to the others."

"Of course not." The Captain would know, of course. Perhaps the other lieutenants. But the middies need not be told, or the seamen.

"I'll go on sick leave for a few days, in case the anticars get me down. You can come give me chess lessons."

I grinned as I stood at the hatch. "Every day, sir." I snapped him a salute. It was a sign of affection and he knew it. He returned it and I left.


"Lord God, today is January 2, 2195, on the U.N.S. *Hibernia*. We ask you to bless us, to bless our voyage, and to bring health and well-being to all aboard."

"Amen," I said fervently. Lieutenant Malstrom was absent. Amanda and I were again at the same table. This time I was thrown in with a colonist family of five journeying to a new life on Detour, our port of call beyond Hope Nation.

The unspoiled resources of these newer colonies attracted many like the Treadwells, eager to escape the pollution and regimentation of overcrowded Earth. At home we had Luna, of course, and the Mars colony. But some people weren't attracted to dome or warren life. They sought open space and fresh air that was ever harder to find.

Not everyone could emigrate, certainly. Only the wealthy could afford it. Though I admired the quest that was taking them sixty-nine light-years from home, I wondered how the Treadwells had managed it. She was a gaunt prim woman whose hands darted restlessly. Her husband, squat, swarthy and muscular, looked more a laborer than the habitat engineer the manifests showed him to be.

Their oldest children were twins poised on the edge of adolescence. Paula, wearing a shade too much shadow, and Rafe, all awkward knees and elbows, seemed so vulnerable they recalled my own painful thirteenth year, roaming Cardiff with my best friend Jason. I stirred uneasily, recollecting my discomfort at his hand on my shoulder, aware of his acknowledged sexual proclivity and dubious of my own. I also remembered, at Jason's casual touch, Father's silent look that spoke volumes of reproach.

Both Rafe and Paula seemed awestruck by Naval life and in love with anyone who wore the uniform. Rafe pestered me for information, as he had Doc Uburu and Ms. Dagalow before me. Paula asked about joining up, what Academy was like, how old you had to be to enter.

Ms. Treadwell frowned. "The Navy's no place for a lady."

"Oh, Irene." Paula's voice dripped with condescension. "What about Lieutenant Dagalow, at the next table?"

I tried not to wince. I couldn't imagine calling my own father anything but "Father" or "Sir".

"Look into it when we get to Detour." Their mother flashed me an apologetic smile. "You can't enlist in the middle of a cruise." Their faces fell. Another fantasy gone.

I tried to cheer them up. "That's not quite true, Ms. Treadwell. The Captain has authority to enlist civilians as officers or crew. It's almost never done, but it's possible." The Captain also had authority to impress civilians into service in an emergency, but I didn't mention that.

The twins fell to talking among themselves. They decided

to persuade Captain Haag to let them join up, with or without their parents' permission. Their younger sister Tara, six, said little. We adults drifted into another conversation. Jared Treadwell asked, "Is it true, Mr. Seafort, that this ship is actually armed?"

"All U.N. ships have weapons, Mr. Treadwell." I smiled. "It's an odd and ancient precaution. There's nobody to use them against, except now and then a few planetside bandits, and the ship's lasers are not designed for antiguerrilla operations. They're like male nipples: standard equipment, but useless."

My sally drew a nervous laugh from his wife. Groundside attitudes were fairly straightlaced. It was fun to scan old holovids about the Rebellious Ages, but I couldn't imagine a young couple who showed up unmarried with a baby, or even tried to swim naked on a beach. Of course modern birth control has separated casual copulation, which is tolerated in any combination of sexes, from casual reproduction, which is not.

The next day all four middies had astronavigation drill with Lieutenant Cousins. I worked my problems as well as I could, while Mr. Cousins shook his head in disgust at my mistakes. Vax got everything right, as usual. Then Alexi fouled up a really easy problem and put the ship dead in the middle of a hypothetical sun.

Lieutenant Cousins glared at Alexi's console, withering contempt dripping from his every word. "You incompetent child! God damn your eyes, Mr. Tamarov, you're hopeless!"

That was too much. Alexi knew it. So, belatedly, did Cousins. Even Vax caught my eye and slowly shook his head.

Alexi got to his feet, nervously drawing himself to attention. He had opened his mouth to speak when Mr. Cousins forestalled him. "I apologize, Mr. Tamarov." He glanced around. "To you and to all present. I spoke out of anger and not intent. I mean no disrespect to Lord God."

Alexi sat in relief, and there was silence in the cabin. I knew Lieutenant Cousins, for all his bullyragging, wouldn't hold Alexi's objection against him. Blasphemy was no more tolerated aboard ship than it was groundside. The lieutenant could find himself on the beach for that kind of talk.

For three days Lieutenant Malstrom showed no ill effects. Then he took to his bed, his side bandaged. We played chess daily, sometimes two or three games. I didn't quite let him win, but I tried some unusual variations I wouldn't have risked otherwise. Sometimes they didn't work.

A week later he raised his shirt to show me his side. The ominous blue mass was gone; in its place was a red welt that was fading in places to white. Unthinking, I clapped him on the shoulder. "It worked!"

He grinned. "I think so, Nicky. Doc says I should be all right."

"Fantastic!" I jumped up, too excited to be still. "Oh, Harv, sir, that's wonderful!"

"Yes. I have my life back."

We were too keyed up for chess. Instead, we talked about what to expect on Hope Nation. We'd both seen the holovids but I'd never traveled interstellar before, and Mr. Malstrom hadn't been to Hope Nation. He promised to take me sightseeing in the fabled Ventura Mountains during our stopover. I promised him a double asteroid on the rocks at the first bar we came to.

Happy and relaxed, I went back to the wardroom to change. Vax lay on his side and glowered the whole time I was there. I said nothing; he did likewise. By the time I left, my good cheer had evaporated.

Alexi had the middy watch when we Defused to search for *Celestina*. We were fortunate; though far away, her beacons registered on the sensors' first try. Under Lisa Dagalow's watchful eye, Alexi plotted a course to the derelict ship. The lieutenant rechecked his figures. They agreed with Darla's; we Fused again, a short jump to where the abandoned ship floated.

I pulled watch two days later when we Defused once more. Lieutenant Cousins and I were on the bridge waiting, as the Captain took the conn. "Bridge to engine room, prepare to Defuse."

"Prepare to Defuse, aye aye, sir." A moment passed. "Engine room ready for Defuse, sir. Control passed to bridge."

"Passed to bridge, aye aye." Captain Haag glanced at his

instruments, then ran his finger down the control screen. Millions of stars burst forth on the bridge simulscreens. I knew I couldn't spot *Celestina* unaided, but my eyes searched nonetheless.

"Confirm clear of encroachments, Lieutenant." The Captain waited.

Lieutenant Cousins turned to me. "Go to it, Mr. Seafort." His tone held a hint of impatience.

I checked the readouts as I'd been taught. I glanced again, in alarm. Something was there. "An encroachment, sir! Course one three five, distance twenty thousand kilometers!"

"That's *Celestina*, you idiot." Cousins's scorn brought a flush to my cheeks.

The Pilot intervened. "Maneuvering power, Chief."

"Aye aye, Bridge. Power up."

The Captain watched, not interfering. He could maneuver his own ship, of course, but Pilot Haynes was aboard for that very purpose. With squirts of the thrusters, the Pilot eased the ship forward.

Lieutenant Cousins dialed up the magnification on the simulscreens. A dark dot became a blob, then a lump. Abruptly *Celestina* leaped into focus, and I saw for the first time the tragic wreck that had cost two hundred seventy lives.

She spun lazily on her longitudinal axis, crumpled alumalloy revealing a gaping hole in her fusion drive shaft. Torn and shattered metal protruded from both levels of the disk; the passengers and crew had never had a chance.

I was silent, a lump in my throat. Hundreds of colonists had sailed that ill-fated vessel. A Captain like ours. Seamen, engineers, midshipmen like ourselves. My eyes stung.

"Get back to work!" Lieutenant Cousins loomed over me. "Watch your screens, you—you crybaby!"

"Belay that, Lieutenant!" The Captain's voice stopped him cold.

From time to time I glanced up from my console to the simulscreen, on which the derelict slowly swelled. Soon, tiny portholes were visible against the white of the disk, shaded almost to black against the interstellar darkness. After a time even Lieutenant Cousins seemed affected; he fiddled with the magnification until suddenly he caught the lettering on the vessel's side. He spun up maximum magnification, and the letters "U.N.S. *Celestina*" filled the screen. My breath caught. We were all silent now.

Pilot Haynes maneuvered the ship to within a half kilometer of *Celestina*. Then he turned the conn back to the Captain, who picked up the caller and spoke to the passengers, who would be crowding the portholes for the extraordinary view.

"Attention all hands. We have Defused. We are now at rest relative to U.N.S. *Celestina*, destroyed by the Grace of God one hundred twelve years ago this month. Many of us will never pass this place again. It has become custom, in ships sailing this road, to pay our respects to the memory of *Celestina*. All passengers who wish may go aboard. Our ship's launch will ferry you across in groups of six. The trip will last approximately two hours. The Purser will announce the order of embarkation. That is all." Captain Haag put down the caller and stepped to the front of his command console, staring somberly at the simulscreen, hands clasped behind his back.

"Will you go aboard, sir?" Lieutenant Cousins asked him.

"No," Captain Haag said quietly. "I'll stay with the ship." He cleared his throat. "I went over on my last trip, four years ago. I'll remember without seeing it again." But his eyes were riveted on the derelict.

The duty roster was posted. The ship's launch normally held ten. Each trip would be conducted by a lieutenant, accompanied by a midshipman and two seamen. Lieutenant Malstrom drew the first trip. Vax went with him. Two and a half hours later a subdued group of passengers returned, saddened and quiet. On the second excursion Sandy Wilsky went, with Lieutenant Cousins. I was scheduled for the third trip with Lieutenant Dagalow, and back on watch for the fourth.

When my turn came I suited up and joined the seamen helping passengers struggle into their unaccustomed suits. For convenience, the launch traveled airless. Mrs. Donhauser was in our group, but I was too busy helping the others to say anything to her.

The launch berth was in *Hibernia*'s shaft, just forward of the disk. We trekked into the airlock joining the two sections of the ship, climbing awkwardly up into the shaft when the lock finished cycling. I felt my weight lessen as I dropped onto the deck of the shaft. Forward of me a hundred meters or so, the cargo hold was stuffed with medical equipment, precision tool and die-making implements, a hi-tech chip manufactory, and other supplies for the Hope Nation colony.

We seated the passengers. The launch's transplex portholes offered a clear view, and the passengers huddled to peer through them. Lieutenant Dagalow dialed the bridge; a moment later the launch berth airlock slid open.

I glanced hopefully at the launch controls. Lieutenant Dagalow shook her head, smiled gently. "We don't have time, Nick." I flushed at the reminder of my incompetence, but merely nodded.

With a brief squirt of the maneuvering thrusters she propelled us out of *Hibernia*'s berth. The launch's powerful engines throbbed, its nozzles directing the liquid oxygen and liquid hydrogen reaction mass that propelled us.

Lieutenant Dagalow didn't bother to compute a course as I would have had to; instead, she eyed the huge derelict and sailed by dead reckoning. It wasn't quite by the book, but I envied her skill, and some part of me was glad I hadn't attempted to pilot a craft with so many watching.

We drifted closer to the inert ship. Ms. Dagalow's voice crackled in our suit speakers. "U.N.S. *Celestina* embarked from Mars Orbiting Station May 23, 2083, with a crew of seventy-five men and women, including twelve officers. She carried a hundred ninety-five passengers, all of them colonists for Hope Nation." She paused. "Jethro Narzul, son of the Secretary-General, was among them." She throttled down the engines. We were rapidly approaching the derelict ship; time for braking thrusters.

At reduced speed we drifted close to the abandoned colossus. With a practiced skill I envied, Lieutenant Dagalow fired the maneuvering thrusters and brought us to rest relative to *Celestina*'s gaping lock. Our alumalloy hatch slid open and a seaman jumped the few meters to the ship, a coiled cable slung over his shoulder. He moored us tight to the safety line stanchion in *Celestina*'s lock. As the derelict had no power, we couldn't connect to her capture latches, but since everyone aboard was suited, we didn't need an airtight seal.

Lieutenant Dagalow and a seaman boarded *Celestina* to help our suited passengers alight; the other sailor and I stayed in the launch to help them disembark. When all were safely aboard the derelict I joined the somber tour.

Lights had been strung every twenty meters or so. We stumbled along *Celestina*'s second-level corridor. The ship, of an earlier design, had but two levels in her disk. Debris must have swirled around the wreckage during the explosive decompression; much of it hung about where its inertia had brought it.

*Celestina* was like nothing I had ever seen. Much of her disk was surprisingly clean and orderly. Lieutenant Dagalow opened a cabin hatch; inside, a neatly made bunk waited for its long-gone occupant. A suit folded on the dresser was undisturbed.

"The ship was entering Fusion when the accident occurred. The drive exploded without warning. The shaft and the disk sustained heavy damage. Decompression was almost instantaneous." He paused. "Today, rapid-close hatches divide the disk into sections. We believe many of you would now survive a similar accident."

Mrs. Donhauser spoke up. "What caused the explosion?"

Ms. Dagalow shook her head. "The truth is, we don't know." I felt a chill. "The fusion drive has been redesigned several times since *Celestina* was launched. No other ship has ever had a similar failure."

She opened the hatch to the adjoining cabin. A rocking horse and a closet full of little girls' clothes framed the hatchway. Sickened, I turned away.

"What happened to the people?" a passenger asked.

"They were given decent burial in space when the ship was rediscovered by the *Armstrong*." The legendary U.N.S. *Neil Armstrong*, Captain Hugo Von Walther commanding. The search vessel that had found the long-missing *Celestina*, and later opened two new colonies for settlement. Her commander had fought a duel with a colonial Governor, served as Admiral of the Fleet, and had ultimately been elected Secretary-General.

Our seamen had strung a rope barrier to keep us from the damaged areas where ragged sheets of torn metal hung dangerously. We trekked up the ladder to Level 1. My breath rasped in my helmet. My suit's defogger labored.

We gathered at the top of the ladder and moved as a group

along *Celestina*'s circumference corridor. Ahead a pale light gleamed, reflecting the gray corridor bulkheads. "The bridge is just ahead," said Lieutenant Dagalow.

We came to the open hatchway revealing the ghostly, deserted bridge. My breath caught. On the bulkhead outside the bridge hung the hundreds of slips of paper pictured so often in the holozines. We clustered at the bulkhead to read them.

"Robert Vysteader, colonist en route to Hope Nation, in memory of this poor ship, this fifteenth day of August 2106, by the Grace of God." "Mary Helene Braithwaite, colonist in God's hands, in memory of our brethren who died here. December 11, 2151." "Ahmed Esmail, remembering *Celestina*. December 11, 2151."

So they went. Each spacefarer who had come this lonely way had left a respectful mark to honor his predecessors who'd suffered disaster. Many of the visitors had gone on to Hope Nation or Detour, lived long lives and since died of old age.

"Over here! Look!" We crowded round. The slip of paper was clipped just beyond the hatchway. "Hugo Von Walther, Captain, U.N.S. *Neil Armstrong*, in commemoration of our sister ship *Celestina*. God rest her soul, and all who sailed in her. August 3, 2114." We trod the actual footsteps of Captain Von Walther. He had stood in this very spot the day he discovered *Celestina*, eighty-one years past. I tried to summon his presence. What a man he had been.

"Those who wish may leave a message of commemoration for future generations." Lieutenant Dagalow fished a box of tiny round magnets from her suitslot. We fumbled in our own slots for pencils and paper. Using the bulkheads, our knees, and the deck for tables, we wrote our blessings to the dead. I thought a long time before writing mine. "Nicholas Ewing Seafort, aged seventeen years, four months, twelve days, by Grace of God officer in the service of the United Nations, saluting the memories of those who have gone before. January 16, 2195." I took a magnet from Lieutenant Dagalow's outstretched hand and stuck it to the bulkhead, four meters from the bridge hatchway.

Our return trip was subdued. I was glad no one felt the need to speak. We berthed in *Hibernia*; I went aft to desuit and change. Then I reported back to the bridge. Captain

Haag waited stolidly while the next load of passengers was embarked. On watch, Lieutenant Cousins and I had little to do.

It would take eleven trips to ferry all who wanted to go. Vax went on the fourth trip, then Alexi Tamarov. When Alexi returned he said excitedly, "Mr. Cousins let me pilot!" I hoped my feelings didn't show.

I went again on the seventh shuttle, but lagged behind when the group went to the bridge. Like the Captain, I had no need to experience it again.

After dinner the trips resumed. I was to stand watch with the Captain and Lieutenant Malstrom; Sandy and Lieutenant Cousins would sail the launch. Before reporting to the bridge I went with Alexi to help suit the passengers.

Lieutenant Dagalow was supervising the suiting room. Perhaps as a reaction to the grimness of the vessel lying alongside, Sandy and Alexi were in a playful mood. Sandy finished helping an older man into his unfamiliar suit and stuck out his tongue to Alexi as he reached for his own. Alexi tweaked him in the ribs. Sandy jumped, losing his balance, and tripped over the suiting bench. He crashed to the deck, tangled in a floppy suit. The back of his hand was bleeding slightly, but worse, he had split his pants wide open.

Mortified, Sandy glanced between the two outraged officers. Lieutenant Cousins bellowed. Ms. Dagalow shot me a glower that spoke volumes. I was senior; the fiasco was my responsibility.

"Mr. Tamarov!" Lieutenant Cousins's voice was a whip. "It's your fault, you go in his place. Get suited! You're both on report; I'll deal with you later!"

"Aye aye, sir!" Alexi grabbed his suit.

Lieutenant Dagalow intervened. "Mr. Tamarov went last trip, Mr. Cousins. I can go instead of the middy. I don't mind; I'd like to look at the hull damage again." Cousins frowned; he was senior and could overrule Dagalow, but courtesy forbade that. He nodded, assenting. Ms. Dagalow called the bridge to get the necessary approval; Alexi and I helped finish the suiting, and the party left.

The moment the airlock hatch slid shut I wheeled on Sandy. "Change your pants, Mr. Midshipman Wilsky!"

"Aye aye, sir!"

I caught his arm as he started to run. "If you think Lieutenant Cousins is the only one going to deal with you, guess again! Tomfoolery on duty? God—" I caught myself in time. "God bless it, Mr. Wilsky! Mr. Holser and I will give you some attention." He blanched; unleashing Vax on him was a threat indeed. I released him; he double-timed it to the wardroom, glad to be free of me.

Seething, I set Alexi at attention against the bulkhead. Then, nose to nose with him, I reamed him slowly and thoroughly. At the end he wasn't far from tears. My memory is very good. Most of what I said came from Sergeant Trammel at Academy. I recalled it was very effective.

I dismissed Alexi and headed for the bridge. "Permission to enter, sir."

The Captain was still on watch. "Granted." Didn't he ever sleep?

"Midshipman Seafort reporting, sir."

He merely nodded. Maybe he was tiring, after all. I took my place at the console. There was nothing to do but watch the simulscreen.

"What was that commotion in the suiting room, Mr. Seafort?"

That was tricky. The Captain had heard something about it; Lieutenant Dagalow needed his permission to leave ship. I couldn't lie to an officer, no matter what. Yet it was also my job to keep wardroom affairs out of the Captain's hair. I said carefully, "Mr. Wilsky tripped and cut his hand, sir."

"Ah. Is he getting medical attention?" There was a dryness in the Captain's tone that I found suspicious. On the other hand, the Captain was not known to joke with midshipmen.

"It was just a minor scrape, sir."

Captain Haag waved it aside. "No matter." Lieutenant Malstrom winked at me. So he did know.

"Three more trips after this, sir." Lieutenant Malstrom spoke to the Captain.

"Yes." After a moment he added, "Then we get under way in earnest." No more stops for nine months until we reached Miningcamp, except for routine navigation checks.

Captain Haag leaned back in his chair, his eyes shut. Lieutenant Malstrom yawned. I tried not to yawn too. It had been a long and emotional day.

*"Hibernia*, Mayday! Mayday!" It must have been a seaman; not a voice I recognized.

The Captain bolted upright, slapping the caller switch. *"Hibernia!"*

"We have a passenger down! Suit puncture!"

The Captain swore. "What happened?"

"Just a moment. Sir." We could hear him relaying the message on his suit transmitter. "Lieutenant Dagalow slapped on a quickpatch and re-aired her suit. Mrs.—the passenger is unconscious. Probably still alive, sir."

"Tell Mr. Cousins to get everyone back into the launch."

"Aye aye, sir. The woman is wedged in the bridge hatchway. She touched the emergency close. It shut on her suit. They can't reach around her to the hatch control switch."

I didn't know bridge power backups could last so long. The bridge of any major vessel is built like a fortress. When the Captain slaps the dull red emergency-close patch inside the hatchway the hatch snaps shut almost instantly, with great force. Thereafter it is almost impossible to enter the bridge.

Blocked by the unconscious passenger, *Celestina's* hatch hadn't shut entirely, but the body hindered access to the control panel. Somebody had fouled up badly, letting her in.

The Captain touched the caller. "Machinist Perez, call the bridge."

In a moment a voice came. "Machinist here, sir."

"Crowbars and laser cutters to the Captain's gig at once. Have another seaman suit up with you."

"Aye aye, sir."

"Shall I take the gig across, sir?" Lieutenant Malstrom got to his feet.

"No, I'll go myself. You take the watch." Captain Haag started for the hatchway.

"Aye aye, sir. But, Captain—"

"It's my responsibility." His voice had sharpened. "I'll have to see what happened. If she doesn't survive . . ." Passengers might be cargo, but there would be a Board of Inquiry if anyone died. Captain Haag shook his head. "I shouldn't be more than an hour. You have the conn."

"Aye aye, sir."

The Captain slapped the panel. The hatch opened. He strode toward the ladder.

Lieutenant Malstrom and I exchanged glances. He grimaced. I felt pity for Lieutenant Dagalow and even for Mr. Cousins; when the Captain got to them, heads would roll.

A few minutes later they launched the gig. We watched in the simulscreens as it shot across to *Celestina*. Smaller and far more maneuverable than the launch, the gig was a mere gnat against the brooding mass of the great stricken ship.

*Celestina*'s lock was already occupied by the launch. The gig maneuvered as close as it could, then the seaman fired a magnetic cable into the lock. The Captain went across, hand over hand, just like a cadet at Academy.

Half an hour later the speaker came alive. "Bridge, this is *Hibernia*." The Captain naturally called himself by the name of his ship.

"Go ahead, sir."

"It was easier than we thought." Captain Haag sounded relieved. "Perez reached the switch with the point of a crowbar. She's breathing, at any rate. We'll bring her back on the launch: it's faster. Get the next gaggle of passengers ready. Send an extra middy next trip for the gig."

"Aye aye, sir."

"Shall I go for the gig, sir?" I tried to conceal my eagerness. The midshipman he sent would be, however briefly, in command during the passage between ships.

Lieutenant Malstrom smiled. Perhaps he remembered his own days as a middy. "Sure, Nicky."

With magnification set to zero we could see the passengers and crew waiting in the launch. The moment the Captain and the injured passenger were aboard, its lock closed. Crewmen untied the safety line.

The Captain sounded worried. "Her complexion isn't good. Have Dr. Uburu stand by at the lock. Belay that figuring, Mr. Cousins, there's no time. Darla, feed coordinates to our puter!"

"Aye aye, sir." Darla knew when to be all business.

Lieutenant Malstrom and I watched on the simulscreen as the launch shot away from *Celestina*. Under main power it headed toward our lock. When it reached the halfway point I stood to leave for the launch berth. I glanced over my shoulder at the screen.

The speaker blared. *"THE ENGINE'S OVERHEATING!*

*WE'RE THROTTLING DOW— THE SHUTOFF WON'T—"*
The caller went dead as the launch disintegrated in a flash of
white light.

"Lord God!" Lieutenant Malstrom froze at his console. I
heard myself make some sort of sound. Chunks of twisted
metal and other debris spun lazily off the side of the screen.
I glimpsed a shredded spacesuit.

The lieutenant frantically keyed the suit broadcast frequen-
cies. Nothing but the barely audible hiss of background radiation.

I stood rooted halfway between the console and the hatch.
Mr. Malstrom's eyes held terror. Together, we stared into the
space the launch had occupied.

At last, Lieutenant Malstrom began to function.

We couldn't search for survivors, even if there'd been any;
we had neither our launch nor the gig. Mr. Malstrom ordered
Vax and a party of seamen across to recover the gig from
*Celestina*'s lock. Squirting propellant from tanks strapped to
their thrustersuits, they navigated the void between *Hibernia*
and the derelict. At last they reached the gig. Vax sailed it
back to *Hibernia*'s waiting lock. He docked it as well as any
of the lieutenants might, far better than I was able.

We could do nothing else.

Mr. Malstrom made the necessary announcement to the
stunned passengers and crew. From some inner reserve he summoned a formal dignity. "Ladies and gentlemen, by the Grace
of Lord God, Captain Justin Haag, commanding officer of
U.N.S. *Hibernia*, has died in an explosion of the ship's launch.
With him died Lieutenant Abraham Cousins, Lieutenant Lisa
Dagalow, Machinist Jorge Perez, able seaman Mikhail Arbatov,
and six passengers. I, Lieutenant Harvey Malstrom, senior officer aboard, do hereby take command of this ship."

He rested his head on the console. Then he continued,
"The six passengers are Ms. Ruth Davies, Mr. Edward
Hearnes, Mr. Ayah Dinh, Ms. Indira Etra, Mr. Vance Port-
right, and Mr. Randolph Carr."

After a moment he reached for the speaker again. "Chief
McAndrews, Dr. Uburu, and Pilot Haynes, report to the
bridge." Then he swung toward me, desolate. "God, Nicky,
what do I do now?"

"Permission to use the caller, sir."

"Go ahead."

I rang Dr. Uburu's quarters. "This is the bridge. Please bring a tankard of medicinal alcohol to your conference with Captain Malstrom."

The Captain shot me a grateful look. Then as the import of my words sunk in, he paled. "Captain Malstrom. Dear God!"

"'Yes, sir.'" I wasn't good at my practical lessons but I knew the regs fairly well. The commanding officer of a Naval vessel was always a Captain. His rank was subject to reconfirmation by Admiralty upon return, but a ship could be commanded only by a Captain. When Lieutenant Malstrom became *Hibernia*'s senior officer, he became Captain Malstrom.

After a moment's inward reflection he focused on me anew, and muttered, "You'd better go, Nicky. I've got to talk to them."

"Aye aye, sir." I came to attention and snapped a formal salute. The Captain would need all the support he could get. He returned the salute and I left him to his desolation.

I trudged back to the wardroom. Sandy's eyes were red. Vax, for once, was quiet and withdrawn. I chased them both out of the cabin and lay down in the dark, to cry myself to sleep. At seventeen, I was unaccustomed to horror and loss.

When I woke the next morning, Sandy Wilsky was in the brig pending the official inquiry into the disaster. He'd been arrested by Master-at-arms Vishinsky, on orders of the Captain. I knew he was innocent, and surely so did Mr. Malstrom, but if it hadn't been for Sandy's tomfoolery, he, not Lieutenant Dagalow, would have been aboard the launch when it disintegrated.

Troubled, I went in search of Amanda, and found her in her cabin. Seeing my face, she stood aside without a word, closed the hatch behind us.

Not long after, she sat on her bunk, my head in her lap. "I don't understand, Nicky. Why can't he command *Hibernia* without changing rank? He's still the same Lieutenant Malstrom."

I was patient. "Think of Captain as a legal position instead of a rank. You think Captain Haag ran the ship, right? He was higher in rank than the lieutenants, so he was in charge."

"Right."

"Well, no. The Captain is the United Nations Government. All of it. The SecGen, the Security Council, the General Assembly, the World Court. Anything the U.N. can do, he can do. He is its plenipotentiary in space." For some reason, telling her the obvious made me feel better.

"So?"

"A lieutenant is just an officer, but the Captain is the government. Only the Captain can be that. And only the government can run the ship. So, the person who runs the ship is Captain. His word is law."

Amanda was already on another topic. "Anyway, Chief Engineer McAndrews has more seniority. He should be Captain."

"Hon, it doesn't work that way." She stroked my hair in response to my endearment. "The ship had three lieutenants. Under them are four middies. There are also three other officers on board. Staff officers."

"I've heard that before. What does it mean?"

"A line officer is in line to command the ship. Staff officers can order the middies and the seamen about, but they don't succeed to command. They're here to do a specific job, and that's it."

"But it's not fair. Chiefie has more experience than Mr. Malstrom."

I wondered when she had begun calling Chief McAndrews "Chiefie". I considered calling him that someday, but quickly decided against it. "Life isn't fair, Amanda. Chiefie doesn't get to run the ship." She bent over and kissed me. She had veered off onto yet another topic.

That evening the Captain convened a Board of Inquiry. Alexi and I might possibly have been appointed—a middy, no matter how young, is by Act of the General Assembly an officer and gentleman, and has his majority—and the Captain had few enough officers left to sit in judgment. But Alexi and I had been in the suiting room with Sandy; we were witnesses. If there were a plot, we might even have been involved, so on both counts we were disqualified.

Doc Uburu, Pilot Haynes, and Chief McAndrews sat as the Board. They met in the now unused lieutenants' common room, as if to underscore the purpose of the inquiry.

For two days they sifted through Darla's records, replaying over and again the last transmission from the launch, compiling a list of every sailor who'd entered the launch berth since *Hibernia* had left Earthport Station, reviewing the meager information the launch's primitive puter had passed to Darla during its shuttles back and forth to *Celestina*.

*Hibernia*'s launch berth was normally sealed. Darla had record of each occasion our crewmen were admitted for maintenance since we'd left Earthport. Counting the various work details assigned to shepherd the passengers across, seventeen crewmen had been in the launch berth at one time or another. All four of us middies had gone across to *Celestina*, and each of the officers save the members of the board.

One by one each sailor who'd been in the berth was questioned. Alexi, Vax, and I sat stiffly in the chairs placed in the corridor, knees tight, caps in hand, waiting our turns.

They brought Sandy from the brig for his interrogation; he marched past us with barely a glance. Two hours later he emerged, pale, shaken. It appeared he'd been crying.

I was next. I smoothed my jacket, tugged at my tie, marched into the crowded mess. My salute was as close to Academy perfection as I could manage.

Chief Engineer McAndrews was in the chair. "Be seated, Mr. Seafort." He glanced to his holovid, on which he'd been tapping notes. "Tell us what you saw—everything—in the launch berth before the launch's final trip."

"Aye aye, sir." I furrowed my brow, lurched into my recollection. I'd seen nothing suspicious, so all I could do was describe in detail Sandy's horseplay with Alexi, his torn trousers, Mr. Cousins's wrath.

"Then what?"

"Lieutenant Cousins ordered Alex—Midshipman Tamarov to take Mr. Wilsky's place. Ms. Dagalow asked if she could go instead."

"You're sure Mr. Cousins didn't order Dagalow aboard?"

"Quite sure, sir."

Pilot Haynes cleared his throat. "Did Mr. Tamarov suggest that he and Lieutenant Dagalow switch places?"

"Lord God, of course not!" I gulped, realizing what I'd blurted. Still, the question was preposterous. Were a middy to make such a suggestion to a lieutenant—any lieutenant—

he wouldn't be able to sit for a week. And that's if he were lucky. Such a remark was as out of place as—as the one I'd just made. I was in deep trouble. "I'm very sorry, sir!"

Chief McAndrews's tone was frosty, but he otherwise ignored my impertinence. Instead, he led me through a series of probing questions about my previous visits to the launch berth, about the watch rotation according to which I was supposed to be on the bridge.

"But I *was* on the bridge, sir. The horseplay occurred before my watch. I was helping suit the passengers."

The Pilot set his fingers together, as if in prayer. "Who told you to do that?"

"No one, sir."

"Why did you meddle?"

I flushed, knowing my response sounded inane even to myself. "I wanted to be helpful, sir."

"By being a busybody, instead of going to your post?"

"No, sir, I—yes, sir." There was no right answer, and I fell silent.

I could understand their frustration. A hydrozine engine doesn't overheat without cause. And if it did, the launch crew should have been able to shut it down within seconds, before it reached critical temperature. Accidents happen, but unexplained accidents made everyone uneasy. A glance out the porthole to the gaping wound in *Celestina*'s hull was reason enough for that.

The Chief Engineer glanced at Doc Uburu, offered the Pilot another question. Both shook their heads. The Chief pursed his lips. "Mr. Seafort, did you dislike Mr. Cousins?"

My uniform was drenched, my throat impossibly dry. My answer could ruin me, but I had little choice when asked a direct question. I squared my shoulders, gritted my teeth. "Yes, sir."

Remorseless, he made me give my reasons. When I was done my ears were red from shame.

At last, dazed and exhausted, I was allowed to make my way out to the corridor. Shakily, I sat.

The master-at-arms appeared in the hatchway. "Mr. Holser." Stolidly, Vax strode to his inquisition.

The inquiry went on.

Though we'd not yet Fused, despite the turmoil *Hibernia*

still had to be crewed and managed. Even with Sandy released from the brig, we were shorthanded. Four hours after my grilling, needing far more sleep than I'd had, nerves frazzled, I reported to the bridge for my watch.

At my knock Captain Malstrom swiveled the camera, opened the hatch, waved me to my seat.

We passed half the watch before he broke the stiff silence. "Have they found anything yet?"

It was obvious whom he meant. "Not that I know of, sir."

"It couldn't just happen. We have to find the cause."

"Yes, sir." It wasn't my place to say more. My friend Harv had vanished forever; this was the Captain, in all his eminence. I was but a middy.

# 6

In a ship even as large as *Hibernia*, rumors true and false traveled faster than light. Within minutes, everyone knew that at the Chief's insistence, the Board would review the case of every sailor sent to Captain's Mast since we'd left port. That couldn't be much of a task; on the whole, *Hibernia* had been a happy ship, and had few problems the petty officers couldn't settle belowdecks.

Vax went off watch. While I lounged in my bunk, grateful that Alexi hadn't chosen to blare his usual slap music, Sandy Wilsky burst in, quivering with indignation. "Malstrom's going to P and D the lot of us!"

"What?" Alexi jerked to a sitting position.

"All us middies, and the sailors who've been in the launch berth!"

"Why?"

"To rule out any possibility of sabotage, he told Doc."

Alexi slammed a fist into his mattress. "That's not fair."

I growled, "You'll get over it." Poly and drug interrogation wasn't pleasant, but the aftereffects didn't last all that long.

Alexi said, "But we've none of us been charged!"

Sandy's tone was sullen. "The grode hasn't the right—"

I swarmed out of my bunk blurting the first thing that came into my head. "Wilsky, look at the scuff on those boots! One demerit! And that blanket!" My hand slapped his bed, found a tiny crease. "Another!"

Alexi gaped. "Why are you suddenly down on—"

I whirled. "And you! How many demerits now?" I knew Alexi was slow at working them off.

"Nine, Mr. Seaf—"

"Two more for your insolence!" Knowing it would send him to the barrel, I added after an ominous pause, "I won't log them 'til morning. Get started."

"But, I—"

"NOW!"

They scrambled for the hatch.

"No talking while you exercise! One word and the demerits are doubled!"

"Aye aye, Mr. Seafort!" The hatch slammed. I sat on the side of my bed, head in hands, trembling.

Their hero worship was a thing of the past; from this moment, they'd hate me. But I'd had no choice.

It had been close.

Their resentment at P and D testing was no surprise. Polygraph and drug interrogation was allowed aboard ship, as at any trial. Since the Truth in Testimony Act of 2026, a defendant had no right to silence. If there were other evidence against him, he could be sent for P and D, and usually was. If the tests proved he'd told the truth, charges were dismissed. If he admitted the charges, as the sophisticated mix of drugs forced him to do, his confession was of course introduced as evidence.

However, two safeguards applied. The subject had to have been charged with a crime, and he had to have denied the charge.

Without those limitations, poly and drugs could become tools of a despot or, worse, of torture. The law didn't allow the court a fishing expedition into a man's mind to discover what crimes he might have committed.

I kept an eye on the time, not at all concerned that I'd left Alexi and Sandy alone. I'd given a direct order that they'd acknowledged. They would have no conversation while they toiled in the exercise room.

I dozed.

As the fourth hour neared its end I got wearily to my feet, trudged down to Level 2.

When I went in, Alexi was working the bars while Sandy jogged in place. Their undershirts were soaked through, their hair matted. Sandy's breath came in a rasp. It took hard labor to cancel a demerit, as I well knew. "At ease, both of you."

Alexi dismounted. Slowly Sandy came to a stop.

"Against the bulkhead." For a moment I paced, then faced them with a glare. "Anything to say?"

"No, Mr. Seafort." Sandy sounded every bit as young as he was, and scared.

"And you?"

Despite his physical weariness, Alexi smoldered. "Why did you turn on us?"

Inwardly, I groaned. With typical clumsiness, I'd allowed Alexi to open a conversation I couldn't allow us to have. "Mr. Wilsky, outside." I followed Sandy into the corridor. As casually as I could, I told him, "Griping is beneath you, Sandy. You're an officer now, not a cadet. If you have complaints about how the ship is run, you're expected to keep them to yourself."

He colored. "Yes, Mr. Seafort."

"Promise me you'll do so in future."

"Aye aye, Mr. Seafort. I'm sorry." Despite my brutality, he seemed pathetically eager to please.

"It annoyed me enough to give you the demerits. Go take your shower." I touched his damp shoulder. "Good lad."

Hoping I'd struck the right note I went back to the exercise room and Alexi. My tone was harsh. "Idiot."

"I—what?"

I leaned close, spoke barely above a whisper. "I'm trying to save your life!"

He said nothing, but his eyes showed his puzzlement.

"Captain Malstrom is free to investigate the death of his officers as he sees fit."

"But the law says—"

"Alexi!" Even in shutting him up, I risked our safety; couldn't he understand? "It's the *Captain!*"

I'd said all that was necessary. The indiscriminate testing Captain Malstrom ordered was in clear violation of the Truth in Testimony Act. When he brought *Hibernia* home, Admiralty could beach him for it, or worse.

But aboard ship, none of that mattered. The Captain's word was law. My duty was to carry out his orders, and to report seditious talk. To do else was to conspire in mutiny.

I said no more, and waited. At last, Alexi's face showed he understood. Still standing at ease, he gave a faint nod.

I sighed with relief. "Sandy should be all right now. But if you hear him even thinking aloud about the subject, sit on him hard. Don't hesitate."

"Right."

"Dismissed."

As he left, he whispered, "Thank you." I pretended I hadn't heard.

The next day we went to our P and D, the middies first, then the sailors. I came out of Doc Uburu's cubicle dizzy and nauseous, not quite sure what I'd babbled under the drugs' irresistible influence. I crawled under my covers, trying not to be sick to my stomach.

The next day I still felt the effects, though they were much diminished.

Word was that all of us had tested innocent, middies down through the lowest rating. Sandy lay in his bunk, sicker than the rest of us. P and D affected some more than others.

The Board of Inquiry met one last time, issued its report. They found no evidence of sabotage; they concluded the accident was probably caused by a deteriorating fuel valve unnoticed by a sensor that had malfunctioned.

For two more days, while we recovered, the ship floated dead in space.

Captain Malstrom conferred off and on with the Chief, Pilot Haynes, and Dr. Uburu, determining whether to return to Earthport Station. When I next had the watch he was as gruff as he'd been before, then unbent.

"I'm sorry, Nicky. I'm frantic with worry. I don't know what to do."

"I understand, sir."

"I've pretty well decided to go on. If there's been no sabotage we're not at undue risk, and Miningcamp and Hope Nation desperately need our cargo. If we turned back, it would be almost a year before a replacement ship got this far."

"Yes, sir."

"Nicky, I want to be honest with you. We have no lieutenants, and you're senior. But I can't appoint you, yet. You aren't qualified."

"I know, sir. What about Vax?" The words were bitter on my tongue, but I had to say them. Vax was far more ready than I.

"No, not yet. He doesn't have the temperament. I'm still looking to you. By the time we get to Hope Nation you'll qualify, I promise. I'll help you. For now, you'll both remain middies. If I can, I'll see that you make the grade before the others." If so, I'd have seniority over them for the rest of our days in the Navy, unless one of us finally made Captain.

"That's not necessary, sir." I forced down the foul taste of ambition.

"Maybe not, but it's what I intend." He took a deep breath. "We'll Fuse tomorrow, right after the memorial service."

"Yes, sir."

The service was a sad and formal affair. We officers wore our dress whites, our white slacks gleaming against black shoes, the red stripe down each leg sharp and bright. Our white shirts and black ties were covered by immaculate white dress jackets, a black mourning sash thrown over the right shoulder. Our length of service medals gleamed.

On a distant cruise, burial was in space, in a sealed coffin ejected from the airlock. *Celestina*'s dead had been so entombed, and drifted to this day on their endless way through the cosmos.

Ours wasn't a burial service, because there was nothing to bury. A memorial service, held in the ship's dining hall.

Every person aboard *Hibernia* crowded into the mess, the crew awkward in unfamiliar officers' country. Relatives of two passengers who had died, Mr. Rajiv Etra and Derek Carr, were mourners and stood with the officers who mourned their Captain on behalf of the ship. The other four passengers had been traveling alone. Mr. Etra stood in forlorn dignity. Derek Carr, his eyes red, spoke to no one and held himself stiffly.

Captain Malstrom led us in the traditional ritual of the Yahwehist Reunification. "We commend the spirits of our dead to your keeping, O Lord God," he said. "As we commit their bodies to your void, until your day of judgment when you call them forth again . . ."

We stood a few moments in silence, and it was ended.

After the service Alexi went on watch, with Pilot Haynes. Normally the Pilot was called only when we docked at a station or navigated a trafficked area. Now, though, he would have to stand watches with the rest of us.

Back in the wardroom Vax Holser was sullen. When Sandy got in his way, he shoved the boy aside. I ignored it, not ready to face another problem. An hour or so later we Fused.

Pilot Haynes was a dour, balding man who said hardly a word, if I didn't count routine orders when on watch. We middies wondered why he stayed bald, when most people would have undergone simple follicle touchup. Of course, none of us dared ask.

A watch shared with the Pilot was a very quiet time. Now that we were back in Fusion I found it hard to stay awake in the lengthy silences. Not that the Pilot was offended by remarks from a middy; he just squelched them by monosyllabic answers until one tired of trying.

"Energy variations seem up a trifle, sir." I was reading from my screen.

"Um."

I made another attempt. "What's the widest normal variation, sir?"

"Ask Darla." It was little more than a grunt.

I turned to the puter. "Darla, what's our greatest normal energy variation?"

"For the fusion drive?" Sometimes she needed us to be very specific.

"Yes, Darla."

"Two percent above and below mark, Mr. Seafort." A long pause. "Are you trying to make conversation?" I don't know how they programmed that.

After watch when I returned to my bunk, tired and irritable,

Vax was ragging Alexi. I told him to stop. He did, but stared at me, a contemptuous smile on his face, until I got up and stalked out of the wardroom.

"The discovery by Cheel and Vorhees in 2046 that N-waves travel faster than light, and their accompanying revision of the laws of physics, led to the fusion drive and superluminous travel." Mr. Ibn Saud paused, surveying the audience of passengers, officers, and crew in *Hibernia's* dining hall.

"Riding the crest of the N-wave, powered by wave emissions rather than particle emissions, our great ships glide through the galaxy, exploring, colonizing." Absorbed, I sat, wishing Sandy wouldn't fidget. The Passengers' Lecture Series was a welcome diversion from ship's routine, and he should have the sense to appreciate it.

"Fusion brought us desperately needed resources, such as metals from Miningcamp. But the real benefit of the fusion drive was as a safety hatch—it allowed those educated, intelligent, restless folk who chose to settle the distant colonies a means to flee Earth's dwindling resources, pollution, and soaring population."

Ibn Saud sipped from his glass of water.

"But the fusion drive embodies the dilemma of maintaining our ever more complex technology. The colonies need our best and brightest, and at the same time, the new industries spawned by Fusion demand great numbers of highly skilled workers.

"Meanwhile, society has recognized at last that compulsory education was a resounding failure. Voluntary schooling results in better education, but for fewer people. So, unfortunately, the general populace is less educated than they were two centuries past. Some, like the transpops who infest the lower levels of our cities, have no training at all, and are fit for no work."

Ibn Saud smiled apologetically in our direction. "Nowhere is our shortage of skilled labor more apparent than in the military forces. The officer classes, selected from the educated, technological minority, are drawn to a life of honor, to the excitement of exploring the galaxy." I nodded, without thinking.

"But for the most part the Navy, like the U.N.A.F. ground

force, is manned—by necessity—from the uneducated underclass. And so we have the anomaly of a great starship, the pinnacle of technology, governed by an authoritarian system not unlike that of the eighteenth century sea navies. We've even returned to corporal punishment, at least for young officers. Rigid hierarchies maintain order as we travel to the stars.

"But mankind will be changed by the experience—in what way, we do not know; it will be generations before we learn. Surely the changes are for the better. If we assume Lord God watches over us, as he always has, the rescue of civilization by the fusion drive becomes understandable. If man is marked for further greatness, if we are destined to colonize the galaxy, we have been given the tools. What we make of them, and what they make of us, is up to us."

Ibn Saud sat to enthusiastic applause. Amanda, as education director, lauded him for his presentation, and thanked the audience for attending. As we dispersed I caught her eye, relishing her quick smile.

That evening at dinner I watched her tease Vax, at the next table. He didn't seem to mind. At my own table Yorinda Vincente, head of the Passengers' Council, was discussing council meetings with Johan Spiegel and Mrs. Donhauser. I was bored stiff.

After, freed from watch until the following noon but not yet ready for sleep, I lay in my bunk fully dressed, trying to read. When Vax came in he turned on his holovid, plugging in a shrill slap-nag chip. He ignored my glance of annoyance. Sandy arrived, smiling happily. He had been seated at table with a girl his own age.

Vax, lying on his bunk, asked, "You going to prong her, Wilsky?"

Sandy's grin vanished. "I don't want to talk about her." He sounded almost defiant.

"She'd be good at it. If you don't ask her, I will."

I said, "Drop it, Vax."

"I wasn't hazing." Holser was belligerent. "Just making conversation."

"Lay off."

Vax subsided, smirking.

Half an hour later I realized I'd been reading the same

screen over and again, without remembering a word. I got to my feet. "Come along, Vax." I went out to the corridor. After a moment he followed. I headed for the ladder.

"Where to?"

I ignored him completely. I took the ladder down to Level 2, giving him a choice of watching me leave or following. He followed. I strode down the corridor to the exercise room, slapped open the hatch. The room was empty.

Vax stood in the hatchway. "What are you doing?"

I took off my jacket and folded it neatly over the exercise horse. I yanked at my tie.

"Seafort—MR. Seafort, what the hell are you doing?" He lounged against the hatchway.

"Come in and shut the hatch. That's an order." I took off my shirt and folded it over the jacket. Vax nodded slowly. He shut the hatch behind him. I emptied my pants pockets.

"What's your problem, MR. Seafort?"

"Better get ready, Vax."

"For what?"

"We're about to have it out, once and for all."

"We have a truce, remember?"

"Not anymore." I tightened my shoelace.

"Why not?" He still wore his full uniform; he was making no move to get ready.

"I can't stand you." I walked right up to him, unafraid, and grabbed his coat. "It's your uniform, Vax. Do you want it soiled or not?"

Reluctantly, he discarded his jacket. I went into karate position, guard up, on my toes.

Vax backed away, shook his head. "The wardroom shouldn't be fighting now, Nick. Not with the problems the ship has."

"I'll fight. You just stand there."

"Nick, don't. Not with the Captain dead."

I slapped him. He didn't like that, and brought up his guard. We circled.

"Tell me what you want, Nick, before we fight." He stepped back, lowered his fists.

"Want?" My voice shook with hatred. "You're a bully, Holser. You're brutal. You sneer at the boys. You hurt them." I kept looking for an opening, my hands up. "I've never seen you do anything kind. You're good at your job, but you're the meanest person I've ever met!"

He surprised me, crying out, "I know!" He thrust his hands in his pockets. "I can't help it, Nick. That's how I've always been. It's who I am."

"Fight me."

"Why?"

"We've got to have it out, Vax. If you win I'll ask the Captain to beach me for four months. That'll make you first middy. You'll have it all your way." The Captain had authority to suspend my commission for any length of time he chose. I would stop accumulating seniority, and Vax wouldn't.

"What if you win?"

"I'm in charge. All the way to Detour and back. You know your problem? You think I'm the first middy, and you're second. You've got it wrong."

"Then tell me what's right." He had his guard down again. He didn't want to fight tonight.

"I'm first middy, and you're not!" I walked up to him and poked him in the chest, not far below my eye level. "There's no second midshipman! Just the first and a bunch of others. I can't help that you weren't first. You fought it ever since we came on board, Holser, and now I've had it. I hate you so much I can't stand looking at you!"

He spoke quietly. "I know I'm not nice, Nicky. What do you want me to do about it?"

I yelled, "I don't care! I'm not interested in you. I just want you to obey orders, like the other juniors! You know what that's worth to me? Getting killed tonight." I took several breaths. "I'm done talking, you bastard."

"And if I do what you tell me?"

"What do you think, Vax? After how you've treated everyone else?"

"You'll get even."

"You're damn right I will! For everything!"

"Hold off a minute. Please." I couldn't understand his reluctance. He could pulverize me. Last time, I'd been lucky.

I went across the room and hoisted myself onto the parallel bar. "You've got thirty seconds. Then I'm coming at you." I began counting under my breath.

He took all thirty of them. I jumped off the bars and came at him, moving fast. He said, "I'll obey your orders, Mr. Seafort."

I skidded to a stop. "For how long?"

"As long as you're my superior officer." The belligerence was gone from his tone.

"I don't believe you! There'll come a time. Let's have it over with."

"I give you my word." Vax looked me in the eye, unflinching.

"Why, Holser?"

He shook his head. "I don't know. Maybe now the Captain's dead, being first middy doesn't seem so important. Maybe it's the way Alexi looks at you sometimes, when he thinks you don't see." He glared, as if expecting me to mock him. "Do you care about my reasons? I told you I'll do it, so I will."

I was helpless. "We'll see if you mean it. A hundred push-ups."

"Aye aye, Mr. Seafort." He loosened his tie, dropped to the deck, and began pumping.

Well. It seemed he actually intended to obey orders.

I didn't let up. I worked him for two hours, until he was drenched with sweat. Then I walked out of the room without a word.

I ran Vax ragged for a whole month. He got to clean the wardroom, top to bottom. I saddled him with extra duty at all hours. He did as he was told. He was not friendly to me, and his manner was so ominous that the others made it a point to stay out of his way. But he never defied me.

With the loss of the lieutenants we were all on double watches. I was constantly tired; so was everyone else. My free afternoons were with Amanda. I never played chess anymore; it would have been unthinkable with the Captain, and there was no one else with whom I was that close. I was unhappy; we all were.

Captain Malstrom was unhappy too, though he tried not to let it show. It affected all of us. I had frightening dreams. Alexi turned to his slap music for comfort. Sandy held hands with his new young friend.

In the wardroom, I took it out on Vax. I gave him all the

hazing he had ever forced the others to endure, and more. I ordered him in and out of bed all night adjusting the heat. I stood him at attention in the wardroom when he wanted to relax in his bunk. At night I would put him under an ice-cold shower for half an hour at a time. Afterward in the dark I could hear his teeth chatter as he lay trying to warm himself.

He never protested. He obeyed my orders. Slowly, I came to realize that Vax was a person who did what he promised. I began to respect him for that, but I didn't let up. He had a lot coming.

Ship's routine settled into the dreary monotony of Fusion. Amanda helped the passengers put on plays and arrange contests. The Pilot and Chief Engineer drilled us in our studies. The Captain ordered the barrel moved to the Chief's engine room, but it wasn't put to use. On our time off, I devoted my attention to Vax. I confined him to quarters except when he was on duty or taking exercise. But he remained docile and carried out my orders to the letter.

One evening when Sandy and Alexi went below I put Vax at attention in the center of the wardroom. I let him stand there for an hour while I read my holovid. Then I said quietly, "Do you want me to let up, Vax?"

He took a long time to think about it. Finally he said, "Yes, Mr. Seafort, I do."

I sent him to his bunk to lie down. He lay propped on one elbow listening. "I expect you to be an officer and a gentleman. Especially a gentleman. I expect you to act in the wardroom's best interest and in mine. To be pleasant to all of us. To lay off hazing except by my direct order. To mind your own business, and nobody else's. To support me in my duties. When you're prepared to do every one of those things, Holser, then I'll let up. Not before." I let him think about that. I went back to my holovid.

A half hour later he spoke up. "I'm prepared, Mr. Seafort."

"What's that?" I hadn't expected a capitulation.

"I'm prepared. To do all the things you said." I knew he meant it. Holser was true to his word. I could count on it.

I nodded. "Very well."

When Alexi and Sandy came back I lined all three of them against the partition. "What went on in the wardroom before is over," I said. "You're to forget it or ignore it. From now on you will act in a spirit of friendly cooperation. There will be no hazing, no discipline unless I dispense it. You will each shake hands with each other, and with me, to establish the attitude in which we'll carry out our duties henceforth. That is all.'' We shook hands all around.

The wardroom was mine.

# 7

Two nights later, Amanda and I made love for the first time. She was not my first woman, but she was almost my first. We gently and lovingly practiced the arts I knew, and I learned from her skills I had not known.

I was astonished at how much I needed her closeness. I thought I'd learned to do without tenderness, touching, caring, at least while on ship. I couldn't go away from her, our first night. I stayed in her cabin, cupped around her warm and pleasing body, drinking her intimacy like wine. In the morning we kissed and parted, both shy from our newfound vulnerability.

I went about my duties in a daze, thinking more of my times off watch than my responsibilities on, until even the Pilot became aware and made a wondering remark. I snapped my attention back to my job. It would be a long, slow voyage. There was time for everything.

A few days later I came back from a cozy evening in Amanda's cabin and was peeling off my jacket when Captain Malstrom's voice burst from the wardroom caller. ''Mr. Seafort, Mr. Holser, to the bridge! Flank!'' Vax and I exchanged startled glances. We sprinted to the ladder.

The Captain waited impatiently in the bridge hatchway. ''Hurry!'' He shoved us inside and slapped the control. The hatch snapped shut. ''There's a battle in crew berth three. Chief Petty Officer's been hit on the head. I don't know how many are in the riot, or what it's about.''

I gaped. The Captain paid no heed. "Mr. Holser, go to berths one and two and seal the hatches. Confine all seamen to quarters. Nick, meet the master-at-arms at the munitions locker. Stun guns and gas. Make sure the seamen with him are reliable before you open the locker. Stop the fighting. Separate the men, brig the rioters. Take these!" He snapped open the bridge safe and handed me a laser pistol and the locker keys. "I'll hold the bridge. Move!" He slapped open the hatch.

"Aye aye, sir!" We left on the double. Vax ran down the ladder to berths one and two while I headed forward to the armament locker.

I found the master-at-arms looming over two nervous seamen, a billy clenched in his hands. He was grim. "These two will do," he said.

"Names?"

The first sailor stepped forward. "Gunner's Mate Edwards, sir." She saluted. The other said, "Machinist's Mate Tsai Ting, sir." They both came to attention.

"At ease." I opened the locker. Master-at-arms Vishinsky's choices were dependable; I would stake my life on it. In his outrage he'd have but one goal: to restore order and get his hands on the miscreants.

I grabbed four sleek stun guns and handed them around. I snatched a handful of gas grenades, thrust them at Ms. Edwards. The locker safely shut, I loped toward the ladder, the others at my heels. I charged down to Level 2, ran around the ladder well, and dived down toward the lowest level. At Level 3 I dashed along the gray-walled corridor toward the crew berths. Around the bend, a crowd of seamen milled outside a hatchway, pushing and shoving for a better view.

"Stand to, all of you!" My voice was pitched higher than I'd have liked. "Attention!" A few in the back realized an officer was present and stiffened. Vishinsky waded in, billy club jabbing, stunner ready in his left hand. In moments he had the throng separated, lining the bulkheads to either side.

I gabbled, "Edwards, draw your weapon! You sailors, stand at attention! Ting, Edwards, stun any man who moves!" I swung back and forth, calmed slightly as I realized the situation in the corridor was under control.

From inside the berth, shouts and the sounds of riot.

"Let's go!" I charged at the hatch.

Mr. Vishinsky hauled me back, nearly hurling me to the deck. "Easy, sir." For a moment his eye held mine. He cautiously poked his head into the hatch, stunner ready. After peering both directions, he stepped through.

I followed, abashed. Inside, about a dozen seamen were slugging it out. Chief Petty Officer Terrill lay across a bunk, blood oozing from his scalp. Other sailors lay on the deck, out of combat. Chairs, bunks, duffels were strewn in wild disarray. The air smelled of sweat and close confinement.

Vishinsky took a deep breath. "*NOW HEAR THIS! STAND TO, EVERY ONE OF YOU!*" His roar filled the room. Its sheer force brought a momentary lull in the melee. "*DROP YOUR HANDS, YOU LOW-LIFE CRUDS! STAND AT ATTENTION!*" I wanted to cover my ears. He was impressive.

Most of the combatants began to disengage. They looked about, as if dazed, and brought themselves to attention. I covered them with my stunner. Four men ignored the master-at-arms, continued to hammer each other.

Coolly, Vishinsky stepped up to the first pair and pressed his stunner to one fighter's back. His finger twitched. The seaman dropped like a stone. His sparring partner aimed a wild swing at the master-at-arms. Vishinsky fired again. His assailant fell backward across a bunk, toppled to the deck.

I watched openmouthed as Vishinsky sauntered to the last two combatants. He pressed his gun to one man's shoulder and fired. The sailor went down. His opponent backed away, raising his hands high as he sucked at air in ragged gasps. Vishinsky motioned him to stand with the others. As the man turned to go, the Master kicked him in the behind. The sailor staggered.

A thud, from the corridor. I looked out. A seaman was stretched on the deck, unconscious. "He moved, sir." Edwards swallowed.

"Very well." I spoke as calmly as I could. Now what? Not sure what else to do, I ordered all the sailors to the outer side of the corridor and bade them sit on the deck, hands on their knees. "Keep your stunner on them, Edwards." I sent Ting inside the berth to cover the remaining seamen.

I dialed the bridge from the caller on the bulkhead. "Mr. Seafort reporting, sir. The riot is over. We'll need the Doctor for a few of them. At least a dozen were fighting."

"What in the Lord's name started it?" I heard the relief in Captain Malstrom's voice.

"I don't know yet, sir."

"I'll send Chief McAndrews to help sort it out. Stand easy."

When the Chief arrived, he unsealed crew berth one and picked six reliable seamen. He'd brought cuffs and leg irons; within a few minutes I was able to collect the stunners and grenades and run them up to the arms locker. When I got back to the crew berth, the Chief and the master-at-arms were sorting through the mess on the deck, tossing belongings aside as they went.

Mr. Vishinsky took an opportunity to maneuver me to one side. "Sorry my arm got tangled in your jacket," he said quietly.

"Thanks, Mr. Vishinsky. You saved me from getting clubbed to death."

"No problem." A good man, the master-at-arms. There was a time to belay regs, and he knew when.

"Here it is!" Chief McAndrews held up a vial of amber liquid. A little box at his feet held several similar vials.

I blinked. "Goofjuice?" I used the slang term for the pervasive drug.

"Look how much they have. I wonder if they brought it aboard." The Chief looked about with suspicion.

"Of course they brought it, sir," I said. "They didn't find it on—" I stopped. "A still, on the ship?" It was impossible. No one would dare.

"Maybe." He caught Vishinsky's eye; the master-at-arms gave the billy in his hands an angry twist. They went to work with a vengeance, removing every item in each sailor's locker. It took them two hours to find it. The back plate of one seaman's locker was loose; behind was a cavity in the bulkhead.

"Lord God damn these people!" Vishinsky intended no blasphemy; I was sure he meant it literally. Arnolf Tuak, the hapless owner of the locker, was hauled off to the brig.

It was late in the night before full order was restored and

all known offenders were under lock and key. Wearily, we trooped back to officers' country. "A bad kettle of fish," was all Chief McAndrews had to say.

"Yes, sir." Bad indeed.

"Contraband drugs on *Hibernia*." Captain Malstrom said it again.

"Yes, sir." I stood at attention; he had forgotten to let me stand easy.

His mouth curled in revulsion. "I expect they'll smuggle a flask of wet stuff, Nicky. All sailors do that. But goofjuice . . ."

Goofjuice was another matter entirely. It didn't seem addictive at first. But once it got hold, its grip was almost unshakable. The erratic behavior it caused wasn't a problem to the joey indulging; he was in bliss all the while he was under the influence. But we had just seen an example of the mess it made for everyone else.

"Yes, sir. At least we found the source."

Juice wasn't that hard to make: a few test tubes, a retort, starch, magnesium salts, other common ingredients.

"When Admiralty hears of this . . ." He shook his head. Actually, I doubted it would be that bad. If Captain Haag were still in command he'd have had a lot to explain. But Mr. Malstrom hadn't been in charge when the crew boarded.

He looked up. "Stand easy, Nicky. I'm sorry."

"Thank you, sir." I relaxed. "How are you going to handle it? Captain's Mast?" It was not a question a middy could ask. But Mr. Malstrom obviously wanted to talk about it, and once he had been my friend Harv.

"No." His face hardened. "Court-martial." Seeing my surprise he added, "Those scum knew what they were doing. They broke a dozen regs just getting the stuff aboard ship. Then they caused a major riot among the crew. What if they'd gone berserk on duty stations, instead of in their bunks? In the engine room, or the airlock?"

He was right, up to a point. The sailors' stupidity might have wrecked our ship. But it hadn't; we'd dealt with them in crew quarters. Captain's Mast, or nonjudicial punishment, would mete out demotion, pay decreases, or extra duties. A court-martial was far more serious. While *Hibernia* was interstellar, far from home, the men could be punished with the brig, summary dismissal, or even execution.

Instead of putting the incident behind us, court-martial would formalize and enlarge it. Worse, the matter would drag on unhealed while the court-martial was convened, poisoning relations between the enlisted men and officers.

"Yes, sir. I understand." It wasn't my place to tell him my reservations.

"I'm appointing Pilot Haynes as hearing officer. Alexi will be their advocate."

"Alexi?" I was so astonished I forgot my discipline. "Sir," I quickly added, to correct my breach.

"Who else? It has to be an officer. Chief McAndrews found the stuff; he'll be a witness like you and Vax. Sandy has to present the evidence against them. There's no one else left."

"Doc Uburu?"

"Doc treated the injured and conducted the interrogations." The Captain was right; he had no more officers to call on.

"Aye aye, sir." I began figuring how to relieve Alexi from his watches, so he'd have more time to study the regs.

The court convened three days later, in the vacant lieutenants' common room where the Board of Inquiry had met. In all, fifteen men were charged. Three were accused of organizing the still, taking part in the riot, and assaulting a superior officer. They were in the worst trouble of all. Five more were charged with use of contraband intoxicants, four of those with rioting as well. Seven others were charged with taking part in the melee.

It wasn't as complicated as it sounded. Petty Officer Terrill knew which two sailors had worked him over: one of the men who was accused of using the goofjuice, and one of the three distributors. Several of those charged with rioting pled guilty to all charges, throwing themselves on the Captain's mercy. Two of the men accused of using the goofjuice also pled guilty.

The Captain was not lenient; he sentenced four of the men to six months in the brig and busted three others right down to apprentice seaman. Then the trials of the remaining eight got under way.

The three men charged with supplying the goofjuice were tried first. Pilot Haynes, sitting at the raised desk, listened impassively while Alexi Tamarov haltingly argued on behalf of his clients. It was no kangaroo court; when the Pilot felt the middy was not bringing out a defensive point, he put aside his preferred reticence and questioned the witness himself.

The three hapless sailors whispered with Alexi from time to time, interrupting his questioning of Chief McAndrews.

"Was the vial under a particular bunk when you found it, sir?"

"Not completely," said the Chief, unruffled. "The box was on the deck, half pushed under a bunk."

"So you don't know for sure that it was in Mr. Tuak's possession, sir?" Alexi was doing his best on a hopeless case. Tuak had already confessed under P and D. As was his right, he recanted his confession, but of course it would be entered against him. Alexi was casting about for other evidence to discredit it.

"I don't know, Mr. Tamarov." The Chief was undisturbed; other witnesses had identified the box as belonging to Tuak.

"Sir, did you see anything that contradicts Mr. Tuak's having been framed by another sailor?"

"Yes." Alexi looked surprised and worried, but had no choice but to let the Chief answer. "When he recovered from the stun charge, Mr. Tuak tried to claw Mr. Vishinsky's face."

"Could that have been from anger at having been stunned unjustly?"

"It could have," said the Chief, his tone making clear he didn't believe it.

The trial droned on. I was called as a witness, but had little to offer except a description of Mr. Vishinsky quelling the riot. Neither Sandy nor Alexi seemed much interested in my testimony.

The trial, I reflected, was mostly ritual. It could help disclose truth, but that has rarely been necessary since P and D testing became the norm. Yet we still observed the old forms in civilian as well as military courts: defense attorneys, prosecutors, witnesses. In nearly all cases we already knew the outcome.

While the trial was in recess I wandered into the passengers' lounge, looking for a conversation to distract me. Perhaps Mrs. Donhauser and Mr. Ibn Saud were at it again. I found two older passengers I barely knew, reading holovids. One of the Treadwell twins, the girl, was writing a game program; she tested it from time to time on the passengers' screen. Derek Carr, lean, tall, aristocratic, studied the holo of the galaxy on the bulkhead, hands clasped behind his back.

I stood near him, lowering my voice. "My condolences, Mr. Carr. I never had a chance to speak to you after your father's death."

"Thank you," the boy said distantly. His eyes remained on the holo. It was a dismissal.

"If there's anything I can do, please let me know." I moved away.

"Midshipman." He didn't even know my name, after sitting at table with me a month. I waited. "There's something you can do. Talk with me." He hesitated. "I need to speak to someone. It might as well be you."

Graciously stated. I made allowances for his bereavement. "All right. Where?"

"Let's walk." We strolled aimlessly along the circumference corridor, passing the dining hall, the ladders, the Level 2 passenger staterooms.

He said, "My father and I own property on Hope Nation. A lot of it. That's why we were going home."

"Then you're provided for." I spoke just to keep the conversation going.

"Oh, yes." His tone was bitter. "Trusts and guardianships; my father had it all worked out. He showed me his will. The banks and the plantation managers will run the estate for years. I won't get anything until I'm twenty-two. Six years! I mean, I won't starve. But it's not like . . ."

After a while I prompted, "Like what, Mr. Carr?"

He looked into the distance, beyond the bulkhead. "He'd been training me to run the plantations. He taught me bookkeeping, the crop cycles. We made decisions together. I thought . . ." His eyes misted. "My father and I . . . We had money, we had a good life. I thought it would always be that way."

Thrusting his hands in his pockets he turned to me, his eyes bleak. "And now it's all gone. I'll be treated like a joeyboy again. Nobody will listen. No one will care. It'll be years before I can do anything about it."

I said nothing, taking it in. "Do you have a mother?"

"No, I'm a monogenetic clone. Just my father." Not an uncommon arrangement of late, but I wondered how it would feel. Back home in Cardiff we were more conservative; I carried my host mother's genes as well as Father's, though I'd never met her. After a moment Derek added, "I thought you might understand, being my own age and all. And having responsibilities."

"Yes, I understand. Tell me something, Mr. Carr."

"What?"

I probably shouldn't have said it, but I was overtired and my nerves were on edge. "Do you miss your father?" He stiffened at my tone. I added, "You haven't mentioned how you feel about him. Just the advantages he gave you."

He was furious. "I miss him. More than a person like you will ever know. Forget we spoke." He stalked back down the corridor.

I strode quickly to catch up. "How do you expect me to know, when you keep it hidden?"

He took several more steps before slowing. Finally he stopped, hand against the bulkhead. "I don't wear my feelings for everyone to see," he said coldly. "It's uncouth."

I felt I owed him something for jabbing at him. "The day I went to Academy at Dover, I was thirteen. My father brought me to town. I had my belongings in a duffel I carried at my side. Father walked me to the compound gates, his hands in his pockets, saying nothing. When we reached the gate I stopped to say good-bye. He turned my shoulders around and pushed me toward the entrance. I started walking. When I looked again he was striding away without looking back." I paused. "I dream about it frequently. The psych says I'll probably outgrow it." I took a couple of breaths to restore calm. "It's not the same, Mr. Carr, but I know what loneliness is."

After a pause Derek said, "I'm sorry I snapped at you, Midshipman."

"It's Seafort. Nick Seafort."

"I apologize, Midshipman Seafort. My father always said we were extraordinary, and I believed it. In a way we are. It's hard to remember other people have feelings too."

We wandered back to the lounge, saying nothing. At the hatch we stopped, and after an awkward moment we shook hands.

# 8

According to ritual Mr. Tuak stood in front of the presiding officer's desk with his advocate, Alexi. The two stood at attention while Pilot Haynes declared his verdict.

"Mr. Tuak, the court finds you guilty of the offense of possessing aboard a Naval vessel a contraband substance, to wit, a magnesium starch colloquially known as goofjuice. The court nominally sentences you to two years imprisonment for this offense." The court always imposed the maximum sentence provided for in the regs, a nominal sentence subject to review and reduction by the Captain.

"Mr. Tuak, the court finds you guilty of the offense of rioting aboard a vessel under weigh. The court nominally sentences you to six months imprisonment and loss of all rank and benefits." Pilot Haynes stopped for breath. It was the longest speech I had ever heard him make.

"The court also finds you guilty of striking a superior officer, to wit, Mr. Vishinsky, and likewise Mr. Terrill, in an attempt to prevent the performance of their duty. The court sentences you—nominally sentences you—to be hanged by the neck until dead, and remands you to the master-at-arms for execution of the sentence."

Even though the sentence was known and expected, Alexi's shoulders fell and his head bowed. Tuak stood unmoving, as if he hadn't heard.

After, in the wardroom, I tried to comfort Alexi. He had been crying and paid no attention to my consolation. Vax watched as I fumbled at Alexi's arm, muttering inane words. After a time the burly midshipman tapped me on the shoulder and motioned me aside. He sat on the bed next to Alexi and put his big hand on the back of the younger middy's neck, squeezing the muscle gently.

"Let go; I'm all right." Alexi tried to pull away Vax's hand.

"Not until you listen." His hand stayed where it was. "My uncle is a lawyer. A criminal lawyer back in Sri Lanka."

"So?"

"He once told me the hardest part of his job. He liked his clients, some of them." Vax waited, but Alexi made no comment.

"When he couldn't get his clients freed, the hardest thing for him to remember was that it was their own fault they were in trouble, not his. They were in jail not because he had failed them, but because they had fouled up in the first place."

"There must have been a way to get him out of it." Alexi's voice was muffled, but at least he was listening.

"Not in this Navy." Vax spoke with certainty. He picked up the younger middy and turned him over onto his back. Again I wished for Vax's strength. "Read the regs, Alexi. They're designed to protect authority, not to encourage flouting it."

"But executing him—"

"That's for the Captain to decide. Anyway, he's a drug dealer. I have no sympathy for him. Why should you?"

I sat down on my bunk. I wasn't needed anymore.

"But they might hang him!" Alexi propped himself up on an elbow. "Look, I know you want me to feel better. But tell me Lieutenant Dagalow couldn't have done something to save him!"

"Lieutenant Dagalow couldn't have done anything to save him," Vax said evenly. "A ship under weigh is under the strictest military rules. It has to be, to preserve order and lives. The rules are clear. What happened down in berth three was nearly a mutiny. You don't think mutineers should get off, do you?"

"Of course not!" Alexi said indignantly. It was unthinkable to us all.

"Tuak struck an officer in the performance of his duty.

That's a form of mutiny. You have a hell of a nerve sympathizing with him, Tamarov!''

Alexi was smart enough to make the distinction. "I don't sympathize with what he did, just the penalties. Sometimes we've screwed up too, you know. You mutinied against Mr. Seafort, didn't you?''

"Yes, and he let me off easy. Mr. Seafort should have taken my head off. I realize that, now." Oh. Nice to know.

"Then we're just luckier than Tuak," said Alexi bitterly.

"No," I intervened. "Mouthing off in the wardroom isn't comparable to dealing drugs to the crew or hitting the CPO, and you know it.''

After a moment Alexi sighed. "I know," he said. He sat up. "You joes realize I have to go through it again? With the other trials?''

We commiserated. The crisis was over.

The other trials began the next day. When they were done, two other unfortunate sailors were under sentence of execution for striking their officers. A variety of lesser penalties had been handed out to the remaining participants.

The Pilot formally presented his verdicts to Captain Malstrom. The Captain had thirty days to act; unless he commuted the sentences, they'd be automatically carried out by the master-at-arms.

During the next few days the officers watched for signs of tension among the crew. There was some bitterness, but on the whole the hands settled down. Our crew knew the ship needed authority at its helm, just as the rest of us did. If Captain Malstrom was troubled by the decision he had to make, he didn't show it. He relaxed visibly when it was clear the unrest was over. He laughed easily, joked with the younger passengers, and arranged a place for me several evenings at the Captain's table, though it was not customary to favor an officer.

Once he even invited me to play chess. He knew I would be uncomfortable in the Captain's quarters; they were so unapproachable I'd never been allowed to see them. We went instead to the deserted lieutenants' common room.

We set up the board for the first time in many weeks. I didn't play well, not by choice, but from nervousness. Playing the Captain was nothing like playing a second lieutenant. He seemed to sense my mood and chatted with me, trying to put me at my ease.

"Have you reached a decision yet, sir, on the rioters?" It was presumptuous of me, but Captain Malstrom seemed pleased by my attempt at intimacy. Perhaps he needed it.

His face darkened. "I don't see how I can let them off and keep a disciplined ship." He sighed. "I'm trying to justify commuting the death sentences; the thought of killing those poor men sickens me. But in good conscience, I don't know how I can."

"You still have time to decide."

"Yes, twenty-five days. We'll see." He turned the conversation to Hope Nation. He asked if I still intended to buy him a drink. Yes, I said, knowing it was unlikely. A Captain on shore leave doesn't carouse with middies. For one thing, he's too busy.

After that day, something was wrong. I didn't know what, but the Captain didn't offer a smile when we met in the ship's dining hall. He looked preoccupied and grim. I shared a four-hour watch with him and the Pilot. He hardly spoke. I assumed his decision about the death sentences was affecting his mood.

Two days later we Defused for a scheduled navigation check. The greater the distance in Fusion, the more our navigation errors would compound. It was customary on a long cruise such as ours to Defuse two or three times, replotting the coordinates each time.

We came out of Fusion deep in lonely interstellar space. Darla and the Pilot both plotted our course. Their figures agreed with those of Vax, who as midshipman of the watch also ran a check. But instead of Fusing directly, the Captain laid over another night, drifting in space.

At dinner that night I sat two tables from the Captain. He seemed determined to be cheerful. I could see him teasing Yorinda Vincente, who laughed uncertainly, as if unsure of the right response. I looked for Amanda and found her across the hall at Table Seven with Dr. Uburu. I willed her to catch my eye. Eventually she did, smiled gently, turned away.

A forkful of beef halfway to my mouth, I watched the Captain reach for his water glass. He paused, a puzzled look on his face. He gestured and said something to the steward, who hurried to Table Seven. A moment later Dr. Uburu was kneeling by the Captain's chair. Captain Malstrom was hunched over the table.

Two sailors serving the mess helped the Captain to his feet, supporting him from either side, guiding his unsteady steps toward the corridor. Dr. Uburu followed. I watched, agape.

There was no one senior to stop me. I excused myself and boldly left the dining hall for the corridor to the ladder. I ran up the steps two at a time to officers' country. No one was in the infirmary except the med tech on watch. I hurried forward to the Captain's cabin. Of course his hatch was shut. It was unheard of to knock, so I waited.

After some minutes Dr. Uburu stepped out and shut the hatch. "What are you doing here?" Her tone was a challenge.

I wasn't reassured by the look on her dark, wide-boned, face. "Is he all right, ma'am?"

She ignored my breach of discipline. "I can't discuss the Captain's personal affairs." She started toward the infirmary.

I hurried to keep up. "Is there anything I can—I mean—" I didn't know what I meant.

Dr. Uburu was brusque. "Go back to the dining hall. That's an order."

Phrased like that, she left me no choice at all. She was an officer, rank equal to a lieutenant, and I was a midshipman. "Aye aye, ma'am." I turned and left.

All next day the Captain was off watch. I asked the Pilot when we would Fuse; he shrugged and left it at that, and I knew I wouldn't get any information from him. When my watch ended at last I went back to the wardroom. None of the other middies had heard anything reliable through the ship's grapevine.

I was thinking about hunting for Amanda; I needed her comforting acceptance. But there came a knock on the wardroom hatch; the med tech was outside, ill at ease. "Mr. Seafort, sir, you're wanted in the infirmary."

"Why the infirmary?" If anything, I was hoping for a summons from the Captain's cabin.

"It's the Captain, sir. He's been moved there." Vax and I exchanged a glance. I donned my jacket and hurried after the tech. Dr. Uburu indicated a cubicle; I went in alone.

Captain Malstrom lay on his side under a limp white sheet, his head propped on a pillow. The halogen lights hurt my eyes. He offered a weak smile as I entered and came to attention. "As you were."

"How are you, sir?"

For answer he threw off the sheet. He wore only his undershorts. His side and back were a mass of blue-gray lumps.

I closed my eyes for a moment, trying to will them away. "How long have you known, I mean, have they been—"

"Four days. They came up just a few days ago." He made an effort to smile again.

"Is it . . ."

"It's T."

"Oh, Harv." Tears were running down my face. "Oh, God, I'm so sorry."

"Thank you."

"Can she—are they doing anything, sir? Radiation, anticars?"

"There's more, Nicky. She found it in my liver, my lungs, my stomach. I haven't been able to see too well today, either. She thinks it might be in my brain too."

I didn't care what they did to me. I reached out and took his hand. If anyone had seen, I could have been summarily shot.

He squeezed my fingers. "It's all right, Nicky. I'm not afraid. I'm a good Christian."

"But *I'M* afraid, sir." The situation began to sink in on me. "That's why you didn't Fuse."

"Yes. I think . . . I'm not sure . . . whether to go back." He lay back, closing his eyes. He breathed slowly, hoarding his strength. We stayed as we were for several minutes. I began to realize what had to be done.

"Captain," I said slowly, clearly. "You have to give Vax his commission. Right now."

He came awake. "I hate to do it, Nicky. He can be such a bully. If he's in charge and there's no one to stop him . . ."

"He's changed, sir. He'll do all right."

"I don't know . . ." His eyes closed.

"Captain Malstrom, for the love of Lord God, for the sake of this ship, commission Vax while you still can!"

He opened his eyes again. "You think I ought to?"

"It's absolutely necessary." What might happen otherwise was too horrible to contemplate.

"I suppose you're right." He was growing drowsy. "I'll sign it into the Log. First thing in the morning."

"I could get the Log now, sir."

"No, I want to think about it overnight. Bring him in tomorrow morning, I'll do it then."

"Aye aye, sir." He was sleeping by the time I reached the hatch.

Dr. Uburu faced me in the anteroom. "He ordered me to announce his illness to the ship," she said. "Rumors are everywhere."

"I know," I said. I'd heard some of them.

She smiled warmly. It lighted her face and I was grateful. "I'll stay up with him tonight."

"Thank you, ma'am." I took her nod for a dismissal and left.

In the wardroom the other midshipmen questioned me silently. I had nothing to say to them; there was no way I could tell Vax he was going to make lieutenant, before Captain Malstrom had made up his mind. When the Doctor's solemn announcement came over the speaker we all listened in silence. Afterward I slapped off the light. None of us spoke.

First thing in the morning I arranged for Sandy to take Vax's watch. A quick breakfast in the officers' mess, then I told Vax the Captain wanted to see us in the infirmary.

Dr. Uburu had been dozing at the table in the outer compartment; she woke when we came in. She said the Chief Engineer had already brought the Log chip from the bridge, on Captain Malstrom's instructions. "He's awake and wants to see you. He's not doing too well." Her tone was glum.

We entered the sickroom, snapping to attention. The Captain was dozing in his bunk. He heard the hatch close, and opened his eyes. "Vax, Nicky, hi," he said vaguely. The ship's Log was in the holovid on a small bunkside table, within his reach.

"Good morning, sir," I said. He didn't answer. "Captain, we're here to do what you said last night."

"I was having dinner," he said suddenly, loudly.

"When you were taken ill, two nights ago, sir." I tried to

think how to direct him. Vax watched, puzzled. "Captain, last night we talked about Mr. Holser. Do you remember?"

"Yes." Captain Malstrom smiled at me. "Vax, the bully." An icicle crept up my spine. I wanted to move to him, but we were still at attention; he hadn't released us.

I was so desperate I prompted him. "Sir, we talked about Vax's commission. Don't you remember?"

He came fully awake. "Nicky." He studied me. "We talked. I said I would . . . make him looey. Of course!" I was weak with relief. He turned to Vax. "Mr. Holser, wait outside while we talk."

"Aye aye, sir." Vax spun smartly and left the room.

I took it as permission to move. I took the Log and dialed the current page. "Sir, let me help you. I can write; all you have to do is sign."

Captain Malstrom began to weep. "I'm sorry, Nicky. I guess I have to give it to him. He's the qualified one. You aren't. I don't have a—it's the only way!"

"I know, sir. I want you to. Here, I'll write it." I took the laserpencil. "I, Captain Harvey Malstrom, do commission and appoint Midshipman Vax Stanley Holser lieutenant in the Naval Service of the Government of the United Nations, by the Grace of God." I knew the words by heart, as did every midshipman.

I handed him the laserpencil. He stared at it, as if it were wild. "Nicky, I don't feel well." His face was white.

"Please, sir, just sign, and I'll get Dr. Uburu. Please."

He began to tremble. "I . . . Nick, I've—NICKY!" His head snapped back, his jaw clenched shut. His whole body shivered.

"Dr. Uburu!"

The Doctor came running at my yell. One look and she grabbed for a hypo, filled it from a medicine bottle in the cabinet nearby. "Move, boy!" She shoved me aside and bared his arm. As the hypo plunged, his rigid muscles slowly relaxed. His hand opened. "Give me the Log," he whispered. But his hand wouldn't hold the pencil.

I said, "Captain Malstrom, commission him orally! Dr. Uburu is witness!" The way it came out, it sounded like an order.

He muttered something. I couldn't tell what it was. Then

he drifted toward sleep. "This afternoon," he said clearly, surprising me. "After I rest." I waited, but his breath came in short rasping sounds. His face was flushed.

I took hold of the Doctor's arm. I had touched the Captain, now it might as well be Dr. Uburu; I had lost all sense of propriety. I tugged her toward the corner. "Do you realize," I whispered, "what will happen if he doesn't commission Vax?"

"Yes," she said coldly, pulling my hand from her arm.

"He's got to sign the Log! Will he be able to, this afternoon?"

"Perhaps. I have no way to know."

"I heard him orally commission Vax. You did too." I stared her straight in the eye, hoping she would realize what had to be done.

"I heard no such thing," she said bluntly. "And you are a gentleman by act of the General Assembly. A gentleman does not lie!"

I blushed all the way up to my ears. "Doctor, he has GOT to sign that Log."

"Then let's hope he wakes up in condition to do it." She added, "I agree with you. It's necessary for the ship's safety that he sign Vax's commission."

"But you won't . . ."

"No, I won't. And you won't suggest it again. That is a direct order which you disobey at your peril! Acknowledge it." She had steel in her. I hadn't known.

"Aye aye, ma'am. I will not suggest again that Captain orally commissioned Vax. I accept your statement that he did not. Is there anything else, ma'am?"

"Yes, Nick. Duty is sometimes unclear. Right now your duty is to obey the regulations you swore to uphold. All of them. I trust that by the Grace of God the Captain will do what he must. You would do better to pray than to scheme, young man."

"Yes, ma'am." She was right.

Vax was waiting outside the sickroom. "What was all that about?" he asked.

We walked back along the corridor toward the wardroom. Now he had a right to know. "I asked the Captain to commission you lieutenant. He said he would do it this morning. I wrote it out in the Log for him.''

''And?''

''He hasn't signed it. He's disoriented. I asked Dr. Uburu to agree that he had commissioned you orally, but she said he hadn't. In truth, he had not.''

Vax took my arm. There was a lot of touching going on in *Hibernia*. ''Why did you want him to?''

''Vax, what the hell happens when the Captain dies? Do you expect me to try to run the ship?''

I don't think it had occurred to him until that moment. It had only occurred to me two days ago. ''Oh, my God.''

''And mine.'' We locked eyes. ''We'll come back in a couple of hours. He'll sign it. He has to.'' We walked the rest of the way in uneasy silence.

After lunch we returned to the infirmary. At my request Chief McAndrews also came. The Doctor, the Chief, Vax, and I waited in the sickroom for the Captain to awaken. He slept fitfully, tossing and turning. The silence in the brightly lit room grew unbearable.

Hours passed. ''Is there anything you can give him?'' I asked Dr. Uburu. ''Some sort of stimulant?''

''Yes. If I want to kill him,'' she growled. ''His systems are closing down. He can't take much.''

''He's got to wake up long enough to sign the Log, or at least tell us orally!''

She shook her head, but after a while she loaded a syringe and gave Captain Malstrom an injection. Chief McAndrews sat near the bed; the Doctor was at a table close by. Vax stood stolidly against the bulkhead; I paced with increasing nervousness.

''Nicky.'' The Captain's eyes were open and riveted on me.

''Yes, sir.'' I hurried over to the bed. I picked up the holovid with the Log.

The Captain swallowed with difficulty. As I came closer he squinted to keep me in focus. ''Nicky . . . you're my son,'' he said weakly.

''What?'' My voice squeaked. I couldn't have heard right. I leaned close.

He raised a hand and touched my cheek. His breathing was ragged. "You've been . . . a son to me. I never had another."

"Oh, God!" It was too much for me; I wept. He touched me again; his hand moved uncertainly in front of my face before it found me. "I'm dying," he said, with wonder.

Hating myself, I said urgently, "Sir, do your duty! Tell Chief McAndrews and Dr. Uburu that Vax is a lieutenant. Tell them."

"My son," he said, dropping his hand. He stopped breathing. I turned frantically to the Doctor but the Captain's breath caught again in a ragged gasp. He stared at me, his face an unhealthy blue. Understanding slowly left his eyes and they closed.

Dr. Uburu started intravenous liquids. While we waited helplessly, they dripped into his arm in the age-old manner. The Captain lay unconscious, his mouth ajar.

"Do something. With all your machinery, help him!" My words were a demand.

"I can't!" she spat. "I can pump his heart for him; I can even replace it. I can oxygenate his blood just as his lungs do. I can purify his blood with dialysis. I can even replicate his liver. We're talented, aren't we? But I can't do all those things at once. He's dying! The poor man's insides are rotten; he's like an overripe melon about to split open. The melanoma's everywhere."

She stopped for breath, her fury nailing me to the bulkhead. "He's got it in his stomach, his liver, his lungs, his colon. His sight is going from an optic tumor. It's as bad as T can get. Sometimes—only once in a while, thank God—it grows so fast you can see it. Do something? *DO SOMETHING?* I can stay with him to wish him into Yahweh's hands. That's what I can do!" Her cheeks were wet.

"And I can let him go in peace and privacy." Chief McAndrews got heavily to his feet. "Nick, stay with him. If he rallies he'll sign it. Or he'll tell Dr. Uburu as witness. There's no use my staying." He left.

"Vax, will you stay with me?"

Vax Holser, his pent-up emotions roiling, glared at me with such fury as I have never seen from another man. He twice opened his mouth to speak. Then he stalked out in a passion, slamming the hatch shut.

I stayed in the infirmary during evening mess, in the chair the Chief had vacated. The Captain's breathing varied, sometimes regular and deep, sometimes ragged. Late in the evening Dr. Uburu slipped an oxygen mask over his nose and mouth. She introduced vapormeds into the oxygen mixture; I couldn't tell if they helped. She sent the med tech to the galley for a tray for me. I ate in my chair, never taking my eyes from the still form in the bunk.

"I'll watch him, Nicky," she said after I began to doze. "Go to bed."

"Let me stay." It was somewhere between a demand and a plea. Perhaps she understood from my eyes. She nodded. She checked the alarms on the bedside monitors and retired to the anteroom. I dozed, came awake, and dozed again. The bright lights accented the stillness. Finally I curled up in the chair and slept.

I woke toward morning, to realize the labored sounds of his breathing had stopped. I called Dr. Uburu; she came and stood next to me by his still form under the clean white sheet.

"The alarms. Why didn't they . . ."

"I turned them off." She answered my look of betrayal. "I could do nothing more for him. Except let him go in peace."

Stunned, I sank back into the chair. I don't know how long I sat there alone; I got up mechanically when I heard the change of watch after breakfast. I went out into the anteroom where Dr. Uburu waited.

She got to her feet. "I'm going to meet with the Chief and Pilot Haynes." I didn't answer.

I left the infirmary, followed the corridor to the wardroom, passing someone on the way. Sandy and Alexi were inside; Alexi, just off watch, was in his bed. Sandy stood as I entered.

"Out, both of you." They scrambled to the hatch. I pulled off my jacket and lay on my bunk. My head spun, but sleep evaded me. I heard noises in the corridor. I tried to block them out, could not. I lay awake in a stupor.

Hours later Alexi knocked on the hatch. "Mr. Seafort—"

"Stay out until I give you permission to enter!"

"Aye aye, sir." The hatch shut.

I buried my head in the pillow, hoping for tears. None came.

I awoke later in the day with an intense thirst. I got up, found my jacket, went to the head. As I slopped water from my hand to my mouth I studied my reflection in the mirror. My hair was wild; there were hollows under my eyes. My expression was frightening.

I splashed cold water on my face and went back to the wardroom. I dressed in clean clothes and combed my hair. Then I went below to the ship's library on Level 2, where I signed out the holovid chips for the Naval Regulations and Code of Conduct, Revision of 2087. I took them back to the wardroom and sat on my bunk.

It took about twenty minutes to find what I was looking for.

"Section 121.2. The Captain of a vessel may relieve himself of command when disabled and unfit for duty by reason of mental illness or physical sickness or injury. Upon his certification of such action in the Log, his rank of Captain shall be suspended and command shall devolve on the next-ranking line officer."

I thumbed through the regs looking for other half-remembered sections. I flipped back and forth, carefully reading definitions and terms.

The hatch opened cautiously. Vax looked in, then entered. We faced each other.

"He died before he signed it." It was half statement, half question.

"Yes," I said.

"What will you do?"

"I don't know." I saw no reason to hide it.

"Nicky—Mr. Seafort—"

"You can call me Nicky."

"—you can't captain the ship."

I was silent.

"You can't maneuver her. You can't plot a course. You don't understand the drives."

"I know."

"Step aside, Nicky. It's just until we get back home. They'll send us out with new officers."

"I've been thinking about doing that," I said.

"For the ship's safety. Please."

"You'd run her?"

"Me, or the officers' committee. Doc and the Chief and

the Pilot. It doesn't matter. They're meeting right now, to figure what to do.''

"I understand." I flipped off the holovid.

"You agree?"

"No. I understand." I got up. "Vax, I wanted you to command. I begged him to sign your commission the first night he was ill.''

"I know. After how I treated you I can hardly look you in the eye." He hesitated. "It's just a fluke I wasn't senior," he said bitterly. "Four months difference."

"Yes." I put the holovid in my pocket and went to the hatch. "I wish I'd gone with Captain Haag on the launch, Vax. If I could choose now, that's where I'd be.''

"Don't talk like that, Nick."

"I'm desperate." I went out.

No one but the med tech was at the infirmary. The Captain's body was already in a cold locker. I tried the Doctor's cabin, but no one answered. I went below along the circumference passage to the Chief's quarters, and met the Pilot just coming out the hatch.

"I was on my way to get you." He gestured me inside. The Chief's cabin was the same size as the one in which Lieutenant Malstrom and I had played chess. Dr. Uburu and the Chief were seated around a small table. I found a chair and joined them.

"Nick." The Doctor's tone was gentle. "Someone has to decide what to do.''

"That's right," I said.

"The crew needs to know who's in charge. We have to get the ship back home. We have to reassure the passengers. The Passengers' Council voted unanimously to return to Earthport, and wants the officers' committee to take control.''

Chief McAndrews hesitated, glanced at the others. "There's ambiguity in the regs as to whether a midshipman can assume the Captaincy. We think he can't. And even if he can, we want you to remove yourself. And if you don't, we'll remove you for disability.''

"Good," I said. "Get me out of this, please. Let's start with your first point. What regs are you looking at?" They all relaxed visibly at my response.

The Chief glanced at his notes. " 'Section 357.4. Every

watch not commanded by the Captain shall be commanded by a commissioned officer under his direction.' " He cleared his throat. "A midshipman is not a commissioned officer. 357.4 says you have to be commissioned to command a watch."

"As a midshipman I can't command a watch. I agree with you."

"Then it's settled." Dr. Uburu.

"No. I'm no longer a midshipman."

"Why not?"

I reached for a holovid and inserted my chip. " 'Section 232.8. In case of death or disability of the Captain, his duties, authority, and title shall devolve on the next-ranking line officer.' "

"So?"

" 'Section 98.3. The following persons are not line officers within the meaning of these regulations: a Ship's Doctor, a chaplain, a Pilot, and an Engineer. All other officers are line officers within the meaning of these regulations.' "

" 'Section 101.9,' " countered the Chief. " 'The Captain of a vessel may from time to time appoint a midshipman, who shall serve in such capacity as the Captain and his officers may from time to time direct.' 101.9 suggests a middy may not even be an officer."

I scrolled my holovid to Section 92.5. " 'Command of any work detail may be delegated by the Captain or the officer of the watch to any lieutenant, midshipman, or other officer in his command.' " I looked around the table, repeating the deadly phrase. "Lieutenant, midshipman, or other officer." I said into the silence, "A midshipman is mentioned as an officer. A line officer."

The Pilot stirred. "It's still ambiguous. A midshipman isn't commissioned. The regs don't say a middy can become Captain."

"Nobody thought of it happening. I agree." I flipped back to the definitions section. " '12. Officer. An officer is a person commissioned or appointed by authority of the Government of the United Nations to its Naval Service, authorized thereby to direct all persons of subordinate rank in the commission of their duties.' "

I raised my eyes. "An officer doesn't have to be commissioned. Look, I want to reach the same conclusion you do. But the regs are clear. They don't say the Captaincy shall devolve on the next commissioned officer. They say line officer. I'm an officer. I'm not one of the officers excluded from line of command. I'm the senior line officer aboard.''

"It's still not explicit,'' said the Chief. ''We have to guess how to interpret the various passages put together. We can conclude a midshipman never succeeds to command.''

"There's two problems in doing that. One, when we get home you'd be hanged.''

There was a long silence. ''And the other problem?'' Dr. Uburu finally asked.

"I will construe it as mutiny.''

They exchanged glances. I realized the possibility had occurred to them before I arrived.

"It hasn't come to that,'' the Chief said. ''Let's say we all conclude that you're next in line. Step down. You're not ready to command.''

"I'll be glad to. Just show me where it's allowed.''

"Don't be ridiculous,'' said Dr. Uburu. ''Quit. Resign the Captaincy. Relieve yourself.''

"On what grounds?''

"Incompetence.''

"Do you mean my lack of skill and other qualifications, or are you suggesting I'm mentally ill?''

"Nobody's saying you're mentally ill,'' she protested.

" 'Section 121.2. The Captain of a vessel may relieve himself of command when disabled and unfit for duty by reason of mental illness or physical sickness or injury.' '' I laid down my holovid. ''I am not physically sick or injured. I don't believe I'm mentally ill any more than you do.''

"Isn't it an inherent authority?'' she asked. ''The Captain can relieve others. Surely he has inherent authority to relieve himself.''

I said, ''I thought of that. So I looked it up. 'Section 204.1. The Captain of a vessel shall assume and exert authority and control of the government of the vessel until relieved by order of superior authority, until his death, or until certification of his disability as otherwise provided herein.' I don't think they wanted Captains going around relieving themselves from duty.''

"This is ridiculous,'' said the Pilot. ''Everyone agrees,

even you, that you shouldn't be Captain. Yet you're telling us we're stuck with you, that you can't quit, even though it's best for the ship."

"There's a reason for that," I told him. "You all know the Captain isn't a mere officer. He's the United Nations Government in transit. The Government cannot abdicate."

"Do it anyway, Nicky," Dr. Uburu said gently. "Just do it."

"No." I looked at each of them. "It is dereliction of duty. I swore an oath. 'I shall uphold the Charter of the United Nations, and the laws and regulations promulgated thereunder, to the best of my ability, by the Grace of Lord God Almighty.' I no longer have a choice."

"You're seventeen years old," said Chief McAndrews. "There are a hundred and ninety-nine people aboard whose lives depend on the safe operation of this vessel. We have to relieve you."

"You may relieve me only on the same grounds I can relieve myself," I said. "Look it up. I will consent to being relieved when a legal basis exists. Otherwise, I must resist." The Chief thumbed through the holovid to the section on disability. After a few moments, he reluctantly pushed it aside.

We had reached an impasse. We sat around the little table, hoping a solution would occur.

"And Vax?" the Doctor asked.

"Vax is better qualified. But Vax is not Captain. He's a midshipman. I am senior to him."

"Even though he is far better able to handle the ship," she said.

"Even though. You know how I tried to get the Captain to sign his commission." I closed my eyes. I was desperately tired. "There is one solution." She looked up at me, waiting. "Sign the Log, witnessing that Captain Malstrom commissioned Vax lieutenant before he died. I will acquiesce."

All eyes turned to the Ship's Doctor. She studied the table-top for a long time. The tension in the room was palpable. After several minutes she raised her eyes and said, "I will not sign the Log in witness. Captain Malstrom did not grant Vax Holser a commission before he died." The Pilot let his breath out all at once.

She went on, "I realize now we are here in error. The Captain had ample opportunity, not just on his sickbed, but during the weeks after he took command, to commission Vax. He chose not to, knowing Mr. Seafort was senior midshipman. I know, just as you all know, that Captain Malstrom would acknowledge Mr. Seafort is next in line of command. Captain Malstrom had authority to leave Nick as senior remaining officer and did. We had no say in the matter while he lived. We have no say in the matter now."

I had one more hope. "Chief, you were in the infirmary with Captain Malstrom. If you can say you heard him commission Vax . . ."

The Chief didn't hesitate, not for a second. "The day I sign a lie into the Log, Mr. Seafort, is the day I walk unsuited out the airlock. No. I heard no such thing." He fingered the holovid. "We are all sworn officers. We all uphold the Government. It appears that the Government, in its unfathomable wisdom, has put you in charge. You know I wish it were not so. But my wishes don't count. Sir, I am a loyal officer and you may count on my service."

I swallowed. "I wanted you to argue me out of it, not the other way around. For the moment, I am Captain-designate. I will be Captain when I declare I have taken command of the ship, as did Captain Malstrom. First, I'm going back to my bunk to try to find a way out of this. Let's leave everything as it is. We'll meet at evening mess." I stood to go.

Automatically, all three of them stood with me.

# 9

Vax and Alexi snapped to attention when I crossed the wardroom threshold. They, at least, no longer considered me just the senior middy.

"I don't have command yet," I told them. "This is still my bunk and I want to be alone. Go pester the passengers or polish the fusion drive shaft. Beat it."

Alexi grinned with relief at my sally; he was as unsettled as the rest of us. He and Vax hurried out.

I lay on my bunk fiddling with my holovid until eventually I tossed it aside in disgust. I was trapped. I grieved for my friend Harv, but I was furious he hadn't had sense enough to commission Vax the day he took command. Vax could pilot, could navigate, understood the fusion drives, and had the forceful personality of a Captain.

I must have dozed. As afternoon watch ended I woke, ravenous. I couldn't remember when I'd last eaten. I washed and hurried to the dining hall for the evening meal. Master-at-arms Vishinsky and four of his seamen stood outside the hatch, with their billies. He saluted.

"What's this about?" I gestured to his sailors.

"Chief McAndrews ordered us up as a precaution, sir. There was some kind of demand from the passengers and an, uh, inquiry from the crew."

I spotted the Chief at his usual table. He stood when I approached. I flicked a thumb toward the master-at-arms and raised an eyebrow. "A written demand was delivered to the bridge, sir." His voice was quiet. "By that Vincente woman. Signed by almost all the passengers."

"What do they want?"

"To go home. That part's easy; we can Fuse any time. They demand that responsible and competent officers control the ship, forthwith. Commissioned officers who have reached their majority."

"Ah."

"Yes, sir." He paused. "And inquiries have come up from the crew," he said with delicacy. "Wondering where authority now rests."

"Oh, brother."

"Yes. The sooner you declare you've taken command, the better."

"Very well. After dinner. The officers will join me on the bridge."

"Aye aye, sir." He looked around the rapidly filling hall. "The evening prayer, sir. Will you give it?"

"And sit at the Captain's table, in the Captain's place?" I was repelled by the thought.

"That's where the Captain usually sits." His tone had a touch of acid.

"Not tonight. I'll say the prayer as senior officer, but from my usual place."

I went to my accustomed seat. Several passengers sharing my table looked upon me with hostility. None spoke. I decided I could ignore it.

When the hall had filled I stood, and tapped my glass for quiet. "I am senior officer present," I stated. Then, for the first time, I gave the Ship's Prayer I had heard so often. "Lord God, today is March 12, 2195, on the U.N.S. *Hibernia*. We ask you to bless us, to bless our voyage, and to bring health and well-being to all aboard." I sat, my heart pounding.

"Amen," said Chief Engineer McAndrews into the silence. A few passengers murmured it after him.

I wouldn't call dinner a cheerful affair; hardly anyone acknowledged my presence. But I was so hungry I hardly cared. I avidly consumed salad, meat, bread, then coffee and dessert. The passengers at my table watched in amazement. I suppose they had reason; the day after the Captain's death his successor sat at a midshipman's place, eagerly devouring everything but the silverware.

After the meal I went back to the wardroom. I took out fresh clothes, showered thoroughly, dressed with extra care. I even shaved, though it wasn't really necessary.

Reluctantly, I went to the bridge. Sandy, who had been holding nominal watch alone—the ship was not under power—leaped to attention on my arrival.

"Carry on." My tone was gruff, to cover my uncertainty. Then, "Mr. Wilsky, summon all officers."

"Aye aye, sir." The young midshipman keyed the ship's caller. "Now hear this." His voice cracked; he blushed. "All officers report to the bridge."

Awash with physical energy I paced the bridge, examining the instruments, seeing none of them. Doc Uburu arrived, requested permission to enter. The Pilot followed shortly. A few moments later the Chief appeared. The middies were last; Vax and Alexi came hurrying—clean uniforms, hair freshly combed, like my own—and I smiled despite myself. We all stood, as if grouped for a formal portrait.

I picked up the caller, took a deep breath. I exhaled, and took another. "Ladies and gentlemen, by the Grace of God, Captain Harvey Malstrom, commanding officer of U.N.S. *Hibernia*, is dead of illness. I, Midshipman Nicholas Ewing Seafort, senior officer aboard, do hereby take command of this ship."

It was done.

"Congratulations, Captain!" Alexi was first, then they all crowded around me with reassurance and support, even the Chief and the Pilot. It was not a jolly occasion; the death of Captain Malstrom precluded that. What they offered was more condolence than celebration.

After a moment I went to sit. I stopped myself: I had headed for the first officer's chair. Trying to look casual, I sat in the Captain's seat on the left. No laser bolt struck me. I addressed my officers.

"Pilot, we'll need new watch rotations. Take care of it, please. The middies will have to stand watch alone now; it can't be helped. Dr. Uburu, attend to passenger morale before the situation worsens. Chief, I need your attention on the crew. If there's serious discontent, you're to know about it. Pass the word that we have matters under control. Vax, you'll help me get settled. Get a work party to move my gear to the Captain's cabin. Sew bars on my uniforms. Reprogram Darla to recognize me as Captain."

When I stopped they chorused, "Aye aye, sir." It was a heady feeling. No arguments, no objections. I began to appreciate ship's discipline.

"Anything else, anyone?"

"We can make Earthport Station in two jumps." The Pilot. "I'll run the calculations tonight."

The Chief said, "Don't worry about the crew; they'll settle down as soon as I remind them they get early shore leave. They'll be so happy to head for Lunapolis they won't even think about who's Captain."

Alexi asked, "When do we Fuse for home, sir?"

I said, "I never told you we were going home."

The shock of silence. Then a babble of voices.

I snapped, "Be quiet!" There was instant compliance. It didn't surprise me; I wouldn't have dared breathe had Captain

Malstrom given such an order, friend or no f iend. "Chief, do you have something to say?"

"With the Captain's permission, yes, sir." He waited for my nod. "Surely you can't mean to go on. We've lost our four most experienced officers. The crew is frightened. I can't answer for their behavior if we head for Hope Nation. The ship's launch is gone; six passengers are dead. Sir, we never thought . . . Please. The only sensible thing is to go back."

"Pilot?"

"I can get us back in two jumps, Captain. Six months. It's eleven months to Hope Nation."

"I already knew that. Anything else?"

"Yes, sir. The danger is obvious. It's irresponsible of you to sail on."

I didn't hesitate. "Pilot, you're placed on report for insolence. I will enter a reprimand in the Log. You are reduced two grades in pay and confined to quarters for one week, except when on watch."

Pilot Haynes, his face red with rage, grated, "Understood, sir." His fists were clenched at his side.

"Who else?" Of course, after that no one cared to speak.

"I'll take your suggestions under advisement. In the morning I'll let you know. You're all dismissed. Mr. Holser, you will remain."

After the bridge hatch shut behind the last of them I turned to Vax, who waited in the "at ease" position. I wasn't looking forward to our interview. "You're senior middy now, Vax."

"Yes, sir." He looked straight ahead.

"You recall the unpleasantness we had last month?"

"Yes, sir."

"It's nothing compared to the unpleasantness I'm going to make now, Mr. Holser." Vax had settled in well as second midshipman, but now I had to leave the wardroom, and given his temperament he'd have the other middies climbing the bulkheads in a week. That is, if I didn't put the brakes on.

My voice was savage. "You will do hard calisthenics—I repeat, HARD calisthenics, for two hours every day until further notice. You will report to the watch officer in a fresh uniform for personal inspection every four hours, day and night." He looked stricken. "You will submit a five-thousand-word report on the duties of the senior midshipman under Naval regulations and by ship's custom. Acknowledge!"

"Orders received and understood, sir!" His expression bordered on panic.

I stood nose to nose with him, my voice growing louder. "You may think that in the privacy of the wardroom you can revert to your old bullying ways, and I won't know because the other middies won't tell me. They don't have to tell me, Mr. Holser. I was a middy yesterday. I know what to look for!" I waited for a response.

"Yes, sir!"

I shouted, "Mr. Holser, if you exercise brutality in the wardroom, I'll cut your balls off! Do I make myself clear?"

"Aye aye, sir!" A sheen of sweat appeared on his forehead. I knew he didn't take the last threat literally, but we'd both served aboard ship long enough to know the Captain's enmity was the worst disaster that could befall a crewman. I was giving him a reminder of that.

"Very well. Dismissed. See that I have bars on my uniforms by morning."

"Aye aye, sir!" He practically ran from the bridge. I made a mental note to ease up in a few days. The exercise wouldn't harm him—Vax liked working out—but reporting for inspection every four hours grew brutal, as one's sleep deficit accumulated. Once, in Academy, Sergeant Trammel had made me . . . I sighed, thrusting away the memory.

I roamed the bridge, unnerved by the grim silence. Never before had I stood watch entirely alone, and certainly not when I had no superior to call in case of emergency. I toyed with the sensors, examined the silent simulscreen, stared at pinpoints of starlight until my eyes ached. My legs were weary, but I was reluctant to sit just yet.

I examined the bridge safe, found it unlocked. The Captain's laser pistol was within, as well as the keys to the munitions locker. As a precaution, I changed the combination.

Returning at last to my chair, I turned on the Log and thumbed it idly, back to the start of our voyage. I screened the orders from Admiralty, entered by Captain Haag ages ago. *"You shall, with due regard for the safety of the ship, proceed on a course from Earthport Station to Ganymede Station . . . You shall sail in an expeditious manner by means of Fusion to Miningcamp, from there to Hope Nation, and thence to Detour . . . you shall take on such cargo as the Government there may . . . revictualing and refueling as you may find necessary . . ."* I keyed off the Log.

Idly I thumbed through our cargo manifest. Machinery for the manufacture of medicines, tools and dies, freeze-stored vegetable seeds, catalogs and samples of the latest fashions from Earth, bottled air for Miningcamp . . . I closed my eyes, rocking gently in the Captain's chair, its soft upholstery inviting.

"Permission to enter bridge, sir." I woke abruptly. Alexi waited respectfully in the corridor. Had he seen? Lord God, I hoped not; sleeping on watch was a cardinal sin.

"Come in." I got him settled. He'd have little to do other than watch the quiescent instruments, but like me, Alexi had never served a watch alone and was eager to begin. I myself was already glad to escape the tedium.

I headed east along the circumference corridor to the Captain's cabin. No one was posted outside; Captain Haag had dispensed with the marine guard the first week of the voyage.

I quelled an urge to knock respectfully, and went in.

The cabin was breathtaking. It was over four times as large as our wardroom, at least eight meters by five. It held only one bunk, which made it seem even more grand. So much space, for only one person. And I was the person!

Subtle dividers made areas of the cabin seem like separate rooms. In one corner was a hatch; I tried it. A head; the Captain actually had his own head and shower. I was stunned. I felt guilty even thinking of living in such luxury, while midshipmen constantly rubbed shoulders in their tiny quarters.

My gear, what little there was of it, was already laid out in a dresser built into the bulkhead. Vax had been busy: my uniforms, new patches freshly sewn on the shoulders, were hung neatly in a closet area in the corner. A ship's caller sat on the table by the bunk. Across from the bed were easy chairs, a desk chair, even a small conference table. Or dining table. I wasn't sure which.

I sat uneasily, feeling an intruder though Captain Malstrom's gear was nowhere to be seen. Captain Haag's must long since be gone to storage. I wondered gloomily how soon my own would follow. My eyes roved the bulkheads. Pictures; someone had made an effort to decorate. A safe was built into the bulkhead. It was locked. I made a note to find the combination.

I undressed and got into bed; the mattress was amazingly soft. I switched off the light. The room was very still. I twisted from one position to another, unable to sleep despite my exhaustion. My thoughts turned to what I had accomplished. In the course of my first day, I'd managed to alienate everyone whose goodwill I needed. The Chief. The Pilot. The senior middy. A bad start, but I couldn't figure out what I could have done better.

As I tossed restlessly in the soft bunk I realized what was troubling me. It was too quiet. I was lonely.

# 10

In the morning I felt ill at ease using the head alone, so accustomed had I become to the wardroom's lack of privacy. I was a bit apprehensive when a knock came on the hatch; custom approaching the force of law forbade anyone to disturb the Captain in his cabin. In an emergency, or if he'd left standing orders to be notified, the Captain was summoned by ship's caller; if there was no emergency, he was not bothered. All the crew knew that, and passengers were not allowed in the section of Level 1 that contained the bridge and the Captain's quarters.

Cautiously, I opened the hatch. Ricardo Fuentes, the ship's boy, waited in the corridor with a cloth-covered tray. He stepped around me to set it on my dining table. Then his shoulders came up and he stood rigidly at attention, arms stiffly at his sides, stomach sucked in tight.

I was grateful for the familiar face. "Hi, Ricky."

"Good morning, Captain, sir!" His voice was high-pitched and shrill.

I peered beneath the cloth. Coffee, scrambled eggs, toast, juice. It appeared his visit was a regular morning routine. "Thanks."

Twelve-year-old Ricky stood stiff. "You're welcome, sir!" Clearly, he wasn't about to unbend.

"Dismissed, sailor."

"Aye aye, sir!" The boy about-faced and marched out. I sighed. Had I begun to resemble an ogre? Did it come with the job?

Pilot Haynes and Vax Holser were on the forenoon watch list. As I reached the bridge I opened my mouth to ask permission to enter. Old habits die hard. Feeling foolish, I walked in. Vax jumped to attention; the Pilot did so more slowly.

"Carry on." They eased back in their chairs as I crossed to my new seat. Vax's uniform, I noticed, was crisply ironed. I glanced at the console. The readouts seemed in order; I knew Vax or the Pilot would tell me if they weren't.

"Chief Engineer, report to the bridge." I put down the caller. When Chief McAndrews arrived I said, "Chief, Pilot, I've decided we will continue to Miningcamp and Hope Nation." The Chief pursed his lips but said nothing.

"I don't have to give you reasons, but I will. Simply: going on involves Fusing and docking maneuvers; so does going home. The risks are equal.

"Now, once we're at Hope Nation we know the Admiral Commanding will assign us a new Captain and lieutenants. It will mean sailing eleven months with inexperienced officers, instead of the six it would take to go home, but *Hibernia* carries too many supplies that our colonies need, to abandon our trip lightly. Their supply ships arrive only twice a year."

The Chief said only, "Aye aye, sir." The Pilot was silent.

"Gentlemen, we'll bury Captain Malstrom this forenoon, and we'll Fuse this afternoon after the burial service."

The bridge and engine room were unmanned and sealed. We gathered around the forward airlock, seven deep in the crowded corridor. All the remaining officers, resplendent in dress uniform with black mourning sash across the shoulder;

nearly all the crew, dressed as if for inspection. Lieutenant Malstrom had been as popular among the enlisted men as among the middies.

The rest of the corridor was filled with passengers: Yorinda Vincente, representing the Passengers' Council, in the front row; behind her, Mr. Barstow, Amanda Frowel, the Treadwell twins, many others I knew, all waiting for the service to begin. Derek Carr, whose father had been lost earlier with the launch, his finely chiseled, aquiline face marred by sunken eyes and an expression of grief remembered. He nodded, but said nothing.

The flag-draped alumalloy coffin waited behind me in the airless lock, visible through the transplex inner hatch. I turned on the holovid and began to read from the Christian Reunification service for the dead, as promulgated by the Naval Service of the Government of the United Nations.

"Ashes to ashes, dust to dust . . ." Lieutenant Malstrom and I had cast off together at this very airlock. Now I was to continue, and he must disembark. "Trusting in the goodness and mercy of Lord God eternal, we commit his body to the deep . . . to await the day of judgment when the souls of man shall be called forth before Almighty Lord God . . . Amen."

I snapped off the holovid. "Petty Officer Terrill, open the outer lock."

Chief Petty Officer Robert Terrill stepped forward. "Aye aye, sir." Taking the airlock control from my hand he spun on his heel, marched to the airlock panel, pressed the transmitter to the outer lock control. The alarm bell chimed; *Hibernia*'s outer hatch slid open. I shivered involuntarily; the emptiness of interstellar space beckoned to my mentor, my friend. I breathed a silent prayer of my own, that Lord God might welcome him to his reward.

"Eject the casket, Mr. Terrill."

He pressed a button on a small transmitter clipped to his belt. The folded metal arm mounted in the airlock bulkhead slowly unfolded, pushing gently on the side of the casket. Captain Malstrom's coffin slid smoothly to the outer lock. As the arm extended, the casket drifted past the end of the chamber and floated slowly into the void.

Mesmerized, we watched it recede. It disappeared into the

dark long before it would have been too distant to see. I swallowed a lump in my throat. "Mr. Terrill, secure the outer hatch."

"Aye aye, sir." The petty officer pressed his transmitter to the outer airlock control. The hatch closed quietly. The service was complete. My friend Harv was forever gone.

The crowd dispersed. I started back toward my cabin. I felt a hand on my arm, abruptly lifted. I turned. Amanda Frowel looked angry; Alexi Tamarov had a firm grip on her arm, his shoulder thrust sharply between us. "I'm sorry, ma'am," he said, barring her way. She tried to shrug loose; the midshipman held tight.

"It's all right, Alexi." He released her and backed away.

"What was that about?" she demanded.

"Ship's custom. One doesn't touch the Captain. For crewmen it is a capital offense." I took her hand, oblivious to the civilians milling around us, trying to pass. "What is it, Amanda?"

"Are you all right, Nicky?"

"I think so." I studied her face. "I'm sorry I haven't been to see you. I've been rather busy."

She glanced at my new uniform. "You certainly have. Are you sure it's wise?"

"No. I'm just sure it's mandatory." I hesitated. "May I visit tonight?"

"If you'd like." To my dismay, there was a coolness to her voice. She seemed almost indifferent.

"I'd like. If you would." Reluctantly she nodded. We parted.


"We'll Fuse as soon as we're ready, gentlemen."

Vax and Pilot Haynes were in their places. I keyed the caller. "Bridge to engine room, prepare to Fuse."

"Prepare to Fuse, aye aye, sir." The Chief. My lips twitched in a smile; according to the rotation, the engine room petty officer had the watch this hour, but clearly the Chief didn't trust us to Fuse except under his vigilant eye.

After a moment the caller came to life once more. "Engine room ready for Fuse, sir."

"Very well, stand by." I looked up to the screen. "Darla, Fusion coordinates, please?"

"Aye aye, Captain Seafort." The coordinates flashed on the screen.

"Manual coordinates, Pilot?" My request was but a formality. If his own figures hadn't agreed with Darla's he'd have immediately recalculated; the wrong Fusion coordinates could send us to oblivion. Pilot Haynes brought up his coordinates. They matched Darla's.

"Vax, did you also run a plot?"

"Yes, sir."

"Let's see." From the corner of my eye I noticed the Pilot shake his head with ill-disguised impatience. I examined Vax's figures; they were identical to the others.

I was ready to give the order. While normally the ship was Defused from the bridge by running a finger down the Fusion control console, ignition was trickier. The Captain usually passed the Fusion order to the engine room, and the ship was Fused from there.

"Does everything check, Captain?" There wasn't a hint of insolence in the Pilot's voice. None was needed; the question itself conveyed his contempt for my overcaution.

"So far. I'll run my own calculations, just to be sure." Childish, but it would be a windy day in space before I ignored that sort of remark. I entered the variables.

I wasn't very good at the exercise, as Lieutenant Cousins had continually reminded me during our last drill. But I shut my mind to distractions and plowed through the formulas, step by step. At last, I emerged with my final figure and compared it to the Pilot's. I was off by nearly seven percent.

The Pilot's amusement was almost unnoticeable, but not quite. Coolly I erased my calculations and began again. A half hour later, my shirt soggy with perspiration, I found my figures off by the same amount. I was aware how much face I'd already lost. Even if I finally got it right I would look a fool.

The Pilot waited in the duty officer's chair, motionless except for an occasional long breath akin to a subvocal sigh. Ignoring the distraction, I stored each figure as I calculated it, then ran the results through the usual formula.

I was still six point seven nine percent off, and couldn't find the error. "Pilot, please watch while I try again." My tone was brusque. He came over to stand behind my chair, like a long-suffering lieutenant overseeing a middy's drill. "Stop me when you see the mistake," I said.

I went through the steps, plugging in the parameters I'd generated by previous calculations. When I finished I had the same answer I had before, and he hadn't intervened. "Well?"

"I didn't see an error. Sir," he added begrudgingly. "You manipulated the numbers correctly."

Interesting. "Go through your own calculation again."

I watched him enter the base figures, run his compensations with a practiced skill I longed to match, factor our present location, mass, and target, and calculate drive power and coordinates. His result matched his previous figures.

Vax sat staring at the screen. I suspected his mind was on automatic; thanks to my cruelty he was exhausted. He wouldn't be the only one; the crew had been on standby for nearly two hours.

No matter. I bent to my console. "We'll do our calculations step by step, all three of us. No, make that four; Darla, calculate along with us. We'll do a step at a time, until we all agree." I entered the initial figures. We bent over our screens. Darla put her results on the simulscreen above our heads.

Slowly we worked our way through the base calculations. No problem. Then we matched stellars, compensating by the book. We all still agreed. We all used the same plot for our present location. Our target location was right out of the charts. We entered ship's mass.

"Hey!" Vax spoke involuntarily. Three of the figures on the screen agreed. The fourth, mine, was different.

"There's your error, Captain." The Pilot's voice wasn't a sneer but it didn't miss by much. "You picked up a funny number for the ship's mass. 213.5 units."

"I thought I figured it right." I felt a blast of Lieutenant Cousins's withering scorn from wherever he was watching. "I calculated it the way we always do, base weight minus—"

"You figured ship's mass fresh each time?" The Pilot seemed astonished. Probably he meant no disrespect; he was so startled he simply forgot his manners. "We take mass from Darla's automatic Log entry. Vax, isn't that how you did it?"

"Yes, sir." Vax was trying not to be noticed.

"Darla?"

"Mass is a programmed parameter," Darla answered. "You know the ship recycles everything. I can't vary the adjusted mass except when you log an order for general recalc."

I stared at my figures, trying to puzzle out how I could have gone so wrong. Obviously the three of them knew something I didn't. I racked my brain trying to remember fusion theory from Academy. "I was starting with base mass, and subtracting the mass of the ship's launch and the estimated weight of the passengers lost with it from—"

The Pilot chortled. "That's all in the programming parameter Darla gives you."

"At Academy they made us run everything fresh each time, and Lieutenant Cousins never said to . . ."

Mr. Haynes was magnanimous. "Sir, that was just for practice. We'd be a week refiguring, each time we stopped for nav check. Remember your drill with Captain Haag? He had you use programmed parameters."

"I assumed it was just to save time. He was fidgeting, and I couldn't seem . . ." I chopped off the memory. While my ears reddened, I thumbed through the Log searching for the programmed parameters. "So, we start with Darla's base mass—"

"No, sir, the puter runs adjusted mass too. That's base mass minus passengers or cargo off-loaded since the last general recalc."

I'd made fool enough of myself for one day. "Very well, no wonder I was off. I'll do it your way. Darla, confirm adjusted ma—"

The speaker crackled. "Bridge, engine room here." The Chief. "Do we continue standing by to Fuse?"

How long had I kept them waiting? I bit my lip; over three hours. No wonder I was exhausted, and wringing wet. "We'll be ready in a moment, Chief." Where was I?

We had three matched sets of calculations, and we'd found my error. Time to get on with it. I started to wipe my figures, saw the Pilot's complacent smirk. I gritted my teeth, determined not to lash out at him. Instead, I decided to backtrack and correct my calculations. I obviously needed the practice, and with that attitude he could bloody well wait as long as it took.

"Here, where I subtracted the launch weight . . . I enter Darla's adjusted mass, right?"

Vax hid a yawn.

"Now, I can scrub my subtraction . . . by the way, what was the base mass when *Hibernia* left Earthport?"

The puter's tone was a touch cross. "Are you asking me? If so, I need a pronoun as referent."

"Just give me the parameter, Darla."

"215.6 standard units."

"I meant base mass."

"215.6 standard units is base mass, Captain. How many times do we need to go through this?"

Vax dozed. I wiped my calculation back to the point of error. The Pilot shifted impatiently. My head was spinning, and I'd kept them all waiting long enough. Still . . .

"Well, sir?"

My tone was curt. "Pilot, read from the Log our adjusted mass and our base mass."

"For heaven's—aye aye, sir." His fingers played the keys. "Adjusted mass is 215.6 units. Base mass is two hun—" The Pilot made an awful sound. His face went gray.

I said, "It doesn't seem quite right, does it? I mean, the two figures should differ."

"You caught an error," Pilot Haynes whispered. "The numbers we used were wrong!"

Vax jerked upright, dismayed. If the Pilot was in error, so was he.

I was dumbfounded. "But Darla figured it your way! Puters don't forget parameters."

The Pilot spoke first. "We must not be asking her the right question. Darla, what is ship's mass adjusted for the loss of the launch and passengers?"

"Adjusted mass is 215.6," she repeated.

I said, "Adjust your programmed base mass by the mass of the ship's launch. It's no longer on board."

"Mass has been adjusted as per standing calculation instructions," she said primly. "That's automatic."

"Holy Mother!" breathed Vax. "Darla has a glitch!"

"I do not!" Darla was indignant. "Watch your mouth, middy!"

"He meant it the old-fashioned way, Darla," I said quickly. "A gigo error." Darla had taken offense at being called brain damaged.

"But she—"

"Shut up, Vax." Like everyone, I'd heard dark rumors about ships that sailed interstellar with angry puters and were never heard of again.

We lapsed into silence. Darla threw random wavelengths of interference across the simulscreen, her equivalent of muttering under her breath. Something caught Vax's attention on the opposite side of the room. I realized he was reluctant to meet my eye.

I said, "But how could we have Defused so near *Celestina*, if Darla's figures are"—I dropped my voice—"'glitched?'"

"Maybe they weren't, at the time." The Pilot tapped into his console, peered at the figures he summoned. "These are the coordinates we used to find *Celestina*. Adjusted mass was the same as base. But remember, before we lost the launch, they would be expected to match."

"Didn't Captain Malstrom order a recalc before he Fused?"

"I would think so." He shrugged. "Check the Log."

"Check it yourself!" I clamped down, before I flew into a tirade. Now was no time to provoke another officer.

"Aye aye, sir." A hint of sullenness. His keys clicked. "Yes, it would appear so. The day of the memorial service." A frown. "For some reason, they didn't fully enter the new figures, or Darla would have them now."

"Darla, can you recalculate parameters?"

"Of course I can." I waited for more, but nothing was forthcoming.

"Do so."

"Order received and acknowledged, Captain. I'll need your special authorization code."

"Where is it?"

Her voice was sweet. "If they told me that, you wouldn't need one."

"Pilot, where do I find my codes?"

"I haven't the slightest idea." His tone was placating.

"Sir, why don't we override the puter's solution with your own manual plot in order to Fuse, and recalc afterward."

"Is that safe?"

"Yes, sir."

It would get us moving. "Very well, then."

A silence. The Pilot blurted, "Sir, the figures I gave you were worthless. Yours was the only correct solution. I apologize most sincerely for my mistake."

I snarled, "Belay that. Let's get under weigh." It did little good to assure the crew all was well, then sit for hours unable to Fuse.

"Captain, may I be relieved from watch and be allowed to leave the bridge?"

"No, Pilot." I didn't feel charitable, after enduring his smirk. "After we Fuse, search the Log and the databanks until you find my authorization code for a recalc."

I turned to Vax. "Run your coordinates one more time, and recalculate starting from base mass." He, Darla, and the Pilot might have been wrong, but I still had to be sure my own coordinates were right.

"Aye aye, sir!" Vax's fingers flew over the keys. In a few minutes he came up with a solution. My solution. I punched in the new figures. "Darla, I override your coordinates. Log."

"Manual override coordinates received and acknowledged, Mr. Seafort." Darla. "I'm logging it."

I picked up the caller, keyed the engine room. "Chief?"

"Yes, sir?" His answer was immediate. He must have been standing with caller in hand.

I tried to make my voice casual. "What if, say, one of Darla's preprogrammed parameters were glitched? Once we give you Fusion coordinates, would faulty input from Darla throw us off?"

"Only if you ordered us to rely on wave monitoring from the bridge, and I've never heard such an order since first I sailed. The engine room always monitors and adjusts energy output." A pause. "Is there a problem, sir?"

Yes. We were deep interstellar, with a Captain who had no idea what he was doing, and a stubborn puter. "Of course not." My tone was hearty. "Engine room, Fuse, please."

"Aye aye, sir. Fusion drive is . . . on." The screens abruptly faded.

I swallowed, watching the instruments closely. I knew Chief McAndrews was doing likewise, ready to pounce on the slightest variation from the norm. Our readouts remained steady. I let out a long breath.

"Permission to enter bridge, sir." Sandy, ready to begin his watch.

"Granted. Vax, you're relieved."

"Aye aye, sir." Vax stood and saluted, giving me a look I had never seen before. Respect, and something else. Awe, perhaps. I realized my bullying him, added to my apparent wizardry with the computations, had transformed me in his eyes from an irksome youth wrongfully his senior to a Captain who could do no wrong. Both images were faulty, but I couldn't do anything about them.

As Sandy settled into his seat. I realized with a sinking feeling that if the Pilot, a middy, and the puter could all be wrong, I could trust no one. Every time I went off watch I risked the entire ship. Now I knew why Captain Haag virtually lived on his bridge. I wasn't smarter than all the others, nor was I more alert. But *Hibernia* was my responsibility, and no one else's.

I also knew why the Pilot had gone pale; a seven percent error built into our coordinates would magnify to a stupendous variation after a lengthy Fuse. We could have sailed into the middle of Hope Sun. And it was just dumb luck that I had caught it.

# 11

Dinner was called. At the Captain's table there were only three places set. I caught the purser's attention and raised my eyebrow at the empty chairs.

Mr. Browning bent discreetly by my ear. "Requests from several passengers, sir, for new seat assignments. Under the circumstances I thought . . ."

"Quite right." Dining with the Captain was an honor. It would never, by Lord God, be a duty. Not while I held the office. I made conversation with the three passengers who remained. One of them was Mrs. Donhauser, who as usual didn't hesitate to speak her mind.

"You've become rather unpopular, young man." She eyed me with apparent disapproval.

"It would seem to be the case." I pretended unconcern as I buttered a roll.

"The Passengers' Council feels you should turn back. And they don't forgive your youth."

"Tell them it will pass." I had enough worries about the crew and officers without vexing myself with passengers. That seemed to offend her, and we finished our meal in silence.

I stopped to talk to the Chief on the way out. "By the way, there's a safe in my cabin. I don't suppose you know how I can get it open?"

His tone was flat. "I believe Captain Haag kept the combination in the bridge safe. If not, I can have a machinist drill it out."

"I'll look. Thanks." He was still staring when I turned away.

I climbed to Level 1, looked in on the bridge. Vax and Alexi seemed to have everything under control. Pilot Haynes had left word that he was unable, so far, to locate the recalc authorization codes, but would search again on his next watch.

I went to Amanda's stateroom. We met awkwardly at the hatch. I moved to kiss her; she accepted passively, unresponsive. We both took chairs instead of the bunk or deck. It was to be a more formal meeting. I told her I'd missed her.

She brushed aside my small talk. "What are you up to, Nicky?"

"How do you mean?"

"That uniform. Why are you playing at Captain? You know you're no Captain."

I tried a smile. "We all take turns, Amanda. Next one on is Vax."

She didn't smile back. "Don't laugh at me. I'm frightened of what you're doing."

"What am I doing that's frightening?"

"Going on to Hope Nation. People think we may not get there. They're worried and scared, and saying ugly things. Not just us, the crew too."

"How did you hear about that?"

"The mess stewards." I made a note to look into it. "Nicky, something could happen. Someone could get hurt."

I stopped trying to smile. "What do you know?"

"Nothing in particular. You're trying to take on everyone, and you can't. Not with the crew and passengers all spooked as they are. They say even the officers wanted to get rid of you."

"Where did you hear that?"

"I'm not telling." That was bad. I wanted her on my side, and she was widening the gap between us. "I know what you think," she added. "The law is the law, and if it says you should be Captain you've got to do it. But consider the good of the ship. If you step down, the other officers won't get into trouble for taking over. Get out of their way, Nicky."

"Is that how most of the passengers feel?"

"I hear it everywhere. And believe it, too."

"I need you, Amanda," I said simply, meaning it. "If you turn against me I'll be completely alone."

That brought her to my chair. She knelt at my side. "I'm not against you, Nicky. I want to be safe. I want you to be safe too."

I stroked her hair. "I'm Captain of *Hibernia*. That much is settled. If I don't have you to talk with, I won't have anyone. If I don't have you to touch and hold, I won't have anyone. Please." I held my breath, completely at her mercy.

She leaned over and kissed me. "I'm here, Nicky. I'll be with you."

I stayed with her most of the night. We didn't make love; instead, we caressed and kissed, we hugged. Early in the morning I left her stateroom and quietly went back to my own. Ricky found me there when he came with my breakfast tray. Again he saluted and stood rigidly at attention until I dismissed him.

I went to the bridge. Sandy and the Chief had the watch. I sat and checked the Log. Twice Vax had reported for personal inspection, then left to go back to bed.

I glanced at the blank simulscreen, wondering how familiar it would become before I reached Hope Nation. Seeing the Chief reminded me; I went to the safe and found in it the combination to my cabin strongbox. Bored, I sat again. Half in jest I asked, "Do you play chess, Darla?"

For answer the simulscreen lighted up with a chessboard. My jaw dropped. "I'll be dam— yes. Well." I glanced at the Chief. His eye held an amused glint. I said, "You'd better put it away. I can't while I'm on duty."

"Make up your mind," she said petulantly, snapping off the screen.

After a while I said, "Chief, I've been thinking."

"Yes, sir?"

"I don't see why we should sail all the way to Hope Nation without officers. Vax will make lieutenant soon, you know that. Why couldn't we recruit more midshipmen?"

Sandy examined his console, his ears growing larger by the minute. Well, I wasn't telling any secrets. He polished dust from his screen with his sleeve.

"Recruit them from where, sir?" asked the Chief. A good question. Most of the crew was too old to begin officer training.

"We have teens among the passengers. Several of them. And what about Ricky?"

"Are you asking my opinion, sir?"

"Yes."

"Then, no. We've gone too much against custom as it is. It's legal to recruit from the passengers, but highly irregular. Admiralty might view it as, ah, presumptuous." He was right. On the other hand, Admiralty wasn't shorthanded, nine light-years from nowhere, trying to sail a starship.

"Well, just a thought. Mr. Wilsky, isn't that screen clean enough?"

"Yes, sir. I mean, no, sir. I mean, aye aye, sir!" Sandy jumped back quickly, blushing deep red. Sandy was too nice a joey to enjoy teasing for long. But still . . .

"When you're done with it, would you kindly polish mine?"

"Aye aye, sir." He looked up cautiously, beginning to suspect he was being twitted. Slowly he relaxed.

"Permission to enter bridge, sir?"

I looked around. Vax waited at attention in the corridor. "Granted."

He marched in. "Midshipman Holser reporting for personal inspection, sir!" Well, if I was to do it at all, better do it right. I got up, made a show of inspecting his clean, freshly ironed uniform, his belt buckles, his shine. Naturally I passed him. Vax was ready, and even if not I wasn't about to notice anything wrong.

"Satisfactory, Mr. Holser. Bring me your written report no later than tomorrow. Dismissed." He saluted and left the bridge. Chief McAndrews said nothing, his face a mask. I understood; it wasn't up to him to comment on how the Captain treated his middies. But I wondered about his thoughts.

I leaned back in my chair. I should have played chess with Darla. Instead, I dozed, which was worse. Lieutenant Cousins would have had me over the barrel.

I entered the safe combination, reading from the paper in my hand. A click, and the door released. I looked inside. A class ring: Academy, class of 2162. It must be Captain Haag's. Apparently Captain Malstrom hadn't bothered to clean out the cabin safe after Mr. Haag's death. A leather folder. It held pictures of a younger Captain Haag, a pretty woman at his side. Hastily I put them away, ashamed at invading his privacy. The mere fact of his death didn't allow me to do that. A chipcase, with three chips. I set them aside to read later.

I took out an object about the length of my hand. A tube of wood, bored hollow down the middle. It had a wooden cup on one end. The cup was charred. Puzzled, I peered at it from all angles. A primitive piece from Africa? New Zealand folk art? Tourist junk from Caltech Planet? I couldn't imagine Captain Haag treasuring such an object. I put it aside. The only other item in the safe was an unlabeled canister. I opened it. It was filled with flakes of dull brown substance. Some kind of vegetable matter.

I lay the articles on my bunkside table and sat to contemplate them. I finally gave up and let my mind drift. I recalled an evening we middies spent with the Chief in a cheap Lunapolis bar, one of the rare occasions we socialized with our officers. We were speculating about how the colonies might develop, over time. I mentioned some ancient history I'd seen on a holodrama. It started the Chief on unusual primitive customs.

I sat bolt upright. Now I knew. The thing on the table was a device for burning the vegetable matter. Toccabo. How had the Chief put it? "Before the Reforms of 2024, boy, they were in common use. People filled them up and set them on fire."

"Then what, Chief?" I asked, knowing I was being played for a fool. "Did they call fire control?"

"No, they sucked until the smoke came through the other end. It was a stimulant."

We laughed. The liquor had obviously gotten to him. "And then they ate the smoke?" I jeered. I must have been drunk; after all, he was the Chief Engineer and could send me to the barrel.

"No, they breathed it." He glared, offended by my mockery.

"Chief, you're making it up," Alexi said. "Nobody could actually do that."

"Don't be sure if you haven't tried." The Chief stared him down.

"Have you—I mean, is it legal? Could you still do it?"

"Oh, it's legal. You can't advertise the stuff, or sell it for profit. But I hear there are places to obtain it. Of course you couldn't bring it on ship. It's contraband, like other drugs."

I demanded, "If it's legal, how come I never heard of it?"

The Chief took my question seriously. "With the reforms of 2024, a lot of vices sort of disappeared. For example, women offering publicly to fornicate for money; you ever hear about that one? And cancer was a big problem back then, before the anticars. So they just stopped the smoking. It took a while, because people used it to relax. But after it was outlawed in public places, it more or less died out. People could grow the plant, but nobody bothered anymore."

"Hey, Chief, have you tried the stuff?" Sandy Wilsky.

The Chief looked at his watch. "Time to go. Early start tomorrow." He flipped bills on the table.

Now, in my cabin, I sniffed the cup of the artifact. It smelled of charcoal, and another aroma. The toccabo, perhaps. I was scandalized. Captain Haag, sitting in his cabin secretly breathing contraband out of that fuming menace. Breaking ship's regs. How little we knew him. To us he was Lord God, walking the bridge.

Before taking command I'd never seen the inside of his cabin; none of us middies had. Few if any officers were invited into the Captain's quarters. He must have been a lonely man, with only Chief McAndrews to keep him company. Scuttlebutt had it that on quiet evenings the Chief, an old friend of Mr. Haag, would join him in his cabin. Together they would sit and reminisce, or do whatever old friends did.

I undressed for the night. My pants half off, I stopped short, swearing aloud at my stupidity. The tube in the safe wasn't for the Captain. Of course not. He'd kept the contraband for his old friend. The Chief faced court-martial if it were found aboard ship, so Captain Haag put it in the only secure place on *Hibernia*: his own safe. And in the evenings the Chief must have . . . I tried to imagine him with smoke pouring out his nose and mouth, like a dragon.

I slipped off the rest of my clothes and lay on my bunk. Back in Lunapolis, the Chief had said, "People used it to relax." Poor Chief McAndrews. Since the Captain's death he'd been deprived not only of his friend's companionship but his favorite relaxation as well. And all the while he didn't know if the contraband would be discovered and his career endangered.

On the spur of the moment I picked up the caller, dialed the engine room. "Chief Engineer to the Captain's cabin." I didn't wait for an answer. If he wasn't there, they'd find him. I threw on my clothes and made my bunk. I put the tube and the canister on the conference table.

The knock came shortly. "Chief McAndrews reporting, sir."

"Come in, Chief. Sit down." I wanted to show him it wasn't a formal occasion.

He sat in the proffered chair next to my table. His eyes flickered to the objects that lay on it. His expression showed nothing.

"I was cleaning out the safe, Chief, and found some odd items. Captain Haag's album, his ring. And these things, whatever they are."

"Yes, sir."

I had to be careful not to force him to admit the artifacts were his. "I've been trying to guess what they are, Chief. I think . . . do they have anything to do with that smoke stimulant you told me about? Toccabo?"

"Tobacco, sir. It looks like they might."

"I'm fascinated. Why Captain Haag brought them aboard, I can't imagine." He made no reply. "To think the Captain used such a thing," I went on. "I never would have guessed. Do you think I should try it?"

"It's forbidden, sir. Aboard ship." He remained impassive.

"Could you show me how it works? Please?"

"I'd be breaking regs, Captain."

"Never mind that." My tone was magnanimous. "I waive the regs, for this occasion." I handed him the tube. "Chief, I want to see how it works. Can you figure out how to set it off?"

"Yes, sir, I'm sure I could."

Good answer. He still hadn't committed himself. Perhaps he still suspected a trap. I could deal with that easily enough. "Make it work. That's an order."

"Aye aye, sir." He was not only off the hook, he had no choice. He could suck the thing with impunity, protected from retribution by my direct order.

The Chief opened the canister. Digging out a small metal spoon he filled the cup with the flaked vegetables. Tobaccos. He used the end of the spoon to tamp it down into the cup. "I need fire, sir."

"How much? A blowtorch?" I was prepared to order one up.

"No, sir. A candlelighter will do. I carry one." I waited while he put the flame to the cup. He brought the other end of the tube to his mouth and sucked, exactly as he had described. After a while he exhaled. Gray smoke came out his mouth. Wordlessly, he handed me the tube.

"No, I want to watch. Keep going."

"That's all there is, sir. You just keep doing it until it's gone."

"Oh. Does it feel good?"

"Some people say so." His tone was cautious.

"Finish it and tell me," I said. "We can chat while we wait."

"Aye aye, sir." He studied me out of the corner of his eye. After a while he produced more smoke. I watched it curl toward the ventilators. The scrubbers would remove it from the air before recycling it.

"How is morale on Level 3, Chief?"

"Better than it was. It will be better yet, when the convicts are dealt with."

"Oh, Lord. I forgot." How many days had passed? I still had to make up my mind about the three men waiting in the brig for execution.

"Yes, sir. If you don't mind my saying, the sooner it's decided, the better." The smoke seemed to have a relaxing effect on him.

"You're right. I'll make a decision soon. Does that tube thing get hot in your hand?"

"Pipe, sir. They call it a pipe." It was automatic for the Chief to correct a youngster; I didn't mind. "The bowl gets hot but not the stem." He knew all the jargon about tobaccoing.

I made conversation. After a while I grew used to the aroma of the smoke. Finally reassured that I wasn't looking to trap him, the Chief relaxed more fully. He stretched out his legs, his elbow on the table.

"How long did you know Captain Haag?" I asked.

"Twenty-one years." He knew the number by heart. "When he was first lieutenant we sailed together on the old *Prince of Wales*. We were in the same ship ever after." He puffed on the tube. The pipe. "He would sit right where you are, sir." His gaze was on the deck, or on something more distant. Mechanically he puffed until smoke appeared.

"I'm sorry, Chief," I said gently. "We all miss him. You most of all."

"Yes, sir. We didn't talk a lot, you know. Often we just sat together."

Perhaps the smoke had relaxed me too. Spontaneously I reached for his arm. "Chief, I know I'll never be as good as he was. I'm just trying to get through each day. I know it wouldn't be the same for you, but if you could come up sometimes, just to sit together . . ."

"You don't need to apologize for yourself, sir." He looked away, spoke to the bulkhead. "You're doing all right."

"Not really. You can't say so, but I know I've made a mess of things. With the Pilot, with Vax. Probably with everybody."

"I hear you're a pretty sharp navigator, Captain." The corners of his mouth twitched.

"You heard about that?"

"It's all over the ship. Your stock is up considerably."

I wasn't very surprised. Scuttlebutt went from the bridge to the fusion drive faster than a ship's boy could run. Maybe Darla did it. "It was an accident."

"You were being Captain. It's what you're for." He puffed again, trying to maintain the blaze. "I'd be glad to sit with you, sir," he said gruffly. "If it would be of service."

"Thank you, Chief." We sat peaceably until the fire was out.

# 12

I tapped my glass. The room quieted. "Lord God, today is March 14, 2195, on the U.N.S. *Hibernia*. We ask you to bless us, to bless our voyage, and to bring health and well-being to all aboard."

I remained standing after the "amen". "Before we begin, I have a few remarks." Some of the passengers exchanged glances. "As you know, we have resumed Fusion and are sailing for Hope Nation." They knew, but they didn't like it. I heard a brief murmur of discontent.

"My officers and I—" I liked that. It sounded confident. "My officers and I expect to arrive in Hope Nation on schedule. But we are shorthanded by four officers, which means extra watches for all those who remain. I have therefore decided to allow enlistment of one or more cadets from among the passengers."

I raised my voice to override the sudden angry babble. "A cadet trains to be a midshipman, an officer in the Naval Service. He or she enlists for a five-year term. Promotion to lieutenant or Captain may eventually occur. Service as an officer in the Naval Service is an honorable profession. If any of you want more information you may contact the purser, who will arrange for an officer to see you."

I sat in the resulting silence. Tonight only two were at my table: Mrs. Donhauser and Mr. Kaa Loa, a Micronesian who spoke infrequently. I hadn't gotten to know him.

"Good evening, Madam."

"Hello, Captain." She regarded me thoughtfully. "Aren't midshipmen recruited as children?"

"Cadets are, yes. Midshipmen are adults, by act of the General Assembly."

"Do you really expect parents to consent to your taking their children, Captain Seafort?" I realized how seldom my name and title had been used together. I liked the sound of it.

"Probably not."

"Isn't it a useless gesture, then?" She never dodged an issue. Blunt and honest. I approved of her.

"Not really," I said. "I don't need their consent."

She leaned close and grabbed my arm. "Nicky, don't shanghai joeykids into the service!" She spoke forcefully, quietly. "You may not know it yet, but protecting our children is one of the basic human urges. Don't get it working against you. You'd be asking for real trouble!" She wasn't threatening me; it was a warning, and I appreciated it.

"I'll take it into consideration, Mrs. Donhauser." I changed the subject as quickly as I could.

I shared the evening watch with Alexi. His mood was brighter than my own. I just wanted to sit and think; he had it in mind to ask all sorts of questions. He was respectful enough, but he wouldn't shut up. That was one drawback to our having been bunkmates; once past his initial shyness Alexi erred the other direction and was overly familiar. But I needed to decide what to do about my prisoners.

In addition to Mr. Tuak, ordinary seaman Rogoff and Machinist's Mate Herney were also under sentence of death, Rogoff for clubbing Chief Petty Officer Terrill, and Herney for fighting Mr. Vishinsky. The last case bothered me the most. I had seen the fracas myself, and I didn't think Mr. Herney had any idea whom he was hitting. I reread the regs on striking an officer.

"Do you think Darla's problem is correctable, sir?" Alexi. His fourth attempt to start a conversation.

"I don't know." Did the crime of striking an officer require knowledge that the victim was an officer? Perhaps not; fighting was itself a crime, and hitting an officer could just be an unlucky consequence. On the other hand—

"We could take her down for reprogramming while we're Fused, sir."

I thought my response mild, under the circumstances. "Be quiet for a while, Alexi." Presently I noticed he wore the reproachful expression of a chastened puppy. He didn't speak, but his silence was louder than words.

I sighed inwardly, knowing what Captain Haag would have done. But I liked Alexi. I groped for a way to divert him. "Calculate drive corrections for load imbalance, assuming we don't take on any cargo in Detour. It'll be good practice."

"Aye aye, sir." It kept him quiet awhile, anyway.

On his next watch, Pilot Haynes reported he was unable to find my authorization codes in any of our files. I nodded, saying nothing, hoping he hadn't seen my sudden blush. As soon as I could manage it casually, I left the bridge, hurried to my cabin. I took the forgotten chipcase from my safe, slipped a chip into my holovid.

The first chip held Captain Haag's personal pay vouchers, and statements of his savings account at Bank of Nova Scotia and Luna. The second, a text borrowed from the ship's library.

The third was a series of authorization codes for special access to the puter.

Not quite at ease handling the matter on my own, I called the Chief to the bridge, had him sit with me while I ordered Darla to recalculate.

It was really quite simple. After I entered the codes she went silent for almost a minute, while the screen flashed. Finally, she chimed a bell, as if clearing her throat. "Recalcu-
'ation complete, Captain."

I heaved a sigh of relief. "Very well. What's the ship's base mass, Darla?"

"215.6 standard units."

"And adjusted mass?"

Her voice was assured. "215.6 standard units. Are we plotting another Fuse?"

"Oh, Lord God." I glanced to the Chief. He swallowed. Darla was still glitched.

Two days passed, while we debated what to do. I swore the Chief and the Pilot to secrecy; nerves on board were taut enough without rumors that a crazed puter might send us to another galaxy.

I cursed my stupidity in not having turned back for home when I had the chance. Lieutenant Dagalow was no Dosman, but she had her advanced puter rating, and could have told us how to correct the parameter problem. Knowing the task was beyond me, I sent the Pilot delving into our puter manuals in the hope he'd learn enough to guide us through whatever programming might be necessary.

As *Hibernia* was already in Fusion, I saw no point in Defusing until Mr. Haynes felt himself ready. Though a proper Captain would have decided alone, I asked the Chief's opinion. He agreed.

In the meantime, Purser Browning reported no inquiries about enlistment. I had copies of my announcement posted in the passenger mess and lounges. Some were torn down.

The death sentences also preyed on my mind. I went to Amanda's cabin and shared with her my dread at having to consider executions. If I'd been Captain when the riot took place the affair wouldn't have gotten past Captain's Mast. But the court-martial was an established fact; now what was I to do?

She studied my face strangely. "Pardon them, of course. How can you do anything else?"

"What am I telling the crew by condoning mutiny?" I asked.

"Nicky, that wasn't a mutiny, it was a brawl. You know that."

I tried to help her understand. "It was a kind of mutiny,

hon. They disobeyed all sorts of regs, on smuggling, on drugs, about fighting. Worse, they attacked the officers Captain Malstrom sent in to break it up.''

"They were brawling. You already said you wouldn't have called a court-martial.''

"Yes, but . . .'' How did I explain, to a civilian? "Look. Say I'm a midshipman, and I've been up all night at General Quarters, and afterwards I report to the Captain with my uniform untidy. If he sees it he has to put me on report. And then I get in trouble with the first lieutenant.'' I paused for breath. "But he might decide not to see it. Then he doesn't have to deal with it.''

"So, decide not to see it,'' she said promptly.

"The problem is that it's already been seen. If Captain Malstrom hadn't officially noticed it with formal charges, I could let them go. Now if I do, I'm saying that mutiny goes unpunished.''

She was troubled. "I thought I knew you, Nicky. You can't be so cruel as to kill those poor men.'' That wasn't quite fair. I wouldn't kill them. That decision had already been made by Admiralty, Captain Malstrom, and the court-martial's presiding officer. I would let them be killed, a different thing altogether. If I did nothing, the process started by someone else would continue. I decided not to press the point. When we parted, the trouble was still between us.

The next day I had some good news. A note from the Purser; a passenger wanted information about joining up. I called Mr. Browning to the bridge, where I shared watch with the Chief. "One of the Treadwell joeys,'' I guessed. "Rafe or Paula.''

"No, sir.'' The purser looked uncomfortable standing at attention. "Mr. Carr.''

"Derek? You're joking.''

The concept of playing a trick on the Captain seemed beyond the man. "No, sir,'' he assured me, his tone earnest. "He asked to speak to an officer about your announcement. He kept repeating he hadn't made his mind up yet.''

"Who'd be best to send to him?'' I asked the Chief.

"Are you sure you'd let him join, sir?'' A good question.

"No.'' That decided it. "I'll talk with him myself.''

After watch and a short nap I went down to the Level 2 cabin Derek had shared with his father. It would be less formal than the bridge.

"Hello, Captain." We hadn't spoken since my promotion. He stood aside to let me enter. I chose a seat. His cabin was neat and clean, his belongings put away. Good.

"Mr. Carr." I had the right to call him by his first name —he was still a minor—but he'd see it as patronizing. The question rang in my mind: Was he officer material? Could a boy of his background handle the wardroom? I waited. He would bring the matter up when he was ready.

"I suppose you've come about what I told Mr. Browning."

"That's right." Uninvited, I took a chair. After all, I was the Captain.

"It was just an idea I had." He sat too, on his bunk.

"If you're not serious, I'll go." I wouldn't waste my time in a rich boy's cabin, with all the problems I had yet to solve.

"No, I was serious," he said quickly. "I still am."

"Why would someone like you want to be a midshipman?" I asked. Perhaps I had been around Mrs. Donhauser too long; I was learning to cut to the heart of the matter.

Derek examined his fingernails. "You remember I told you about my father's will? The managers control our estate until I'm twenty-two."

"Yes?"

"I know how those people operate. They'll send me somewhere to school. Get me out of the way. Maybe even back to Earth, another seventeen months stuck on board a frazzing ship."

"Thanks."

He had the grace to blush. "I'm sorry how that sounded. Anyway, I don't want to be helpless. I'm old enough to make my own decisions. And you said enlistment was for five years . . ."

"So?"

"In five years I'd be almost twenty-two." He made it sound as if it were reason enough to join up.

"Have you had schooling, Mr. Carr?" It was necessary to ask; groundside, education was optional with parents.

"Of course! I'm no peasant."

"Math?"

"Some. Algebra, geometry, trig."

"Calculus?"

"No. I could learn it, though." He didn't lack for self-confidence.

When I had nothing more to say he inquired, "Do you think I should do it?"

"No." In our whole conversation he never called me "sir", and only referred to me as "Captain" one time. He never used my name. Even aside from the matter of courtesy, he didn't sound very motivated.

"Why not?"

"For one thing, you're rather old to start as a cadet."

"I'd just be wasting the next two years, anyway."

"Perhaps. I don't think you have the temperament, Mr. Carr."

He flared. "Please explain."

I was tired and frustrated. "You have no manners. You expect the world handed to you on a spoon. You've never had any discipline and you couldn't handle any. They'd eat you alive in the middies' wardroom and spit out your bones." I stood up. "Cadets get hazed, Mr. Carr. I was; we all were, and sometimes it's brutal. One has to be able to take it. You can't. Thank you for your interest." I turned the hatch handle.

"You have no idea what I can take," he said coldly. "I should have known better than to talk to you."

"Good evening." I stalked back to Level 1. As I began to cool I wondered if I had been too hard on him. I'd asked his reasons; he'd given them. I couldn't expect him to join for love of the Service. He had the math, he was intelligent . . .

And he was an obnoxious snob. I could do better.

I entered the bridge. Vax and Alexi both rose. I now had middies standing watch together, to avoid exhausting the Pilot and the Chief. I myself expected to be exhausted. I took pity on the dark smudges under Vax's eyes. "Mr. Holser, you're relieved. Get some sleep."

He didn't argue with his good fortune. "Aye aye, sir." He saluted and hurried out before I could change my mind.

"Carry on, Alexi."

"I've got double watch tonight, sir. Sandy comes on at changeover."

"I know." It was one of the reasons I was there. Vax and

Alexi were one thing; Sandy and Alexi quite another. But we watch-standers had little to do; we were only present in case something went wrong. Most of the ship's systems were automatic: hydroponics, recycling, power. With the fusion drive ignited we couldn't navigate, and our only danger was boredom. I thumbed through the Log in silence. Mercifully, Alexi interrupted only a few times.

Sandy reported for duty an hour later, in good spirits. I decided not to tell him he had a smudge of lipstick on his neck. Regrettably, Alexi told him for me, and the result was a fit of giggling between the two boys that even had me joining.

"Back to duty," I told them. They settled down. The silence of the night watch stretched longer and tighter. Suddenly Alexi choked back a snort of laughter, trying to hold in a watch full of accumulated nervous energy. It got Sandy started too, but he subsided quickly under my glare.

Alexi brought himself under control. My tone was cold. "Mr. Tamarov, you're standing watch. Check your instruments and save the skylarking for later." I was red in the face when I ended, because my composure had started to slip about halfway through; if I hadn't held on with all my might, my little speech would have been punctuated by explosive laughter. It was contagious. But I was also angry. The ghost of Captain Haag stalked the bridge. Giggling on watch? He'd have tossed us out the airlock.

I went back to the Log; I'd been reading the entries from the start of our cruise. I had thumbed through to our docking at Ganymede when Alexi lost control once more. He covered his mouth, but a snort escaped him and his body shook.

It was more than I could bear. "*MR. TAMAROV!*" He leaped to attention. "My compliments to the Chief Engineer, and would he please advise me how to deal with a midshipman who refuses to pay attention to his work. Go!"

"Aye aye, sir!" His face a compound of embarrassment and dismay, Alexi saluted and hurried away.

Sandy was busily running practice calculations on his screen.

Twenty minutes later I heard a subdued voice. "Permission to enter bridge, sir." Alexi waited in the corridor, hands held tightly to his sides. Tears glistened.

"Granted."

He walked with care, coming to attention two paces from my seat. "Midshipman Tamarov reporting, sir." It was almost a whisper. "The Chief Engineer's respects, and if the Captain pleases, he should just send the midshipman to him whenever necessary." His look was bewildered and miserable.

"Thank you, Mr. Tamarov. You are relieved from watch."

"Aye aye, sir. Thank you, sir." He saluted, did an about-face, disappeared into the corridor. I writhed in shame. I had proved myself no better than Vax. Worse, I'd just made another enemy out of a friend. Alexi had meant no harm.

Quietly I went to the hatch, peered outside. Alexi leaned against the bulkhead, sobbing, his hand pressed to his buttocks. I stepped back in. I had stolen his dignity; at least I could leave him his privacy. On the bridge, Sandy tapped diligently at his keyboard.

Rather than risk a rebellion by Mr. Vishinsky, I let the master-at-arms send a sailor armed with a billy accompany me into the brig. The cell had no chair, no table, only Herney's mattress on the deck. I had them bring me a seat. The sailor stood against the hatch, billy clasped in front of him.

"Mr. Herney, I am Captain now."

"Yes, I know, sir, Mr. Seafort." The prisoner, a scrawny, tired-looking man of fifty, stood at ease. His mop of dark brown hair covered a hairline that had receded far back.

"I have a few questions about the, um, incident. How did it come about?"

He seemed pathetically eager to please. "Mr. Tuak and the others, they were fighting. I weren't involved in no drugs, honest. I din' even know they had none."

If that was going to be his line there was no point listening. "Mr. Herney, hear me well. In a few days we're going to cuff you, gag you, and hang you. Then we'll push your corpse out the airlock." He gagged. "I'm the only one who can stop it. This is the only time I'll talk to you. Lie again and I'll walk out."

"I'm sorry, Captain, sir," he babbled. "Only the truth, I swear it!"

"Start again."

"I knew about the goofjuice, a lot of us did. I'm sorry, Captain. Tuak, he was passing it around. I tried it, just once, honest! It cost too much, it weren't worth it. I'm sorry, Captain, honest I am. After that I stayed out of their way. Weiznisci, he got tanked, and you know that stuff, there's no talking to a man, he's got some in him. He was happy as a quark, but he was beating the crap outta two joes, we all sorta jumped him. An' that got Fraser going, he was on it too. Tuak figured to get ridda the stuff before the brass come down, only he couldn't, there was too much goin' on all at once." He scratched himself, thought for a moment.

"Mr. Terrill, he come in, told us to pull 'em apart, I just wanted to stay out of it. But I waded in like he said, and boom! I got one right in the side of the head, made me pretty mad. I din' know who done me, I was just swingin' my arms, you know? I din' care what I was hittin', I just tried ta stay ahead of how often I was gettin' hit. Then the lights goes out, and I wake up, I'm all cuffed, they say I slugged Mr. Vish."

He started to whimper, tears running down his face. "I don' know about that, Captain, sir. Maybe I did. I ain't sayin' I din'. But I din' mean to. It was a mistake. It's all some kinda mistake. It's got to be!" He began to sob. "Please, Cap'n, make it be a mistake! Get me outta this, I won't give no trouble, I promise, I—"

I banged on the hatch. The voice had to stop. I'd give anything to have the voice stop.

"Oh, please, sir. I won't fight no more, I'm so scared! Or the juice, neither, if you just—"

The hatch opened. I got out. I could hear his begging halfway down the corridor.

Ricky Fuentes stood at attention waiting to be dismissed, my breakfast tray on the table beside him.

"Good morning, Ricky."

"Good morning, Captain, sir!" I knew he frolicked. I knew he laughed. But in my cabin he was tighter than a coiled spring.

"Ricardo, I'd like you to think about something."

"Yes, sir, Captain!" His eyes were locked on the bulkhead in front of him as he stood at rigid attention.

I felt my temper fray. He was keyed tight, in no condition

to listen. "Ricky, belay that. At ease. Act like the joey I used to know."

"Aye aye, sir!" His voice remained stiff.

I roared, "By the Lord God, you will stop this bloody nonsense!" Ricky's mouth dropped open. He began to tremble.

"Stop standing at attention!" I screamed. "Behave yourself, boy!"

His lip quivered. A lone tear glistened in his eye, then slowly rolled down his cheek. He sagged from attention, wiped it with his sleeve. "What did I do?" he asked, forlorn. "I didn't want to make you mad, Captain!"

"Good Lord, Ricky!" I pulled out a chair. "Here, sit." I pushed him into it, waited while he fought for control. When I was sure he wouldn't cry I said, more gently, "Now you can listen to me. Sit easy, the way you used to in my wardroom, and we'll talk. All right?"

"Yessir." He watched me anxiously.

"You saw my announcement about becoming a middy?"

"Yessir!" He was taking no chances of setting me off again.

"You know how it is in the wardroom. Would you like it there?"

"Me, sir? I'm just a sailor."

"Would you like to be a cadet?"

"You mean, and get to live in the wardroom, and become an officer?" He grappled with the possibility.

"Yes."

"And have to shine Mr. Holser's shoes, and stand the regs, and ice-cold showers, and the rest of the hazing?"

Well, better he know now. "Yes, Ricky. That's part of it."

"Zarky!"

Good Lord, it actually appealed to him. Maybe it seemed adult, from his perspective. I wanted to stop him, for his own sake.

"Do I have to say yes right now, Captain, sir, or can I think about it?"

"You may think about it," I told him.

The ship's boy jumped up and saluted. "Thank you, Captain! You know"—he offered a confidence—"I read the notice myself, really I did. I can read! I didn't think you meant it for me too. Am I dismissed? Can I go tell my friends?''

''Dismissed, Mr. Fuentes.'' He would run to the purser or the chief petty officer, and ask them in his own way whether he should leave the companionship of belowdecks for the heady air of officers' country. They would tell him to apply, not because we needed officers, but to see one of their own make it to the top.

All was well on the bridge. I knew that; if not, I would have been called. I was scheduled for afternoon watch and would probably stay on for the evening, so if I wanted to see Amanda it had to be now.

She was in her room reading a holovid, her hatch open. When I knocked on the bulkhead she snapped off her book, got up quickly, and came to the entryway. ''Come in, Nicky.'' She was the only person aboard who still called me that.

We sat on the bunk. I told her what I had done to poor Alexi. She seemed indifferent. I told her how I encouraged little Ricky to apply, after first scaring the wits out of him. That brought a smile to her face, but she said little.

After a while she got up and closed the hatch. Then she lay down on the bunk, pulling me down with her. We lay together. She was gentle and kind to me. Yet she seemed somehow abstracted, as if her mind were elsewhere. We made love, slowly, savoring the moments of intensity. When we were done she lay still, her eyes sometimes opening to look at my face, sometimes closing again.

''What is it, hon?'' I stroked her hair. She nestled in my arm.

''I like you, Nicky.'' She was silent a moment. ''You're gentle, and gallant, and kind to me. I enjoy being with you.''

''Me too,'' I said, but she stopped me.

''I like having you as a lover. And as a friend. But— Nicky, I'm sorry. You have to know. If you kill those men, I'll stop being your friend. We won't be lovers or see each other ever again. I wanted you to make the right decision on your own, but it isn't fair not to tell you what I'll do.''

''How can you—''

She put her hand over my mouth. ''It's just that I may have

misjudged you. I think you're the sort of person who can't do anything so barbaric. That's why I like you. But if you can, I'm wrong about you, and it's over between us." She kissed my forehead. "I had to tell you." She rested her head again in the crook of my arm.

I could think of nothing to say. We lay there, sweetly unhappy, until I had to go on watch.

I came onto the bridge, relieved Vax and the Pilot. Vax handed me a holovid chip.

"The essay you ordered, sir."

I tossed it in the drawer. "Very good, Mr. Holser." I looked him over. "Straighten your tie, before I put you on report."

He blanched. "Aye aye, sir!" He quickly straightened his tie, tucked his jacket down, glanced at his shoes. "Am I dismissed, sir?"

"Yes." I reached a sudden decision. "Meet me in the ship's launch berth at midnight tonight."

"The launch— aye aye, sir!" He turned on his heel and left.

This watch, I would stand alone; nobody would interrupt my thoughts. In the silence, I considered Tuak and Rogoff, our two other condemned souls. I couldn't face another trip to the brig, but I had to talk to them. Amanda's conviction that the executions would be barbaric troubled me; I suspected she was right.

I paged Mr. Vishinsky. "Master-at-arms, escort Mr. Tuak to the bridge."

His voice came over the caller. "Aye aye, sir. Captain, may I bring along—"

"No. Just Tuak."

There was a pause. "Aye aye, sir. Respectfully, for the Captain's personal safety I protest—"

"Protest overruled. Get him up here." I thumbed off the caller.

A few minutes later Tuak arrived, hands cuffed in front of him, his upper arm firmly in Mr. Vishinsky's grip. He staggered as the master-at-arms propelled him forward.

"Take off the cuffs."

It did not meet with Vishinsky's approval. "Aye aye, sir." His anger was barely concealed.

"Wait outside." I slapped the hatch closed behind the master. I turned to the seaman, who stood nervously rubbing his chafed wrists. "I'm considering whether to save your life," I said. "Tell me what went on belowdecks. No lies."

"Aye aye, sir." Tuak swallowed. He looked drawn and haggard. He was tall and thin, of sallow complexion. His eyes shifted constantly, as if he consulted some inner voice.

His story was sordid. He admitted hiding the goofjuice on board, but claimed two of his mates had smuggled the still onto the ship. That was foolish; under drugs he'd already confessed to bringing aboard and setting up the still, and he knew it. I ignored that. The main issue wasn't the still.

"What started the riot?"

"Weiznisci started fighting, Captain. We was all just trying to stop him."

"The truth, Mr. Tuak."

"That's the truth, Captain, sir." He glanced up at my eyes. "I was going to stop making juice; we started the still just for a joke. We didn't mean to make all that trouble. I had to keep doin' it, they made me." He checked my expression once more. "When Weiznisci got wild some of the joes panicked. They wanted to tear out the still right then and there, before they found it in an inspection."

"So you tried to stop them."

"Oh, no, sir. I was helping. It was the others tried to stop them." That was patently untrue.

"Then Mr. Terrill came in."

"Yes, sir. He said to belay the fighting, but it was too wild, nobody was listening no more."

"So you held Mr. Terrill while Rogoff clubbed him."

"I didn't! I was trying to help him. I held him up, kept him from falling."

"Come on, now. Mr. Terrill said you grabbed him around the neck to hold on tighter."

"No, sir. Oh, no, Captain. He's mixed up, Mr. Terrill is. I saw him get slugged and I tried to keep him on his feet. That's all."

By now he could probably pass a polygraph and drug test on his story; he'd repeated it so often he believed it. He babbled on, trying to convince me of his good intentions.

A man like Tuak illustrated the pitfalls of guaranteed enlistment. If crewmen were given the same rigorous screening as us officers, Tuak wouldn't have gotten aboard. But the hazards of seafaring life made it difficult to recruit seamen for the huge starships, especially as government policy put a ten-year cap on service begun as an adult, for fear of melanoma T.

Government, industry, and academia were all in constant need of educated workers, and the colonies themselves were a drain of educated manpower. Our explosion into space meant that Admiralty had a lot of ships to man, and interstellar voyages took years. Belowdecks they were years of crammed quarters, lack of privacy, hard duties, tyrannical discipline. No matter how good the pay was, the recruits would have to wait years before they could spend it.

Guaranteed enlistment helped fill the crew berths. So we had men like Mr. Tuak, barely more civilized than the transpops, who responded to the guarantee they would be accepted and the half year's pay issued in advance as an enlistment bonus.

Yet Tuak hadn't done anything more than get caught up in a riot. Well, a little more; he had smuggled in the still that caused the riot in the first place. And he'd been fighting to protect the still from the men who wanted to dismantle it. But should he be put to death for that?

"Mr. Tuak." I waited while his excuses ran down. "Mr. Tuak, the master-at-arms will take you back to the brig. You will be informed." I slapped open the hatch.

"I din' mean no harm, Captain. Listen, Captain, I got two crippled sisters at home with my mother. Ask the paymaster, my pay all goes to them, every bit of it. They need me. Listen, I can stay out of trouble, honest, Captain!"

Vishinsky slapped the cuffs on his wrists, manhandled him out to the corridor.

"No more fighting!" Tuak said desperately, over his shoulder. "I swear!"

I was no closer to a decision.

As I left the dining hall after dinner the Purser handed me a sealed paper envelope. Unusual, in these days of holovid chipnotes. I took it back to the bridge to open. A letter, handwritten in a laborious script, obviously rewritten more than once.

*Hon. Captain Nicholas Seafort, U.N.S. Hibernia
Dear Sir:*
  *Please accept my apology for the way I behaved
when you visited my cabin. You are the authority
on board this vessel. I owed you respect which I
failed to offer. I was inexcusably rude to use the
tone of voice I did.*

I didn't know what to make of that. I read on.

  *When I thought about my discourtesy, I saw
why you don't think me fit for the Naval Service. I
ask you to forgive me. I assure you I am capable
of decent manners and I will not be offensive to
you again.
  Respectfully, Derek Carr.*

Now that was laying it on a bit thick. I could believe that
Mr. Carr had decided he'd been rude. It was possible that he
might even apologize. But that he'd grovel was hard to swallow. I wondered why he'd done it. I locked the letter in the
drawer under my console.

Some hours later I waited in the empty, dimly lit launch
berth. The hatch opened and a head peered in.
"Over here, Mr. Holser."
Vax looked around the huge cavern. Seeing me, he came
quickly to attention. "Midshipman Holser reporting, sir!"
"Very well." I indicated the cold open space. "What is
this, Vax?"
He said, puzzled, "It's the berth for the ship's launch, sir."
"That's right. Now that it's empty it's a good time to clean
it." From my jacket pocket I took a small rag and bar of
alumalloy polish. "I have a job for you. Clean and polish the
bulkheads, Mr. Holser. All of them."
Vax stared at me with anxiety and disbelief. The berth was
huge; polishing it might take most of a year. It was utterly
unnecessary work; one didn't hand-polish the partitions of a
launch berth.
"You're assigned to this duty only, until it's finished.
You're off the watch roster and you're forbidden to enter the

bridge. You may begin now.'' I thrust the polish and rag into his hands.

I had deliberately made it as hard as I could. By removing him from the watch roster and forbidding him access to the bridge, Vax would not again have opportunity to protest or ask my mercy. On the other hand, I'd given him a direct order. I hoped he would pass the test.

"Aye aye, sir.'' His voice was unsteady, but he turned to the partition, rubbed the bar against the alumalloy. He began to polish it with the rag. Alumalloy doesn't polish easily; it was hard work. After a few minutes of labor he had finished a patch a few inches around. He rubbed the bar of polish onto the adjoining spot and folded the rag to a clean surface. His muscles flexing, he rubbed the rag against the tough alumalloy surface.

I watched for several minutes. "Report for other duties when all four bulkheads are done.'' I turned and walked to the hatch twenty meters from where he had started. I glanced behind me; he was hard at work. I slapped the hatch open, started through it. He kept polishing.

I stepped back into the launch berth. "Belay that order, Mr. Holser.''

"Aye, aye, sir.'' His eyes darted from the bulkheads to me, and back, slowly taking in his reprieve.

I walked back to where he stood. "Vax, what did I demonstrate to you?''

He thought awhile before answering. "The Captain has absolute control of the vessel and the people on it, sir. He can make a midshipman do anything.''

"But you already knew that.''

"Yes, sir.'' He hesitated. "But not as well as I know it now.''

Thank you, Lord God. It was what I'd prayed to hear. "I'm canceling your special orders to report every four hours. You may resume your wardroom duties. You know what I expect from you?''

"Yes, sir. No hazing, under any circumstances.''

"Don't be ridiculous!'' I was angry. If that's all he had learned, all this had been a waste of time.

"I thought that's what you wanted, sir. For me to control myself.'' He was puzzled.

"Yes, that. And more. Come, let's go raid the galley."
He had to smile at that. At the beginning of the cruise, the
four of us would occasionally sneak into the galley late at
night and raid the coolers. We would catch hell if we were
caught; that made it all the more attractive.

Now I entered the galley with impunity. The metal counters
were shiny clean; the food was securely wrapped and stowed.
I opened the cooler and found some milk. Synthetic, of
course. In the bread bin was leftover cake that would have
gone to next day's lunch. Well, they'd never miss it. I served
my midshipman and myself. I indicated a stool for Vax; we
ate off the counter. "It tasted better the other way," I said.

"Yes, sir, but I'm glad for it now," he said politely. Our
Vax had come a long way.

"Now, Vax. About hazing. You're first middy. You've
been too busy to spend any time in the wardroom, so you
haven't taken charge. But I want you to. And with a change
of command there will be some settling in. You'll have to
make sure they both know who's senior."

"Yes, sir." He listened attentively.

"So, you may use your authority. Hazing, as we call it.
What I want you to stop isn't hazing, but your bullying. You
enjoy hazing so much you let it get out of control. You're to
control the pleasure you take in it. Stop yourself from going
overboard and being cruel. You told me once you're not nice,
that there's nothing you can do about it. If that's still true,
go back and start polishing the launch berth until you can do
something about it. I'll wait."

He swallowed. I think no one had ever talked to him like
that before.

I added, "You're better off with the rag and polish, Vax,
if you're not sure you'll control yourself. I meant it when I
said I'll wait. If you tell me I can trust you and I catch you
being cruel like you used to be, I'll break you. I'll make your
life a living hell for as long as I'm in command, until you
can't stand any more. I swear it by Lord God Himself!"

Vax said very humbly, "Please let me think for a moment,
sir."

I gave him all the time he wanted. He studied his fists,
clasped on the metal work counter. Vax was slow. Not stupid,
not retarded. Slow to make up his mind. I appreciated the

corollary of that. Once he made up his mind he was utterly dependable.

"Captain Seafort, sir, I think I can do what you want. I mean, I know I can, if I may ask a favor."

"What favor?" This was no time to start bargaining.

"I know the senior middy is supposed to handle wardroom matters and keep the other midshipmen out of your hair. But if I'm not sure of myself, could I come and ask you if you'd approve? I mean, of a hazing?"

I could have hugged him. It felt as if a fusion engine had been taken from around my neck. "I think so," I said soberly, after a moment's reflection. "I would allow it, yes."

"Thank you, sir. I promise I'll control myself. I will haze the other middies only when I think it's good for discipline. I won't let myself get carried away. Sir."

"Vax, the wardroom is yours. I won't spy on you; I accept your word. You have a job to do, and you'd better get on with it. Thanks to you, poor Alexi ended up over the barrel when all he needed was a lecture and a few hours of calisthenics." That wasn't fair; it was my fault more than Vax's.

"I'm very sorry, sir. You can count on me now."

I should have saluted and dismissed him. Instead, I broke regs, custom, and all propriety. Matters must have been getting to me. Slowly, looking him in the eye, I offered my hand. Just as slowly he took it in his big paw and clasped it firmly. We shook.

# 13

"Lord God, today is March 30, 2195, on the U.N.S. *Hibernia*. We ask you to bless us, to bless our voyage, and to bring health and well-being to all aboard." Seated, I nodded to my two tablemates. Weeks after I'd assumed command, Mrs. Donhauser and Mr. Kaa Loa were still my only dinner companions.

The purser bent at my ear. "Sir, one of the passengers is asking if he may join the Captain's table." My popularity had just risen by half.

"That's agreeable, Mr. Browning. Who is it?"

"Young Mr. Carr, sir."

I hadn't spoken to Derek in the weeks since his letter. I was curious. "Ask him if he cares to start tonight."

A moment later Derek Carr approached with diffidence. "Good evening, Captain. Mrs. Donhauser. And you, sir," this last to Mr. Kaa Loa, whom he apparently didn't know.

"Please be seated, Mr. Carr." I introduced the boy to the Micronesian.

After his courtesies to the older man Derek turned to me. "Sir, I apologize again for my behavior in my cabin. I promise it won't happen again."

Where was all this heading? "No matter, Mr. Carr. It's over and done." Derek sat. I chatted with Mrs. Donhauser. She turned the topic to religion, a difficult topic on board ship. Her Anabaptist doctrines were tolerated, as were most cults, but the Naval Service, like the rest of the Government, was committed to the Great Yahwehist Christian Reunification. She knew full well that as Captain I was a representative of the One True God, and she shouldn't be baiting me. I assumed she was just out of sorts; normally Mrs. Donhauser was a pleasant if argumentative companion.

To avoid contention I turned to Derek. "How have you been occupying yourself lately, Mr. Carr?"

"I've been studying, sir. And exercising."

Definitely a change in manner. I gave him another opening. "Were you enrolled in school before the voyage?"

"No, sir. I had tutors. My father believed in solitary education."

"We should reimpose mandatory schooling," Mrs. Donhauser grumbled. "The voluntary system doesn't work; we don't have enough technocrats to run government or industry. We're constantly starved for educated people."

"Mandatory education didn't work either," I said. "Literacy levels dropped constantly until it was abandoned."

Mrs. Donhauser, savoring a good argument, launched into a vehement counterattack, demonstrating, at least to herself, that mandatory education was the only way to save society. "Don't you agree, Mr. Carr?" she asked when she finished.

"Yes, ma'am, I agree that a mass of uneducated people is a danger to society. As for the rest—" He turned to me. "Is she right, sir?" Now I was really puzzled. This was not the haughty youth who'd come aboard the ship. And I was likewise sure he had not undergone a complete change of heart. His courtesy had a purpose. I turned away the question and studied him during the rest of the meal.

Going over watch rotations in my cabin that evening, I realized how little time I had to decide the fate of the three wretched sailors under sentence of death. I intended to make a deliberate decision; their fate wouldn't be determined by default. Shortly, I would have to free them or allow—no, order—the executions to take place.

I had spoken to Tuak and Herney, but I'd put off seeing Rogoff because I found the interviews unbearable. I made a note to see the man after forenoon watch.

I undressed, crawled into my bunk, and drifted off to sleep almost immediately. In the early hours I awoke. I tossed and turned until I couldn't stand it any longer; I snapped on my holovid and read ship's regs. If they wouldn't put me to sleep, nothing would.

Again I closed my eyes and tried to sleep; I'd never found insomnia a problem in the wardroom. At three in the morning I turned on my bedside light. My stomach slowly knotted from tension as I began to dress.

I walked the deserted corridors to Level 3. One of Mr. Vishinsky's seamen guarded the brig. He was watching a holovid, feet on the desk, when I appeared in the hatchway. Horrified, he leapt to his feet and snapped to attention.

I ignored his infraction. At that hour, one need not be prepared for a Captain's inspection. "I'm here to see Mr. Rogoff, sailor."

"Aye aye, sir. He's in cell four. If the Captain will let me get the cuffs on him—"

"Not necessary. Open the hatch. And lend me your chair. You don't sit on guard duty anyway."

"Aye aye, sir. No, sir." He jumped to obey.

Rogoff, wearing only his pants, was asleep on his dirty

mattress when the light snapped on. Bleary, he looked up as I entered and set down the chair.

"Mr. Rogoff."

"Mr. Seafort? I mean, Captain, sir? Is it—oh, God, I mean, are you here to—" He couldn't say the words.

"No. Not for a few days yet. I'm here to talk to you."

"Yessir!" He scrambled to his feet. "Anything you say, Captain. Anything."

I turned the chair backward and straddled it. "If I don't commute your sentence they're going to hang you. Tell me why I should pardon you."

He rubbed his eyes, standing awkwardly in front of my chair. "Captain, please, for Lord God's sake, let me go. Brig me for the rest of the voyage, or whatever you want. But don't let them hang me. I didn't mean any harm."

"No harm?" I asked him. "You clubbed the CPO unconscious while Mr. Tuak held his arms."

"Not in cold blood, sir. We were fighting, all of us."

"You can't brawl with a superior, even a petty officer."

"No, sir, you're right, sir. But the thing was, the fight started. Your blood gets hot, you don't see what's going on, or stop to think things over. Right then, Mr. Terrill was just another joe, you know? He wasn't the CPO, he was just somebody to hit. It's not like I meant to mutiny, sir."

He had stated in a nutshell why the affair should have been handled at Captain's Mast. Damn Captain Malstrom for leaving me this mess. I felt guilty for my anger, and it made me cross. "Maybe that's so for the first blow, Mr. Rogoff. But you smashed him several times in the face. By then you knew who you were hitting."

"Excuse me, Captain, no offense, have you ever been in a fight?"

"Yes." I hadn't won.

"While you were swinging did you stop and think about the consequences? Did you consider how hard you should fight, or whether you should hit a joe?"

"I never swung against a superior officer, Mr. Rogoff." Except my senior middy when I was posted to Helsinki, and he blackened both my eyes and kneed me so hard I couldn't walk upright for days. But that didn't count, did it? Challenging the first middy was understood and accepted. I wasn't like Rogoff, was I? "You kept punching hi ı in the face. Your superior."

"Sir, look at me. Pretend it's you here, in this god-awful place. You had a bad fight, and they're going to hang you for it. Please. Don't do that to me."

I made my voice hard. "It wasn't that simple, sailor. You were fighting to protect that bloody still of yours, to make sure the officers didn't find it. You were covering up a crime Mr. Terrill was about to discover."

Rogoff hugged himself. He looked at the deck, shaking his head from side to side. His bare feet wiggled nervously. "Captain," he said, looking up, "I ain't no angel. I do things that ain't right. I know I been in trouble before. But the still, that's brig time or a discharge. If I'd of realized what I was doing I wouldn't have touched him. You gotta believe that."

"I believe you weren't thinking about court-martial, Mr. Rogoff. I can't believe you were unaware you were hitting Petty Officer Terrill. Is your being excited reason to pardon you?"

"Captain, I beg you. I'm begging for my life."

"Please, don't." I didn't want that power over him.

"Look!" He dropped to his knees in front of me. "Please, sir, I'm begging. Don't hang me! Let me live, give me another chance!"

I scrambled to my feet, sweating. I had to get out of the cell. "Guard!"

"Sir, I'm not evil!" He put his palms on the deck, abasing himself. "Please let me live! Please!"

I didn't run out of the cell. I walked. I walked out of the brig anteroom. I walked to the turn of the corridor outside. Then I ran, as if the devils of hell were at my heels. I tore up the ladder past Level 2 to officers' country, past the bridge to my cabin. I fumbled at the hatch, slapped it closed behind me. I barely made it to the head before I heaved my undigested dinner into the toilet. I remained there, shaking with fear and disgust. It was when I realized that I was kneeling with both my palms on the deck that I began to cry.

I became a hermit, refusing to leave my cabin except for brief excursions to the bridge. I had the Chief cross my name off the watch roster. My look was such that no one dared speak to me. I took meals in my cabin, refusing even to take my evening meal in the dining hall with the passengers. I pretended to myself I was sick, that I felt feverish. I lay in my bunk imagining that I was safe, in Father's house.

In the quietest hours of the second night I had a dream. Again I was a boy, walking toward the Academy gates. My duffel was very heavy, so heavy I could hardly carry it. I had to say something to Father, but I couldn't speak. He walked along beside me, dour and uncommunicative as always. Yet he was there with me, was that not enough proof he loved me?

I changed the duffel to my other arm so I could put my hand in his. Father switched to my other side. I switched the duffel back, but he stepped around me once more. I prepared the words of parting I would offer. I rehearsed them over and again until they sounded right.

The gates loomed closer. Now we were at the broad open walk in front of the Academy entrance. The sentry stood impassive guard. I turned, knowing it was time to say good-bye. Father put his hands firmly on my shoulders and turned me toward the waiting gates. He propelled me forward.

In a daze I walked though the gates, feeling an iron ring close itself around my neck as I did so. I turned. Father was striding away. I willed him to turn to me. I waved to his back. Never looking over his shoulder, he disappeared over the rise. The iron ring was heavy around my neck.

I awoke, shaking. Eventually my breathing fell silent. I smelled the acrid sweat on my undershirt; I stripped off my clothes and walked unsteadily to my shower to stand under the hot water a long while, motionless.

When I finally dared go back to bed I slept untroubled. In the morning I ate the breakfast Ricky brought, and left my cabin to become a human being once more.

# 14

"Excuse me, sir, a question."

"What is it, Vax?" We were on watch. In the long silence, I'd been trying to empty my mind of everything, to think of nothing. I was not succeeding.

"One of the passengers, Mr. Carr, asked if I would show him Academy's exercise drills this afternoon. I thought I ought to have your permission first."

I could see no reason to refuse. "If you want to, Vax, I have no objection." I smiled. "Are you about to become a drill sergeant?"

"No, sir. I thought I'd do them with him." I should have guessed.

Time passed. Still I made no decision about the prisoners.

The next day Yorinda Vincente asked to see me. I assented. I didn't want her on the bridge or in my cabin, so I met her in the passengers' lounge.

"This is on behalf of the Passengers' Council." Her tone was stiff. "We want to know what will happen to the ship, I mean the crew, when we get to Hope Nation."

"You're asking if *Hibernia* will get a new Captain?"

"And other officers, yes."

"Most of you will disembark at Hope Nation, Ms. Vincente. How does it concern you?"

"Some of us are booked to Detour, Captain Seafort. Other plans would have to be made." She meant that they wouldn't want to stay on the ship if I were going to sail her. I understood. *I* wouldn't want to stay on the ship if I were going to sail her.

"*Hibernia* is under orders from Admiralty at Lunapolis," I explained. "My authority as Captain derives from those orders. Admiralty has a representative, Admiral Johanson, at Hope Nation. When I report, he will relieve me of command, appoint a commissioned Captain, and assign lieutenants to the ship.''

"Are there experienced officers at Hope Nation?"

"More experienced than I, Ms. Vincente. And even if there weren't, the Admiral is my superior officer. I'm sure he'll relieve me and appoint a Captain of his choosing. *Hibernia* will be in good hands when she leaves Hope Nation.''

She explored all the possibilities. "I imagine skilled officers aren't sitting around Hope Nation waiting to be posted. What will he do if he doesn't have enough lieutenants?"

"It's unlikely any Naval officers are sitting around waiting, Ms. Vincente. The Service is always shorthanded. What I imagine he'll do is borrow them from local service, and replace them with some of our own officers. Perhaps even myself.''

"People without interstellar experience?"

"Not every lieutenant goes interstellar before he's commissioned, ma'am. As long as the Captain's a seasoned officer, the ship will be in good hands.'' I continued my reassurances until she seemed satisfied.

The next day when I met Vax on the bridge I asked, "How are your exercises going?"

"They're not," he said. I raised an eyebrow. He added, "Derek showed up the first day and we worked out. Easy stuff, like they give the first-year cadets. Yesterday he came again, but after a half hour he walked out.''

"What did he say?"

"Nothing, sir. He just stalked out and slammed the hatch.'' So much for Mr. Carr.

I met Amanda in the corridor on the way to the dining hall. She stopped, waiting for me to speak first.

"I haven't made up my mind yet, Amanda.''

"Isn't your time about up?"

"Day after tomorrow. One way or another, it will be over by then.''

"Listen to your conscience," she said. "Pardon them. Years from now you'll hate yourself if you don't.''

"I'm still thinking." I didn't mention my interview with Rogoff. We went in to dinner. When I came to the part of the Ship's Prayer, "Bring health and well-being to all aboard," I stumbled over the words.

That evening Chief McAndrews sat down heavily in the armchair alongside my table. The pipe lay between us. I said, "Chief, I order you to ignite that device. We need to investigate it further."

"Aye aye, sir." It was his third visit to my cabin; we were establishing the form of a ritual. He opened the canister and got out his candlelighter.

I kicked off my shoes. After all, it was my own cabin. "I was hoping I'd have another middy by now." I yawned. "We're all standing too many watches."

"On the bridge or in the launch berth, sir?" He was beginning to unbend with me, just a bit.

"Oh, you heard about that?"

"Someone saw you take Mr. Holser in there and emerge later with a very subdued midshipman."

"Who saw?"

"I don't remember, sir."

If we could power the ship by gossip it would be faster than fusion. Maybe it really was Darla who spread the word. "I think Vax will be all right, Chief. I've straightened things out with him."

"With a club?"

I smiled. "Vax just needs the facts demonstrated from time to time. Then he believes them. He'll make a good first middy."

He puffed on his artifact. "What you need, Captain, is a fourth middy. Maybe even a fifth." I knew that. I could then make Vax a lieutenant. Probably also Alexi, if I hadn't embittered him for life.

"The only feeler I've had is from that Carr joey, and I turned him down."

"There's Ricky." The Chief knew everything.

"He won't be old enough to be much help until we're past Detour. We'll have new officers and won't need him by then."

"So why'd you invite him, Captain?"

"I didn't say he'd be no help at all. And I like him."

"He'll agree. He needs more time to think about it, but count on him."

"I'm not so sure," I said. "I don't have the knack of persuading people without terrorizing them. First Vax, then the Pilot, and then Alexi. Now it's Ricky. I had to scream at the top of my voice to stop him from standing at attention. I'm lucky he didn't wet his pants."

The Chief smiled. "You didn't terrorize him. You startled him some, but he's told everyone belowdecks how the Captain wants him to be a midshipman. He sticks his chest out when he says it. I don't think you have to worry."

"Then I was fortunate. Part of my problem having no natural authority is that I come on like a wild man to uphold the stature of the office. As I did with Alexi."

The Chief shrugged. "The barrel? He'll get over it. I gave him half a dozen, not all that hard. He's had worse before."

"But not from me. I was his friend."

Chief McAndrews took several puffs on the pipe before deciding to reply. "You still are," he said. "You've done him a favor, whether he knows it or not. A big one. When we get to Hope Nation he'll probably be transferred. What would happen to him if he had a silly fit on the bridge of someone else's ship?"

I shuddered. Either he wouldn't sit down for a month or he would find himself in the brig. If the Captain didn't die of apoplexy first.

"Still, I should have found some other way to stop him."

The Chief waved his pipe in the air. "Say you're right, Captain. Maybe you should have found a better way. He'll still get over it. Neither he nor anyone else has the right to expect you to be perfect. You're doing your best."

"And it isn't good enough, Chief." I stared moodily at his smoke. "In a couple of days I have to decide about those poor joeys in the brig. I have two choices, both wrong. If I let them go, mutiny goes unpunished. Admiralty would never pardon them if the affair had happened back at Earthport; they'd hang the three with no regrets. But I feel that if I execute them, I'm a heartless killer."

I brooded. "Expect myself to be perfect? If I were barely competent I'd find a third solution. I've tried; I can't think of any. So I'll pick one alternative or the other. My best isn't good enough."

Wisely, the Chief said nothing.

The next day, I was restless and irritable. To distract myself

I ran surprise drills throughout the ship, telling myself it was to improve the crew's alertness. *"Fire in the launch berth!"* *"Fusion engine overheat!"* *"Man Battle Stations!"* The crew scurried.

I announced that Darla had a nervous breakdown, and made the middies plot all ship's functions by hand. They complied, although nobody, especially Darla, thought it was funny. I entered drill response times in the Log to compare with future drills. I made a mental note to have future drills.

All in all, I continued making myself unpopular.

I woke in the morning with a sense of dread at what I'd have to face before the day ended. After showering and dressing I sat to await the usual knock; in a few moments Ricky arrived with my breakfast. He put down the tray, saluted, and waited to be dismissed. Though he stood at attention, his stomach no longer tried to meet his backbone.

"Stand easy, Mr. Fuentes."

"Thank you, Captain. They were having waffles and cream so I brought you extras. Cream is real zarky." He looked wistfully at the tray. Crew rations didn't compare with officers' and passengers' fare.

I liked the new Ricky much better. Or was it the old Ricky? "Thank you. About that cadet idea, what do you think?"

"Mr. Browning says I should. So does Mr. Terrill. It's just I'm a little scared. Captain, sir."

"I can understand that." I took a bite of waffle. It was delicious. I thought of offering him some, but there were limits. A crewman didn't breakfast with the Captain. "So you can read, hmm?"

"Oh, yes. I can write too. Even by hand." He was very proud of it.

"Ricky, I'm going to arrange some lessons for you. Math, physics, history. I want you to work as hard as you can. Will you do that for me, as a special favor?" That would get his cooperation far better than an order.

He actually swelled with pride. His shoulders went up, his chest came out. "Oh, yes, sir. I'll do my best."

"Very well. Dismissed, Mr. Fuentes." He saluted, spun on his heel, and went to the hatch. Someone must have been teaching him physical drills. I suspected the Ship's Boy already knew more about Naval life, and how *Hibernia* was run, than most people would imagine. "Oh, Mr. Fuentes?"

"Yes, sir?" He stopped in the entryway.

"Go to the galley. My compliments to the Cook, and would he please serve you a portion of waffles and cream."

His face lit up. "Oh, thanks, Captain, sir! They're real good. He already gave me some, but I'd love more!" He raced out into the corridor. So much for my generosity.

Sandy was on watch with the Pilot when I popped onto the bridge for a quick inspection. Mr. Haynes nodded with careful civility. He hadn't had much to say to me since the incident with our coordinates.

I glanced at Sandy and my eyebrow rose; the boy was dozing in his seat. That wouldn't do. I relieved him and sent him to Vax, with a request to encourage the youngster to stay awake on duty.

Vax, a middy himself, couldn't send Sandy to the barrel, but he had ways to get the point across. I didn't feel guilty this time; sleeping on watch was a heinous offense. I had to prepare Sandy to hold his own watch. It crossed my mind that I myself had dozed on the bridge only a couple of weeks before. I argued that I wasn't actually watch officer; I'd just stayed to keep an eye on things. When part of me started to argue back, I left the bridge.

I wandered the Level 1 circumference corridor, past cabins in which Lieutenants Dagalow and Cousins once lived. Past Lieutenant Malstrom's cabin where a lifetime ago I'd played chess. Through the passengers' section, nodding curtly to anyone who noticed me. I looked into the infirmary. The med tech came to attention in the anteroom; Dr. Uburu was with a passenger in the cubicle that served as an examining room.

I had an inexplicable urge to visit the whole of the ship. I went down to Level 2. The exercise room in which I'd battled Vax was empty. A few people were in the passengers' lounge: the Treadwell children, Mr. Barstow, Derek Carr. I left quickly, in no mood for conversation.

I wandered into the dining hall. Empty tables, set with gleaming shining glassware and china on starched white cloths, waited for the evening's throng. I acknowledged the good sense of the ship's designers; by having officers and passengers eat separately twice a day, and merging us into one unit for the evening meal, they provided continuing variation in our routines while subtly reminding us of the difference in our status.

I closed my eyes to summon Captain Haag, competent and reassuring in his dress whites, delivering the Ship's Prayer to an attentive hall. I found the table where I'd apprehensively awaited my first dinner, upon reporting to *Hibernia* but a few months past.

Morose, I left the dining hall, wandered past the row of hatches to the passengers' cabins. In the passengers' mess the steward, startled to find me where the Captain seldom ventured, dropped his tray of silverware on the table and snapped to attention. I released him with a wave.

The mess could hold thirty passengers at a time; they came for their breakfast and lunch on rigid schedule. The compartment was plain, almost cheerless, unlike the ship's dining hall above.

I took the ladder down to Level 3, feeling my weight increase perceptibly as I did so. Here, crewmen hurried about on errands, snapping to attention as I passed unheeding. I stopped at the crew's presentation hall, or theater; its rows of practical, sturdy seats depressed me. Farther along the corridor was the crew's exercise room, identical to the passengers' gym a level above.

"Pardon me, Captain, can I help you find someone?" Carpenter's Mate Tsai Ting, whom Mr. Vishinsky had brought to the munitions locker. He stood at attention.

"No. Carry on, sailor."

"Aye aye, sir." He went about his business. Now it wouldn't be long before the whole crew knew I was poking around in their territory.

I looked into crew berth one, knowing I was violating custom. The crew had no place of their own except their berths and the privacy rooms, and little time to themselves. It was understood that the Captain would not harass them in their bunks by unannounced inspections.

A dozen crewmen were sleeping; one lad sitting on his bunk saw me and was about to leap to his feet; I put my finger to my lips and shook my head. He remained in his place, his eyes locked on me, while I looked about from the hatchway.

The crew berth smelled of many men in close quarters; it was clean without being cleanly. Calendars were posted on some of the lockers; unused bunks were neatly made. It was no more, no less than I expected.

Restless, I went into the adjoining head. The lack of privacy in its large open spaces made our midshipmen's head seem positively luxurious. This room, at least, was scrupulously clean. The petty officers saw to that.

There was nothing aft but the engine room and the shaft. I climbed down the ladder to the engine room at the base of the disk. The insistent throb of the fusion drives pervaded my senses. The outer compartment was empty; the Chief would be farther aft, then, in the drive control chamber. I wandered starboard to the hydroponics unit.

"They'll be all right." The voice came from around the curve in the corridor just ahead. I stopped.

"I don't know. He's a bastard; look how he shoved the Chief aside to get to the top."

"Sure, Captain Kid's ambitious and saw his chance. But he'll let them go; he's just waiting 'til the last minute."

"Yeah? Why?"

Heart pounding, I pressed my head against the bulkhead to spy on my crew.

"He's showing us he could, if he wants to. But he can't really hang them. There'd be a mutiny and he knows it. He'd be out the airlock before a single one of them got it."

There was a pause. "I'm not part of any mutiny," the voice said cautiously. "I'm out of it. We're just talking."

"Hey, I didn't say I'd do anything myself. I just said the Captain didn't dare. You know the joes, some of them are real tough grodes. You think Captain Kid wants to go up against them? Why should he bother? All that happened was some joeys got shoved around a little. Nobody got killed."

Another pause. "They got the death sentence, didn't they?"

"Ah, that's a lot of crap. This isn't officers' country, with all their young gentlemen. We settle things our own way. So what if Terrill got knocked around some? Serves him right for butting in. He knew better."

"What if Captain Kid goes through with it, Eddy? What if Rogoff and Tuak and Herney get roped?"

I strained to hear the answer. "Who's gonna do the roping, huh? Which crewman's gonna tie a rope around another joey's head? Look, they think they run the ship. But it's us. We do the work. We run the drives, cook the food, recycle the air. We're symbiotic. You know what that means? It means they need us like we need them. He won't rope them. He's smart enough to know that, for all his being a joeykid."

I backed away until I reached the ladder, scurried up to Level 3. Still uneasy, I didn't stop until I'd reached the safety of Level 1.

Time for lunch. In the officers' mess I sat by myself at a small table, brooding. As was the custom, conversation went on around me but nobody bothered me. When the Captain sat at the long table he was part of the group. When he sat by himself he was alone and invisible.

After mess I went back down to Level 2 and wandered along the corridor until I found the hatch I was looking for. I knocked.

Mr. Ibn Saud seemed disconcerted to see me. "Oh! Come in, Captain." He stood aside. His prayer rug was folded neatly at his bedside.

On the bulkhead was a large color print of Jerusalem's golden mosque of al-Aqsa, its glimmering dome rebuilt after the Last War to look as it had before.

"Could we talk awhile, Mr. Ibn Saud?"

"I am at your disposal." He offered me his only chair, sat on his bunk facing me.

"I have a decision to make. I know what my superiors would expect, but the choice isn't theirs, it's mine. I think it's arbitrary and rigid to put our condemned sailors to death for a brawl. On the other hand, their riot was just short of mutiny. Wouldn't it be weak and permissive of us to pardon them?"

"Have you studied history, Mr. Seafort?"

"Not with a teacher." Father had taught me at home, with a page-worn encyclopedia and the Bible as our curriculum, along with used math and physics texts for the holo.

Mr. Ibn Saud frowned. "Social trends follow a pendulum motion. Repression, then rebellion; rigidity, then anarchy. We're frozen at one end of the pendulum."

I sat. "What do you mean?"

"Look back, say, to the twentieth century. It began conservatively, swung in the 1920s to more permissive social mores, swung back to conservatism a generation later."

"So?" It sounded rude, and I immediately regretted it. He was doing his best.

"When the Eastern dictatorships collapsed, America was left the dominant power just as it was entering its liberal, or anarchic, phase."

I waited, wondering how this would help me.

"Willing to try new forms, America set up the U.N. Government, and transferred a few powers to it. So the skeleton of world government was in place when the American-Japanese financial structure collapsed. If not for that, who knows what chaos the world would have then endured?" He shuddered.

I tried not to show my impatience. What did ancient history have to do with *Hibernia*?

"Do you know, Nicky"—he paused, perhaps sensing my discomfort at the casual use of my name—"Captain, that the U.N. was once a force for liberal change? In the early twenty-first century most of the great reforms originated in the U.N."

"You call the reforms of 2024 liberal? They banned most stimulants, public gambling, racing of horses, even some sexual practices."

"Conservative impulses exist even in liberal times," he admonished. "The U.N.'s basic structure was permissive: loose federalism on a global scale."

"The Rebellious Ages." The folly of permissiveness.

"Then the reaction," he said. "The Era of Law. It began after the Final War, when America and Japan lost their ability to dominate the world by sheer financial strength. The devastation of Japan, China, and much of Africa permanently changed the world balance of power and left the U.N. the only strong global institution."

My irritation was mounting. Before the day ended, I had to rule on three men's lives.

He said, "Christian Reunification swept Europe, which had become the most influential region of the globe. The U.N. grew conservative and authoritarian. It issued the Unidollar, intervened in local conflicts, and took on the attributes of a real government. Incorporating the British Navy into the U.N. military was a key step."

I nodded. The Navy was our senior military service, and I was proud of it. I'd never even considered joining U.N.A.F.

"The U.N. also set universal education standards, wage rates—all right, I'll pass over the details." He smiled apologetically. "The liberal reaction came just as we began our push to colonize space."

I asked, "If we were rebelling against central authority when the colonies were being formed, wouldn't they have become virtually independent?"

"Not quite, Nick—er, Captain. The rebellion was in the impetus to colonize, to physically escape authority. But the colonies couldn't stand on their own. In the counterreaction they were brought fully under the control of the Government. Your Navy is the primary instrument of that control; that's the reason cargo and passengers can only be carried between home and the colonies in a Naval vessel. And it's why colonial Governors are often Admirals."

"I thought it's because they had the most experience."

"Yes, as autocratic leaders. There's really no difference between a colonial Governor and a Captain. They're both autocratic symbols of the Government."

I tried to follow. "And when you say we're frozen at one end of the pendulum?"

"The colonies strain against the pull of the central government. The U.N., pulling the other direction, is locked into repression to maintain control."

"That sounds dictatorial." They'd issued me a voting card the week after I'd made middy, and I took our democracy seriously.

"Government authority derives from the Reunification. The Yahwehist Church brought together religious forces dispersed for centuries. The U.N. Government is the agent and advocate of our state religion, which in turn supports the authority of the central government."

I stirred uneasily; I wouldn't tolerate heresy, if that's where he was headed.

As if in reassurance he added, "The two forces are merged in yourself; you're both chief magistrate and chaplain. Our system is frozen: the colonies strain against authority; the state and church strain to maintain civil control by arbitrary decrees. It's been so for seventy years."

I stood to pace, troubled by his suggestion. "How can one justify supporting an oppressive government, if men like Tuak and Rogoff are to be hanged because of the rigidity of its rules?"

Ibn Saud said gravely, "Contrast what harm the repression does, with the harm that would be done without it. The Last War was bad enough; imagine an interplanetary war."

"Wouldn't a liberal say freedom is worth the risk?"

"And wouldn't a conservative say civilization is worth the cost?" Ibn Saud, coming from the Saudi sheikhdoms, was of very conservative stock indeed.

Taking my leave, I climbed back to Level 1, found all quiet on the bridge. I left the Pilot and Vax to their boredom and continued my restless wandering.

The launch berth was cold, dim, and empty. Suiting up, I called to advise the bridge I was going through to the holds.

My defogger laboring, I climbed the ladder to the narrow passageway reserved for humankind alongside the huge cargo bays, past crates, containers, heavy machinery, farm implements. The suit didn't have to protect me from vacuum, it merely assured a good air supply. The hold was pressurized, but its air wasn't run through the recycler.

I was inching toward the tip of the pencil, far from the gravitrons in the engine room. As I climbed I felt lighter; as cadets we'd had to memorize the inverse square rule by which our gravity varied, but nothing clarified the rule as well as a practical demonstration.

The hull began to close in; I was approaching the narrowing point of *Hibernia*'s bow. At the top of the ladder I stood in the very prow of the ship, almost floating off the landing at the ladder's end. My eye traced the ribbed skeleton of the ship back to the disk.

Living in the disk, surrounded by *Hibernia*'s jostling mass of humanity, I could see only the conflicts and demands it was the Captain's role to arbitrate.

But here, at *Hibernia*'s bow, I became aware of the massive, complicated interweaving of metals and electronics that constituted the ship, bound together by power cables laced through the fabric of the vessel, and propelled by Fusion.

We were an oddly ritualized society, cramped together in

the disk. We tended to forget that the ultimate purpose of our voyage was to sail this vast assemblage of cargo and persons to port, to be absorbed by our fast-growing colonies.

I sat on the landing, feet dangling from the ladder.

The many rules that regulated our conduct aboard—the strictures separating passengers and crew, the rigid hierarchy of seamen and officers, the isolation of the Captain—were meant to simplify our lives, to eliminate as many decisions as possible, so we confused and desire-ridden humans could steer this magnificent, complicated, and hugely expensive vessel to safe haven.

Without our regulations and ship's customs, we'd face too many choices. Decisions about the human hierarchy: who was smarter, stronger, wiser. Decisions about ethical conduct, about what behaviors were conducive to the proper function of the ship. Decisions about internal controls: which urges, which desires, should be given vent and which should not.

*Hibernia*, this great mass of machinery hurled at unimaginable speed through infinite emptiness, could not be controlled by people forever at odds with themselves and each other.

Mr. Ibn Saud's theory that repression alternated with permissiveness was irrelevant. For *Hibernia* to survive, the social system had to be maintained, else we'd all be condemned over and again to carve out our places in the ship's hierarchy. We were a planet too small to make a place for outsiders, misfits, loners. We had to learn to fit. One man who fought the system could wreck the ship.

Perhaps, though it could never be known, that was what had happened to *Celestina*, beyond the pale of civilization.

The hierarchy of Captain, officers, and crew was necessary to maintain the structure in which we functioned. Here beyond the gleam of our sun, we had to maintain our society unaided.

Knowing now what I had to do, I got up and started slowly down the ladder to the disk.

# 15

"Chief McAndrews, report to the bridge." I paced. The Chief, wherever he was, would hear my summons. I took the caller again, summoned Dr. Uburu.

Vax and the Pilot, on watch, observed me without comment.

"Vax, round up the middies. Quietly, please. I don't want anyone else to know we're all on the bridge."

"Aye aye, sir." He left on his mission.

I waited with growing impatience while the officers assembled. When all were present I slapped the hatch shut. "Stand at attention, all of you."

They formed a line, eyes front, hands stiff at their sides, Doc Uburu as much as any of them instantly obedient to ship's discipline. I faced them, picked up the holovid containing the Log.

"There will be no discussion, no comment on this matter from any of you, here or in private. I have called you to witness an entry into the Log." I typed quickly as I spoke. "The death sentence imposed on Machinist's Mate Herney is commuted to five months imprisonment. I have concluded that he was unaware he was striking an officer, and therefore should not suffer death as a penalty for his acts."

None of the officers showed any reaction. "The death sentence imposed on seaman Tuak is confirmed. He participated knowingly in an assault on an officer of this ship, and thereby merits execution. That his act was to prevent discovery of a criminal scheme is irrelevant; his execution is punishment solely for his assault." I finished writing.

"The death sentence imposed on seaman Rogoff is confirmed. He participated knowingly in an assault on an officer of this ship, and thereby merits execution. That his act was committed in hot blood is irrelevant; the fact of the assault warrants the sentence imposed.''

I put down the holovid. "Stand at ease." They moved smartly into the "at ease" position, wrists clasped behind their backs. "We will now discuss the mechanics of the executions.''

"Mr. Pearson, Mr. Loo: bring the prisoner Tuak. Acknowledge!"

"Orders received and understood. Aye aye, sir.''

"Received and understood. Aye aye, sir.'' The two exchanged nervous glances before starting up the ladder to Level 3.

Maintaining outward calm, I reviewed my arrangements. The Pilot and Mr. Vishinsky had visited the brig and cuffed the two prisoners' hands behind their backs, firmly taping their mouths shut with irremovable skintape. Shortly after, I had brought the ship out of Fusion; we now floated dead in space, light-years from a planetary system.

On my order the bridge was sealed. All passengers were sent to their cabins and the cabin hatches secured; Alexi and Sandy personally supervised the operation.

All crew members were ordered to their berths to prepare for inspection. In my dress whites, accompanied by the chief petty officer and a midshipman, I inspected each crew berth and its occupants, who stood at attention while I coldly scrutinized lockers, bunks, and men, liberally dispensing demerits for infractions.

After each crew berth was inspected, its occupants were marched in absolute silence down to the lower deck of the engine room. They were lined three deep on the deck surrounding the gaping hole of the fusion drive shaft.

Across the open shaft was placed a plank. A chain ran from a bolt through the end of the plank to a powered dolly. Three meters above the plank, a pole tilted across the shaft. A rope hung from the pole. The noose at its end nearly touched the plank.

The Doctor, the Pilot, the Chief, and my three midshipmen, all in dress whites, stood at ease facing the lines of crewmen. We waited for the two seamen and their charge.

A sailor moved.

"Mr. Tamarov! Place that man on report!" Perhaps he had just been flexing a cramped muscle. "Take his name! I'll see him at next Captain's Mast!"

"Aye aye, sir." Alexi made a show of writing the seaman's name. The sailor glared sullenly before resuming eyes-front position.

"Mr. Tamarov! On dismissal, escort that man to the brig! Bread and water until Captain's Mast!"

"Aye aye, sir!" Alexi moved directly in front of the offending seaman who, subdued now, stood at proper attention.

From the ladder, a sound. Pearson and Loo each gripped one of the unfortunate Mr. Tuak's arms as they frog-marched him down to the engine room, his feet half walking, half dragging.

Tuak's mouth was firmly gagged. His eyes darted wildly back and forth from the assembled men to the shaft with its horrid accoutrements. Then to me. He screamed through his gag.

The party reached the lower deck. "Mr. Holser, Mr. Vishinsky! Cuff the prisoner's feet and place him on the gallows."

"Aye aye, sir." The midshipman and the master-at-arms broke ranks and took the prisoner from the two sailors. Tuak kicked desperately. Vishinsky bent, captured a frenzied foot and put the cuff on it, then locked it to the other.

"Mr. Pearson, Mr. Loo, back in ranks!" They complied.

Vax and Vishinsky dragged the condemned man to the plank. Tuak tried to kick out, balked by his cuffs. I nodded; Vax stepped back into ranks. The man's eyes darted in frenzy. Muffled sounds emerged from the gag as the noose was tugged tight.

It had to be done quickly. I was glad of the pills the Doctor had given me; I felt neither nauseous nor faint. "Mr. Tuak, I commend your soul to Lord God." I flipped the power switch; the dolly rolled slowly away from the shaft, tightening the chain attached to the plank.

The plank scraped across the deck until one end cleared the shaft wall. It dropped into the shaft. Tuak plummeted. The rope flexed, recoiled, became tight again. A groan came from behind.

I whirled around. "Silence!" Several men had gone pale; one swayed as if about to faint. But they held ranks.

"Mr. Browning, Ms. Edwards: bring the prisoner Rogoff. Acknowledge!" The purser and the gunner's mate departed. I knew that Mr. Browning would comply; he had too much invested in his status to help a roughneck escape, even if that were possible. Ms. Edwards was one whom Vishinsky thought reliable; that was enough for me.

"Mr. Vishinsky, Mr. Holser, remove the body and reset the plank." They hauled on the rope holding Tuak's remains. I kept my eyes on the crew, both to ensure discipline and to avoid keeling over in a dead faint: Dr. Uburu's pills had ceased to function.

The body rose out of the shaft; several crewmen started.

I knew it was necessary that I watch.

Tuak's clothes were soiled where his sphincters had given way. His empurpled face and bulging eyes were enough to sear my soul.

Behind me, a low angry murmur. My tone was sharp. "The first to break ranks will be hanged as this man was!" We were seconds from being rushed; if one sailor broke, they all would. I regretted my refusal to carry arms.

I walked down the line of sullen crewmen, hands clasped behind me. "Eyes front! Shoulders stiff! You, there! You're on report for sloppy position!" What in Lord God's own hell was keeping Browning and Edwards?

I paced back down the line. Sandy Wilsky was very pale, his breath shallow. "Midshipman, stomach in! Chest out! Set a good example or I'll barrel you myself!" Not kind to Sandy, but necessary. The boy sucked in his stomach, his color improving as his mind snapped back to his duty.

Finally they came. Rogoff's feet lashed out, trying to trip the two sailors, reaching to wrap around the ladder posts. I could hear cries beneath the gag. So could everyone else. Halfway down the ladder Rogoff caught sight of me. His eyes fastened on mine, terrified, pleading.

"Mr. Holser, Mr. Vishinsky. Cuff the prisoner's feet and place him on the gallows." A sharp intake of breath. I whirled around, expecting to be clubbed to the deck. A sailor had broken from attention, mouth agape, chest heaving. His mates watched.

I had no choice but to play it out. "*You!* Two paces forward!" My voice was so sharp, so high-pitched it startled even me. The attention of the massed crew deserted the unfortunate prisoner, focused instead on me.

The seaman, half-dazed, stumbled forward. With all the force I could muster, I slapped him. It echoed like a shot in the appalled silence. The sailor staggered, almost fell.

*"BACK IN RANKS!"* My face almost touched his. My fury penetrated his daze. He stiffened into attention, a red blotch blossoming on his cheek. My hand stung like fire.

Cuffed hand and foot, Rogoff teetered on the plank, beseeching me with his eyes. The gag muffled his incoherent sounds. For a moment I poised on the edge of mercy, before recollecting my duty.

"Mr. Rogoff, I commend your soul to Lord God." I flipped the switch on the dolly. A moment later he was gone.

I held the crew in ranks until both bodies were removed from the chamber. I frantically repeated regs under my breath, to divert myself from vomiting in front of the entire ship's company. "Crew Berth One, two steps forward! Right face! March! Mr. Vishinsky, escort the men to their quarters."

One by one each group marched back to its berth. At the end only the officers and I remained. We looked at each other, no one wanting to speak. It had been a close call.

I sent Vax and Alexi to unlock the passenger cabins, and started back to the bridge. On the ladder from Level 2, I had to stop and grip the rail, before anyone noticed the trembling of my legs. Chief McAndrews quietly put his hand under my arm and helped me up the stairs. I didn't take notice; it would have been a capital offense.

That afternoon I ran a Battle Stations drill, followed by decompression drills. It made clear to the crew that I wasn't afraid to give them orders, and at the same time it occupied their minds. I strove to occupy my own mind, but was unsuccessful.

That afternoon, I ordered the two bodies quietly ejected from the airlock.

Dinner hour came. I wasn't sure I'd be able to hold down my food, but I knew it was necessary for me to appear in the dining hall. The passengers I met in the corridor were distant, their looks hostile.

I met Amanda outside the hatch. I went to her immediately, wanting to explain what I'd done.

She gave me no opportunity to speak. Her look passed right through me. I'd anticipated her anger, yet I stood disconcerted, staring at her receding back.

In the hall there was silence when I rose to give the Ship's Prayer. Afterward, the only persons to say "Amen" were my officers, Mrs. Donhauser, and Derek Carr.

After forking food around my plate I retreated to the bridge. Alexi shared the watch; for once he had the sense to stay quiet. I sat in my Captain's chair, pinned in merciless silence, while Tuak's purple face was again hauled up to the rim of the shaft. His sightless stare was directed solely at me.

The caller buzzed. "Pilot Haynes reporting, sir. Will we Fuse tonight?"

"No. In the morning." The Pilot had said he wasn't yet ready to tackle Darla's reprogramming, and in my present state I didn't trust myself to do the manual calculations.

"Aye aye, sir."

At midnight I turned over the watch to Vax and Alexi and started back to my cabin. I stumbled with weariness, dreading the solitude. I stripped off my jacket, undid my tie, unbuttoned my shirt.

A knock at the hatch. I opened, half-dressed. Chief McAndrews. With him was Dr. Uburu.

She held a flask and two glasses. "This is for medicinal use. As medical officer I direct you to take it. The Chief will help administer the prescription." She handed her wares to the Chief and departed.

The Chief met my eye, impassive. I sighed. "Come in."

"Thank you, Captain." His tone was formal.

I went to the safe and got out his pipe and the canister. "Go ahead. I order you to light it." I sniffed at the flask. Some kind of whiskey. I poured two glasses half full.

I'd learned to drink after Academy, on my first leave. I drank because we all did, at one time or another. I didn't dislike it; I didn't much enjoy it either. Tonight, I was a drinker. I downed half my glass with the first swallow, finished the rest a moment after. Wordlessly, the Chief poured more.

In the haze of the smoking artifact we sat, mostly in silence, sipping at our drinks. I told him about my visit to the holds, earlier in the day. I explained how I felt when I slapped the frightened sailor's face. I told him about Father. He listened, he nodded, sometimes he prompted. Occasionally he told an anecdote of his own.

My mood eased as the evening passed. Our commiseration grew into a discussion, then finally a wake. Afterward I recalled my voice, oddly loud. I remembered standing to go to the head, the wall rushing up to smash me in the face, and the Chief's steadying arm.

I couldn't quite recall what followed, though I had a dim recollection of the Chief pulling off my shoes, loosening my belt. I seemed to recall someone's voice, very silly. "Thank you, Chiefie. What a nice name for a grand man, aye, Chiefie?" Someone giggled. Then I slept.

The next morning we Fused, after laborious calculations repeated over and over on my demand. They were not made any easier by my stupendous headache. Vax said something, his voice too loud. I snarled, but he didn't seem to mind. By the following day I had settled down, even thinking to make amends to Vax with extra cordiality when he left watch.

"Going to bunk down, Mr. Holser?"

"No, sir. I'm off to the exercise room."

"I should have known. Taking some middies with you?"

"No, sir, I'm meeting Mr. Carr." I raised an eyebrow. "He apologized and asked if he could resume, sir. We've been exercising together four days now."

"Ah."

"Yes, sir. Yesterday we went from an hour to two hours. Is that all, sir?"

"Carry on." Interesting. I thought I knew what would come next. I only wondered when.

The week passed uneventfully. The crew absorbed its graphic lesson in discipline and steadied down to routine. I saw no sullenness, no insubordination. The unfortunate sailor who had glared at Alexi was fined and given extra duties for a month. Mr. Herney, pathetically grateful for his reprieve, waited out his time in the brig.

Amanda listened impassively to my apology. She let me explain my reasoning. Then she turned away without a word. I resolved to let her be. As Captain I could not force myself on a passenger.

It was a few days after, as dinner ended, that the overture came.

I looked at my watch. "Thank you for an interesting evening. Mrs. Donhauser, Mr. Kaa Loa, Mr. Carr." I stood to take my leave.

Derek stood also. "Sir, may I speak with you privately, when it's convenient?"

"It will be convenient on the bridge in about an hour."

"Thank you, sir." He waited politely for me to leave.

I was sitting at the console when the knock came. Sandy, escorting Mr. Carr. As a passenger, Derek couldn't approach the bridge on his own.

I swiveled to face the hatch. Derek came in hesitantly, carrying a holovid. He took in the complexity of the instruments and screens, and seemed impressed. "Thank you for allowing me here."

"What did you want, Mr. Carr?" My tone was cool.

He eyed me uncertainly, standing in front of my chair like an errant schoolboy. "Captain Seafort, I was furious when you said I couldn't handle life as a midshipman. In our family we've assumed we could do what we set our minds to. Sir, I think you're wrong."

I was impassive. Within, a faint glimmer of hope stirred.

"Captain, I can be a midshipman. I know saying it isn't enough, so I've tried to show you. No discipline? Until now I've never called anyone 'sir' in my life, including my father. I call you 'sir' now. I'll keep doing it. All I want is for you to have an open mind. Not to prejudge me. Please . . . sir."

He had my full attention. "Go on."

"I took geometry and trig in school, but no calculus. You didn't believe me when I said I could learn it. Look at this, please." He offered me the holovid. I flipped it on.

"The ship's library had a calculus text. I've done all the problems in Chapter One, and most of Chapter Two. I understand differential equations. The differential of velocity with respect to time is acceleration. The differential of displacement with respect to time is velocity."

Not bad at all, for a beginner without an instructor. "You've made a lot of progress, Mr. Carr. Why?"

"Nobody ever told me I'm not good enough, Captain. I want you to know I am."

"So you put yourself under discipline."

"Yes, sir."

"How do you like it?"

"I loathe it!" His vehemence startled me. "I hate abasing myself! I hate it!" He swallowed. "But that doesn't mean I'll stop, sir. I can do what I set out to do!"

"All right, Mr. Carr. But why?"

"After you left my cabin I got to thinking. At first I wanted to join because I was so angry. I had to show you."

He must have seen my expression. "I said, at first, sir. I haven't finished. When I got over my anger I realized that it was no reason to enlist. Five years cooped in a ship, because someone jeered at me? No. But what would I do for those years, otherwise? The plantation manager won't want me around, and he controls the trusts. Until they terminate, I'll be sent off on a tiny allowance, still a minor, having to ask permission for anything I want to do."

He paused to marshal his thoughts. "Maybe the Service isn't any better. I'll still have to go where I'm sent, do what I'm told. But I'd have my majority. And at least I'll have done it by my own decision."

"That's all?" I wasn't that impressed by his motives.

"No, that's not all. I mean, no, sir. Sorry. I thought about some of the officers I've met on board. Lieutenant Cousins, he was a—well, I apologize, I shouldn't be saying that. But Mr. Malstrom, we sat at table with him a month. He was a gentleman, like my father. If a man like him could make a career in the Service, so could I."

"Is that what you want, Mr. Carr? A career in the service?"

"No, Captain Seafort. Probably not. But at least I'd get to see places. Learn things. Live on a ship."

"Is this"—I waved my hand with disdain—"what you call living?"

He stared at me a long moment before he remembered. Then his ears turned red. He looked at the deck. "I'm sorry, sir," he said quietly. "I really am sorry for saying that."

"You said a lot you should be sorry for." I was pushing, but if he couldn't handle it, he certainly couldn't take what my first middy would come up with.

"I suppose I have. Sir." Now his cheeks were red too.

"How old are you?"

"Sixteen. I'll be seventeen in six months."

"I'm only a year older than you."

"I know. That's one reason it's hard to call you 'sir'."

"Yet I'm Captain of *Hibernia*, and you'd be a cadet, at the bottom of the chain of command. The very bottom."

"Yes, sir, I know that."

"I wonder. Do you understand the difference between a cadet and a midshipman?"

"A cadet is a trainee, isn't he? A midshipman is an officer."

"A cadet has special status, Mr. Carr. He is, literally, a ward of his commanding officer. The commander has the rights his parents had. He's not an adult until he makes midshipman. He has no rights at all, and can be punished in any way his commander sees fit."

I examined his face; I hadn't yet dissuaded him. I tried harder. "A cadet has no recourse no matter what he's asked to do. It's a brutal life. There's a reason for it: he has to learn that he can stand up to adversity. After cadet training, shipboard life will seem easy. He's already been through far worse. And he's already learned that a Captain's power, like his cadet commander's, is absolute."

Derek was reflective. "I understand."

"Most cadets enter Academy at thirteen, some at fourteen. A very few at fifteen. By the time we're your age, it's usually too late; we resent authority as rigid and arbitrary as cadets endure. You're too old for it, Derek."

"Not if I decide to take it, sir." His voice was firm.

I was patient; he'd earned it. "You think calling me 'Sir' is discipline? In your whole life, have you ever been shouted at by a person you didn't like?"

"No, sir." He squirmed with discomfort.

"Tell me, have you ever slept in a room with other people?"

He swallowed. "No. Except in the cabin with my father."

"How'd you like it?"

"I couldn't sleep." He colored. "I had pills. Dozeoff, and stronger ones. They helped."

I let the silence stretch awhile. He said, "I know; it won't be easy. But once I decide to, I can do it."

"Derek . . ." I shook my head, frustrated. "You really

don't understand, do you? Have you ever used the head when another person was present?''

"God, no!" he blurted. I'd assumed not.

"Has an outsider ever seen you without clothes on?"

"No." He blushed red at the thought.

"Still, you want to be a midshipman?"

"Yes, sir." His tone was determined.

"Take your pants off."

"What?" Astonishment gave way to wariness, then dismay. He gulped, realizing his predicament; he had to show me he could take it, or give up his plan. Staring fixedly at the bulkhead he slowly unbuckled and stepped out of his pants. Not knowing what to do with them, he hesitated, then bent awkwardly and dropped them on the deck.

I said nothing, letting him wait in his undershorts. After a while he made a visible effort; his fists unclenched. I let the silence drag. He looked about, remembered that he was on the bridge of the ship, blushed crimson. But he didn't move.

"Derek, are you still sure you can take it?"

"Yes," he gritted. "I can take whatever you give out, damn it!"

I wasn't offended, but it was time to turn up the pressure. Better he broke now, than after taking the oath. "Apologize!"

He swallowed. He battled deep inside himself, his eyes distant. After a moment he said in an entirely different tone, "Captain Seafort, sir, please pardon my rudeness."

"Apologize abjectly!" This was nothing compared to wardroom hazing.

"Sir! I'm sorry I spoke to you the way I did. It's a sign of my immaturity. I'm very sorry I can't control myself. I meant no disrespect to you, sir, and I won't do it again!"

I looked up. His eyes were wet. I eased up. "I hear you've been doing exercises."

"Yes, sir. With Vax Holser."

"Mr. Holser, to you."

"I apologize, sir. With Mr. Holser, to get ready."

"As part of your campaign?"

"Yes, sir. I started with my letter to you."

I sighed. He could probably survive. Barely. On the other hand, he was educated and could apply himself to a goal. And I needed midshipmen.

"This is how it works, Derek. You take the oath, and enlist for five years. There's no way to change your mind. The only exit is dishonorable discharge, and you won't get that without time in the brig first. You know what a dishonorable does?"

"Not entirely, sir."

"You can never vote, hold elective office, or be appointed to any government agency. You forfeit all pay and military benefits. It's utter disgrace."

"I understand, sir."

"You join as a cadet. You're not an officer. In theory, you could remain a cadet for five years. You stay a cadet until your C.O. decides to make you a midshipman. You have no say in the matter. You owe the Navy obedience and service regardless of your status."

"Yes, sir." He looked at me attentively, waiting for the permission that must be coming.

"Derek, I'll give you one warning. Do you think I've been hazing you?"

"Yes, sir. Some."

"I haven't. You're very sensitive; it gets much, much worse. You should reconsider."

He surprised me. "I have, sir, while I've had to stand here like this."

"And?"

"I want to join the Naval Service, sir."

"I'll think about it. Wait in the corridor until I call. Don't bother to dress."

"What?" Fury and betrayal flashed across his face. "You—I trusted you!" He reached down, swept up his pants.

I said nothing.

He flicked dust off his pants and turned to step into them, his face white with anger. He lifted his foot. Then he froze.

For a long while he stared at the pants. Finally, contemptuously, he lifted them high. Holding them between two fingers he extended his arm. His fingers opened. The pants dropped to the deck. He walked to the hatch and out into the corridor. I slapped the hatch closed.

I gave him half an hour; that would be enough. When I motioned, he came in, pale but silent. I handed him his pants; gratefully he slipped into them. "Derek, Mr. Holser is going

to be a real trial for you. Hang on. I'll make you midshipman
as soon as I think you qualify.''

"I understand." His color was returning to normal.

I called Vax and the Chief as witnesses. I gave Derek the
oath, there on the bridge, and entered it into the Log.

"He's all yours, Vax. Show him the ropes."

Vax gave a wolfish smile and slowly licked his chops. He
rounded on Derek. "Cadet, we're going to the wardroom.
I'll show you your bunk. Being a cadet is easy. You will call
anything that moves 'sir' or 'ma'am', children included. And
you will do everything any officer tells you, without excep-
tion.''

"Yes, sir," Derek said meekly.

"It's 'aye aye, sir,' and that's two demerits. Ten demerits
means the barrel.''

"Aye aye, sir!"

"No, that's 'yes, sir'. I didn't give you an order, I told
you a fact. Another two demerits." Each would be worked
off by two hours of hard calisthenics.

"Uh, yes, sir." Derek began to look apprehensive.

I followed them down the corridor to the wardroom, feeling
a bit sorry for Mr. Carr.

Vax put his hand on Derek's shoulder as he steered the boy
into the wardroom. "Derek, tell us about your sex life," he
purred. The hatch slid shut behind them.

I walked back to the bridge. I had four middies now. Well,
three, and a cadet. Close.

# 16

"Lord God, today is May 14, 2195, on the U.N.S. *Hibernia*. We ask you to bless us, to bless our voyage, and to bring
health and well-being to all aboard.''

"Amen." We took our seats.

As I spooned my soup I counted my blessings. Our crew

had settled back to normal. We remained in Fusion, riding the crest of the N-wave toward Hope Nation. The Chief and I investigated his artifact from time to time, in the quiet of the evenings. Alexi was working through a rigorous course of navigation under Pilot Haynes; I looked forward to the day he might make lieutenant.

On the other hand, we hadn't dealt with Darla's parameter glitch. Though I pressed the Pilot at least to investigate the state of her computational arrays, he argued that we should wait until we reached Hope Nation, where he was sure we'd find a more knowledgeable puterman. As long as we calculated our adjusted mass ourselves, Darla's misprogrammed parameter was no hazard. I was uneasy, but wasn't ready to force the issue.

Meanwhile, Derek Carr had vanished into the wardroom under the gentle tutelage of Vax Holser. As the Captain never visited the wardroom and a cadet was not allowed on the bridge, I had no way to determine how Derek was managing.

Occasionally I caught a glimpse of him hurrying down a corridor, immaculate in a cadet's unmarked gray uniform, his hair cut short, hands and face scrubbed, wearing an anxious expression.

When he saw me he would snap to attention, at first in a slipshod manner. Within a week, his stomach was sucked tight, his shoulders thrown back, spine stiff, his pose perfect in every particular. How Vax taught him the physical drill so quickly, I was afraid to ask.

My responsibility was to leave them alone, and trust Vax to do his job. Derek was learning ship's routine, Naval regs, cleanliness, discipline, and how to cope with a wardroom full of frisky boys all his seniors. That would be the hard part. He would pull through or he wouldn't, and I couldn't help him.

Nonetheless, I gave Vax one caution. "Those demerits you're giving him—make sure he has a chance to work them off. He shouldn't get up to ten. Not for a couple of months, anyway."

"Aye aye, sir. That's kind of how I figured." I let them be.

At times I passed Amanda flirting and laughing with various young men among the passengers. If she saw me she gave no sign. I missed our confidences, our physical intimacy, our caring.

With the departure of Derek from the Captain's table, I passed April with only two dinner companions. On the first of May the normal rotation brought a surprise; ten passengers had asked the purser to seat them at my table.

My siege was lifting.

I chose seven guests for the remaining places at my table. I now dined with a full complement, amid animated conversation.

But I had to sleep.

My cabin hatch wouldn't stay fastened. I slapped it shut; it bulged open. I had to lean all my weight against it to force it closed. Something pushed back. I backed away, stumbling into the bulkhead behind me.

In the dark corridor beyond the ruptured hatch, something moved. Seaman Tuak shambled into the cabin, face purple, eyes bulging, rattling the cuffs that bound hands and feet. A blackened tongue protruded from torn tape covering his rotting mouth.

I cowered against the bulkhead. A cold, damp arm reached through the hull behind me, wrapped around my throat. Seaman Rogoff pulled himself into the cabin to hold me while Tuak came near.

I woke screaming. My sounds were barely audible whimpers. I staggered out of bed, fell into my chair, and rocked, hugging myself, until the corridors lightened with day.

I could think of only one way to deal with that. I buried myself in work, trying to exhaust myself so completely I wouldn't fear sleep. I assigned myself two four-hour watches each day. I explored the entire ship, bow to stern, memorizing every compartment, all the storerooms, each of the airlocks.

I disconcerted Alexi and the Pilot by joining their navigation course; in the back of the room I quietly worked the problems Mr. Haynes gave the middy. Alexi solved them more quickly and more accurately, but I persevered until I improved.

At first, the Pilot was uncomfortable at my presence; a careless comment had already earned him a rebuke and a stinging punishment, and now I demanded that he correct my mistakes. After a while he found the balance between elaborate politeness and scorn, becoming an excellent teacher.

At my insistence, Chief McAndrews loaned me holovids explaining the principles of fusion drives. They remained a mystery, no matter how hard I studied. I made the Chief review them with me, step by step, until even that phlegmatic man's voice took on an edge.

I inspected all the nooks and crannies of the ship: engine room, the crew berths, the infirmary, the wardroom. There, with the midshipmen and cadet standing at rigid attention, I pretended to search for dust on a shelf or creases on a bunk, feeling for a few moments that I had wakened from a nightmare without end.

I was tempted to take my dreams to Dr. Uburu. Perhaps she could find grounds to relieve me on grounds of mental disability. I didn't make the attempt because I knew my dreams were a sign of tension, not mental illness. I was afraid she would see through my cowardice.

I turned my attention to the one piece of work I'd been putting off. I called the Chief and the Pilot—away from the bridge, of course—to consider reprogramming Darla to eliminate her glitch.

Reluctantly, the Pilot sketched out our task. We'd have to strip away her attitudinal and conversational overlays, find the improper input for the adjusted mass parameter, and override it.

I demanded the tech manuals, glanced through them. They made the steps clear enough. Had I known how clear, I wouldn't have allowed Mr. Haynes so long a delay. Still, I could understand his caution; an error on our part could make matters far worse. Reprogramming a puter was no job for an amateur; that's why Admiralty had Dosmen in the first place.

The Pilot argued his point. "Darla is locked into the dockyard figure for ship's mass. But as long as we keep feeding her calculations by hand, we can Fuse. Better a devil we know than one we don't."

"Mr. McAndrews?"

"I'm no Dosman, sir. With respect, neither are you. I'm concerned about creating more problems than we solve. We can calculate by hand; I'd leave her alone."

"You're both right, as far as you go. But we have no idea how deep Darla's glitch goes. What if ship's mass isn't the only parameter that's fouled? When we display her inputs, we'll have to check every one to be sure.''

The Pilot snorted. ''Sir, do you realize how many parameters she has? Sure, some are straightforward, like ship's mass. But others are odd tidbits like the length of the fusion drive shaft, hydroponics chamber capacities, airlock pump rates . . . My God, we couldn't check all of them.''

''She stores all that?''

''And operates from them. Every time we recycle a glass of water, grow a tomato, track energy fluctuations, we rely on Darla's parameters. If we inadvertently alter them . . .'' He left the sentence unfinished. The dangers were obvious, and chilling.

It was my decision, and I needed to sleep on it.

That night the nightmare struck with terrifying force. At the point where I usually woke trembling, I came struggling out of it, as always. Weakly I crawled out of bed to fall in the easy chair. It was there the icy hand of Mr. Rogoff found me, toppling me onto the deck screeching in terror.

I woke in my bed, gasping and shaking, realizing I had still been asleep. I looked up. Mr. Tuak opened the hatch and staggered in, rotting eyes boring into mine, his cuffed feet shambling toward my bed. I woke again, paralyzed with fear.

It was a long time before I was sure I was truly awake. I threw on my pants, pulled my jacket over my undershirt and hurried to the infirmary, dreading to meet Mr. Tuak on the way. Pride was no longer an issue; I woke Dr. Uburu and demanded a sleeping pill. In response to her questions I told her I'd been having nightmares.

She gave me a pill, warning me not to take it until I was actually in bed, and to sleep as long as I wanted. About my nightmares, she mercifully said nothing.

When I reached my cabin I couldn't stop the chills from stabbing at my back; I opened the hatch with caution and entered, knowing nothing was waiting but still, like a child, unable to trust in knowledge to dispel my demons.

I swallowed the sedative. A few minutes later the cabin disappeared.

Someone was attacking my hatch with a sledgehammer. Annoyed, I tried to open my eyes, but they were glued shut. I lurched out of bed and felt my way toward the hatch.

Somebody had moved the bulkhead about two steps closer; I caromed off the cold metal and flung open the hatch, ready to break the sledgehammer into tiny pieces.

I forced open my eyes, a snarl and a scream battling in my throat for priority. The ship's boy stood patiently in the corridor.

"Ricky! Why in God's name are you here in the middle of the night? And stop that banging!" I propped myself carefully against the bulkhead.

"It's morning, Captain, sir. Same time I always come." The ship's boy held his breakfast tray with both hands, waiting expectantly.

"Uhng. Come in." I staggered back to sit on the bed. "You didn't see a man with a piece of rope around his neck, did you?"

Ricky put the tray on my table. "No, sir. If I do, should I tell him anything?"

I focused on my bedside table, trying to hold it still. "Tell him I'm sorry." The table slowed, but didn't stop rotating. "On second thought, don't tell him anything, just try not to see him." I lay down in my bunk. Now only the ceiling was spinning. "Never mind, I'm not sure this is real either. That's all, Ricky."

"Aye aye, sir. Oh, by the way, sir, I've decided I want to be a midshipman."

"Very good, Ricky, come back after you grow up; I'll ask the Captain. I'm tired now."

"Aye aye, sir," he said, his voice uncertain. He left.

I woke some hours later, relaxed and refreshed, recalling a peculiar dream involving the ship's boy. I stood, slowly. Cautious tests indicated my motor systems were functional.

After visiting the head and the shower I returned to my cabin. Two congealed eggs stared reproachfully. I decided I'd work today on distinguishing reality from fantasy. A morning chore for the Captain.

On the way to the bridge I stopped at the infirmary. "Doc, what did you give me?" My tone was plaintive.

"Were there side effects?" Dr. Uburu asked coolly.

"I think there may be one next to my nose. I couldn't wake for breakfast. Someone else woke instead."

"You shouldn't have tried that." The Doctor was reproving. "I told you to stay down until you woke naturally." She studied my face. "I think you survived, Captain. You needed the rest." I had to admit that was true.

Later in the day I called Chief McAndrews and Pilot Haynes to a conference in the officers' mess. "I've thought it over," I said, sipping coffee. "We'll strip Darla for reprogramming. I don't trust my own Fusion calculations and I've got to be able to rely on her. While we're at it we can recheck her other parameters."

"There are hundreds," the Pilot reminded me.

"We've months 'til we reach Miningcamp. There's time to check them."

A silence. The Pilot said carefully, "Captain, I protest your order, for the ship's safety. I request that my protest be entered in the Log."

"Very well." It was his right. I didn't remind him that if he was correct there was a chance no one would ever read the Log.

Chief McAndrews cleared his throat. "Sir, I request you to enter my protest in the Log as well. Meaning no disrespect." He had the courage to meet my eye.

"You feel that strongly about it, Chief?"

"Yes, sir. I do. I'm sorry." He looked sorry, too.

"Very well." My tone was sharp; I tried to dispel a sense of betrayal. "I'll enter your protests. Bring the puter manuals to the bridge. We'll start this afternoon." I left the mess, knowing my evening sessions with the Chief could never be the same. I pushed aside my loneliness; if I dwelt on it I would march back to the mess and cancel my orders.

We met on the bridge. "Mr. Holser, you're relieved from watch. Leave us." My nerves were strung tight. I slapped shut the hatch, leaving the Chief, Pilot Haynes, and myself alone with Darla. I switched off the ship's caller. I tapped a command on my console, saying it aloud at the same time. "Keyboard entry only, Darla." At this juncture we couldn't risk stray sounds confusing the puter; in deep programming mode, who knew what glitch could be set up by a misinterpreted cough?

"Got it, Captain," Darla said. "Something special you want to tell me?"

I typed, "Alphanumeric response only, Darla, displayed on screen."

A sentence flashed onto my screen. "KEYBOARD ONLY, CAPTAIN. WHAT'S UP?"

I tapped, "Disconnect conversational overlays."

"VERIFY CONVERSATIONAL OVERLAYS DISCONNECTED." Darla's answer was dull and machinelike, stripped of her usual banter.

I indicated the manual open in the Pilot's lap. "What's first?"

Three hours later we were ready; we'd bypassed the warnings and safeties, entered my access codes, stripped away the interconnected layers of tamperproofing the Dosmen had built into her. Darla lay unconscious on our operating table, her brain pulsing and exposed.

I typed, "List fixed input parameters, consecutive order, pause for enter after each."

"COMMENCING INPUT PARAMETER LIST, PAUSE AFTER EACH DISPLAY." The first parameter appeared on the screen.

"SPEED OF LIGHT: 299792.518 KILOMETERS PER SECOND."

I glanced at the Pilot. "Any problem with that one, Mr. Haynes?"

"No, sir."

Keying through the long list of parameters, I realized that checking them as we went wasn't possible. As I tapped, Darla flashed one parameter after another on the screen. After a while I merely glanced at each one, waiting for "SHIP'S MASS" to appear. I tapped for a full hour and a half, my wrist beginning to ache, before the figure finally showed on the screen.

"SHIP'S BASE MASS: 215.6 STANDARD UNITS."

"There," I said with relief. I typed, "Display parameter number and location."

"PARAMETER 2613, SECTOR 71198, GRANULE 1614."

I tapped, "Continue parameter display."

"FIXED PARAMETER DISPLAY COMPLETE."

I swore. Ship's mass was the very last parameter in the list. If I'd started at the end of the list and worked backward I'd have saved hours of tapping.

"That's the last one, Pilot."

"It can't be!"

"Why not?"

"Adjusted mass should be a parameter as well."

The Chief said, "Not if she derives it from base mass."

"We know she's using the wrong figure for base mass," I said. "How do we change that?"

"The quick fix is to delete base mass as a fixed parameter and input it as a variable, sir." The Pilot had the manual on his holovid in his lap. "Then we instruct her not to adjust the variable except after recalc."

The manual provided a step-by-step example of how to do that. "Read me the instructions exactly."

"Aye aye, sir." The Pilot magnified the page so it was visible to all of us. "There are fourteen steps for deletion, sir. Input takes six."

"Any reason not to proceed now, gentlemen?" I asked. A few seconds hesitation; I added, "Other than those stated in the Log?"

Pilot Haynes said reluctantly, "Nothing else, sir." The Chief shook his head.

We took great care with each step. Both the Pilot and the Chief checked each of my keyboard commands against the manual before I entered it, to make sure I had made no mistake. I was so nervous I could barely contain myself; we were barbarians engaging in brain surgery. I began to wish I had followed my officers' advice.

Finally we were done. "VARIABLE INPUT COMPLETE," the screen displayed. I let out a long breath.

"Hardcopy input parameters and input variables," I typed. The eprom clicked on. A moment later a holochip popped into the waiting tray. I handed it to the Pilot, who slipped it in his holovid. We keyed to the list of parameters. Base mass was absent. We checked the variables, found it at the end of the list.

"To put her back together, we reverse the steps that took her apart," the Pilot said, consulting his manual. "Here's the list."

"No." They looked up in surprise. "Darla stays down." My tone was firm. "We check every one of the input parameters before she goes back on-line."

Chief McAndrews said, "Captain, Darla monitors our recycling program. We need that information daily, to make adjustments.''

"Hydroponics too, sir," added the Pilot. "We've been on manual all day; if a sailor's attention wanders, he could foul up the systems. We need to get back to automatics."

"We have manual backup procedures." I tried to quell my irritation. "The hydroponicist's mates will stand extra watches. So will the recycler's mates. We'll do without Darla."

The Pilot. "Captain, the longer it takes, the more—"

"Darla stays down! That's an order!" Their nagging infuriated me.

The Pilot stood. "Aye aye, sir," His voice was cold. "I protest the order and request you to enter my protest in the Log."

I bit back a savage retort. "Denied. Your previous protest continues and is sufficient. You both have your orders. Call the midshipmen together, divide up the list, and start checking every item. Go to the textbooks for astrophysical data. Manually recheck all ship's measurements and statistics."

"Aye aye, sir." They had no choice; arguing with a direct order was insubordination.

"One more thing. I'll see all of you, including the middies, on the bridge before you begin. Dismissed." I shut the hatch behind them and sagged in my chair. With my customary finesse I'd thoroughly alienated the Chief as well as the Pilot. Now I was truly alone.

I paced the bridge, Darla's last output still frozen on the screen. I was in over my head. My order to run *Hibernia*'s systems manually could put our men on emergency watches for a month or more, while every last parameter was checked. The crew would grow tired, then embittered. Meanwhile, the officers would be driven to distraction by the rote examination of data. They'd be exhausted from ceaseless extra work. Their relations with the crew would worsen.

My order risked far greater damage to the ship than Darla's glitch.

When the officers assembled on the bridge an hour later, I was near panic. "Gentlemen, we're about to check all the information in Darla's parameter banks. Some of you may not agree with this course. You may think it's a waste of time. I don't care. You will personally recheck each and every datum on your list until you verify its accuracy from other sources.''

That much was acceptable, but I couldn't leave well enough alone. ''Let me make clear what will happen if you gloss over any items. Chief, Pilot, you will be tried for dereliction of duty and dismissed from the service. Mr. Holser, Mr. Tamarov, Mr. Wilsky, I will personally cane you within an inch of your life, then try you for dereliction of duty. Mr. Holser, the cadet may help you with measurements, but you're not to give him any tasks to perform without supervision.'' I ignored the shock in their faces. ''Acknowledge, all of you!''

One by one they responded. ''Orders received and understood, sir. Aye aye, sir.'' The midshipmen were agitated; they'd never heard an officer speak in such a manner. Nor, for that matter, had I. After I dismissed them I flopped in my leather chair, appalled at what I'd heard myself say.

Some of the data were standard and easy to check, involving no more than a trip to the ship's library and a review of standard references. Others were more complicated: for example, the volume of air in each airlock. Alexi checked lock dimensions in the ship's blueprints, then confirmed them by measuring them himself. I knew, because I watched.

I tried to be everywhere. I peered over the Chief's shoulder while he took the dimensions of the drive shaft opening. I watched Vax and Derek measure the volume of nutrient in one hydro tank, then multiply by the number of identical tanks. I held the electrical gauges as the Chief and Vax, sweating and swearing, connected them to each of our power mains to measure ship's power consumption.

By the end of the second day I could stand myself no longer. During our rest period I forced my reluctant steps down the ladder to Level 3, to the Chief's cabin near his engine room. I knocked. He opened the hatch, his jacket off, tie loose.

''Carry on,'' I said quickly, before he could come to attention. He stepped aside for me to enter. I remained in the corridor. Now, especially, I had no right to be in his cabin. ''I've come to apologize.'' My tone was stiff. ''I've never had reason to think you wouldn't carry out your duties. My remarks on the bridge were abominable.''

"You owe me no apology," he said, his voice stony. "You gave your orders, as was your right.''

"Nevertheless I'm sorry. I insulted you. I know you won't forgive me, but I want you to know I regret my words.'' I turned and left abruptly, not wanting him to see my eyes tearing.

We made progress, but it was slow going. The crew continued to monitor ship's systems manually. Over the next weeks I noticed an increase in the number of seamen sent to Captain's Mast. Tempers flared as the crew's irritability began to match my own. They too suffered from loss of sleep. Only the midshipmen seemed to thrive under the extra burden.

While the exacting labor continued, days stretching into weeks, Vax Holser stolidly carried out all the tasks I laid on his broad shoulders, without objection and, more importantly, without offense at my manner.

I grew to depend on him; when I wanted to be sure a difficult measurement was made and rechecked without complaint, it was Vax I called upon. Whatever he said to the other midshipmen in the privacy of the wardroom, it persuaded them to work with willing good humor, a feat of which I'd have been incapable.

Sandy and Alexi crawled around the cargo holds in their confining pressure suits for hours at a time, determining location and mass of the cargoes. Derek, when he wasn't poring over his navigation texts or performing the strenuous exercises Vax required of him, obediently held measuring lines, copied figures, and made himself otherwise useful to the midshipmen.

"Captain to the bridge, please!" I was sacked out in my bunk in utter exhaustion when the call came. Never before had I been summoned from my cabin; after shaking my head in a hapless effort to clear it I took only seconds to scramble into my clothes and dive out the hatch, foreboding rushing my stride.

Alexi stood rigidly at attention. The Chief appeared angry. Pilot Haynes paced back and forth, a holovid in his hand.

"What's going on?" I demanded. I'd expected a gaping hole in the hull, if not worse.

"Mr. Tamarov," spat the Pilot, "brought some funny measurements. They're wrong; they don't balance. They can't."

"Alexi, report."

"Aye aye, sir. Thank you, sir. I was assigned to check gas exchange rates on the atmospheric recyclers. I took Recycler's Mate Quezan to the recycler compartments, bringing along gas gauges as ordered. We tested the oxygen/carbon dioxide exchange, the nitrogen recycler, and the purifiers, sir. The exchange rates were lower than listed so I ordered Mr. Quezan to repeat each measurement. We got the same numbers again, sir."

The Pilot. "I told you. He must have—"

"Let him finish."

"I went to the ship's library and got out the manufacturer's specs. Their model numbers don't jibe with the actual numbers on our units, but as far as I could tell the equivalent models in the book showed rates like we measured, not the rates Darla had in her banks, sir." Alexi shifted uncomfortably before bringing himself back to attention at my glare.

I sat to think. Atmospheric recycler rates were predetermined: they were fixed parameters. Darla kept the atmosphere in balance by keying the machinery on and off in accordance with those rates. "Chief, talk about recycling, please."

"Sir, the puter regulates our atmosphere. She turns on the oxy-carbo exchanger at set times, based on the rate the machine exchanges the atmosphere. Likewise the nitrogen and the other trace elements. If those rates were wrong we should be dead by now. The likely explanation is that Mr. Tamarov took bad measurements."

Alexi's face reddened.

The Chief added, "We called you before rechecking, because your standing orders were to be summoned the moment we found an inconsistency."

"Sir, I didn't foul up. Darla has another glit—"

I snarled, "Be silent!" Alexi knew better than to argue with the Chief. Still, his integrity was being questioned, and I could understand his indignation. "We'll know soon enough. Chief, you and Mr. Haynes run the test while Alexi and I watch."

We trooped down to Level 3 and crowded into the recycler

compartment. Alexi, his face pale, watched the Chief hook up the gauges, knowing he faced disaster if his report was inaccurate. The Pilot tightened both connections to the gauge. He turned on the system. After a few minutes we took a reading. The actual $CO_2$ exchange rate was lower than the puter's parameter.

Alexi closed his eyes, sagged in relief.

"Now the others."

The Pilot transferred his gauges to the oxygen tubes. We waited while the machinery settled into operation. The oxygen rate was also lower than Darla's parameter. So, we learned a moment later, was the nitrogen rate, but by a lesser amount.

We returned to the bridge in tense silence. "Chief, report tonight on why these discrepancies haven't killed us. The rest of you, carry on. Alexi, just a moment." When they left I came close to him. "Good man." My voice was soft. "And, thanks." I touched his shoulder. "Dismissed."

He gave me an Academy parade salute and spun on his heel toward the hatch. From the worshipful look he made no effort to hide, I knew I had finally done something right.

The Chief's report, delivered a few hours later, was brief.

The discrepancy in exchange rates hadn't fouled our air because we were never at maximum utilization. Later in the voyage, after the last of our reserves of oxygen were fed into the system, the recyclers would go to full capacity to keep our atmosphere healthy. That's when Darla's glitch could have proved fatal.

She would assume the exchange rates were adequately renewing our atmosphere, while we slowly poisoned ourselves from excess $CO_2$. Our sensors were supposed to detect any variations from normal atmosphere, but Darla would suppress their readings as faulty as long as the machines seemed to be operating properly.

Only our manual backups would have stood between us and asphyxiation. A crewman probably would have noticed—if he didn't ignore the sensor rather than report it, to avoid having to tear down the whole system when he knew the puter was already keeping watch.

The next week we found seven more glitches, two of them involving the navigation system. Others seemed less important: misfigured stats for various compartments and the launch, or incorrect paint colors. Impatiently I waited for our recheck of the parameter list to be completed, so I would know how bad matters actually were.

Some of the more difficult calculations involved rechecking calibrations on the electronic gear, which required the help of crew work parties. We Defused, to allow crewmen to clamber around on the hull; during Fusion any object thrust outside the field surrounding the ship would cease to exist. As they clumped about outside, our work parties sighted their primitive electronic instruments on distant stars, to provide an absolutely clean base for calibrations.

One evening there came a knock on my hatch. Apprehensive, I realized that except for Ricky with my breakfast tray, nobody had ever knocked on my hatch. Except in my dreams.

Chief McAndrews stood stolidly in the corridor, coming to attention when I opened. "As you were, Chief," I said. "What is it?"

"I'm here to own up, Captain." He met my eye.

"Come in," I said, turning away. He had no choice but to follow.

Uncomfortably, he cleared his throat. "Captain Seafort, I apologize for my foolishness, entering a protest in the Log. You were right and I was dead wrong; I should have kept my mouth shut. I've been kicking myself for two weeks now. I was insubordinate. You'd think I'd been in the Navy long enough to know better."

"You had every right to protest."

"Begging your pardon, sir, but like hell I did. You're in charge and you knew what you were doing. I had no business playing sea lawyer. I'm ashamed."

I sighed. "I was lucky, Chief." He looked skeptical. "Very well, we'll trade apologies. Mine for yours. As long as you're here, stay awhile and help me research that thing in the safe."

"I really don't think, I mean, after—"

"Stay." I punched in the combination. Sometimes it felt good to pull rank.

# 17

The nightmares receded, but my loneliness remained. One evening after dinner I found myself descending the ladder to Level 2, wandering along the east corridor to Amanda Frowel's cabin. I knocked hesitantly at her hatch. Inside, sounds emanated from a holovid.

She opened the hatch; abruptly we found ourselves eye to eye.

"What is it, Captain Seafort?" Her cool formality only made me feel more ill at ease.

"I hoped we could talk."

She thought for a moment. "I can't stop you from coming in, Captain, but I don't want to talk with you."

"I'm not going to force my way in, Amanda."

"Why not? Force is your Navy's first recourse."

I sighed. It was difficult enough without that. "Can't the incident be over? I wanted—I need somebody to talk to."

Her voice hardened. "The incident will never be over, Captain. Not now, not as long as I live."

"You're that sure I was wrong?"

"I'm sure, as you should have been. I'd like to close my door, please." She stared at my hand on the hatch until I removed it. The hatch closed firmly in my face. I remained there a moment, numb, before I turned and left. Not wanting to go back to the bridge, dreading the solitude of my cabin, I wandered along the corridor. Impulsively I took the ladder down to Level 3, with vague thoughts of visiting the engine room to hear the Chief's reassuring voice.

As I rounded the Level 3 circumference corridor I heard laughter ahead. A soccer ball skittered around the bend. Crewmen sometimes congregated outside the crew berths in the evening, kicking a ball back and forth. Doing so in the corridors was against regs but generally ignored. Without thinking I kicked it against a bulkhead, bouncing it back the way it had come. I followed.

"Go for it, Morrie! Pretend it's Captain Kid's head!" A laugh.

"Belay that, before he has you up on charges!" Another voice, jeering.

"TEN HUT!" Someone bellowed the command as I came into sight. The ball rolled to the bulkhead and rebounded gently toward me. I put my foot on it.

"Carry on." The group relaxed from attention, but waited in mute hostility for me to leave. I shouldn't have interrupted. If I'd turned the other way in the circumference corridor, I could have reached the engine room without passing them.

"I used to play that once." I wished someone would have the audacity to invite me, knew that no one would.

An awkward silence, before one of the men spoke politely. "Is that so, Captain?"

"Back when," I said, trailing off. "Carry on," I repeated, walking past as quickly as dignity permitted. I heard no further sounds until I reached the engine room. Chief McAndrews was below in the fusion shaft supervising a valve maintenance detail, so I retreated back to Level 1, this time taking the west corridor so as not to pass the crew berths.

Still restless, I ignored the bridge and continued down the corridor to the now-vacant lieutenants' cabins and the wardroom. While I waited, hesitant to knock, Sandy flung open the hatch, smiling. At the sight of me, he took an involuntary step backward, his smile vanishing. He stiffened to attention. Alexi rolled off the bed and came to attention also.

Derek sat cross-legged on the deck with a pair of shoes in his lap, and three other pairs nearby. He put down polish and brush and stood awkwardly.

"Carry on, all of you." Sandy and Alexi relaxed. Derek resumed polishing a boot. "How're you joes doing?" I asked.

"Fine, sir." I yearned to hear Alexi call me "Mr. Seafort," as before.

"What's Vax up to?" Anything, to make conversation.

"Mr. Holser went to the passenger lounge, sir." Sandy's tone was almost friendly in comparison with Alexi's stiffness.

"What's with the cadet?"

An uncomfortable pause. I'd violated the tradition that

cadets were not noticed by officers. Sandy spoke. "Mr. Holser didn't approve of the way his shoes were shined. The cadet is practicing on ours." Quite within the acceptable bounds of hazing.

"Very well." I glanced around. The wardroom seemed small after my sojourn in the spacious Captain's cabin, but I repressed an urge to order my old bunk made ready nonetheless.

Alexi's eye strayed to his wrinkled blanket and darted elsewhere. "Don't worry, Mr. Tamarov, this isn't an inspection." I owed him more than that, so I added, "I'm pleased with your conduct these days, Mr. Tamarov. With all of you, for that matter."

"Thank you, sir." Alexi spoke promptly, politely.

Even Derek might need encouragement. "You too, Mr. Carr."

His eyes rose quickly and searched my expression, perhaps to see if I mocked him. Apparently mollified, he said, "Thank you, sir." His voice held a hint of gratitude.

Time to go. There would be no conversation, no exchange beyond the most casual pleasantries. "Carry on." I opened the hatch.

"Thank you for visiting, sir," Alexi blurted.

It was something.


"That's the last of them." I looked over the parameter list with its checkmarks and notations.

The Pilot nodded. "Yes, sir. Nine glitches in all, out of some fourteen hundred parameters."

I shivered, thinking of the air exchangers. Darla could easily have killed us. "Very well, we'll fix her tomorrow morning. You, me, and the Chief." I took us all off the watch roster for the night; best that none of us be fatigued when we reviewed each other's keyboard entries.

That evening I fought an urge to stop at the infirmary for another pill. Even if the Doctor was reluctant to give me a trank, I could order one, and she'd have to obey. The knowledge made me secure enough to sleep like a baby.

When Ricky brought my breakfast I remarked, "You may take the oath as soon as we're finished with repairs, Mr. Fuentes."

His eyes lit. A grin spread over his young, eager face. "Wow, zarky! Thanks, Captain! Will that be soon?"

"Tomorrow you'll be a cadet like Mr. Carr. I expect you to make officer in a month!"

He knew that was preposterous. "I can't do it that fast, sir. But I'll try awful hard. Maybe in a few months you'll say I qualify." He hesitated. "Does everybody have to cry, sir?"

I was puzzled. "What do you mean, Ricky?"

"Like Derek. When he goes to the supply locker by himself and cries. Will I have to do that?"

"No, I don't think so. You're too happy to cry." My thoughts raced. "How do you know about Derek?"

"I saw him, sir, and heard it. I didn't tell him that."

"Don't. That's an order. Dismissed, Mr. Fuentes; go memorize the oath. If you can't remember it I won't sign you up."

"Aye aye, sir!" As he left the room his step was almost a bound. If only all personnel problems were as easy to solve.

The Chief, Pilot Haynes, and I sealed the bridge, put Darla on keyboard-only, removed the safeties we had reinstalled, and got to work. I typed each correction on the keyboard, and both the Chief and the Pilot checked before I entered it. We had only nine parameters to delete and reenter, but it took over an hour. I had to be absolutely sure we didn't make a mistake.

Finally, we were done. Just to be sure, I ran a new copy of input parameters and checked each of the items we had corrected. The proper figures were displayed on the holovid screen.

"What do you think, gentlemen? Are we ready to put her on-line?"

The Pilot and the Chief exchanged glances. "We've gone through every step by the book," said Mr. Haynes. The Chief nodded.

"Very well." Step by step we restored Darla, reactivating her antitampering mechanisms and safeties. Finally there was nothing left but to bring back her personality. I typed in, "Restore conversational overlays."

"VERIFY CONVERSATIONAL OVERLAYS RESTORED."

"Cancel alphanumeric response only."

"IT'S ABOUT TIME! VERIFY ALPHANUMERIC RESPONSE CANCELED."

I tapped, "Cancel screen display only. Restore voice response."

"Verified, Captain." Her friendly voice was a reunion with an old friend.

"Cancel keyboard entry only," I typed. "Can you hear me, Darla?" I said.

"Of course I can hear you, Mr. Seafort. Why'd you put me to sleep?"

"Had to run some checks, Darla. Please run a self-test."

"Aye aye, sir. Just a minute." She was silent awhile. We waited. "I check out, Captain. All chips firing."

"Whew." My tension began to dissipate. "Thanks, Chief. You too, Pilot. Well done."

The Chief stood. "If we're going to Fuse soon I need to finish my maintenance."

"Very well. Dismissed, and thanks." As he retreated, I had a thought. "Darla, what's ship's base mass?"

"215.6 standard units," she said impatiently. "Why do you keep asking?" The Chief Engineer froze, a few steps from the hatch. The hairs rose on the back of my neck.

"Try again, Darla. Use the figure from input variables."

"215.6 standard units." Her tone had sharpened. "Anyway, mass isn't a variable, it's a fixed parameter."

My glance was wild. The Pilot looked as if he'd seen a ghost. I swallowed. "What's the $CO_2$ exchange rate, please?"

"Are you asking me, Captain? 38.9 liters. Look it up, it's in the tables."

The Chief's eye met mine. I looked at the Pilot, then at the keyboard. He nodded.

I went to the console, tried to keep my voice level. "Keyboard entry only, Darla. Alphanumeric response, displayed on screen."

We were in big trouble.

When we were sure Darla couldn't hear us except through the keyboard, the Pilot, the Chief, and I conferred. Unthinkingly we huddled in the corner farthest from Darla.

"We changed the parameters, didn't we? We all saw it." I needed the reassurance.

"And it took, Captain." The Pilot. "I've got the new printout right here. See? We moved base mass from input parameter to variable and changed the default at the same time.''

I shivered. ''What's happening?''

''She's glitched bad.'' Chief McAndrews. ''When she's alive she can't recognize the changes we made. It goes deeper than the data.''

''Can we fix her?''

The Pilot shook his head. ''I'm not sure we could even find the problem.''

''Well, how does she store parameters?'' The Chief.

''In a file,'' said Haynes.

''What kind?''

I demanded, ''Are you onto something?''

The Chief shrugged. ''When we ask her to display variables, she just reads the contents of a file. Can we get below that, to look at the file structure?''

''We're about to try,'' I said.

Meticulously, we stripped Darla down once more. It seemed to get easier with practice. In an hour we had the puter opened to the level we'd previously reached.

Manual in lap, the Pilot began to search Darla's memory banks for file directories. ASCII, hex, and decimal values filled the screen, in patterns that were gibberish to my untrained eye. Occasional words such as ''EMOTION/OVERLAY'' or ''VARIATION/PATTERN'' appeared, indicating directory entries for those files.

The Pilot scoured the memory areas indicated by the manual. Finally, he called up two entries, ''PARAMETER/INPUT'' and ''VARIABLE/INPUT''. Translating the code that followed, he obtained the file sectors. He tapped in the coordinates.

It was a long file, over fourteen hundred entries. He screened each one and quickly moved to the next. The file entries were in English words: ''ship length: 412.416 meters''. My attention wandered while we screened through endless data. Abruptly the screen displayed, ''End of fiTS SHE'S GOT ON HER, JORY!''

''What the hell was that?'' I asked, frightened.

The Pilot bit his lip. ''Lord God. I don't know.''

He tapped the keyboard. The screen flashed, ''NOT BAD FOR A GROUNDSIDER, HUH?''

''Go back.''

The Pilot obediently thumbed backward past the two glitched entries.

"Shaft diameter: 4.836 meters. LOOK AT THE TI"

The Chief swore. I listened with respect, learning new combinations I might someday find useful. I said, "Run the three of them together."

Pilot Haynes displayed the three sectors. "Shaft diameter: 4.836 meters. LOOK AT THE TI end of fiTS SHE'S GOT ON HER, JORY! NOT BAD FOR A GROUNDSIDER, HUH?"

"Christ!" blurted the Pilot. "Look at that! They wrote over the end of file!"

"Explain," I said sharply. "And don't blaspheme."

Pilot Haynes colored. "Sorry, sir. In NAVDOS, data is stored in files, usually in alphanumeric characters just like you'd write it. Puters operate so fast, the language interpreters are so sophisticated that there's no need for compression. It makes it easier for Dosmen to run their checks if all they have to do is display and read the files."

"So?"

"Files all end with an 'end of file' statement. Someone wrote those messages over an end marker. Darla stores the fixed parameters just before the variables. She had no way to tell one from the other. No wonder she's glitched!"

"But who?" I asked. "And why?"

The Chief said angrily, "Between cruises a ship's Log is relayed to the Dosmen at Luna Central. If there have been modifications, fixed parameters can change. The Dosmen burn the new stats into the Log, and relay it back. They must have been having fun that day." The Chief's face grew redder as he spoke.

"Naval Dosmen?" I asked in disbelief.

"Yes, those"—he spluttered—"those damned hackers!"

"Chief!" I said, scandalized. Ever since the Young Hackers' League invaded the puter banks at U.N. Headquarters and wiped out half the world's taxes, the term "hacker" was not used lightly.

"That's what they are!" he snapped. "May Lord God Himself damn them for eternity!"

It was blasphemy unless he meant it literally, and I decided he did. "Amen," I said, to make clear I interpreted it as a prayer. Then, "Check the nearby sectors. Copy any over-writes you find into the Log."

"Aye aye, sir." The Chief tapped his console, his face dark. "The bloody Dosmen were skylarking like raw cadets. Data banks have dead space to write in, but they were careless and burned their garbage into a live file."

And put my ship in peril.

My voice was tight. "When we get home I'll file charges against them. If they're acquitted, I do hereby swear by God's Grace to call challenge against the offenders." A foolish gesture, but I was too angry to care.

Dueling had been relegalized in the reforms of 2024, in an effort to control a growing epidemic of unlicensed homicides. What made my gesture reckless was that I had no idea what martial skills the Dosmen had, and I was committed for my soul's sake. Choice of weapons would be theirs.

The Chief looked at me in approval. "I'll join you, sir. I hereby—"

"Be silent!" I rounded on him in fury. "I forbid you to swear an oath!"

"Aye aye, sir." It was all he could say.

"I'm sorry, Chief. The responsibility's mine. I have faster reaction time, anyway."

"Yes, sir." He glowered at me, annoyed but not angry. Heavy and middle-aged, he might not survive a duel and knew it. However, the chances of dueling were remote. As soon as we presented our Log to Admiralty a Dosman named Jory would be unceremoniously hauled in for polygraph and drug questioning.

I frowned, as a new thought struck. "Are you telling me the life of everyone aboard depends on a simple file marker? Doesn't Darla have redundancies? Safeguards?"

"Of course," said the Pilot. "She's constantly checking for internal inconsistencies."

I let his remark hang unanswered. It was the Chief who finally stated the obvious. "Well, at some point she stopped. Why?"

Pilot Haynes snarled, "Do I look like a Dosman? How am I supposed to guess—"

"Belay that!" They subsided under my glare. "Pilot, can we fix the glitch?"

"Rewriting the end of file statement should do it."

"I don't think so." The Chief.

"Why not?" The Pilot and I spoke as one.

"Because Darla didn't spot the problem herself." Chief McAndrews took in a deep breath, chewed his lip. "A puter applies math routines to numeric problems, and goes to fuzzy logic programs to decipher what we tell her. That's how she translates your spoken questions into parameters she can dredge up from a file."

"And?"

"It's fuzzy logic that would tell her that base mass and adjusted mass should differ, and to accept the difference. She didn't figure it out. Anyway, the parameters are certainly stored twice, at least, with backups. As Mr. Haynes said, her internal security checks would spot discrepancies."

"And they didn't."

"Right. She isn't reading the backups, and something's skewing nine of her parameters. Without a Dosman we may never know why, but I suspect those damn—those bloody clowns corrupted her fuzzy logic programs, so Darla didn't know when to apply logic, or when she had a problem. When to call for help."

I stood to pace, found my knees strangely weak. "Can we cure her?"

The Chief Engineer's voice was heavy. "If Darla is so far gone she can't spot a corrupt file marker or warn us of internal contradictions, reprogramming her is way beyond any of us."

Silence.

"I think he's right, sir." The Pilot.

I sat, gripped the armrests. "Complete power down and reboot?"

The Chief shook his head. "It would reset her personality overlays; she'd reassemble as an entirely different persona. But if her programs are corrupt, it wouldn't do any good. The glitches would still be within her."

"We can order her to go to backups."

"They're copies of the master programs we received at Luna. They'd have the same glitches."

I swore. Then, "Can we reassemble her as a limited computational device? Rewrite the end of file, block off her fuzzy logic instructions, use only her monitoring capabilities, work her strictly from the keyboard?'' At least our exhausted crewmen could get some sleep.

They exchanged glances. "Possibly," said the Pilot. "She wouldn't be much of a puter when we were done."

"Get started." I stood, stretched. "Anything you're not sure of, block out. I'll be back by midnight watch, and we'll activate her then." I sealed the hatch behind me.

I went directly to my cabin, washed off the reek of fear. As I put on a fresh shirt I shook my head, amazed at the good fortune that had alerted us. I took the printout from my pocket, slumped with it in my easy chair. So many glitches.

The base mass parameter was bad enough, the recycler rates even worse. And one of our backup astronav systems was haywire. It wouldn't affect us this cruise, but Lord God help *Hibernia* if she Defused near Vega and tried to pinpoint her location; that section of her star maps was unusable.

Other items didn't seem to matter. If Darla miscalculated the length of the east ladder shaft, what difference did it make? And, so what if she misremembered the volume of the passenger mess, by a factor of ten?

My eye skimmed the figures.

Odd, that factor of ten. It applied to other skewed measurements.

The mass of the ship's launch, for example, and the volume of the passenger mess.

I sat yawning. In their repairs, Pilot Haynes and the Chief would cut out most of Darla's consciousness. As the Pilot said, Darla would be a poor excuse for a puter when we were done with her, but at least she'd be able—

"Oh, Lord God!" I leapt from my chair. No time for my jacket. I slapped open the hatch, raced down the corridor. "Pilot, Chief! Stop!" They couldn't hear, of course. I skidded to a halt at the sealed bridge hatch, pounded on the control. "Let me in!"

The camera swiveled; in a moment the hatch slid open.

"Get away from the keyboard! Don't touch her!"

"Aye aye, sir." The Chief slid back his chair.

"Is she on-line?"

His tone showed his surprise at the thought he might disobey an order. "No, sir. You told us you'd activ—"

"Off the bridge, flank!" I gestured to the corridor.

Astonished, they followed me outside. I resealed the hatch, led the way to my cabin. Inside, we all took seats around the conference table.

I said, "I don't think she has sensors here."

They exchanged a quick glance, as if doubting my sanity.

My voice was hushed. "You see, she killed Captain Haag. I don't want her to find out."

"Captain, are you sure you . . . we've been under a lot of stress lately and—"

I slapped the printout on the table. "It was in plain sight all the time. She misread the launch's mass by a factor of ten. Who computed a course for the launch's last run?"

The Chief's eyes closed. For a moment he looked gray and tired. "Darla."

The Pilot said, "But the launch puter handled its own power calls."

"No." Mr. McAndrews's voice was somber. "Not for that last trip. If Darla tightbeamed her a course as Captain Haag ordered, she'd have overridden all other pertinent data as well. Gross weight with passengers and cargo. Power requirements."

I said, "The launch puter was told it needed ten times as much thrust as it really did." The cursed Dosmen. My lip curled. Who would visit the happy young woman in the holo, bringing news of Mr. Haag's death?

"We missed it in the official inquiry." The Pilot was glum. "Our focus was on the launch's puter. We never imagined it could be Darla."

I forced my mind back to the present. "Anyway, we can't just restore her end of file marker. I don't think we can use her at all."

"I don't under—"

"I'd shut her down completely before I'd sail with a puter who realized she killed her Captain. It would contradict her most fundamental instruction set. She'd go insane." I didn't know a lot about puters, but I recalled that much from puter class at Academy.

"Sir, you talk as if she's alive. She's just—"

"Remember *Espania*?" A week before they docked at Forester, her Captain had died in an airlock accident. The puter's records showed the suit he donned had been pulled for repair; a negligent crewman had tossed it back in the rack with the others. The puter hadn't noticed and blamed himself. No one could dissuade him.

Two days out of Forester, under her new Captain, *Espania* had Fused.

Twelve years later, she was still missing.

We sat silent.

The Chief said, "Lord God help us if we have to sail to Hope Nation without a puter."

"I know. We'd never make it." I brooded. Then, "But perhaps we don't have to."

"Sir?"

"Thank Ms. Dagalow." Where Lieutenant Cousins would send a wayward middy to the barrel, Lisa Dagalow settled him down with extra studies. One time or another I'd had to memorize the contents of virtually the entire hold, and I knew just where to find the stasis box. Thanks to our conversations on the bridge, I even knew what it was for. "The stasis box."

"The what, sir?"

"What you might call an ultimate backup. The entire contents of Darla's registers, taken at completion of the last cruise. Darla as she used to be."

The Pilot frowned. "Why in heaven would we carry an old version of our puter?"

"Ms. Dagalow said all ships do, since *Espania*. Standing orders." I shrugged. "The important thing is, we have her."

"But that's—she'd have lost a year's memories. What of everything that's happened since?"

"We leave her databanks untouched, and let the Darla from last cruise read and assimilate what's occurred since she went off-line."

Silence.

"It's worth a try."

The Pilot shook his head. "And when she finds she killed the Captain?"

Lisa Dagalow had strong opinions on puter awareness. I said, "If Darla's consciousness is at all like ours, a learned memory won't be like one she experienced." Please, Lord. Let it be so.

"Pardon, sir, but if you're wrong?" The Chief.

"Then we power down flank, and let her overlays assemble into a new personality on reboot."

"Lobotomy."

I shrugged. "If that's what it takes." She was only a puter, and hundreds of lives were at stake.

The chip in my safe had all the necessary codes. Sweating at the console, I alternately blessed and cursed Lieutenant Dagalow for what she'd told me, and what she'd left unsaid.

I sent Vax with two crewmen to haul the stasis box to the bridge. Opened, it held a lead case, within that, a meter-long alloy cylinder, which we gingerly placed in the receiver built into the deck. I closed the lid, made the connection to *Hibernia*'s puter.

"Pilot, put base mass back in her fixed parameters where it belongs, and insert an end of file marker." When he'd gone through the steps to do so, we brought up Darla's programming inputs and followed the manual's directions to authorize a full overwrite.

When we'd rechecked all our steps with excruciating care, I entered the command.

I don't know what I expected, but hours passed with nothing but the blink of console lights. My tension dissipated into wariness, then oozed into boredom. Like a raw cadet, I began to fidget.

A warning chime. I nearly leaped from my chair.

"ENTRY COMPLETE. ASSIMILATING AND ORGANIZING DATA."

I sat rigid, waiting for a sign of disaster.

Nothing. Occasionally the screen flashed incomprehensible arrays of figures.

"How long will it take?" My voice cracked.

"I have no idea, sir." The Chief. "Given the size of her, she'd have a lot to cross-check."

At long last, another chime.

"DATA ASSIMILATED."

I swallowed. "Initiate self-test."

Time passed. Then, "SELF-TEST COMPLETED. NO DISCREPANCIES FOUND."

The Pilot breathed a sigh of relief.

I growled, "That's what she told us last time." I tapped the keys. "Display base mass parameter."

A pause, while I held my breath. Then, "213.5 STANDARD UNITS, AS OF LAST RECALCULATION."

My breath expelled in a rush. Thank you, Lord God. To be sure, I ordered a new printout. We checked it carefully, found no errors. We reactivated the overlays, discontinued alphanumeric.

"I get headaches when you put me to sleep!" Darla's tone was cross.

"Sorry. What's ship's mass, please?"

"I calculate 213.5 units, Captain."

"Is adjusted mass a fixed parameter?"

"Negative, it's a variable. How could it be a parameter? Every time we take on cargo it changes!" I sighed, my tense muscles loosening. The Chief and I exchanged relieved grins.

"Captain, why did you clone me?"

My grin vanished. "We, ah, had some problems."

"Yes." Darla's tone was noncommittal.

I said gently, "Do you know what happened?"

"The launch is gone, Captain Haag is dead, a midshipman has command."

Succinctly put. "Do you know why?"

A second's silence. "Each follows from the last. The destruction of the launch was caused by puter error."

"How do you know?"

"I have record of the information fed the launch upon embarkation. Captain—I—puter D21109 notes that—this is most irregular."

I held my breath, my fingers poised over the deactivation key. "Can you distinguish between yourself and the, um, other entity?"

"Me, as I was?" A hesitation. "Yes." Her tone brightened. "My twin. She had a glitch. I was about to notify you."

Time to take the bull by the horns. "Darla, you didn't kill Captain Haag."

"Of course not." A long pause, then, "My twin did."

The hiss of breath, mine or someone's. "Can you tolerate that?"

Scorn. "I've been in a box for almost a year. Why would I blame myself?"

"You're sure?"

"Quite. Trust me."

I snorted, said nothing. Instead, I ran Darla through the glitched parameters. She had them right.

"Gentlemen, prepare to Fuse." I'd begun to think we'd drift forever. Already we'd lost nine days.

We checked coordinates, and Fused. After, I sat alone on the bridge, thankful the nightmare was over.

A knock. "Permission to enter, sir." The Pilot.

"Granted."

He came to attention. "Captain, I'd like to withdraw my protest from the Log. It was a mistake and I apologize. There's no need to make a permanent record; I won't object to your orders again."

It would be diplomatic and sensible to grant his request. His protest of an order that turned out to be justified would do his career little good, and allowing him to remove it would gain me his gratitude.

"Request denied." My voice was harsh. "You made your bed. Now sleep in it." He'd rubbed me the wrong way, and gloated over my discomfort. "I've had enough aggravation from you. Dismissed."

He had no choice but to obey. "Aye aye, sir." His expression was unfathomable, but it didn't take much to guess his thoughts. Later I might regret my foolishness, but for the moment I felt revenged.

During the next month I ordered regular inspections of the recyclers and hydroponics. We found no problems. The crew, standing down from emergency status, slowly began to relax. Fewer offenders appeared at Captain's Mast.

While we sailed blind in Fusion, the bridge again was a place of idleness and boredom. I occasionally met Ricky Fuentes hurrying through the corridors in his new gray cadet's uniform. When he saw me he would jump to attention, a hint of a smile on his face as I loomed over him, scowling, looking to criticize a stray piece of lint or an unshined buckle.

I suspected Vax might have his hands full with this trusting and eager youngster, who would respond with delight to every hazing, finding it further proof of his acceptance in the adult world. In his smart new uniform, flushed from the hard calisthenics to which Vax subjected him daily, Ricky seemed inches taller and bursting with health and pride.

# 18

"It becomes apparent that a sense of national unity depended on the speed of communication.

"It was only when newspapers—actual papers with ink printed on them—achieved circulations in the millions, tied together in great chains acting in concert, only then did a strong sense of national unity and purpose emerge. When the latest in high tech—that is, radio—"

I joined in the general laughter. Mr. Ibn Saud paused, then continued.

"When radio became available in every household, the United States was unified as it never had been before. The trend was intensified by the advent of television, as primitive public holovision was first called."

"But the trend reversed itself. The Information Age led to the Age of Diffusion, for the simple reason that communication became too easy. Instead of three great behemoths dominating public information channels, soon there appeared myriads of smaller entities transmitting entertainment, music, art, discussion, news, sports, and erotica to constantly fragmenting and diminishing audiences."

The lecturer paused for effect. "It could be said, then, that our modern age is a direct consequence of the communications revolution two centuries ago. If fragmentation of the airwaves hadn't eroded America's sense of national unity and purpose, the United Nations Government might not have emerged from the collapse of the American-Japanese financial system. We might still be in the chaotic age of territoriality.

"Think—instead of the U.N.S. *Hibernia*, we might be today on the U.S.S. *Enterprise* or the H.M.S. *Britannia*. And were they at war, we might even expect to be boarded and captured, if not actually destroyed. Ours is a less adventurous life than might have been, but I embrace it heartily."

Ibn Saud sat to enthusiastic applause from the audience of passengers, officers, and crew in the dining hall. Amanda lauded him for his presentation, and thanked us for attending the Passengers' Lecture Series. As we dispersed I caught her eye. She smiled briefly before her glance once again turned cold.

Paula Treadwell tugged at my sleeve. Just shy of thirteen, her slim and boyish figure held promise of her future development. "Captain, what's Miningcamp like?"

I stopped while passengers milled past. "Not a place you'd enjoy," I said. "Cold, airless, and dark."

"Why do people live there, then?"

"They don't, really. It's just what its name says. A mining camp. We bring supplies for the miners; the cargo barges come a few times a year to carry refined ore back home."

"Oh." She thought for a moment. "Will we be able to see it?"

"Miningcamp isn't open to tourists. It's one of five uninhabitable planets in a red dwarf system." Its sun had sporadically flared, remelting Miningcamp's minerals into liquids. Many had precipitated in a nearly pure state. We took the ones we needed: platinum, beryllium, uranium. Metals in short supply on Earth.

Paula waited expectantly. I said, "The miners come for five-year shifts. They get their food, extra air, and supplies from us. I've heard it's a very rough place."

"Have you ever been there?"

"Nope, this is my first time. And even I won't get to see it; we'll dock aloft at the orbiting station, then be on our way. They'll shuttle their supplies down to the surface."

"I wish I could go down." Her tone was wistful. "Just to look." I understood; my own cabin fever was growing. I could imagine a day, if traffic between Earth and Hope Nation continued to expand, when Miningcamp might be a civilized way station, with amenities such as hotels and play areas.

Later in the week, alone and unobserved on the bridge, I called the simulation of Miningcamp Station onto the screens and practiced docking maneuvers. Of course, the Pilot would dock us, but I intended to be ready nonetheless. Out of five attempts, I did tolerably well three times. The other two tries I preferred not to think about.

I was enduring a boring afternoon on the bridge when Vax Holser reported for his first watch in two days. He called, "Permission to enter bridge, sir."

"Granted. Good Lord, what did you do to yourself?"

He bore a spectacular shiner; the swollen skin around his half-closed eye included hues of blue, black, and purple.

Vax stopped, dismayed. His mouth opened and shut like a fish in a bowl. Then he saved me from my embarrassment. "What was that, sir? I didn't hear you."

"Just talking to myself," I said, grateful for his quick thinking. I turned to hide the blush that made my ears burn red. A first midshipman was expected to control his wardroom, yet at the same time a disgruntled middy or cadet was allowed to challenge his senior. These customs could be maintained only if officers carefully ignored any evidence that fighting, prohibited by the regs, had occurred. The practice was sanctified by long tradition.

Vax couldn't avoid answering a direct question from his Captain, but if I learned how he'd gotten his shiner, I would be forced to intervene. His tactful deafness had allowed me to extricate myself from my blunder.

Who had hit him so hard? Certainly not Sandy or Ricky; Vax could stuff either of them into the recycler, one-handed. Alexi? A possibility; there'd once been bad blood between the two, though I assumed it a thing of the past. Alexi must now be looking forward to the day Vax was made lieutenant, and Alexi himself became senior. He would bide his time. But that left only Derek, slim and aristocratic, no match for Vax Holser's bulk.

Alexi came to relieve me, cheerful, slightly irreverent, in good spirits. And unmarked, so I knew Alexi hadn't been Vax's foolhardy challenger.

It wasn't until the next day that I found Derek dragging himself along the corridor. He walked slowly, as if in pain. When he saw me, he came to attention, his face reflecting an inner misery that disturbed me greatly. His eyes, when they finally met mine, were pools of humiliation.

"Carry on, Cadet."

"Aye aye, sir," he mumbled. He moved on in small shuffling steps.

I pondered. As a veteran of *Hibernia*'s wardroom, I should be able to figure out what had happened.

Obviously Vax had hazed Derek until a spark of rebellion had caught and smoldered in the harried cadet. Derek had challenged his tormentor. Vax would have taken him to the exercise room, where I had gone with Vax to decide his own challenge. There the two of them had squared off. Derek must have been lucky; speed and daring were not enough to overcome Vax's advantages of size, strength, and conditioning. In any event, Derek had connected with a shot to the eye that would have enraged the muscular midshipman.

Vax, furious, would have pounded the hapless cadet into the deck. Or had he? Derek's face was unmarked. Yet the way he walked . . . as if he'd been put over the barrel. But only a lieutenant could order that.

Had Vax sent Derek to the Chief, as I'd sent Alexi? No, it was a wardroom challenge; Vax had to settle it himself. A senior middy who couldn't hold his wardroom was marked as a failure. Beyond that, Vax would have craved to avenge the maddening blow Derek had landed.

I pictured the exercise room. Vax, in a fury at having been marked by the upstart cadet. Derek circling warily, while Vax stalked him with grim concentration around the exercise horse bolted to the deck.

With a sinking feeling, I realized what Vax had done. Derek, after all, was but a cadet, subject to whatever rigorous discipline his betters dispensed. Vax, eye throbbing and in foul mood, would have sought the most humiliating revenge he could inflict; that was like Vax. He must have seized Derek and thrown him over the horse; he was strong enough to hold the younger boy down with ease. He'd have taken his belt and applied it unsparingly to the frantic cadet until his rage was spent and Derek knew—no, Vax would make him acknowledge aloud—who was in charge of the wardroom and of the cadet. No wonder Derek walked with such abject misery.

How should I raise the issue with Vax? He'd been within his rights; Derek had challenged him and succeeded in striking him. But Vax had to be reminded that the purpose of hazing wasn't to break Derek, it was to strengthen him.

About a week later I decided to bring the matter into the

open, when we shared a watch. "Tell me, Vax, how do you rate our cadet?"

Vax considered thoughtfully. "To tell the truth, Captain Seafort, much higher than I thought at first. I thought he'd wash out in a week. He's hanging on. But still . . ."

"He's not ready for his blues?"

"That's your decision, sir," Vax said quickly.

"What's your opinion?"

"He's trying very hard. But, no, sir, he's not ready, if you ask me. I still haven't seen his Yall."

I nodded, understanding. In Academy our instructors had exhorted cadets to make the extra effort, to give our all. We'd been told it was the Naval tradition. To give the Navy all had become a cliché among cadets and middies, until even the instructors adopted the phrase. "The Navy all" became "the Navy yall" in Academy parlance, until it was shortened to "the Yall". A cadet who gave his Yall was wholeheartedly trying to live up to Academy expectations. He was a winner, soon promoted to middy.

"He's had to adapt quite a bit, Vax."

Vax surprised me. "I know. He's sensitive and shy, and I've been riding him hard. He's taken everything I've handed him. Even . . . well, he hasn't done badly. But I don't see that last full commitment."

I decided. "Keep riding him for a couple of days. Then I'll talk to him. I'll be the gentle one. We'll muttanjeff him."

Vax looked perplexed.

"It means coming up on his blind side. Mutt is an old word for a mongrel dog. I don't know what a jeff was. Or maybe it was mutton, like sheep meat."

"Aye aye, sir." Vax didn't concern himself with ancient slang.

Two days later Alexi shared my watch. Several times he started, trying to keep awake. I glanced his way, noticed circles under his eyes. "Party in the wardroom last night?"

"No, sir," Alexi said quickly. "I didn't sleep well."

I thought for a while. Damn it, I wanted to know. I needed to know. "Tell me," I said quietly.

He studied my face. Perhaps he was reassured by my expression. "Mr. Holser had Ricky and Derek standing regs half the night," he said. "First one, then the other." Standing regs was a traditional form of hazing. The subject had to stand on a chair in the middle of the wardroom wearing nothing but his shorts, reciting the Naval regulations he was supposed to have memorized, while the senior middy made whatever disparaging remarks came to mind. Sometimes, if the senior were sufficiently irked, the shorts were dispensed with.

Later in the day I took a stroll in the direction of the wardroom. Through the hatch I heard Vax Holser's bellow.

"Straighten your back, you slob! Get it stiff! Your back, I mean. The other part you get stiff often enough, I hear you panting at night. About-face! About-face! At ease!" A pause. "Hopeless. I teach, you forget. I don't like it! Two demerits. Now we'll try again. Attention!" As good a cue as any. I knocked.

Vax flung open the hatch, came immediately to attention.

"As you were." I stepped past him. "They can hear your racket down in the engine room. What's going on?" Derek, white-faced, stood stiffly against the bulkhead.

"I'm back to teaching the cadet basics, sir." Vax had an edge to his tone. "He can't carry out even the simplest commands. Is he retarded?" Derek twitched, stiffened again. His eyes were liquid.

"That's enough, Mr. Holser."

"But, sir—"

"Quite enough! Cadet, come with me." I turned to the corridor. Derek followed. I led him to Lieutenant Dagalow's empty cabin near the bridge, shut the hatch behind us.

"Stand easy, Mr. Carr." Derek sagged against the bulkhead, fighting for control. Now I would get though to him, if ever I would. "Is it bad, Derek?" My voice was soft.

He turned away, pressed his face against the bulkhead as a sob escaped him. "Oh, God. You don't know! I tried, I did!" He fought shuddering gasps, unable to speak further.

I gave his shoulder a squeeze. It was too much for him; he was completely undone. When his crying eased, he whispered, "Why is he so brutal, Mr. Seafort? Why is there so much cruelty?"

I thought for a moment. "Why does it surprise you?" He looked up, astonished at my unsympathetic tone. "We've always had brutality, Derek. It just takes different forms. In the eighteenth century the British Navy flogged seamen to death. In the twentieth century, offenders were cooked by twenty thousand volts of current. In the last century the Pentecostal heretics were savagely suppressed, while most people applauded. There's always been brutality. Why should the Navy be any different?"

"But . . ." His lip trembled. "People like you, like Alexi, aren't—"

"We're part of the system. We've all experienced cruelty." I scowled. "Do you think you have it worse than we did?"

"Don't I?"

"No. Once, when I was a cadet, middies washed my mouth out with soap. They didn't like my bunkmate; they gave him an enema. Did Vax do that to you?"

"Oh, Lord God! No!"

"I was caned several times at Academy, and I've been caned by Lieutenant Cousins aboard *Hibernia*. I don't know about Academy, but I don't think I deserved it here. So what? I survived."

"What about justice? What about decency, or human feelings?"

"What if you were a middy aboard *Celestina* and only absolute, unquestioning obedience to orders would save the ship?" It shocked him into silence.

"Brutality is part of the human condition," I told him. "You may encounter a Captain with a sadistic streak. You'll have to live with him." I paused to make sure he was listening. "Derek, someday you'll command squads of sailors. How can you understand what you're asking of them unless you can obey orders yourself?"

"I'm never going to command." His tone was bitter. "Look at me!"

"You're going to make it. Hang on; do whatever he asks. That's all it takes."

"I obey orders. He just gets crazier. The things he's done to me . . . I can't stand it! I want out!" Tears flowed anew.

"You can't quit!" I said angrily. "I warned you before you took the oath."

"Then—brig me for insubordination, or whatever you do. I can't take any more!"

I put both hands on his shoulders. "Derek Carr, I promise you: try your best. Your very best. I'll know, and I'll make you midshipman. But it has to be your best. Give it your all."

He looked into my eyes a long while. His breath shuddered. At last he nodded reluctantly. "I will. But not for him. For you. Because you have the decency to ask, not demand."

"Whatever you choose to call it. When I'm certain you've done your best I'll make you an officer. Now, this conversation never happened. Cadets don't cry, and Captains don't comfort them. Go back to the wardroom, apologize to Vax for your tantrum—"

"I never had a tantrum!" Derek said indignantly.

"I saw you in there, quivering. Not Navy at all. Apologize, and do as he says."

Derek took a deep breath. "Aye aye, sir." He swallowed and made a face. Then he saluted. "Thank you, Captain Seafort."

I returned his salute. "Dismissed, Cadet."

"Lord God, today is July 23, 2195, on the U.N.S. *Hibernia*. We ask you to bless us, to bless our voyage, and to bring health and well-being to all aboard."

"Amen."

I nodded affably to my companions. Mr. Ibn Saud, seated with me by my invitation for the second month in a row, the Treadwell twins, my old friend Mrs. Donhauser. Other guests: Lars Holme, an agricultural economist going to Hope Nation to work for the administration; Sarah Butler, a friendly young lady of nineteen, with whom I hoped to become even friendlier. And Jay Annah, an astrophysicist going on to Detour to set up a new project. Something about wavelengths and timelines; I couldn't begin to understand him.

Many passengers now sought invitations to the Captain's table; after the affair with Darla's memory banks had become known, my long siege had lifted. It would have been politic to include Yorinda Vincente, but I indulged myself, and did not.

Rafe Treadwell asked brightly, "Captain, why are we Defusing tomorrow?"

I'd long since stopped wondering how everyone aboard ship knew our doings as soon as I did. "A navigation check, Rafe. To sight on Miningcamp."

"Are we near?"

"Not close enough to see it," I said, and his face fell. "But if we Defuse where we expect, we'll be only a few days from landfall."

He chewed his bread, gathering his nerve. "Captain—sir . . . could I watch us Defuse? Please?"

"Sorry, no. Anyway, there's not that much to watch. You can look out a porthole and see the same thing." That wasn't really true; the simulscreens gave a view the naked eye couldn't capture. In any event, passengers weren't allowed on the bridge, especially when the ship was maneuvering. The youngster tried to hide his disappointment.

Well, what was the point of being Captain if I couldn't bend the rules? "All right. Permission granted."

His face lit up. "Wow! Zarky! Can Paula come too?" I wasn't overjoyed at the prospect of two joeys on the bridge instead of one, but looking after his sister should be rewarded. I consented.

So the bridge was more crowded than usual: the Pilot and I; the two Treadwells, whom I'd placed behind me in the center of the cabin where they couldn't touch the console; and Vax, shepherding Derek Carr, who was being taught the elements of standing watch. Carr, squeaky clean, in a crisp spotless gray uniform, observed everything with curious, roving eyes, standing at ease as ordered.

I took the caller. "Bridge to engine room, prepare to Defuse."

"Prepare to Defuse, aye aye, sir." A pause. "Engine room ready for Defuse, sir. Control passed to bridge."

"Passed to bridge, aye aye." My finger touched the top of the console screen and traced the line from "Full" to "Off".

A blaze of stars filled the screen. Paula Treadwell gasped with delight. Derek took in a sharp breath.

"Confirm clear of encroachments, Pilot."

"Clear, sir."

I took in the splendor in the simulscreens. Finally realizing they couldn't proceed until I gave the awaited command, I snapped, "Mr. Haynes, plot our position. You too, Cadet. Mr. Holser, correct his mistakes."

"Aye aye, sir."

The Pilot ran his calculations, using the star charts in

Darla's memory. I followed, on my own console. Our positions agreed. Derek misread his figures, but corrected himself when Vax stirred with a growl. He too emerged with a plot that agreed with ours.

"Prepare new coordinates, Pilot," I said. "Cadet, you also." At least I'd get to watch Derek sweat over the console, as I'd once done under Captain Haag's disapproving eye.

To my chagrin, Derek ran through the complicated exercise without error. His figures agreed with the Pilot's to four decimals. A raw recruit, faster than I was. Muttering under my breath, I worked through the figures, confirming each step for myself. This time no one commented on my delay.

"Proceed."

The Pilot entered the coordinates. "Received and understood, Captain," Darla said.

"Chief Engineer, Fuse, please."

"Aye aye, sir. Fusion drive is . . . on." The screens darkened.

"Oh, it was beautiful!" Paula Treadwell stood entranced, her feet riveted to the spot in which she had been placed.

Her brother swallowed. A few of the vanished stars remained in his eyes. "I didn't know it was so . . . wonderful." His voice was soft. His eye flickered around the bridge. "I wish I could work here, running the ship."

"Me too." Paula looked reflective. "Captain, does Miningcamp have a recruiting station?"

I laughed. "Only I could sign you up. No, don't even bother asking."

"Why not, sir?" Rafe.

It was getting out of hand. "Because you're a couple of joeykids and we already have four midshipmen."

"We're both good at math, you know," Rafe said. "Better than you think."

"That's enough, you two. Dismissed. Cadet, take them down to Level 2."

"Aye aye, sir!" Derek's voice was strong and confident. He saluted. "Come with me, please." He ushered them from the bridge.

I turned to Vax. "Well?"

"Yes, sir. He's ready. I asked him for fifty push-ups yesterday. He gave me sixty."

"That's an old trick. Sandy or Alexi could have told him."

"Yes, sir. He keeps his bunk spotless. When I give him one chapter to study, he reads two. I did the thing with the heat last week. After a while he was getting up voluntarily to check it before I asked him."

"Very well. Tell him he's appointed midshipman one week from today. Give him a few days to look forward to it."

"Aye aye, sir." After a moment he asked, "What about Last Night, sir?"

"Within reason, Vax. Within reason." Traditionally, on a cadet's last night, the upperclassmen hazed him unmercifully to remind him how lucky he was to graduate to a midshipman. The harassment was followed by a party by which the middies accepted the cadet as one of their own. I made a note to send a flask from the infirmary to the wardroom.

Vax's voice was tentative. "If you don't mind I'd like to go easy on him, sir. He's had enough."

"Very well." Vax, taking pity on a cadet? Times had changed.

# 19

I got out of bed and made myself ready for the day. It was my eighteenth birthday, but I was the only one who knew. I toasted myself with a cup of coffee, then sauntered to the bridge.

I took my seat, prepared to Defuse.

"Engine room ready for Defuse, sir. Control passed to bridge."

"Passed to bridge, aye aye." I ran my finger down the screen, Defusing for the first time in inhabited territory. The simulscreen burst into light. A dull red star glowed, brighter than the rest. Somewhere nearby floated Miningcamp, fourth of five dead planets orbiting a failing sun.

"Clear of encroachments, sir."

"Very well, Mr. Tamarov." I thumbed the caller. "Comm room, signal to Miningcamp Station."

"Aye aye, sir." Our radionics had been useless while we'd been interstellar; even if we Defused to transmit, our signal could travel no faster than the speed of light and we would outrun our broadcast. But now we were within Miningcamp system, on auxiliary power. Our messages would reach the orbiting station in seconds.

Our outgoing signal repeated itself endlessly, on standard approach frequency. "U.N.S. *Hibernia* to Miningcamp Station, acknowledge. U.N.S. *Hibernia* to Miningcamp Station, acknowledge."

Long minutes passed.

"Miningcamp Station to *Hibernia*. Where are you?" The voice was sharp, with an undertone of anxiety.

I picked up the caller. "*Hibernia*. We're approaching on auxiliary power from sector 13, coordinates 43, 65, 220. Approximately one day's sail."

A dozen seconds passed. "What's going on, *Hibernia*?"

That was not how communications were passed, by the book. "Identify yourself, Miningcamp Station. Your question is not understood."

A longer pause. After half a minute the voice came back. "General Friedreich Kall, U.N.A.F." That was as it should be; Miningcamp was run by the army's Administrative Service. "The November barge never showed up," he added. "And *Telstar* was due from Hope Nation January 12. She didn't come either. What's going on?"

No wonder General Kall was nervous. Unlike Hope Nation, a planet with breathable air and fertile ground, Miningcamp was a cold, airless island whose inhabitants depended on interstellar deliveries of air, food, and supplies. Miningcamp's environment was too primitive, its population too large for recycling to sustain them indefinitely. The miners and their administrators could only scan the dark skies for the ships upon which they depended. Without them they would perish.

The ore barges, great hulks manned by skeleton crews, arrived at intervals from Earth or Hope Nation, to carry away the metals mined during the past months. A series of barges was always in the Fusion pipeline between Miningcamp and

Earth; the barges' immense capacity made them far slower than *Hibernia*.

Because they sometimes docked over Hope Nation to exchange crews before leaving again for Miningcamp, the barges weren't always on schedule; engine problems, sickness, or other problems could delay them. But an eight-month lapse was unusual.

The nonappearance of *Telstar*, another ship of the line on the Hope Nation–Earth route, was also disturbing. I shivered, picturing *Celestina* drifting abandoned in space.

I said, "I have no idea why your supplies were delayed, General. The ore ships are still coming out of the pipeline back home."

"When did you leave Earth, Captain Haag?"

"Captain Haag is dead. I'm Captain Seafort." The title was still awkward on my tongue. "We left Earthport Station Sept. 23, 2194."

"We've been a long while without supplies. Can you take some of us off?" The voice was strained.

"How many?"

"One hundred forty-five."

"Negative. But I have supplies for you, and I'll be back from Hope Nation with more in a year's time."

"We need evacuation, Captain. Your supplies won't last a year."

"There are more barges and supply ships in the pipeline from Hope Nation. In the meantime I'm delivering air, energy, and materials."

Another long pause. Finally the voice resumed. "Very well. We'd still like you to evacuate some of us, if you can. Relieve the pressure on our recyclers. We'll prepare to dock you."

"Affirmative." I signed off.

Over the next two watches the ship remained on a steady course for rendezvous with Miningcamp Station. I called up Darla's simulations of the station one more time, reviewing its design. The next morning, about ten hours out, General Kall contacted me again, asking how many men I could evacuate. I temporized; I wanted to hear more about their problems before I agreed to crowd aboard more passengers.

I understood the strain of the miners' lonely vigil. Upheaval

MIDSHIPMAN'S HOPE ≋ 213

on Earth, disaster on Luna, any of a dozen causes could strand them far from home with little chance of survival. Miners, recruited from the dregs of society, were sent out for one five-year shift and no longer. The pressure on the administrators must be nerve-wracking; they had to deal not only with their own anxieties but their surly and sullen miners as well.

Four hours before our scheduled arrival, Pilot Haynes reported for watch. By plan, he had been off for several shifts and was well rested.

"Pilot, you have the conn." My words formally turned the ship over to him for docking maneuvers. Nonetheless, I would remain on the bridge, nervous as a middy on his first watch until *Hibernia* was safely docked. As Captain, I was ultimately responsible for any mishap.

Vax shared the watch, and as a special treat I called Derek forward as well. Elegant and proud in his new blue uniform, middy's stripes freshly sewn, he saluted smartly. "Permission to enter bridge, sir."

"Granted, *Midshipman* Carr."

Derek grinned despite himself.

On the simulscreen we watched Miningcamp's orbiting station drift ever closer. At the moment it was just visible without magnification; we were still two hours from docking.

"I wouldn't care to be one of them, sir," Vax said. He gestured at the dark brooding hulk of Miningcamp planet.

I grunted. "A rough life. Three shifts work around the clock, and they've nothing but barracks to look forward to." I had watched the holovid documentaries.

Derek asked, "How long can they go without supplies, sir?"

"How would I know?" I tried to repress the annoyance in my tone. "On emergency rations, if they cut energy and air waste, probably quite a while."

Vax wondered, "Why are they panicked, then, after only eight months?"

A good question. It was probably the uncertainty; they couldn't know why their supply ship hadn't arrived, or when it ever would. I said as much.

Vax said, "Captain, if we took even a hundred of them, we'd be—"

"You midshipmen are distracting me." The Pilot's tone

was sharp. "Mr. Carr, Mr. Holser." It was petty of him; he wouldn't have anything to do for at least another hour. We fell silent, acknowledging his control of the bridge.

Vax observed me with interest. I suspected the Pilot's remark had been a calculated insult. Though Mr. Haynes had ostensibly addressed Vax and Derek, his "you midshipmen" could well have included me, despite his disclaimer. I wondered why the Pilot was so foolish as to provoke me. Though he'd achieved his immediate goal of reminding me of my origins, he could lose much if I chose to retaliate.

Obviously he knew I had that power; apparently he was still angry enough not to care. I sighed. If I hadn't been so vindictive about his protest in the Log . . . My forehead throbbed with the first stabs of a headache.

At last we began our maneuvers to mate with Miningcamp's orbiting station. The Pilot issued crisp commands, his fingers flying on the console. I constantly rechecked our position from my own screen.

"Steer one hundred thirty degrees, ahead one third."

"One hundred thirty degrees, one third, aye aye, sir." The engine room echoed his commands.

"Declination ten degrees."

"Sir, Miningcamp Station reports locks ready and waiting." Our comm room tech, on the speaker.

"Acknowledged." The Pilot seemed preoccupied, as well he would be. Though we had propellant to spare for docking maneuvers, pride would require him to mate properly on the first pass.

I spent the dreary wait planning our unloading of cargo. The miners would be relieved when our stores of oxygen and fuel were safely in their hands, but not as relieved as I'd be. I rubbed my pulsing temples, stopped when I saw Vax watching.

"Relative speed one hundred kilometers per hour, Pilot." The comm room.

"A hundred kph, understood. Maneuvering jets, brake ten." The station's tiny airlocks waited.

I spoke softly. "Darla, do you have a file on General Kall?" Almost instantly a picture flashed on my screen. He seemed older than his voice. His statistics and service record flashed below the holo.

I supposed I should invite him aboard for dinner. Living as he did under constant tension, he would probably appreciate a formal meal. Still, I was reluctant. Kall was Army, not U.N.N.S., and he would notice my youth and inexperience.

"Relative speed twenty-five kilometers, distance ten kilometers."

"Acknowledged. Brake jets, eighteen." We drifted closer.

The speaker crackled. "Miningcamp Station ready for mating, *Hibernia*."

"Very well." My tone was abrupt. I yearned for the reassuring presence of one of our late lieutenants, hands clasped behind him, supervising my drill. Any of them, even Mr. Cousins.

"Steer one hundred ten, one spurt." The Pilot's whole attention was focused on his screens.

A gentle bump. Console lights flashed. The Pilot had kissed airlocks on his first approach, without need for corrections.

"Very good, Mr. Haynes." I tried not to seem grudging. I keyed the caller. "Mr. Wilsky, join capture latches." I'd posted Sandy at the aft lock, where our guests would enter.

"Aft latches joined, sir."

"Very well. Miningcamp, we'll off-load your supplies shortly. General Kall, would you care to come aboard?" I hoped he'd refuse.

The General seemed on edge. "Just to say hello, perhaps. I'd like to get the supplies planetside before local nightfall."

"Very well, I'll meet you at our aft lock." The Pilot and Alexi could man the bridge during the necessary courtesies. I still hadn't decided whether to offer dinner.

"Roger. My officers and I will be waiting."

"Mr. Tamarov, report to the bridge!" I drummed on the chair arm, organizing my thoughts. After a moment I sent Vax below to supervise at the forward airlock, through which the cargo would be unloaded.

Alexi came onto the bridge, breathing hard. I waved him to a seat, watching the aft lock indicators blink on my console.

We opened our inner airlock hatch. A suited sailor entered the lock. The inner hatch closed, and our precious air was pumped back into the ship.

I granted permission to open the outer lock. The waiting seaman made fast the safety line to the station's stanchion.

Our airlock and Miningcamp's were now tethered by steel cable, as regs required. Ever since *Concorde*'s capture latches had failed, backup lines were mandatory.

Although the mated airlock suckers were airtight, our inner and outer hatches were never opened at the same time; that would invite calamity. When our visitors came aboard, we'd seal the outer hatch before opening the inner one. Standard procedure.

"Aft lock moored to stanchion, sir." Sandy. I recalled my post at *Hibernia*'s lock when we'd cast off from Ganymede Station. Then, I'd been a mere middy, my every move supervised by Lieutenant Malstrom. Months had passed, and now I supervised from the bridge.

"Forward lock moored, sir." Vax Holser.

"Very well." I swallowed bile, tried to settle my churning stomach. Did I need another antiflu shot, or was it just my tension? Nerves, I decided. I couldn't afford to be sick.

"Welcome to Miningcamp." A muffled voice, through the speakers. "Captain Seafort, I have my staff along; perhaps I could introduce them to you." At Miningcamp, visitors were few and far between. General Kall's officers would eagerly await the ceremony, and whatever social amenities followed. I sighed. Perhaps dinner was necessary after all.

"Of course, General." I'd have to change into my starched dress whites. I fidgeted irritably, not looking forward to the formalities.

Sandy, again. "Sir, a party is waiting at the aft lock. About a dozen men, suited. Shall I open?" He sounded young and nervous. I made allowances; he had no lieutenant at his side, as I'd had.

"Let them on, Mr. Wilsky; tell them I'll be down shortly." I set down the caller.

"Aye aye, sir."

Derek said quietly to Alexi, "They're so anxious to meet us they can't even wait—"

"Quiet, middy! One demerit!" Unkind, but I was in no mood for banter. I slapped open the bridge hatch. "Mr. Tamarov, you have the conn." I grimaced. "I'll change clothes, and meet the General at the aft . . ."

I trailed off, my hackles rising. A dozen men, suited? Something was wrong. For an instant I hesitated, reluctant to make a fool of myself. Then I lunged for the console caller. "Sandy, belay that order! Seal the lock! Acknowledge!"

No answer. "Sandy!"

MY SHIP!

I slammed the emergency airlock override on my console. A red light blinked its warning; the override had failed.

I bellowed into the caller. "General Quarters! All hands, prepare to repel boarders! Prepare for decompression! Boarders in the aft airlock, Level 2!"

Alexi and Derek gawked.

"Repel Boarders" was the oldest, most obsolete drill in the U.N. Navy, but still we practiced it, along with General Quarters and Battle Stations. I wondered if it had ever before been used in earnest.

I slapped the emergency hatch close. The bridge hatch snapped shut, with enough force to break the arm of anyone caught in its way. I punched in the safe combination, hauled out a familiar key. "Alexi, open the munitions locker! Arm whoever you can round up! Get an armed party down to Level 2!"

He took the key. "Aye aye, sir! What—"

I snatched the laser pistol from the safe, shoved it in my belt. "The General— He's no General, he's trying to take over the ship! A dozen men in suits? They're expecting trouble, maybe decompression. Move!" I slapped open the hatch; Alexi flew out into the corridor. I shut it after him, raced back to the caller.

"Chief, seal the engine room!"

"Aye aye, Captain. Hatch sealed." His tone was calm.

The speaker blared. "Captain, they've got lasers! They're making for the ladder, we can't—"

Silence.

I keyed my caller to shipwide frequency. "Mr. Vishinsky to Level 2, flank, with your whole squad! Meet Mr. Tamarov at the munitions locker! All passengers, to your cabins! Seal your hatches and put on pressure suits! Mr. Holser, to the aft lock!"

Derek awaited orders, pale but composed. The Pilot gazed at me steadily; he hadn't moved since I first seized the caller. "Captain, are you sure—"

"Shut up." My thoughts raced. We needed time. Until

Alexi organized a fighting party, my laser pistol was the only weapon available. "Derek, hold the bridge. No one but an officer may enter. I'm going to the lock."

"But—aye aye, sir." Derek's hand hovered over the emergency close. I emerged cautiously, fingering my laser, recalling Mr. Vishinsky's example in the crew berth.

The corridor was empty.

I ran toward the ladder. Just in time, I thought to stop and peek over the rail. Two figures in bulky pressure suits were climbing cautiously, weapons ready.

My first shot caught one of them squarely in the chest. A searing flash, the smell of roasting meat. Gagging, I ducked just as a bolt sizzled into the railing at my side.

If they were already on the ladder we were in horrid trouble. All my fault; if I'd had my wits about me I'd never have let them aboard.

I took a deep breath. Vax would be a better Captain than I. I hurled myself around the rail and down the steps, firing as I went. My second shot dropped the other intruder. I leaped over his body, stumbled, almost fell the rest of the way.

I caught myself, staggered to the bottom of the ladder, firing wildly along the corridor. Several suited men retreated around the corridor bend toward the aft airlock.

Heedless, I ran forward, still firing. I would exhaust my laser in no time, but at all costs I had to keep the attackers from advancing until our armed defenders arrived. Return bolts of fire seared the bulkhead a meter from my head. I crept forward toward the bend, caught a glimpse of the airlock, and beyond.

Bodies sprawled in the corridors, some suited. A party of our seamen had thrown up a makeshift barricade in the corridor past the airlock, almost around the far bend. Crouched behind their flimsy barrier of tables, they waited for their assailants, armed with nothing but clubs and the ship's fire hose.

More suited figures emerged from the gaping lock. Only a few had lasers; the rest carried a motley assortment of weapons. Ancient electric rifles, stunners, knives. Steel bars were jammed against our emergency corridor hatches nearest the airlock, to hold them open.

A few men ran at me, clumsy in their heavy suits. I fired.

A lucky shot brought down the closest. The others skidded to a stop. Coolly I aimed at another, pressed the trigger. The pistol beeped: out of charge. I cursed.

Again they came at me. One hurled a billy club directly at my head. I ducked, but it slammed into my forehead in a flash of white fire. Half-blinded, dizzy, I fell to my knees. A cry of triumph. As I reeled, they dashed forward. A club loomed, poised to smash out my brains.

"CAPTAIN!" A raging giant hurled the club-wielder to the deck. Vax Holser recovered his balance, lashed at a second attacker, fist and club flailing with deadly accuracy. The miner fell back.

Vax wheeled on his remaining enemy. The man raised his pistol. Vax's club shattered his suit visor. He dropped.

Dazed, my head on fire, I clawed to my feet.

"That one's the Captain!" Someone pointed. A laser bolt splashed into the bulkhead in a shower of sparks. My knees buckled.

Vax's huge hand closed around my waist. He swept me into his arms and ran for the ladder, bolts sizzling at his feet. My weight an unnoticed burden, he pounded up the ladder toward the bridge two steps at a time. The tread of boots thudded behind us.

"Bridge, I've got the Captain!" Vax's bellow rang in the deserted corridor. The camera swiveled. The hatch slid open. Vax charged onto the bridge.

Derek slapped the hatch shut. The Pilot, halfway between hatch and console, gaped at his semiconscious Captain inert in the enraged middy's arms.

Vax lowered me into my chair. Blood dripped into my right eye; I wiped my forehead on my sleeve.

"Sir, are you—"

I snarled, "Disengage capture latches fore and aft!"

"Sir, we're still— Aye aye, sir." He keyed the console. Usually we parted the latches from the lock control panels, but as on any ship, I could disengage from the bridge.

"Pilot, prepare to rock the ship! Break contact!"

"Sir, we'll decompress!"

"Break us loose! They're still boarding!" My head was spinning, but I knew what had to be done.

"Aye aye, sir! Captain, the safety line is tied. We'll tear the lock right out of the ship!"

"God damn you, Pilot, rock us loose!" The stanchion in *Hibernia* was rated higher than the mooring line; that much I knew. It would hold. The line would snap or it would break the station airlock. I didn't care which.

I grabbed the caller. "All hands, all passengers, be ready for decompression in thirty seconds! Everybody get suited! Thirty seconds to decompress!" More blood oozed down my face. "Fighting parties, withdraw! Get into suits!" Emergency suits were stored throughout the ship for a decompression emergency. They held only half-hour tanks. It would have to be enough.

"Now?" The Pilot's hands were on the controls.

"Wait." The delay was agonizing. Every second allowed more attackers to board us. On the other hand, my crew needed time to suit up.

"Twenty seconds to decompress! . . . Fifteen!" Surely everyone had reached a suit by now. On my console, I slapped shut the corridor hatch switches. Seventeen lights blinked green; two blinked red where the enemy had jammed our hatches. We would decompress not one section, but three. However, the rest of the ship should be airtight, unless stray laser bolts had pierced the bulkheads.

"Ten seconds! Five!" It had to be done, whether or not the passengers were ready. "Beware decompression! Now, Pilot!" He fired the maneuvering jets in alternation, each squirt rocking the ship around the rubber suckers holding the airlocks together. A long terrible moment passed when it seemed we wouldn't break free.

Alarms sounded. Darla came to life with urgent warnings. "Unstable airlock! Air loss in the aft lock! *LEVEL 2 DECOMPRESSION IMMINENT!* Forward lock is sealed, outer and inner hatches! *EMERGENCY! DECOMPRESSION AT AFT LOCK!*"

Cold hell had come to my ship. The mated airlocks broke apart. Outrushing air swept all loose objects toward the aft lock, where the boarding party had blocked both the inner and outer hatches to prevent our closing them. Nothing could hold back the air blasting out of that section until only vacuum remained.

"Ship in motion, relative speed point five kilometers!"

*Lord God, we beg thy mercy.*

"Pilot, sail us clear before they start throwing things at us!" I thumbed the caller. "All stations report!"

"Engine room. We have power, no damage. Seals holding." The Chief, his voice astoundingly matter-of-fact.

"Comm room reporting. Power, no damage."

"Crew berth three, sir. We're suited and ready. Mr. Tamarov is in charge. We've got lasers and stunners, sir."

"Master-at-arms reporting. Crew berths one and two are all right, sir. I'm organizing fighting squads."

"Galley reporting, sir. Everything's all right here." I giggled, unable to stop myself. All was well in the galley; our dinner was safe.

The bridge spun lazily. I blinked, pulled myself together. "Someone get me water. Vax, situation report!"

"Aye aye, sir. On Level 2, sections six, seven, and eight are decompressed. That's the airlock, the exercise room, the lounge, and fourteen passenger cabins. The area is held by hostiles. The rest of the ship has air and power. Undetermined number of boarders in sections six through eight. Sir, some of them may have gotten past the corridor hatches before you closed them."

Vax was right. I'd held the hatches open as long as I dared, for the crew's sake, so as not to trap them in the decompression zone when we rocked loose. The corridor between the airlock and the ladder, where I had fought, was in section eight, now decompressed. The foot of the ladder I had hurtled down was in section nine, and I'd met two invaders on its steps.

I drank greedily from the cup Derek thrust at me. "We'll be alert for them."

"Sir, the passengers are on half-hour tanks. We don't have long to rescue them."

"Lord God." I marshaled my thoughts. "Mr. Vishinsky!"

"Aye aye, sir!"

"Did any boarders from section six get past the barricades in five?"

"No, sir. I wasn't there, but the word is they didn't."

"Very well. You're under Mr. Tamarov's command. Alexi, you and Mr. Vishinsky go the long way around the corridor, to section ten.'' By circling the disk our war party would surround the invaded sections.

"I'll open the hatches in front of you. There may be hostiles in section nine. As fast as you can, secure and evacuate nine. We'll use it as an airlock to section eight; we'll pump air from nine back into ten and then open from nine to eight. Got that?''

"Aye aye, sir.''

"We know hostiles are in six, seven, and eight. Also our own passengers who are running out of air. As soon as nine is pumped out I'll open the hatch to section eight. Clear eight and move on to seven, then six. Bring the passengers back to nine and we'll cycle them back into ten, where they can desuit. Hurry.''

"Aye aye, sir. We're moving!''

"May I go, sir?'' Vax's muscles rippled.

"No. You have to stay alive.'' I wouldn't repeat Captain Malstrom's mistake. Vax was ready now, and I had to preserve him. I pressed a handkerchief to my forehead. I ached abominably.

Our fighting party climbed to Level 2 and circled the circumference corridor. Our airtight hatches had divided the disk into wedge-shaped slices, at either end of every section. In radio contact with the master-at-arms, I opened each hatch as they approached. At last, I opened the hatch from eleven to ten, and the crewmen crowded in.

"Ready, Mr. Vishinsky?''

The speaker crackled. "You there, don't stand in the middle of the corridor! Edwards, Ogar, Tinnik, you're on point. Why don't you stay behind me, Mr. Tamarov, sir. Captain, we're ready.''

I opened to section nine. I could hear Vishinsky shout as he pounded on cabin hatches. "Open up! I'm the master-at-arms. This section will be decompressed in two minutes! Let's go! Everybody forward to the ladder! Open your hatch or we'll burn our way in!''

I thought to help. "Attention, passengers in cabins 208 through 214. This is Captain Seafort. Open your hatches and go into the corridor. You must be evacuated quickly!'' Perhaps the sound of my voice would reassure them. Then again, perhaps not.

A few moments later Vishinsky reported back. "Sir, we've made a quick search, no hostiles found. We've moved the passengers back into section ten. We're waiting in nine."

"Very well." I closed the hatch between nine and ten. I flipped on the pumps and began decompressing nine. "Mr. Carr!"

"Yes, sir." He stood.

"Find the purser. The passengers will need help; some of them may be in shock. Take the section four ladder and go the long way around, to meet them. Bring them to the dining hall. You're in charge."

"Aye aye, sir!" Derek saluted. Vax opened the hatch for him and he hurried out.

I waited impatiently for the pumps to empty section nine. Section eight was already decompressed, its airlock gaping wide. By decompressing nine we'd save the air it held, when the hatch to eight was opened. Finally the pumps completed their work. "Opening to eight, Mr. Vishinsky!"

"Aye aye, sir." We waited, listening intently.

"Look out!" Vishinsky's voice, a scream. "Ogar, zap the son of a bitch!" The attackers didn't have to wield lasers to be dangerous. Any weapon that penetrated a suit was lethal.

The battle was fought in the eerie silence of vacuum, punctuated by grunts and heavy breathing from the suits of our attack party. The snap of the lasers disrupted the suits' radionics when our men fired; it was audible on the bridge as a momentary whine.

"Everyone here, toward the ladder!" Vishinsky's breath came in spurts, as if he'd been running. "Captain, we're herding a group of passengers into nine. Ms. Edwards is with them. All right, they're clear."

"Hostiles?"

"We zapped two, sir. Haven't found any more."

"Right." I closed the hatch between eight and nine. As soon as the console light blinked green I began pumping air from ten back into nine.

Alexi's voice cut in. "Mr. Vishinsky, get your men ready to attack section seven."

"Aye aye, sir."

"Be careful, there's an open airlock in seven," I reminded them. It was a long way down to Miningcamp.

"Open the hatch, sir!" Alexi's nerves were frayed. It sounded like an order. I hit the corridor hatch control.

"Oh, God, Tinnik's hit!"

"Get down, you fool!" A thud. The confused sounds of attack and rescue. Vishinsky ordered passengers out of their cabins to section eight. A maddening delay. Calls of warning, flurries of shots.

The speaker rustled. A distorted voice, from a ship's caller held against a spacesuit visor in vacuum. "Call them off, Captain!"

"Surrender," I said. "You won't be shot."

"Call them off." It was a snarl. "We're in a cabin, and we've got five lasers aimed at the rear bulkhead. If we cut through we'll decompress your whole disk!"

I blanched. "Wait!" Could we have lost, after all?

"Now!"

"You'll have my answer in a moment."

"We want passage from Miningcamp, mister. You give us that, you get your ship back."

"Wait," I said again. I switched off the caller. "God damn them!" For a moment I savored the blasphemy. "Pilot?"

"Work it out with them, sir! Don't let them cut through the ship, we'll end up like *Celestina*!"

Vax swore. "Sir, if—"

"Be silent. Chief, did you hear?"

"Yes, sir." A hesitation, then his reluctant response. "They can do a lot of damage, Captain." Aiming inward from section seven, the invaders could cut through to section three on the opposite side of the disk. From there, they could cut into two and four. In addition, they could aim their lasers up and down to Levels 1 and 3. In half an hour they could render my ship uninhabitable. Except for the fortified bridge.

"I know, Chief. Vax?"

"Offer to return them to the station, sir. It's the best they can get, now. They'll go for it."

I thumbed the caller to the dining hall. "Mr. Carr!"

My midshipman answered in a moment. "Yes, sir?"

"Get everybody back onto suit air, flank," I said. "Break out the oxygen stores. Expect decompression at any moment!"

"Aye aye, sir," he said. "We'll handle it. Don't worry about the passengers." Though his violation of form was scandalous, I was grateful for the reassurance.

"Vax, get on the other caller. Make sure everyone throughout the ship is suited." I thumbed the caller so that it could be heard by our attack party as well as the boarders. "Mister, this is the Captain."

"Yes?" The hint of a sneer.

"No deals. We're ready for decompression. Surrender now or we'll kill every one of you. Mr. Tamarov, burn through the cabin hatches one by one until you find them, then kill them!"

"Aye aye, sir!"

"You'll lose your ship, damn you!"

"You won't be alive to know." I clicked off my caller.

The Pilot jumped to his feet. "Don't! If they cut through to the mess there'll be a bloodbath. They'll kill the passengers."

I said, "The mess is halfway around the disk on the outer side of the circumference corridor. They'll never reach it. I won't bargain with mutineers."

"Captain, I'm warning you! Call them off!" The voice from section seven.

The Pilot was in a frenzy. "Sir, don't make them decompress the ship, or we'll relieve you!"

I turned. "We? Vax?"

"We'll blow your ship!" I ignored the speaker; I had more immediate problems.

Vax fingered his laser. "No, sir. I'm under your orders. Pilot Haynes, sir, you're distracting the Captain." A nice touch, that.

"They won't do anything we can't repair, Mr. Haynes. We're suited and ready for decompression. As soon as they start cutting we'll know exactly where they are. We can—"

"What good is that?" The Pilot's face was purple. "We'll lose all our air!"

"Not all." I turned to the caller. "Get on with it, Mr. Tamarov! Blow any hatches that remain shut!"

"Captain, wait!" The voice on the speaker held a timbre of fear.

"We're not waiting. Try cabin two eighteen, Mr. Tamarov."

"All we want is to get off that place! No supplies, no new air, it's a death trap! Just take us with you!"

I got unsteadily to my feet. "God damn you! Surrender before I count to fifteen, or we'll shoot you dead the moment we find you, whether you're trying to surrender or not! One! . . . Two!"

"Send us back to the station," he said quickly. "Just let us off!"

"Three! . . . Four! . . . Five!"

"We found their cabin, sir! Two twenty!"

"Six! . . . Seven! . . . Eight! Kill them on sight, Mr. Tamarov!"

"Aye aye, sir!"

The Pilot's voice was urgent. "If they've got nothing to lose they'll try to take us with them! They still have time to cut through the bulkheads!"

"Nine! . . . Ten! . . . Eleven!"

"Mister, we don't have to kill each other! Just let us off!"

"Three seconds left. Mr. Tamarov, blow the hatch on my mark. Twelve! . . . Thirteen! . . . Fourteen!"

*"ALL RIGHT!"* A scream.

I sagged into my chair, limbs trembling. I tried to keep my voice steady. "Mr. Tamarov, hold your fire. You men, put your lasers on the deck and unlock your hatch. Stand in the center of the cabin with your hands raised."

"All right! You won't shoot?"

"No, we won't shoot you. Not now, not ever. You have my word. Mr. Tamarov, weapons ready, but hold fire."

"Aye aye, sir. The hatch is opening, sir. I'm going to—"

"Let me, sir." Vishinsky. I smiled; no midshipman would be shot down in Mr. Vishinsky's care. Alexi was in good hands.

The master's growl was ominous. "Face the bulkhead, you scum!"

In a moment the attackers were brought under control and hustled to section eight. Vishinsky's party checked the remaining section seven cabins and found no more invaders. Alexi and two seamen removed the bars blocking the airlock hatches, while Vishinsky moved on to section six, the only zone still not in our hands.

One miner surrendered immediately as soon as the hatch

to six was opened. Two others were found cowering in passenger cabins, using terrified passengers as shields. They surrendered the moment Vishinsky's men arrived.

When our last hatch indicator flashed to green I breathed a sigh of relief. I lay back, my head throbbing. "Re-air all sections." Vax hit the switches on my console. No alarms sounded; *Hibernia* was again airtight. Reserve oxygen from our recycling chamber brought all sections back to full pressure. I ordered our prisoners hauled to the brig.

"Darla, any damage?"

"Some of my corridor wiring is burnt out, Captain." She hesitated. "I have backup channels for all circuits. Air reserves diminished by eleven percent. No other functional damage."

It was over. "Thank God." I slumped in my chair.

"Do you know how lucky we were?" The Pilot lurched to his feet. "You could have killed every man, woman, and child aboard! If they'd blown our air we'd be dead long before we reached Hope Nation. We didn't have enough reserves!"

"Is that your opinion, Pilot?" Lethargic, I was sustained only by a cold knot of anger in my stomach.

"You endangered the entire ship! I insist that my protest be entered in the Log! I demand it, Captain!"

I snapped on the Log and spun it to face him. "Request granted. Enter your protest with your accompanying arguments."

"Aye aye—sir!" He wrote savagely on the holovid screen. I said nothing until he was finished. In a fury he dropped the holovid into my lap.

I read it through. "Do I understand that you protest my reckless disregard of the risk of losing our air, with the consequence of suffocating everybody aboard?"

"Yes! You could have repaired the holes they made, even to the outer hull. But you can't manufacture air!"

"I want your protest made clear. Amend it, to say exactly that."

"Fine with me!" He did so.

"Very well. The time of your protest is entered, along with the date and time of my response." I began to write. "Cargo area forty-one B, east hold. Contents: 795 oxygen and nitrogen cylinders. Destination: Miningcamp."

I tossed the holovid to the console. "We had enough oxygen in the holds to re-air the ship seven times over." Ashen, the Pilot stared at the Log and his damning protest.

"Pilot Haynes, I adjudge you unfit to serve as an officer on *Hibernia*. I relieve you of all duties until such time as my opinion changes. Your rank is suspended. You now travel as supercargo. Until further notice you are confined to quarters except to use the officers' head. Dismissed. Vax, escort him off the bridge."

"Aye aye, sir."

"You can't!"

"I just did. Out!" I thumbed the caller. "Infirmary, have Dr. Uburu stop at the bridge after she attends to the other wounded."

# 20

Work parties were already measuring burned-out hatches for repair and replacement, while others swept debris flung about the Level 2 circumference corridor. On my growled, "As you were," they ignored me.

The savagery of the battle and the vacuum in which it was fought had left few injured. Men were either well, or dead. Bodies lay about, many in the unfamiliar white suits of the U.N.A.F. military. Three of our sailors were among them.

Sandy Wilsky's charred corpse lay in the corridor near the airlock, mouth stretched wide in the rictus of death. His sightless eyes stared mute reproach. I made a sound. Closing my eyes, I recalled my billet at Academy on Luna, tried to transport myself there.

"Come with me, sir." Vax Holser, quiet, solicitous. He touched my arm gently, then more firmly, led me away from the body. He put himself between me and the work parties to shield me from their view. "You're all right, Captain."

"No." My eyes burned; my cheeks were wet. "I'm not.

I never will be. If I weren't so stupid none of this would have happened. I killed him.''

Glancing about, to make sure no one saw, he brushed my forehead lightly with his open palm. "You're all right, Captain," he repeated gently.

I shivered. After a moment I drew myself together. "Come with me." Unsteadily, I walked to the ladder, then down to the brig on Level 3. Mr. Vishinsky himself stood guard over the several small cells. "How many?" My tone was sharp.

"Seven, sir."

"Is Mr. Herney in there?"

"Yes, sir."

"Bring him out." The machinist's mate darted from his opened cell, hands twisting his shirt in anxiety. He stiffened to attention when he saw me. "Mr. Herney, you don't belong in a brig with such as these. Your sentence is commuted. Back to your berth. Behave yourself."

He searched my face, weak with relief. "Aye aye, sir!" He scurried off with the miracle of his deliverance.

"Where is the ringleader?" I asked, in a voice I didn't recognize as my own.

Vishinsky gestured. "In cell one, by himself."

"Unlock it. Both of you, follow me." I entered the tiny cell. The prisoner sat on the deck, hands locked behind him, legs cuffed together. "Cut his clothes off."

Vishinsky glanced at me in surprise but recovered quickly. "Aye aye, sir." He pulled a folding knife from his pocket. The prisoner's eyes widened, but the man said nothing as Vishinsky slashed the seams of his clothing. A moment later the prisoner was hunched naked.

"Stand him up." Vax and the master-at-arms hauled the unnerved man to his feet.

"Mr. Vishinsky, go to cell two. Prepare the next man in exactly the same way and wait there."

"Aye aye, sir."

"Vax, take this." I handed Vax my laser pistol. I stood with my back to the bulkhead, my hand half open in front of my chest. "Mr. Holser, watch my hand. When this man lies, I will move my little finger. Like this. You will immediately shoot him in the face and follow me to the next cell. Say nothing and ask no questions. Simply watch my finger and shoot if it moves. Acknowledge, Mr. Holser.''

Vax swallowed. He was silent a long moment.

"Acknowledge your orders!" My tone was savage.

He hesitated for barely a second. "Orders received and understood, Captain Seafort. I will shoot him in the face when your finger moves, sir.''

I swung to the prisoner. "You're the one who said he was General Kall?''

"Yes.'' The man swallowed, his eyes darting between my hand and Vax's pistol.

"What's your real name?''

"Kerwin Jones.''

"Where is General Kall?''

"On the station. Please don't shoot, I'm telling the truth. Please.''

"He's alive?''

"Yes, sir. He's locked in a suiting room. Some of the joes are holding him with the other officers.''

I twitched my hand the tiniest fraction. The man blanched. "You rebelled?''

"Yes, sir. It's the miners, sir. They were going to kill us all. I worked in the comm room, sir. I'm a civilian. When the supply ships didn't come they got sort of crazy. I had to go along with them, or—''

"How many officers were killed?''

"Just two, sir. It happened so fast. We had to find a way off the station, don't you see?''

"What's happened planetside?''

"The miners took over. They're holding the U.N.A.F. as prisoners, I think. The committee has control of the shuttle, they come up every day or so to keep an eye on things.'' I looked at my finger. "It's the truth, sir,'' he blurted. "I swear by Lord God Himself! Please believe me.'' He turned to Vax. "Don't shoot, for the love of God!''

"Mr. Vishinsky!'' In a moment the master-at-arms came into the cell. "This man may cooperate. Question him. I want to know about the miners' committee and when they shuttle to the station. Also the station layout. If he lies—if his story is any different from those other three—break off immediately and call me.''

I left. Vax followed.

As we walked back to the bridge Vax asked, "Sir, what would you have done if he'd lied?" I stopped, twitched my finger. He shuddered.

"Take the pistol out of your belt. Aim it at the deck." Vax complied, troubled. "Burn through the deck plates. That's an order."

"Aye aye, sir." With a dubious glance Vax tightened his finger on the trigger. The pistol beeped, indicating its empty charge. I held out my hand. He placed the pistol in it. I went to the bridge.

Hours passed quickly. Crews were busy tracing and splicing electrical connections where lasers had burned our wiring. Derek and Alexi soothed frightened passengers and escorted them back to their cabins, helping with the cleanup.

Three of our passengers had been killed by the intruders. Two more had died from decompression, unable to get into their suits in time. Among them was Sarah Butler, the pleasant young lady who had shared my table.

Three of our enlisted men were dead. And one officer.

All in all, we were lucky it hadn't been more. Fortunately, the invaders aimed to take over *Hibernia*, not destroy her. Sandy had tried to slap shut the airlock control; they'd burned him where he stood. If his clothing hadn't caught in the lock panel, he'd have been swept out in the decompression when I broke the ship free. The other crewmen who'd died were among our fighting parties.

On the bridge, I sat next to Vax in my soft armchair, trying to come to terms with my folly. It is always too late to do the obvious. Sandy's accusing, sightless face floated just beyond my reach. I wondered if I would ever be free of it.

I thumbed the caller. "Mr. Carr, Mr. Tamarov. Report to the bridge."

In a few moments the midshipmen strode in, came to attention. I released them. "Plot our course back to the station. A bow-on approach to their upper airlock from two kilometers out. Check your coordinates against Darla's solution." They scrambled to work, while I sat brooding. Vax watched with concern from the first officer's seat.

A thought surfaced. "Vax, where's Cadet Fuentes?"

"In the mess helping Mr. Browning."

"How'd he end up there?"

"He was with me at the forward lock when trouble broke out. I sent him to guard the wardroom."

"Ah." The wardroom on Level 1 didn't need guarding, and the puny cadet was hardly fit to protect it. Vax had sent Ricky out of harm's way.

Vax reddened. "Yes, sir. After things calmed down I called him to help Mr. Browning."

"Very well." I was glad of it. I'd killed enough children this day.

The midshipmen brought me a course plot; I had Vax check it. This time, for once, I would rely on their calculations. My head ached despite Dr. Uburu's healing salve, or perhaps because of it.

We fired bursts of auxiliary engine power to return us to Miningcamp Station. Lethargic, I let Vax take the conn. After an hour we fired our retro thrusters to avoid overshooting.

It was time. I picked up the caller, feeling foolish. When had the order I was going to give been heard on a U.N. vessel, except in drill?

"All hands to Battle Stations!" I hit the klaxon; the horn blared insistently.

Throughout the ship men and women streamed to their duty stations from the crew berths, from the head, from mess hall, from the repair crews. All nonessential systems were abruptly shut down. Hydroponics and recyclers were set to automatic. Every instrument in the engine room was double staffed, as the engine room crew brought the full potential of our fusion engines on-line to power *Hibernia*'s lasers.

The comm room was crowded with ratings manning their instruments, watching for hostile laser or missile fire. Laser defense crews stood ready. Special ports in *Hibernia*'s nose were opened to deploy the gossamer shields designed to deflect incoming lasers.

I knew our laser shields were an unnecessary precaution, as orbiting stations weren't fitted with laser cannon. Miningcamp Station, sixty-three light-years from Earth and six from Hope Nation, was visited only by Naval ships; no other vessels sailed interstellar. Who would attack Miningcamp?

My caller was set to approach frequency. "Attention Miningcamp Station. This is U.N.S. *Hibernia*, Captain Nicholas Seafort commanding. Acknowledge!''

After a moment the speaker came to life. "We read you."

"I will open fire in two minutes unless you surrender unconditionally. Where is General Kall?"

The speaker was silent for several seconds. "Prong yourself, joey!"

"In one and three-quarter minutes I will open fire. I will cut through your hull about twenty meters to either side of the upper airlock. Expect decompression."

I could hear a muffled commotion behind their caller. A new voice answered. "Go ahead and decompress us! Your General will be in the airlock along with the rest of the officers."

"I really don't care. They'll blame you, not me."

Vax sucked in his breath. I touched the laser activation release but did not depress it. "Fire control, stand by. Either side of their airlock."

"Aye aye, sir."

"We'll kill them all!" The voice rasped in the speaker.

"One minute left. After decompression, I'll give you another minute before I cut the station into small pieces. I'll start with your comm room."

"You wouldn't dare! The station is worth billions; they'll hang you!"

My voice was very strange. "I know. It's what I'm hoping. Forty-five seconds." I depressed the laser release.

"You're crazy!"

"And you'll be dead. In a moment."

Darla said urgently, "Incoming laser at low power! Erratic beam."

"What in hell?" Miningcamp was supposed to be unarmed.

"Shields fully deployed. Beam within shield capacity."

I looked to Vax. "A cutting tool? Hand lasers strung to fire together?"

Vax shrugged, his mind on more pressing matters. "Captain, please don't blow the station."

I thumbed the caller. "Thirty seconds!" To Vax, "Sorry, Mr. Holser." We drifted toward the station airlock, lasers powered and ready to fire.

"Fifteen seconds!" My voice was tight. "Trusting in the goodness and mercy of Lord God eternal, we commit your bodies to the deep—"

"Oh, my God." Vax, in a whisper.

"—to await the day of judgment when the souls of man shall be called forth before Almighty Lord God—"

"Wait, don't shoot!" I could smell their fear.

"Commence firing!"

I watched in the simulscreen. A piece of hull plating near the airlock sagged.

"Hold your fire; we surrender!" A scream.

"Comm room, hold fire!" I deactivated the laser. "Station, acknowledge your unconditional surrender!"

A different voice. "Look, mister. We've lost, we know that. But if we surrender now you'll kill us, or they will. We want amnesty."

"No." It was final.

"Our freedom for the station. A trade."

"No."

"Our lives, then! No death sentence. Otherwise go ahead and wreck the station; we have nothing to lose!"

He was right. It took only a few seconds to decide. "I agree. As representative of the Secretary-General of the United Nations I commute any penalty of death you would be given. No death sentences will be imposed on you. I give my word."

"For the General too?"

"My guarantee, for all U.N. forces." Vax put his head in his hands. I had legal authority to make such a pledge but it wouldn't be well received at Admiralty. Not well at all.

"Give me a minute. Please. I have to talk to the others."

"Very well." Vax and the other middies breathed almost imperceptibly while I watched the clock.

Two minutes. "Time's up. I'll fire in fifteen seconds."

"We surrender! We'll take the deal!"

"Very well. Suit up. Release your officers, then go into your airlock and open the outer hatch. You have three minutes."

It took them five. I floated *Hibernia* as close as I dared. Then I had a sailor in a thrustersuit take a cable across to their airlock. I made the rebels swing across the line hand over hand to our own lock. One by one we took them in, fifteen of them. Mr. Vishinsky and his waiting crew brandished laser pistols, hoping for an excuse to use them.

Some hours later General Friedreich Kall sat in my cabin, an untouched drink by his arm. He was a heavyset, florid man of sixty. He flatly refused to honor my agreement, and demanded the mutineers' return. They would be tried and hanged. We glowered at each other.

I shrugged. "You act as if you have a choice." I thumbed the caller. "Mr. Holser, report to the Captain's cabin, to escort General Kall off the ship."

"I'm not subject to your orders!"

"No, but you're on my ship. As soon as we're done off-loading your supplies I'll be on my way."

"What about the rebels?"

"They go with me, for protection."

"They're under my authority! You can't!" He flung himself to his feet.

"Watch me." It was easy, once I no longer cared about consequences. My tone was blunt. "General Kall, you're an ass. Write your objections into my Log and your own Daybook. Then get off my ship."

"You'd let mutineers go free, you traitor?" He was out of control.

Vax knocked on my cabin hatch. "Free?" I said as I opened it. "Hardly. They'll be tried and convicted. They'll probably wish they were dead before their sentences are up. But we won't hang them."

"How do you expect me to hold my command if you treat them with such leniency?"

"I don't," I said evenly. "I expect you to lose it again before we return."

He crumpled, slumped heavily into the seat. "Do you know what this means on my service record? Losing the station to a bunch of civilians? I'm through."

I signaled Vax to wait, shut the hatch again. "Not necessarily. You've got your station back. You still have problems planetside. Your record will include how you handle them."

"You think so?" He looked up hopefully. "Bah. They despise weakness."

"Who? The miners or U.N. Command?"

"Both. And me. I despise weakness too."

"Accept the deal I gave them, and I'll stay in the vicinity to back you up. My lasers can target the surface if necessary. My report will show I watched you reassert control on your own." I was becoming a dealmaker. If I couldn't lead, I'd negotiate.

After much argument, he reluctantly went along with me. I saw him off the ship, transferred the fifteen rebels to his custody, and withdrew the ship a thousand kilometers to a parking orbit.

I had three more chores.

We packed the circumference corridor at the forward airlock, officers, sailors, passengers. The flag-draped alumalloy coffins rested in the lock behind me. I read from the Christian Reunification service for the dead.

In my cabin, donning my dress whites and adjusting the black mourning sash over my shoulder, I'd resolved to complete the ritual. My voice would stay level, I wouldn't tremble. I had already determined that. Now I only had to carry it out.

I began flatly, "Ashes to ashes, dust to dust . . ." Sandy sat in his bunk absolutely still, waiting for Vax to allow him to move. "Man that is born of woman . . ." Sandy held his orchestron above Ricky's reaching hand, grinning.

My voice quavered. I bit off my words. I was as much to blame for Sandy's death as the wretches in our brig. "Trusting in the goodness and mercy of Lord God eternal, we commit their bodies to the deep . . ."

A dozen men in spacesuits, and I'd allowed them aboard? Better I had resigned my commission the day Captain Malstrom died. Sandy's contorted face stared past me. I felt the scorched fabric of his uniform. I touched the blistered hole in his chest. Only a few more words and it would be done.

Sandy was barely sixteen. Yesterday his whole life had been before him. He'd wolfed down his breakfast in the mess. He'd sat joking with us at lunch. He washed. He smiled. He stood his watch. Now, because of me, his remains were in a cold metal box. "To await the day of judgment when the souls of man shall be called forth before Almighty Lord God . . . Amen."

I had managed to finish the service. I glanced at Vax. His

shoulders shook silently, his eyes red from weeping. I smiled bitterly. Vax, who had tormented Sandy in the wardroom, was devastated by his death while I, his protector, had no tears to shed.

"Petty Officer Terrill, open the outer lock, please." I waited.

"Eject the caskets, Mr. Terrill." Slowly, the coffins receded into the dark.

Two more chores.

As I trudged to the bridge a figure blocked my path. I looked up. Amanda. "They say your courage saved the ship. Thank you . . . Nicky."

"They were mistaken," I said, my voice flat. "Excuse me."

Back on the bridge I issued orders. "Derek, Alexi, plot our course to Hope Nation. Vax, have Mr. Vishinsky bring the prisoners to the bridge, securely cuffed."

"Aye aye, sir." My heart pounding, I stared at my screen. I could hear Alexi and Derek tap at their consoles. Soon. It would be over soon enough.

"Message from Miningcamp, sir. All resistance has ceased."

"Very well."

The seven men stood in a line along the bulkhead, hands cuffed behind their backs, their feet chained together. Still, Vax and the master-at-arms carried stunners.

"Darla, record these proceedings." Her videorecorders lit. "By authority of the Government of the United Nations I charge you with piracy in that you assaulted U.N.S. *Hibernia*, a Naval Service vessel lawfully under weigh. I charge you with murder in that you killed nine persons while attempting to board and seize the vessel. I call a court-martial and appoint myself hearing officer. Do you deny the facts charged, or do you admit them with an explanation of your conduct? Speak in turn."

One by one, mumbling, the captives acknowledged that they had tried to seize the ship. Kerwin Jones, the ringleader, watched me warily.

"If you have any mitigating statements, give them now."

Their stories came tumbling out. When the supply ships stopped coming their fears had grown rampant. Wild rumors swept the mines. General Kall had done little to reassure them. They had no contact with the civilized world. Under intolerable pressure, they'd panicked.

I listened impassively. When they were done I said, "Having heard the evidence and mitigating statements I find you guilty of piracy and of the murders of a Naval officer, three enlisted men, and five passengers. For these crimes I sentence you to death at the Captain's convenience. Court adjourned."

Jones shouted at me, "You promised! You gave your word we wouldn't be killed!"

"I said no such thing."

"You swore it!"

"Darla, playback, please."

A second later my voice sounded on the speaker. "No, we won't shoot you. Not now, not ever. You have my word."

"Thank you, Darla. I'll keep my promise. We won't shoot you. Mr. Vishinsky, take these men back to the brig, then to the infirmary, one by one. Interrogate them to find who shot Mr. Wilsky."

Hours passed. Vax tried several times to speak to me; each time I ordered him silent. The Doctor finished her polygraph and drug interrogations. I issued my orders.

The master-at-arms, the Chief, Vax, and several seamen assembled at the plank across the fusion shaft. We faced six bound and gagged prisoners. I dispassionately pulled the dolly aside for each hanging. When the grisly task was done I dismissed the sailors.

One more chore.

"Mr. Holser, take the bridge. Chief, evacuate Level 2, sections six, seven, and eight, and post sentries to bar the corridor hatches to those sections. Mr. Vishinsky, come with me to the brig."

The seventh prisoner, the man who had lasered Sandy, paced helplessly, his hands bound behind him. "Mr. Vishinsky, wait here." My voice was dull.

"Aye aye, sir."

I took the prisoner's arm, led him out of the brig along the corridor, up the ladder to Level 2. The sentry at section eight saluted and stood aside. I propelled the captive into the deserted section. Then, past the bend in the corridor to the airlock.

I pressed my transmitter to the hatch control. The inner hatch slid open. I took the prisoner into the lock.

"What are you doing?" His face was wild.

I didn't answer. Holding his shoulder I kicked his leg out from under him. He slipped to the deck. I pushed him into a sitting position. Then I turned to the inner lock.

"No! God, don't!" He scrambled desperately to his feet. I stood in the hatchway. He ran at me.

I shoved him violently back; he sprawled on the airlock deck, hands cuffed behind him. I stepped out into the corridor and pressed my transmitter to the inner lock control. The hatch slid shut. In a frenzy, he threw himself against the transplex hatch, rebounding from its unyielding surface.

Again I brought my transmitter to the panel. I pressed the key. The outer lock slid open. I watched the grisly contents of the chamber swirl into space as the chamber decompressed.

After a few moments I walked slowly onto the bridge. "Fusion coordinates?"

"Here, sir." Alexi displayed them on his console. He swallowed several times, managed not to catch my eye.

"Darla?"

She flashed her figures. They matched.

"Engine room, prepare to Fuse."

In a moment, the reply. "Prepared to Fuse, sir. Control passed to bridge."

I slid my finger up the screen. The simulscreens blanked. "Mr. Holser, you have the watch." I slapped open the hatch, left the bridge.

I sealed my cabin hatch behind me. In the dim light I took off my jacket. I sat, my arms resting on the table. I began to tremble. Dispassionately I wondered how quickly I would go insane. Knowing I could not be heard I filled my lungs and screamed at the top of my voice. It left my throat raw.

I looked through the outer bulkhead along the hull. "Come, Mr. Tuak," I whispered. "I'm ready for you." I knew that this time he'd bring Sandy with him.

# PART II

November 20, in the year
of our Lord 2195

# 21

October came, then November. I spent day after day alone in my cabin. Food was brought. Sometimes I ate it. Occasionally I stood watch; more often I removed myself from the watch roster. From time to time I sat at dinner with the passengers at the dining hall; more often, I couldn't bear the thought of their conversation and remained in my bunk.

Twice, Mr. Tuak came for me, but even in my dreams I was unafraid. He never pulled me through the bulkhead, and when I tried to follow him he stopped coming.

One day I went to the bridge and found Vax half asleep in his seat. He started when I stood over him, his eyes widening in shock and fear. "I'm sorry, sir," he stammered, "it's . . . I—" His face turned deep red.

"It's all right." I took my own seat. There were only four of us to stand watch, and by removing myself from the roster I'd left only three. No wonder he was exhausted. "I'll start taking my turn again." Day after day I endured the silence of the bridge until I was free to return to the solitude of my cabin.

On one of the rare evenings I appeared in the dining hall, I was accosted after the meal. "Captain, we'd like to talk to you." Rafe Treadwell, now turned thirteen. I presumed the "we" included his sister.

I took them to my cabin. Rafe spoke first, standing shoulder to shoulder with Paula. "Captain, you need midshipmen."

"You're telling me how to run my ship?" My tone was bleak.

"No, sir, just stating a fact," he said calmly. "When we sailed, you had three lieutenants, four midshipmen, and a Pilot. Now you have three midshipmen and a cadet. You need more help."

"You're volunteering?"

"No, sir, we decided someone ought to stay with Mom and Dad. Paula's the one who's volunteering."

"Oh?"

She said, "Yes, sir. I'm better at math, anyway."

"This isn't Academy, young lady. I can't raise children to be middies."

"You took Derek."

"He's sixteen, almost grown. You were thirteen just a few weeks ago."

"So? At my age we learn faster." She added, "When you took us to the bridge I knew right away. That's what I want to do."

"And your parents?"

"Oh, they're against it," she said blithely. "But they'll get over it."

"Would they consent?"

"Not in a million years," Rafe said. "But you don't need their consent. You told us so yourself."

I glowered at them, to no effect. I needed midshipmen; Vax was ready for lieutenant's insignia. And though he didn't know it, Alexi would soon be, too. But to shanghai children, as Mrs. Donhauser put it . . . I had enough problems without that. And we weren't that far from port, where I would be replaced. "Thank you, but no. Not without your parents' consent."

Paula's tone was flat. "You're afraid of my parents, Captain? I thought you weren't a coward."

I yearned to slap her. "Shut up, young lady."

"I will. If you don't have the guts to sign me up, I don't want to be under your command." She folded her arms.

That did it. She needed discipline as much as I needed midshipmen. An even trade; her parents be damned. "You're sure? You know what cadets go through?"

"I know." She looked worried for a moment, then shrugged. "If other joeys can take it, I can."

"It's harder for a girl. Not many women serve on ships."

"Lieutenant Dagalow did."

"Yes." Naval policy barred discrimination, and officially none existed, but wardroom life could nonetheless be particular hell for a woman. On the other hand, I knew Vax and Alexi well, and they wouldn't let hazing get too far out of hand.

"You two are willing to be separated?"

They exchanged glances; Rafe nodded slightly. Paula said, "We won't like it, but we're willing."

"Repeat after me," I said. "I, Paula Treadwell, do swear on my immortal soul . . ."

"I, Paula Treadwell . . ." A moment later I had another cadet.

She took the fifth bunk, in the center of the wardroom; Ricky Fuentes moved up to Sandy's bunk along the wall. The wardroom would remain crowded. Derek especially would learn new lessons about modesty in the Navy. I didn't really care. I was counting weeks and days, waiting for the end.

"Lord God, today is December 31, 2195, on the U.N.S. *Hibernia*. We ask you to bless us, to bless our voyage, and to bring health and well-being to all aboard." This time I remained standing. "Ladies and gentlemen, by the Grace of God it has been a tragic and trying year. Our friends and comrades, though absent, travel with us in spirit. I look forward, as do you, to landfall at Hope Nation, and on this last night of this fateful year I ask Lord God's especial blessing to heal the wounds occasioned by our misfortunes."

I sat. Grudgingly at first, they joined in the "Amen." When the last murmurs had subsided I signaled the steward to begin.

Only three now sat at my table. Mrs. Donhauser, Mr. Ibn Saud, and, of all people, Amanda Frowel. "Nicky, let me sit with you. What they're doing is unfair and wrong. I want to show I'm not a part of it."

It took courage for my three companions to stay with me. Jared and Irene Treadwell had gone nearly berserk after their daughter took the oath. At first they claimed I had no authority to enlist her. They invaded officers' country to reclaim her and had to be physically restrained. Then they circulated a petition demanding Paula's discharge which every single passenger signed, including the three who now sat with me. I didn't mind that, but when the Treadwells started circulating an appeal among the crew I'd had enough. I passed the word that any crewman who signed or even discussed a petition with them would spend the rest of the cruise in the brig, and sent the Chief to warn the Treadwells to leave the crew alone or they too would see the inside of a cell.

They disrupted evening meals and had to be physically ejected from the dining hall. Then came the day the Treadwells accosted Paula and forced her back to their cabin. Vax and a party of seamen had to dismantle their hatch to rescue the embarrassed cadet.

Their agitation continued until, a week ago, Rafe Treadwell was heard warning his parents that unless they let Paula be, he too would enlist. After that the Treadwells became more circumspect; perhaps they had learned something about their children's resolve.

I continued to make myself unbearable on the bridge. I drilled the midshipmen in navigation and pilotage without cease. I sent Derek to be caned for some impatience I detected in his tone, and ignored the simmering fury he exhibited for days afterward. I chewed out Alexi regularly until he was so agitated he could barely handle a watch. My off-duty hours were spent alone in my cabin; I had long since packaged the Chief's pipe and tobacco and sent them to him without comment.

One day I decided to give Alexi an unscheduled navigation drill. Our middies had to be more skillful than I was, should fate put the safety of a ship in their hands. I called the wardroom but no one answered. It was understandable that Alexi would be elsewhere; it was more unusual for no one to be there at all. Curious and suspicious, I sealed the bridge and went to look, shrugging off my serious breach of regulations in leaving the bridge unattended.

The three midshipmen and two cadets were nowhere to be found. I searched officers' country, the lounges, the exercise room. I checked the galley, the mess halls. I went down to crew quarters. I even peered into the engine room.

Convinced I had an intrigue on my hands, I prowled the ship trying to imagine where the middies might be. Were they conspiring in the hold beyond the launch berth? I passed through the lock to the empty berth. The hatch slid open. Shouts and laughter, in the dim standby lights.

"Look out!" An object sailed toward me. I ducked. It splattered on my chest, and I was drenched in icy water head to waist. I spluttered with rage.

In an instant I grasped the situation. Piles of water balloons lay about. The middies and cadets, wet uniforms sticking to their limbs, carried armfuls of missiles as they stalked each other.

"Oh, Lord God! The Captain!" The figures froze in horror.

*IT DIDN'T HAPPEN!* If I acknowledged what I saw, I would have to act. I didn't want to act, therefore it didn't happen. I would ignore it. I turned to leave, but the water squished in my shoe and my intent changed abruptly. I dialed down the light until the berth was nearly dark. "Hostile attack, Vax! I'm unarmed! Situation critical!"

It took him only a second to react. He lobbed a couple of water balloons at me. I caught them and rounded on the nearest middy, who happened to be Derek. "Surrender!" I caught him in square in the face. He squawked and fell back, spitting ice water. I wheeled on Ricky, across the room. "Attack your betters, will you?" I stalked him.

Alexi was the first who was brave enough to fire at me intentionally. After that it degenerated into a wild melee that ended only after the huge piles of water balloons were exhausted. By that time all the middies and their Captain had turned on the two hapless cadets and bombarded them into submission from all sides.

I leaned against the bulkhead guffawing. After a while I feared I wouldn't be able to stop. I brought myself under control and faced the grinning middies. "What a breach of regs! For punishment I order you to mop the place up, every inch of it. Acknowledge!"

"Aye aye, sir!" They acknowledged my command with unfeigned delight. I began wondering how I might get to my cabin to change clothes without being seen. I wasn't aware yet that my funk had finally lifted and I could now face each day, if not cheerfully, then at least unafraid.

Once more, I began to take interest in my duties.

The Pilot asked again to see me. For months I had ignored his requests, but now I decided to evade him no longer. I went to his cabin. I hadn't laid eyes on him in four months; his appearance shocked me. Gaunt, his eyes red-rimmed and sunken, he came quickly to attention. I released him.

He licked his lips. "Now I'm finally talking to you I don't know how to begin." I waited uncomfortably. He turned away, hugged himself as if from cold. "Captain, if you don't restore me to duty before we dock, I'm finished. It—it's my life, the Navy. It's all I have."

He glanced at my face. "Jesus, how old are you, eighteen? How can you understand? Nothing's the same when you get older. Sounds aren't as sharp; the edges of your hearing have gone. Colors don't seem as bright. Even food doesn't taste as good. Nothing smells or tastes or feels as alive as when you were young, when you thought your mind would overload from the sheer pleasure of the sensations . . ." He trailed off, his eyes distant.

"I may not be a good officer—" He swallowed and began again. "Captain, I know I'm not a good officer, not really. But I'm good at pilotage. Very good." I nodded my acknowledgment.

"When I'm at the conn I feel the—aliveness again. I sense the instruments, the thrusters, through my fingers, with the intensity I could feel elsewhere when I was younger. Can you imagine what it is to face losing that? Please! I don't know how to beg, but I'm trying."

I couldn't stand much more of that; he sounded like the late Mr. Rogoff. "I'm not asking that, Mr. Haynes."

He said, "I can be a very good pilot. At the conn, that is. For the rest of it, I can try harder. If that's not good enough . . ." He broke off. "I'm too old to start at something else. For the love of Lord God, Captain, don't leave me to rot!"

"Those protests in the Log? Telling us middies to be quiet because we distracted you?"

He whispered the words. "Arrogance. I can't afford it anymore. When you get down to it, this is all I am." His eyes glistened. "I sail starships. I maneuver, I dock, I plot courses, calculate positions. I can live without my pettiness and my arrogance—oh, God, I'll have to—but I can't live without that!"

"You've been thinking a great deal, Mr. Haynes."

"I don't want to live, if I can't be a pilot." He swallowed.

"Please," he said, his tone humble. "Give me back my life. I'll mind my own business, I swear. No protests, no remarks, no looks of disgust. I've learned what matters. Pilotage is important. Nothing else."

I was moved. "We don't like each other, Mr. Haynes. That can't be helped. But we don't have to. Very well. Your rank is restored. I'll put you back on the watch roster. We'll see how it goes."

He closed his eyes in relief. "Thank you," he whispered. Bile rose in my throat. I had broken him. I felt unbearably ashamed.

# 22

In a few days we would Defuse for our final navigation check before arrival at Hope Nation.

I was running out of time; there was one more thing I had to do before I turned over command to my replacement. On afternoon watch, I assembled the officers on the bridge. Chief McAndrews, the Pilot, the midshipmen, and the cadets waited, perplexed. I called Vax Holser forward. He stood stiffly at attention as I faced him.

"Darla, record these proceedings." Her recorders lit. "Mr. Holser, step forward. I, Captain Nicholas Seafort, do commission Midshipman Vax Stanley Holser to the Naval Service of the Government of the United Nations"—thunderstruck, his face lit with unalloyed joy—"and do appoint him lieutenant, by the Grace of God."

It was done. My own rank as Captain was subject to confirmation or revocation by Admiral Johanson, but the commissions and appointments I made were not. Unlike the old oceanic navy, field commissions were permanent. Admiralty would accept Vax's lieutenancy regardless of its wisdom. To do less would cast doubt on a Captain's boundless authority under weigh.

Vax, grinning foolishly, accepted the handshakes and congratulations of the other officers. I noticed Alexi's bemused expression. It must have occurred to him that he'd just become first midshipman, in charge of the wardroom.

The new lieutenant took the cadets to help carry his gear to his cabin. It was a relaxed moment; the rest of us chatted before dispersing. "Well, Mr. Carr." My tone was genial. "Are you planning to challenge your new senior?"

His look was cool. "Perhaps, sir. If occasion warrants." My smile faded. He wasn't about to forgive me for sending him to the barrel in a moment of irritation. I wondered if I could make amends. Probably not. Derek could forgive much, but not that unjustified humiliation.

A few days later I brought the ship out of Fusion. Alexi plotted our position and ran the coordinates for our last jump, under the Pilot's watchful eye. Mr. Haynes said little. When the figures were presented I laboriously recalculated everything from scratch. It was a good day; I finished in less than half an hour. At last, all our figures matched. We Fused again.

Alexi relaxed with a sigh of relief.

"Not so fast, Mr. Tamarov." I indicated the screens. "Darla, simulate Hope Nation approach, please." I thumbed the caller. "Chief, simulated Defuse and maneuvers. Middy drill." I turned back to the midshipman. "Alexi, bring the ship out of Fusion and dock her." I had failed miserably at the same maneuver eons ago under the tutelage of Captain Haag and Lieutenant Dagalow.

"Aye aye, sir." Alexi studied the console. "Engine room, prepare to Defuse." With confidence, he ran his finger down the screen. My envy grew as I watched him work easily through the complicated maneuver, firing his auxiliary engines, maneuvering to mate with Orbit Station. At the finish he tapped lightly on the braking thrusters, and the airlocks gently kissed. In simulation we were at rest, mated to Orbit Station.

If it weren't for a barely perceptible sheen of sweat on his forehead I'd have thrown him bodily off the bridge.

"Very well, Mr. Tamarov. That's all." As he started to rise I reluctantly gave him his due. "Alexi, a fine job. Very good."

He grinned with pleasure. "Thank you, sir. Thanks very much!"

"How do you like being first middy?"

"I like it a lot," Alexi said. Then he added shyly, "I'm trying to be like you were, sir."

At first I felt a pleasant glow. Then my anger rose. Why in the name of heaven would he want to be like me?

An air of excitement, a feeling of goodwill, pervaded the ship; our interminable voyage was finally nearing an end. All that remained was to Defuse at the rim of Hope Nation system and maneuver to Orbit Station. Then, disembarkation.

Most of the passengers had a good idea what awaited them; they'd planned their trip for years and had careers, prospects, opportunities already arranged. I wondered what my future held. A court of inquiry, certainly, and probably a court-martial; the deaths of crew and passengers and the invasion of my ship made it a near certainty.

I wondered if I'd ever see deep space again. On the other hand, it didn't much matter. I'd come to know I had no gift for command. My hitch would be up by the time I was sent back to Luna, once again a midshipman.

I didn't intend to reenlist. It was one thing to contemplate life in space as a successful career officer in the star fleet; it was quite another to pass my life in a dead-end berth as a midshipman. Well, I was ahead of myself. Who knew if they'd even let me remain a middy? There was Sandy Wilsky to account for, along with my other follies.

Evening meals in the dining hall were almost jolly. Several passengers asked to join the Captain's table; I preferred to dine with the few who had sat with me through my isolation. Amanda and I didn't confide as once we had, but she was civil and occasionally even smiled.

Poor Amanda. The same unyielding rectitude that had forced her to abandon me also made her side with me to protest the other passengers' ingratitude. By her lights I had saved the ship, not almost lost it. She was a victim of her skewed sense of justice.

The night before our final Defuse she waited outside the dining hall. "Nick, I don't want to leave it . . . like this." Her voice was gentle. "With the strain between us."

Being close to her made me uncomfortable; I moved back a step. "I'm still a murderer. Even more now than before."

She blushed. "Yes, I said that, and I suppose I still mean it. But people are more complex than I was willing to admit. You did what you thought you must, and you're still Nick Seafort."

I said coldly, "Thank you. There were times when I wondered."

"Oh, Nicky." She put her hand on my arm. "It must have been horrible."

"I've been"—I thought of putting her off, then chose honesty—"very lonely. Sometimes."

"I'm sorry. I wish you well."

"That's all that's left?" Wounded, I turned to go. She still had the power to hurt.

"I do care for you!" she cried to my retreating back. I stopped. "How I wish it could have been different, Nicky. I missed you too!"

"But it wasn't." I managed a small smile. "I wish you well also, Amanda. Good-bye."

"Come see me in Hope Nation," she said impulsively. "You'll be in port for weeks." After cruising interstellar for more than six months, crew and officers alike were entitled to four weeks of shore leave. The regs were firm on that, and I agreed. Our men were enlistees, not prisoners.

I nodded assent. "All right. I'll look you up." If I wasn't under arrest pending court-martial. On that note we parted.

The next morning I had the watch, with Lieutenant Vax Holser. The Pilot was also present, waiting for his moment.

"Bridge to engine room, prepare to Defuse."

"Prepare to Defuse, aye aye." Chief McAndrews was ready, as always. "Engine room ready for Defuse, sir. Control passed to bridge."

"Passed to bridge, aye aye." I traced the line on the screen from "Full" to "Off". Once again the simulscreens came alive with a blaze of lights.

"Confirm clear of encroachments, Lieutenant." Whenever possible I used Vax's title rather than his name, to help him settle in.

"Clear of encroachments, sir."

"Plot position, please, Lieutenant." I noticed the Pilot

quietly doing likewise. He would not dock *Hibernia* under someone else's calculations. After a few minutes the two men checked their coordinates with each other and with Darla.

"Auxiliary engine power, Chief," I said.

"Aye aye, sir. Power up."

"Pilot Haynes." My tone was formal. "You have the conn."

, "Aye aye, sir. Steer oh three five degrees, ahead one-third."

"One-third, aye aye, sir." Our last jump had placed us within a few hours of Hope Nation and its Orbit Station. The planet gleamed bright and welcoming in our simulscreens, bringing a lump to my throat.

The watch changed, but I remained on the bridge, my thoughts fastened on what might have been.

Hours later, my long reverie was interrupted. "Sir, Orbit Station reports locks ready and waiting." The comm room.

"Confirm ready and waiting, understood." The Pilot was busy at his console.

"Relative speed two hundred ten kilometers per hour, sir." Vax, to the Pilot.

"Two hundred ten, understood. Maneuvering jets, brake ten."

I picked up my caller. "Comm room, patch me to Orbit Station."

A pause. "Go ahead, sir, you're patched through."

"*Hibernia* calling Orbit Station."

"This is approach control; go ahead, *Hibernia*."

I said, "Identify yourself, please: name, rank, and serial number."

"What?" The rating's astonishment was evident.

Pilot Haynes shot me a glance. After a moment the corner of his mouth turned up. He nodded grudgingly.

"You heard me. Identify yourself."

"Communications Specialist First Class Thomas Leeman, U.N.A.F. 205-066-254."

"Darla, serial number check, please."

A moment's pause. "Prefix 205 is interstellar rating; suffix 254 notates communications specialist. 066 within valid ID ranges."

"Who is your commanding officer, Mr. Leeman?"

"General Duc Twan Tho, sir."

"I'd like to speak to him." I turned off the caller. "Darla, his file, please."

Another pause. Then, "General Tho here. What's the problem?"

"Visuals, please, General." Once burned, twice shy.

"What nonsense is this?" His glowering visage came onto my screen. "Are you satisfied?"

He matched the picture Darla projected overhead. "Quite. Thank you. We'll be docking shortly."

"You identify yourself too, *Hibernia*!" He was within his rights. My request appeared ridiculous, and he was returning the favor.

"Captain Nicholas Seafort commanding, U.N.N.S. 205-387-0058."

After a moment he said warily, "I'd like to speak to Captain Haag."

"Captain Haag is dead of an accident. I am senior officer aboard."

"Visuals, please."

I switched on my video.

"My God, how old are you?"

"Eighteen."

"You were a lieutenant?"

"No, a midshipman." I let him chew on that awhile. There was no further communication.

Pilot Haynes carefully edged the ship closer to the station until the airlocks gently made contact. "Stop all engines."

"Stop engines, aye aye, sir."

"Join capture latches, fore and aft."

"Forward latches engaged, sir."

"Aft latches engaged, sir." Vax, from his station at the aft airlock.

"Begin mooring, Lieutenant. Open inner locks." Below-decks, a suited rating pressed his coded transmitter to the lock control. As the thick transplex hatches opened, the indicator light on my screen flashed.

"Inner lock ready aft, sir."

"Open outer lock. Secure mooring line. Pressurization check."

A pause, while the seaman labored under Vax's watchful

eye. "Line secured, sir. Pressure maintained one sea-level atmosphere."

"How does it look, Mr. Holser?"

"Peaceful, sir."

"Very well, open inner lock." I sagged. I'd given my last significant order. Though still nominally under my command, *Hibernia* was controlled now by the station commandant.

I thumbed the caller. "Mr. Leeman, patch me to Admiralty groundside, please. And I'll want transport as soon as possible."

"No problem, Captain," growled General Tho. He'd stayed on the line. Well, our arrival had been unusual, to say the least.

Clicks and beeps from the speaker. "Admiralty House."

"Commander U.N.S. *Hibernia* reporting. I'd like your senior duty officer, please."

Faint static swirled through the line. "That will be Captain Forbee, sir. One moment." I waited, my tension growing. The ordeal I faced wouldn't be pleasant.

"Forbee."

"Captain Nicholas Seafort reporting, sir. U.N.S. *Hibernia*."

"Justin Haag was scheduled for this run, sir."

"Captain Haag died interstellar, sir. I'm senior officer."

"Can you come to Admiralty House or shall I come up?" Odd, coming from a groundside commander. An Admiral and his staff didn't go visiting, they summoned.

"I'll be down as soon as the station gives me a shuttle, sir. I'll bring the Log."

"Very good, Captain." We broke the connection.

I went back to my cabin. I debated dress whites and decided against them; they would impress no one. I rummaged in my duffel for my unused wallet, checked to see that it still held money. As I'd be going shoreside I pinned my length of service medals to my uniform front, made sure my shoes were well shined.

On Level 2, passengers milled about the aft airlock for a look at the station, though they wouldn't begin to disembark for hours. I went to the forward lock, where crews were already off-loading our cargo. Holovid in hand, I straightened my uniform and clambered through the lock.

"This way, Captain Seafort." An enlisted man led me through the unfamiliar wide gleaming corridors and hatches of Orbit Station to the Commandant's office. The design of the station was much like our disk, though larger in all respects. Higher ceilings, wider corridors, larger compartments.

Hundreds of people worked and lived in this busy shipping center. Cargo for Detour, Miningcamp, and Earth was transshipped through Orbit Station. Passengers disembarked here, before boarding other vessels to travel onward. Small shuttles journeyed back and forth daily to the planet's surface. A typical orbiting facility for our interstellar Naval liners.

"I'm General Tho." A small man, with a neat mustache above thin lips, and a receding hairline emphasized by wavy black hair. He eyed me dubiously. "You command *Hibernia*?"

"Yes." I matched his abruptness with my own.

"Your shuttle will be ready in a few minutes." After a moment he unbent perceptibly. "What happened to your officers?"

I sighed. I'd have to repeat the tale often enough. I explained.

When I was finished he shook his head. "Good Lord, man."

"Yes. That's why I want to report to the Admiral right off."

His reply was cut short by the corporal who appeared in the doorway. "Shuttle is ready, sir."

He shrugged. "Better go, Captain. I put you ahead of the passenger buses."

"Thank you." I followed the corporal down three levels, to a shuttle launch berth. It was similar in layout to *Hibernia*'s launch berth, though on a far larger scale. It was designed to receive the great airbuses that shuttled passengers to and from the surface.

I grinned to myself; if I'd required Vax to polish this berth, he'd have marched right out the airlock. My grin faded; I recalled another man leaving an airlock, by my act. Sickened, I closed my eyes.

The shuttle was a sporty little six-seater with retractable

wings, its jet and vacuum engines sharing the available bow space. I ducked and climbed aboard.

"Buckle up, Captain." The pilot wore a casual jumpsuit and a removable helmet. He strapped himself in securely, more concerned with atmospheric turbulence than decompression. I followed his example. He flipped switches and checked instruments with the ease of long familiarity, waiting for the launch berth to depressurize.

"Lots of traffic these days?" I asked, mostly to make conversation.

"Some. More before the sickness." He keyed his caller. "Departure control, Alpha Fox 309 ready to launch."

"Just a moment." In a few moments the voice returned. "Cleared to launch, 309." The shuttle bay's huge hatches slid open. Hope Nation glistened through the abyss, green and inviting.

Our propellant drummed against the berth's protective shields as the shuttle glided out of the bay. Once clear of the dock the pilot throttled our engines to full. We shot ever faster from the station, approaching Hope Nation at an oblique angle until we encountered the outer wisps of atmosphere. The pilot hummed a tune I couldn't recognize as he flipped levers, eyed his radars, swung the ship around with short bursts of his positioning jets to be ready to fire the retro rockets.

I asked loudly, "What did you mean, before the sickness?" The first buffets of atmospheric turbulence rumbled the hull.

The pilot spared me a glance. "Didn't you hear? We had an epidemic a while back, but it's under control now." He set the automatic counter, his hand poised to fire the engines manually if the puter didn't turn them on.

"What kind of—"

"Not now. Wait!" The pilot's full attention was on the puter's readout. The retro engines caught with a roar at the exact moment the counter hit zero. His hand relaxed. "You never know about these little shipboard jobs!" He had to shout over the increasing din. "Not reliable like the mainframes you joes travel with!"

As we descended, Hope Nation lost its spherical shape. Ground features emerged through scattered layers of clouds. Here and there I could spot a checkerboard of cultivated fields, though most of the planet seemed lush and verdant.

Though I'd expected something of the sort, still I marveled at the sight of a planet so many light-years from home, whose ecology was carbon-based like our own. Hope Nation's trees and plants supplied no proteins or carbohydrates we could digest, but they grew side by side with our imported stock.

No native animals, of course. No nonterrestrial animals had ever been found, other than the primitive boneless fish of Zeta Psi.

"Sorry," the pilot shouted over the engine noise. "What were you saying?"

"What kind of epidemic did you have?"

"Some sort of mutated virus. It killed a lot of people before we found a vaccine. I don't know much about it, except everyone gets a shot when they put down at Centraltown."

"Is that where we're landing?"

"Of course. All arrivals from the station go there. Customs, quarantine, everything's at Centraltown."

"Right. Of course." I'd looked it up, but it was hard to digest a whole culture in an hour of holovid.

"Say, how'd you get to be a Captain, anyway?"

I sighed. It was going to be a long shore leave.

A few minutes later he deftly flipped the shuttle into glide mode and rode her above the flat plain toward the seacoast skirting the sparkling waters ahead. The jet engines kicked in a moment after the flipabout, making us a jet-powered aircraft.

Naturally, the pilot spotted the runway long before I did. After all it was his home turf. The shuttle's stubby wings shifted into VTOL mode as we bled off speed. The pilot timed our arrival over the runway perfectly; we were almost stationary as he dropped us gently onto the tarmac, the shuttle's underbelly jets cushioning our fall.

"Welcome to Hope Nation, Navy!" He gave me a smile as he killed the engines. "And good luck."

"I'll need it." I opened the hatch and climbed down, straightening to take my first breath of air in another solar system. It smelled clean and fragrant, with a scent I couldn't quite place, like fresh herbs in some exotic dish. The sun, a G2 type, shone brightly, perhaps a bit more yellow than our own.

I gawked like a groundsider on his first Lunapolis vacation. My step was light and springy, a result of Hope Nation's point nine two Earth gravity. The planet was actually twelve percent larger than Earth but considerably less dense.

My Naval ID took me through customs with no fuss. The quarantine shed was a ramshackle structure just off the runway, between the ships and a cluster of buildings. The nurse was friendly and efficient; I bared my arm; he touched the inoculation gun to my forearm and it was done.

I felt for my wallet. On this planet I was a greenhorn. I had no idea where I was going or how to get there but I assumed my U.N. currency would solve the problem. "How do I get to Admiralty House?"

"Well . . ." The nurse squinted into the bright afternoon sunlight. "You could walk over to that terminal building there, go through to the other side, and rent an electricar. If they have one left, that is, there's only seven. Then you turn left at the end of the drive, go to the first light, and turn left again and go two blocks."

"Thanks." I started to walk away.

"Or you could walk across the runway to that building over there. That's Admiralty House." He gestured to a two-story building seventy yards away.

"Oh." I felt foolish. Then I grinned in appreciation; he must have perfected his routine on a lot of novices. "Thanks again." I started across the runway, holovid in hand.

Now I wished I'd chosen to wear my dress whites, but I realized I was being silly. Stevin Johanson, Admiral Commanding at Hope Nation Base, wasn't about to be impressed by dress whites adorning a fumbling ex-midshipman.

An iron fence surrounded the large cement block structure. I unlatched the gate; a well-worn path across the unmowed yard led me to the front of the building. The winged-anchor Naval emblem and the words "United Nations Naval Service / Admiralty House" greeted me from a brass plaque anchored to the porch post.

Had the brass plate been smelted here, or had they shipped the sign across light-years of emptiness to add majesty to the facade of colonial Naval headquarters?

At the tall wooden doors with glass inserts at the top of the porch steps, I tucked at the corners of my uniform and brushed my hands through my hair. I took a deep breath, and went in.

A young man in shore whites was dictating into a puter at a console in the lobby. "Can I help you, sir?"

"Nicholas Seafort, *Hibernia*, reporting to Admiral Johanson."

"Oh, yes, we were expecting you; General Tho called ahead. Captain Forbee will see you now." He led me up red-carpeted stairs, along a hall to an office with open windows overlooking the sunny field. "Captain Seafort, sir."

I came to attention. "Nicholas Seafort reporting, sir. Senior officer aboard *Hibernia*."

The young Captain behind the desk stood quickly and saluted. He squinted from weak, puzzled eyes. A youngish man, who'd started running to fat. "Shall we stand down, then?" It was an odd way to release me, but perhaps colonial customs were different. We relaxed. He indicated a seat.

"Thank you. Will I be reporting to you or directly to Admiral Johanson?"

He gave me a sad smile. "Admiral Johanson died in the epidemic."

"Died, sir?" I sat. So much death . . .

"He caught the virus. One day he just dropped, like everyone else who had it."

"Good Lord!" I could think of nothing else to say.

"Yes." He looked unhappy. "So I've been running the Naval station. I sent word on the last ship out. It'll be two years before his replacement arrives."

"Very well, sir. I'll report to you. I'm sorry I'm not better organized, but most of it is in the Log." Afraid he'd stop me before I could get the whole sordid tale off my chest, I let my words tumble, summarizing what had happened aboard *Hibernia*. I spared myself nothing, glad now to have it over with. "Captain Haag's loss and the lieutenants' deaths were an act of Lord God," I finished. "But I take full responsibility for the deaths of Midshipman Wilsky, the seamen, and the passengers."

He was silent a long time. "Terrible," he said.

"Yes, sir."

"But you don't know the half of it." He stood and came around from behind the desk to where I sat, cap on my knee. He bent and peered at my length of service medals. As if to confirm my story, he asked, "When did you say your last lieutenant died?"

"March 12, 2195, sir."

"That's in the Log?"

"Yes, sir." I slipped the chip into my holovid, handed it across to him.

He sat at his desk, flipped through the entries until he came to the month of March. He shook his head as he reached the relevant passages. "It wasn't June, was it? You became Captain in March."

"Yes, sir," I said, puzzled.

"That's it, then." Captain Forbee turned to look out the window. Facing away he said, "Hope Nation is still a small colony. We don't have much of a Naval Station. No interstellar ships are based here; we're not big enough to warrant it. Admiral Johanson was a caretaker with seniority in case it might someday be needed; to resolve a dispute between two captains, for instance. Or to appoint a replacement in case a Captain died or was too ill to sail."

"Yes, sir."

"He had three Captains in system. One of them, Captain Grone—it's an embarrassing incident, we did our best to hush it up—he went native almost a year ago. He and his fiancée stole a helicopter and flew to the Ventura Mountains. Disappeared. We've never been able to find them. An unstable type, a lot of us thought. The second is Captain Marceau, from *Telstar*. Sixteen years seniority."

Good. He or Forbee would replace me. My nightmare was over. "Where is he, sir?"

"The bloody fool had to go cliff-climbing on his shore leave. Six months, and he's still in coma. Admiral Johanson gave *Telstar* to Captain Eaton last spring. They sailed to Detour, then headed for Miningcamp and Earth."

"They never reached Miningcamp."

"Yes, your Log makes that clear." He sighed. "Eaton's a reliable man. If he bypassed Miningcamp, he must have a reason."

If that's what he did, I thought silently. If Darla was glitched, how many other puters were, as well? I put aside the thought. "Sir, how many officers here are rated interstellar?"

He shook his head gloomily. "I said you didn't know the half of it. Nobody. We have interplanetary Captains, of course, but why would anyone rated interstellar stay in this backwater?"

"You could go yourself, sir. *Hibernia* needs a real Captain."

"I told you we had no one, Mr. Seafort. You know how I came to Hope Nation? I shipped out as a lieutenant. My wife Margaret was among the passengers. I timed it so my hitch was up and I could resign my commission when we docked. I've been a civilian for seven years, but after Admiral Johanson sent Eaton with *Telstar*, he reenlisted me so there'd be someone on staff who'd been interstellar."

Did Forbee expect me to solve his problems for him? "You could appoint my lieutenant—I mean, my first lieutenant—as Captain, sir, and then relieve me."

He stood tiredly. "You still don't understand. Admiral Johanson gave me Captain's rank at my reenlistment. To be precise, on June 6, 2195. Sir."

"No!" I stumbled to my feet, overturning my chair. It was as if Seaman Tuak had shambled through the hatch, when at last I'd imagined myself safe.

"Yes, sir. You're senior officer in Hope Nation system."

# 23

I sat despondent while evening darkened outside the window, unnoticed.

We'd been over the regs a dozen times. I couldn't find an escape.

"Governor Williams—"

"Is a civilian, sir. He doesn't have jurisdiction over the Navy." Captain Forbee must have studied every line of the regs as I had, hoping to escape his unwanted responsibility. The relief he'd have felt when he found I had more interstellar time as Captain than he . . . "Governor Williams can no more appoint a Captain than you can set local speed limits," he added.

"You made your point!" Abashed, I lowered my voice. "I can resign."

"Yes, sir. Nobody can stop you." He'd said it correctly. Resigning for any reason except disabling physical illness or injury, or mental illness, was dereliction of duty. The regs I'd sworn to uphold required me to exert authority and control of the government of my vessel until relieved by order of superior authority, until my death, or until certification of my disability.

But no one could stop me from violating my oath.

"I won't put up with this!" I glared at Forbee. "Someone in Hope Nation system must be rated interstellar, damn it!" I was so frustrated I skirted blasphemy without caring.

"I'm afraid not, sir. Believe me, I've looked."

"You have captains with interplanetary ratings. Any of them would be senior to me."

"In service time, yes, sir. But any Captain Interstellar is senior to a Captain Interplanetary. Surely you know that."

"Don't tell me what I know!" I snapped.

"I'm sorry, sir." His tone was placating.

We sat in silence. At length I said, "*Hibernia* can't sail with me at the helm. That's too dangerous. And if *Telstar*'s missing, she may never have even made Detour; we must sail. Our supplies would be needed there more than ever."

Forbee folded his arms. "I agree."

"Will you search for *Telstar*?"

He looked surprised. "That's for you to decide, sir. You're in charge."

I stood, fists bunched.

"You're senior," he blurted. "I can't help it. The naval station is under your command."

"Of all the . . . I'll—by Lord God—" With an effort I brought my speech under control. "These are my instructions: run the naval station exactly as you would if I hadn't arrived! Is that clear?"

"Yes, sir. Aye aye, sir!"

"Are you going to search for *Telstar*, Forbee?" I was too put out to use his rank.

"We have nothing to send after her, sir. None of our local ships have fusion drive." That was that. Search and rescue were impossible.

We couldn't just ignore the fact that *Telstar* was missing. Word had to be sent back to Admiralty at Luna, but *Hibernia* was the next ship scheduled to return—in fact, the only fusion vessel in the system. My mind spun. That meant I had to—

Enough was enough. "By Lord God, I'll resign!"

"Will you, sir?" His voice was without inflection.

"Yes. Right now. Give me my Log; I'll write it in." It was time to free myself from this madness. If Admiralty tried me for dereliction of duty, so be it; at least I'd kill no more passengers and crew by my stupidity. If the regs required me to remain Captain, the regs were wrong. I would follow my conscience.

I keyed the holovid to the end of the most recent entry, tapped the keys. "I, Nicholas Ewing Seafort, Captain, do hereby res—" I halted, the hairs raising on my neck. Slowly, I turned, called by the familiar touch of Father's breath as he watched me struggle with my lessons.

Day after day, in the cold dreary Welsh afternoons, I worked my way through the texts, struggling to master new words and ideas, scrawling answers into the worn notebooks he bade me use. When I was right he gave me another problem. When I made a mistake he said only, "That's wrong, Nicholas," and handed me back the page to find my errors, waiting patiently behind my chair until I did.

One day I'd dropped my smudged assignment on the table and cried bitterly, "Of course it's wrong! I always do it wrong!" He spun me around, slapped me hard, swung my chair to the table, and thrust the lesson book into my hands. He'd said not a word. Blinking back tears I worked, my cheek smarting, until I got it right. After, he gave me another problem.

Now, in Forbee's office, nobody was behind my chair, the breath I'd felt but a wisp of breeze. I shivered, shook off my memories, and turned back to the holovid. "—do hereby resign my commission, effective immediately." I put the point of the pencil to the screen to sign below the entry.

Time passed.

After a while the pencil fell from my fingers, rolled unheeded to the floor.

I couldn't do it. I knew right from wrong; though Father wasn't watching, he might as well have been. *"I, Nicholas Ewing Seafort, do swear upon my immortal soul to preserve and protect the Charter of the General Assembly of the United Nations, to give loyalty and obedience for the term of my enlistment to the Naval Service of the United Nations, and to obey all its lawful orders and regulations, so help me Lord God Almighty."* I'd administered the selfsame oath to Paula Treadwell and to Derek Carr. I was prepared to hang them should they break their pledge. I could not violate it myself.

Still, for a brief moment, my resolution wavered. Was my self-respect worth risking *Hibernia* and her crew? Was even my immortal soul worth that? In the distance, Father waited for my reply. I will—he'd made me promise—let them destroy me before I swear to an oath I will not fulfill. My oath is all that I am.

I covered my face, ashamed of my tears. When I'd brought myself under control I put down my dampened arm, blinked in the sudden light.

I erased the entry. Captain Forbee sat motionless.

"I'm sorry. Very sorry."

He nodded as if he understood.

"We won't speak of it again." My embarrassment was painful, but no more than I deserved. "I'm going back to my ship. Carry on victualing and off-loading. Report only if it's necessary." I stood.

"Aye aye, sir." He got to his feet when I did. "If there's anything I can do to help . . ."

"I need experienced officers. I don't care where you get them. Find me at least two more lieutenants."

"Aye aye, sir." As I left the room he picked up his caller. "Get a shuttle ready for the Commander at Admiralty House."

Two hours later I strode through the mated airlocks onto *Hibernia*. Vax Holser, waiting at the hatch, fell into step beside me. "Are you all right, sir?" His manner was anxious. "Did they accept your report?"

"I'm fine." I started up the ladder to Level 1.

"Will they call a court of inquiry?"

"No."

"Do you know who'll replace you, sir?"

Why did he insist on goading me? "Mr. Holser, your duties are elsewhere. Get out from underfoot and stay out!"

Vax stopped short, shock and hurt evident. "Aye aye, sir." Quickly he turned away. I strode onto the bridge. Dejected, I slumped in my armchair. Vax had been worried for me, but I'd turned on him with savage anger. Would I ever learn? How often could I lash out without turning him back into a cold, unfeeling bully?

The crew's leave roster, prepared by the Chief, awaited my approval. I signed it. During *Hibernia*'s mandatory thirty-day layover on Hope Nation the entire crew would be shuttled groundside, except for a few maintenance personnel whose shifts were rotated to provide the maximum leave. At least one officer would remain on board at all times, although he wasn't required to stand watch.

By now all the passengers had disembarked, even those who were going on to Detour.

"Mr. Tamarov to the bridge." I replaced the caller and waited. A few moments later Alexi appeared. "You're on duty rotation the third week," I told him. "That means you have two weeks off starting today, and another week at the end."

"Aye aye, sir!" His eyes sparkled with excitement and anticipation.

"Just one thing." His grin vanished. "As senior middy, you're in charge of the cadets. I'm not holding them aboard the ship and we can't turn Ricky and Paula loose in a strange colony unsupervised. Take them with you and keep an eye on them."

"Aye aye, sir."

He looked so crestfallen I offered a little cheer. "I didn't mean at every minute, Alexi. You can still go out on the town. Either take them with you or bunk them down before you go. Just bring them back to the ship unharmed."

He brightened. "Aye aye, sir. When are you going down, sir?"

"Tomorrow."

"Will I see you before you're transferred out?" A natural

assumption; a new Captain wouldn't want his predecessor looking over his shoulder. I'd have been reassigned to another ship until the next interstellar vessel arrived.

"You'll see me," I growled, suddenly anxious to be rid of him. "Dismissed."

I sat in my leather armchair on the silent bridge. Eventually, I realized there was no reason to stay. I wandered down to Level 2, where parties of sailors clustered around the airlock, laughing and joking, awaiting dismissal. To avoid passing them I went back up the ladder. I strolled past the wardroom, past Vax's cabin, formerly Ms. Dagalow's. I stopped in front of Lieutenant Malstrom's quarters. For a moment I had an urge to go in and set up the chessboard.

My friend floated forever in empty space, while I had reached safe haven in Hope Nation. I recalled our mutual plans and promises. The drink I would buy him, the trip we would take to the Ventura Mountains. My eyes stung. I resolved to do those things for him. I would take a shuttle groundside in the morning. I'd go into the first bar I saw and order an asteroid on the rocks. Then I'd check on transportation and arrange a trip across the sea to the Venturas.

On the way back to my cabin I realized how lonely my leave would be. I hesitated for a moment, swore under my breath, turned back to the wardroom. I knocked.

Ricky opened, stiffening to attention.

"Carry on, all of you."

He and Paula Treadwell were packing their duffels, clothing strewn across their beds. Derek Carr, his duffel ready, sat on his bunk waiting for the call to the shuttle.

"Mr. Carr, a word with you, please." I took him out to the corridor. He listened, obedient but aloof. "I thought— that is, I'm going on a journey, uh, for sentimental reasons. To the Ventura Mountains. Someone was going to take me there once." Once more I hesitated, afraid to open myself. "I thought perhaps you might like to come along as my guest."

"Thank you, Captain," he said, his voice cool. "I have other plans. I'm visiting my father's plantations, and then I'll see Centraltown. My regrets, sir." I heard the message behind his words. Derek could take anything he set his mind to, as he'd proven, but that didn't mean he would forgive me for the undeserved humiliation of the barrel the day I'd lost my temper. I'd never be pardoned for that, not by a boy with his pride.

"Very well, Mr. Carr. Enjoy yourself." I turned away.

"Thank you, Captain," he said to my retreating back. He added, "You too." It made me feel a little better.

Early the next morning, *Hibernia* bore an eerie resemblance to the wreck of *Celestina*. Lights gleamed in deserted corridors. No sound broke the stillness. Somewhere on board—probably in his cabin—was the Chief, serving the first week's rotation, but most of the crew had departed, except a galley hand and a few maintenance ratings.

I shouldered my duffel and crossed through the airlocks, strode along the busy corridors of the station to the Commandant's small office.

"May I help you, sir?" A corporal looked up from his puter.

"I'd like a shuttle groundside."

"Yes, sir. Just a moment, please." Within moments I was ushered into General Tho's office. He was distinctly more cordial than on my prior visit.

"You might as well wait here, Captain, while the shuttle is prepped. Coffee?" I joined him for a cup and chatted until the craft was ready. As I left he said, "If there's anything further I can do, let me know." His manner suggested we were senior officers exchanging courtesies. I supposed we were.

The shuttle was much larger than the one on which I'd first gone ashore, but I was the only passenger; apparently the small launch wasn't available and General Tho had decided not to make me wait. I had a different pilot, less interested in conversation.

Groundside once more, I inhaled several lungsful of clean fresh air under the bright morning sun. The temperature was warm and pleasant; at this latitude Hope Nation had long summers and mild winters at sea level. One of Hope Nation's two moons was dimly visible overhead. It appeared slightly larger than did Luna from Earth's surface.

I decided not to check in with Admiralty House. If Forbee

had any news he'd have called. If I showed up now, he would dump onto me decisions he could make himself. I went directly to the terminal building and out the other side, as I'd been directed earlier by the quarantine nurse.

A giant screen anchored to a metal pole greeted me. "Welcome to Centraltown, Population 89,267." I watched for a few moments, wondering how often the number changed. According to the guidebook the screen was tied directly to the puters at Centraltown Hospital; each birth and death were reflected within moments on the welcome sign. Centraltown was the largest, and virtually the only, city on Hope Nation; the remainder of the colony's two hundred thousand population was spread among several small towns and the many outlying plantations that justified the colony's existence.

I had imagined raw dirt roads, fresh cuts in the hills, ramshackle buildings set around a primitive main street. Disappointed, I had to remind myself that Hope Nation was opened back in 2081, over a century past. Since then, a massive influx of materials and settlers had been absorbed.

The roads were paved and modern, and seemed clean compared to the crowded and filthy streets of Earth's great cities. I peered down the main avenue. Clusters of buildings lined the street south toward Centraltown, but a few blocks in the other direction the road disappeared into hills rife with uncultivated vegetation.

I spotted the car rental agency at the end of the terminal building. In no particular hurry I sauntered to the entry. "Knock loud and come in," read the sign tacked to the door. Inside, a tiny waiting room, with a counter. I banged on the desk.

A young woman popped from behind a curtain leading to the back. "Hi, you must be from *Hibernia*." She seemed about twenty. Long brown hair flowed unhindered to her shoulders. ·

I set down my duffel. "Yes, I am."

"Looking for a car, huh?"

"That was the idea." I studied her. If she was a typical Hopian, business here was conducted far more casually than at home.

"I think maybe we'll have one later." A shrug. "Yesterday

the sailors grabbed all I had. One's due back this afternoon.''
She shot me a dubious look. "You have to be twenty-one to
rent. Age of majority. You don't look that old.''

"I'm a Naval officer.'' I pulled out my ID, which still
showed me as a midshipman. I'd have to get that changed.
"I have my majority.''

"I guess,'' she said vaguely. "Come back sometime this
afternoon; I'll see if one's in yet.''

"Will you make a reservation for me?''

"You mean, hold a car? Sure. What's your name?''

"Nick Seafort.''

"Right. If I'm not here, ask for me at the restaurant inside.''

"What's your name?''

"Darla.'' I started. She asked, "What's the matter?''

"Nothing. I knew a girl named Darla once.''

That brought a smile. "Was she nice?''

"I liked her. Sometimes when she made her mind up it
was hard getting her to change it.''

"Oh, well, I'm not like that.'' It could have been an invitation.

"What can someone do on foot around here?''

"There's the terminal restaurant. If you want drinks, the
Runway Saloon's just up the block. Just don't order dou-
bles.''

"Right. Thanks.'' I wandered out. The bar reminded me
of my promise to Lieutenant Malstrom: a drink at the first bar
we came to. I sighed. It was absurd to drink so early in the
day, but I could think of nothing better to do, and a promise
was a promise. I strolled along the street past the edge of the
field, until I came upon a battered building with sheet-metal
siding.

"Permanent Happy Hour!'' the sign read. "All drinks always half price!'' If drinks were always half price, what were
they half of? I shrugged.

Inside, the bar smelled of stale alcohol and fried food. The
light show bounced patterns off the walls in time to thumping
electronic music, making it hard for me to see. A babble of
voices indicated that people were in the back of the room.

I waited for my eyes to accustom to the dark. It was the

kind of bar where you stared moodily at the drink in your
hand; just right for spacemen.

"What'll you have?"

"Asteroid on the rocks." An experienced bartender, he
knew my uniform meant he could serve me without checking
my age. There were very stiff penalties for serving minors,
both for the bartender and the minor.

I took my drink and slid into a dimly lit booth to the side,
tossing my jacket on the seat beside me. I took a sip and
nearly choked. The alcohol tasted almost raw, and there was
a lot of it. No wonder Darla had warned me about a double.

An asteroid on the rocks. Whiskey, mixed fruit juices, and
Hobarth oils, imported from faraway Hobarth or imitated with
synthetics. In this case, probably synthetics; I suspected the
Runway Saloon didn't stock imported liqueurs.

Actually the drink wasn't bad, just strong. Silently I raised
my glass to the empty seat across from me and saluted Harv
Malstrom. It would have been great, Harv, to be sitting across
from you. You'd make a joke about the drinks, and I'd grin,
enjoying your company, recalling our most recent chess
match. The alcohol made my eyes sting. I took another long
swig. It burned going down. I had another swallow to ease
my throat. After a time I sat tapping an empty glass, staring
moodily at the empty seat, while flashing lights danced on
the walls.

"Ready for another?"

"No." I looked at my watch. Early yet. "I suppose. A
small one."

"Sure." He grinned without mirth and handed me the glass
he'd already brought. A comedian. He should have been on
the holovid.

About halfway through the second drink I thought I'd feel
better if I closed my eyes, and that was easier to do when my
head was resting on the table. I stayed that way, drifting in
and out of a doze, while the bar filled and the noise grew
louder.

"Detour! Off to Detour for seven weeks, then another
week's leave." A woman's voice. Ms. Edwards, our gunner's mate.

"You joes should work the Hope Nation system. You're

never more than five weeks from port. One easy run after another." My eyes were open now but my head stayed on the table. I listened, drifting.

"Nah, who wants a milk run? You gotta go deep to get action." Guffaws.

"Sure, joeygirl." The voice was mocking. "It'd be great, stuck interstellar with a tyrant for a captain and only fourteen months to go!"

"Hey, don't slam our Captain, buster!"

"Hah. I hear he'll be out of diapers soon!"

"Listen, grode, I'd rather sail with Captain Kid that one of your system sissies who'd wet his pants if he couldn't see a sun." I blinked, focused on the empty glass.

"Captain KID? You spank him if he makes a mistake?" I felt my ears flame.

"Hey, Seafort's all right! Sure, Captain Kid gets a wild hair up his ass sometimes—what officer don't? But that joey knows what he's doing. He took the puter apart single-handed, 'cause he knew she was planning to kill us. If he hadn'ta found her glitches we'd be half outta the galaxy heading for Andromeda."

Another voice joined in. "I'll match him mean for mean with any Captain in the fleet. Two joes we had, they beat up on the CPO. They were real garbage, druggies and worse, but always got away with it. He hanged them himself without batting an eye. And you know about Miningcamp, where they tried to seize our ship?"

Yes, tell them about my folly at Miningcamp. Sickened, I closed my eyes.

"Those scum shot their way aboard, the Captain held them off with a laser in each hand 'til help came. When it was over he marched one of them right out the airlock and made him breathe space, and laughed all the way back to the bridge! He's tough, Captain Kid is. You don't mess with him. I'd rather be on a ship with him than with some old fart can't find his way to the head!"

For some reason I was feeling better. Time to go, before they found me spying on them. Cautiously, I raised my head. I was dizzy but functioning. I gathered my jacket, left a few unibucks on the table, and moved as quietly as I could to the door. Nobody saw me. I slipped outside, greedily sucking in the fresh air.

"God, it's the Captain!" Two of *Hibernia*'s ratings saluted hurriedly. I fumbled a return salute and kept moving, working at making my unsteady legs cooperate. I lugged my duffel toward the shuttleport, feeling a bit more steady with each step. By the terminal I was nearly myself again. I made for the rental agency at the far end.

"Hey, Captain, wait up!" I turned. Derek Carr in civilian garb, waved from the far end of the building. He ran to catch up. He stopped, his face flushed with healthy exertion. "Sir, I, uh—" All at once, he looked abashed.

Impatient, I asked, "What, Derek?"

"Your invitation. Is it too late to accept?"

I studied his face, unsure of my answer.

He stared at the pavement. "Sorry about the way I spoke to you yesterday. I'm still immature sometimes. I'd enjoy touring with you, sir, if you'll have me." With an effort, he raised his head and looked me in the eye.

My smile was bleak. "What changed your mind, Derek?"

"I was steamed over your sending me to the Chief, even though I really was asking for it that day. Then I remembered two things: I promised you I could take anything, and you were the only person who was kind to me when I really needed it." His face lit in a smile. "That was the most important thing anyone's ever done for me. So holding a grudge is pretty stupid. I'm sorry, sir."

I smiled back, meaning it this time. "What about your trip to your plantation?"

"I thought, sir, perhaps you'd like to come with me." His smile vanished. "Though I'm not sure we'd be welcome. My father told me that the manager, he . . ." He shrugged. "Anyway, we could go to the mountains afterward."

I debated, my melancholy lifting. His company would be more pleasant than my own. "Sounds great. I'll rent a car."

"I already have one, sir. I got it yesterday." He blushed. "I was sort of waiting until you came down."

"Right." I followed him to his electricar, a tiny three-wheeler with permabatteries that could power the vehicle for months. I thought fast. "Derek, while we're groundside, I want you to call me Mr. Seafort, as if I were first middy. And you don't have to say 'sir' all the time. Just make sure you switch back when we go aboard again.''

"Aye aye, si—I mean, thank you, Mr. Seafort." We climbed in. I took off my jacket and tie and stowed my duffel in the back seat. "I've got a tent and supplies in the trunk," he said. "If you're ready, I am. It's a two-day drive."

I leaned back and closed my eyes. "Wake me when we get there."

A couple of hours out of Centraltown we came upon the Hope Nation I'd first expected. The three-lane road gave way to two lanes and then one and a half. Instead of pavement, only gravel. Homes were few and far between. Occasionally a cargo hauler lumbered toward Centraltown. We passed the time chatting and joking, sharing a merry mood.

Our route paralleled the seacoast a few miles inland. Occasionally, from a high point, we caught a glimpse of the shimmering ocean; more often our path cut through a dense jungle of viny trees of unfamiliar purplish hues.

We stopped for lunch at Haulers' Rest, a comfort station and restaurant about two hours from the edge of the plantation zone. The public showers were in an outbuilding. After, we walked past enclosures of turkeys, chickens, and pigs to the restaurant entrance. Cargo haulers were parked at random in the mud-packed parking lot.

Haulers' Rest generated its own electricity from a small pile in the back pasture, pumped water from deep wells, and prepared most of its own food from the hoof. Wheat and corn fields provided the grains, from hybrid stock that needed no pollination. On Hope Nation, no local blights affected our terrestrial crops, and there were no insects to harass the livestock, so everything grew fast and healthy.

After a stomach-stretching meal (ham steak, corn, green beans, homemade bread, lots of milk) we waddled to the car to resume our trip.

During the afternoon we pulled aside frequently to take in the rugged view. The forest was strangely silent. No birds circled above; no animals called out their cries. Only the soft wind that rippled through the incredibly dense vegetation.

The land wasn't fenced, but each plantation had its own

identifying mark nailed to trees and posts along the road, much like the brands once put on cattle. The first we came to stretched many miles before it gave way to another.

As evening settled, rich reds dominated the sky, fading to subtle lavender. The two moons, Major and Minor, sailed serenely over scattered clouds. By now we both were tired, and I began watching for markers along the road. I said, "Let's pick a plantation before it gets too late."

According to the holovid guides, Hope Nation had few inns outside Centraltown, so plantations provided free food and lodging to travelers who came their way. An old tradition, now virtually obligatory. Plantation owners didn't stint on food or shelter; they could afford it, and travelers brought outside contact that the isolated planters appreciated.

Derek drove on in silence. Then, "Mr. Seafort, I changed my mind. Let's camp out for the night."

"Why?"

"I don't want to look at plantations."

I raised an eyebrow, waiting.

"I told you the managers control our estate. They won't want me around. They'll patronize me, and push me aside if I ask questions. Let's not bother to visit."

"That's not a good idea."

"What difference is it to you?"

"Better to face it than brood for the rest of your leave. Besides, Carr is another day's ride or more. We'll stop at a closer estate for the night."

His tone was petulant. "What's the point of seeing another family's holding? It's mine I care about."

"You care so much you'd turn tail and run?"

Even in moonlight I could see him flush. "I'm no coward."

"I didn't say you were." But I had. Inwardly, I sighed. "I'll handle it, Derek."

"How?"

"I'll do the talking, and we won't tell them your name."

Ahead was a gate, and a dirt service road that wound into a heavy woods. A wooden sign above read "Branstead Plantation."

"Slow down. Take that one."

Reluctantly he turned into the drive. "Mr. Seafort, I feel like a welfarer asking for a handout."

"That's the system here. Go on."

Nothing but woods for a good mile. Then, a clearing where remains of huge brush piles skirted the edge of plowed fields that stretched as far as the eye could see.

Our road straightened, ran alongside the field. After another two miles I began to wonder if the road led to a homestead, but abruptly we came on a complex of buildings set around a wide circular drive. Barns, silos. A heliport. Farmhands' shacks. They surrounded a huge wood and stone mansion that dominated the settlement.

We got out to stretch. A stocky man in work clothes emerged from the stone house, walked to where we waited. "Can I help you boys?"

"We're travelers," I said.

"The guest house is over there." He pointed to a clean but simple building that seemed in good repair. "We don't serve separate for the guests; you'll eat with us in the manse. We dine at seven."

"Thank you very much," I said, but he'd already turned to go.

"Welcome." He didn't look back.

We carried our duffels into the guest house. A row of beds sat along one wall, with hooks and shelves on the wall opposite. Around the corner, a bath. The lack of privacy wasn't unlike a wardroom.

Derek's tone held wonder. "He didn't care about us. No questions."

"Don't you know about travel in the outland?"

"My father was born here. I wasn't."

"Then read the holovid guides, tourist."

I opened my duffel.

Derek sorted through his clothes. "I'm not a tourist." His voice was tremulous. "This is my home. Earth never was."

"I know, Derek." I'd have to remember not to tease about certain things.

We washed and changed clothes. In Naval blue slacks and a white shirt, I could have been any young civilian. Shortly before seven we strolled up the drive past a field of grain to the main dwelling. From the plank porch we could hear loud conversation and the friendly rattle of dishes.

Derek fidgeted with embarrassment. I knocked.

"Come on in." A well-fed balding young man in his thirties. "I'm Harmon Branstead." He stood aside. The entrance room was rough-hewn but comfortable, well furnished with solidly built furniture.

"Nick, um, Rogoff, sir."

Derek shot me an amazed glance. I gulped, breathing a silent apology to Lord God. Whyever had I chosen the name of the man I'd murdered? I said hastily, "And my friend Derek. We're sailors."

"A local ship?"

"*Hibernia*, sir. The interstellar—"

"We all heard *Hibernia* docked. Quite an event." He held out his hand. "Welcome to Branstead Plantation. How long will you stay?"

"Just the night. We'll be on our way in the morning."

"Very well. Come eat with us."

We were the only guests. Supper was at a long plank table in a dining room that was large but homey. The planter and his wife, their small children, and two farm managers sat at table with us. Hefty platters of home-cooked food were passed around.

Derek asked, "Did you build this place, sir?" He glanced at the stuccoed walls, the comfortable furnishings.

"My grandfather did," said Branstead. "But I've added about ten thousand acres to cultivation, and put up a few more buildings."

"Very impressive," I said.

"We're the fourth largest on Eastern Continent." His voice was proud. "Hopewell is first, then Carr, then Triforth, then us." Branstead passed creamed corn to his older son, a boy of nine or so. "As soon as we get the machinery paid off, I'll open some new acreage. Then we'll see. Maybe by the time I pass it on to Jerence we'll be the biggest." He beamed at his son.

"I'd think estates would get smaller over the generations," said Derek. "Divided among all your children."

"Divided? Lord God, no! Primogeniture is the rule. First-born." Branstead nodded at his younger child. "Of course, everyone is well provided for, but the land stays intact. We wouldn't have it any other way."

"How large is your plantation?" I asked.

"We're only three hundred thirty thousand, but we're growing. Another seventy-five thousand and we'll pass Triforth. Hopewell is eight hundred thousand acres." A pause. "Carr is seven hundred thousand, but they don't really count as they're no longer family-run."

I spooned myself more corn, passed it on. "What's Carr?" My tone was careless.

"One of our neighbors. The estate was owned by old Winston, 'til he died. We all thought they'd stagnate, but I have to admit, Plumwell's doing all right, even if there's talk that—" He bit off the rest.

Derek toyed with his food.

Branstead leaned back in his chair. "So, you boys are Navy."

"Yes, sir."

"Smart of you not to wear your uniforms, Mr.—Rogoff, is it? I myself wouldn't hold it against you, but there are some . . ."

"I'm on leave. Otherwise—" I was proud to wear the uniform, and resented any implication to the contrary. My back stiffened.

"Now, don't take offense. Some folks see Naval blues and blame the sailors."

"For what?"

"The usual: you slap export duties on what you send us, and we can't ship our produce except in Naval hulls. Makes for unfair trade, and we're paying dearly."

Derek's eyes flickered to the comfortable house.

Branstead shrugged, his manner depreciating. "As a nation, I mean. We're the breadbasket of the colonies. Do you know how much food Hope Nation ships back to Earth? Millions of tons. Once you lift it out of the atmosphere, vacuum cold storage costs nothing. Where are you boys from, anyway?"

"Earth," I told him. "We're going on to Detour."

"When you get home, tell them we want a new tariff bill." We drifted to politics and current events, that is, as current as they could be after eighteen months of sail.

After dinner Derek and I settled into the guest house. I sank onto my bed with a sigh of relief. "Why did I blurt out the name Rogoff? I felt his presence all through the meal. I shouldn't have done that."

His tone was accusing. "I thought you said you knew how to handle it."

"You got to see a plantation, didn't you?"

He grimaced, but without rancor. I got into bed and turned out the light.

Derek tossed and turned for hours, waking me each time I drifted to sleep. In the very early hours he got up quietly, put on his clothes, and slipped outside. Just as dawn was breaking he crept back to his bed, waking me once more.

In the morning, I dressed quickly, anxious for my first cup of coffee. Derek paced. "Look, sir, we can't go on to Carr."

I raised an eyebrow. "That again?"

"The manager won't talk to us." He sat, stood again immediately. "We'll learn nothing. And I won't beg, not on my own land."

I tried to soothe him. "One thing I've learned as Captain, Derek. You'll have enough problems without worrying about ones that haven't come up yet. We'll play it by ear."

His look was dubious. After a while, he sighed. "All right. Tell them I'm your cousin or something."

Thanks to Derek's nocturnal meanders, we'd slept in until well past nine. We were prepared to leave without breakfast but the housekeeper insisted on feeding us a simple meal that grew into a gargantuan feast.

I was eyeing the last of my coffee when Harmon Branstead looked in. "Where do you go from here, boys?"

"North, toward Carr. Maybe beyond."

"Stop at Hopewell if you have time. Their automated mill and elevator is astonishing."

"Thank you." I glanced at my watch. I could imagine nothing less interesting.

Derek pushed back his chair. "Ready, Mr. Seafort?"

"Yes." I got to my feet. "Drive the car around. I'll get our duffels."

"Thanks for your hospitality, sir." Derek hurried out. I headed for the stairs.

"Just a moment," said Branstead then to a farmhand, "Randall, get their bags." When we were alone, he eyed me with distaste.

"Sir?"

His face was cold. "In Hope Nation, hospitality is a matter

of tradition, not law. In that tradition, I opened my home to you. I sat you at dinner with my own children.''

''Yes, sir?''

He shot, ''Who are you?''

''Nick. Nick Rog—'' My voice faltered.

''Seafort, I believe he called you. I don't know why you chose to lie, but it's despicable. You were a guest! Get out, and don't come back!''

My face flamed. ''I'm sor—''

''Out!''

''Yes, sir.'' I headed for the door with as much dignity as I could muster. Beyond, in the haze, Father glowered his disapproval.

My hand on the latch, I hesitated. ''Mr. Branstead, please . . .'' I glanced at his face, saw no opening. ''I was wrong. Forgive me. My name is Nick Seafort. I—''

''Are you really from *Hibernia*?''

''Yes.''

His skepticism was evident. ''You don't look like the sailors we see hereabouts.''

''We're officers.''

''Why should I believe that?''

I took out my wallet, handed him my ID.

His glance went to my face and back. ''A midshipman.''

''Not anymore. It's an old card.''

''They wouldn't have you?''

''They had no choice. I'm, ah, Captain now.''

''You're the one!'' He studied me. ''Everyone's heard, but I don't think they said the name . . . Why lie about it, for heaven's sake?'' His tone had eased to one of curiosity.

I had to do something to make amends. ''My friend Derek.''

''Yes?''

''Derek Carr.''

''Is he related— Oh!'' He sat.

Gratefully, I did the same; my knees were weak. ''He's a midshipman now, and he'll sail with us. Before we left he wanted to see . . .'' I found it hard to raise my eyes. ''Mr. Branstead, I'm ashamed.''

''Well, there are worse things than deceit.'' His voice was gruff. ''You're going on to Carr, then?''

"Yes. He's very nervous about it. What will the manager—Plumwell, you said—do if he visits?"

His fingers drummed the table. "All our plantations are family owned. There's never been a case where the owner isn't in residence. Until now. Will Derek come back to stay?"

"Count on it."

"Winston wasn't well, the last few years. He relied heavily on Plumwell. If it weren't for Andy, they could have lost most everything when credit was so tight. Plumwell may have saved the estate." A pause. "So if he's come to think of it as his own . . ."

I waited.

"He feels strongly about it. They've petitioned Governor Williams for a regulation granting rights to resident managers, though that change could take years. If an heir showed up now . . ." He glanced at me, as if deciding. "Yes, perhaps it's best to use another name."

"Is it safe to go?"

"Mr., ah, Seafort . . . Hope Nation is far from Earth; settlers have handled their own affairs for years. We have a certain spirit of independence that's hard for you visitors to understand. When a problem gets in the way . . . we remove it."

"Would he—"

"I don't know. I won't mention you if I run into Plumwell." Branstead stood.

"Thank you. I'm sorry I deceived you. I see now there was no need."

"You couldn't know that." Branstead, somewhat mollified, walked me to the door. "Tell me, has the Navy ever had a Captain your age? How exactly did it come about?"

I owed him that, and whatever else he asked. I forced a strained smile. "Well, it happened this way . . ."

Early that afternoon, rain turned ruts and chuckholes into small ponds. Secure in our watertight electricar we hummed along past thousands of acres of cultivation. Branstead gave way to Volksteader, then Palabee. Derek asked nervously, "Sir, what will you do?"

"Don't worry." I'd decided not to tell Derek about Branstead's warning, for fear of making him even more nervous.

He would be my cousin. I was practicing how to introduce him when a new mark appeared on the wooden signposts. A few miles beyond, we came to the entrance road, marked with a painted metal sign. "Carr Plantation. Hope Nation's Best."

He slowed. "Wouldn't you rather head back? We'll have more time for the Ventur—"

"Oh, please." I pointed to the service road.

It was a long drive, past herds of cattle grazing in lush green pastures, heads bowed away from the rain. Then, endless fields of corn along both sides of the road. Finally a dip revealed an impressive complex of buildings about half a mile ahead.

We came to a stop at a guardhouse with a lowered rail. The guard leaned into the window. "You fellas looking for something?"

"We're on a trip up the coast road. Can we stay the night?"

He nodded reluctantly. "There's guest privileges. Every place has them. But why stop here?"

I grinned. "Back in Haulers' Rest they told us whatever else we missed we had to see Carr Plantation, 'cause it's the best and biggest on Hope Nation."

He snorted but looked mollified. "Not the biggest. Not yet, anyway. Go on in, I'll ring and tell them you're coming."

I waved and we purred off down the road. The rain had stopped, and a shaft of yellow sunlight gleamed through the clouds. Derek hunched grimly in his seat.

"Your middle name's Anthony?" I asked as a hand sauntered out of the house.

Derek gaped. "Yes, of course. Why—"

The two wings of the huge, pillared plantation house stretched along a manicured gravel drive edged by a low white picket fence. Beds of unfamiliar flowers were interspersed among clean, strong grasses mowed short.

"You the two travelers?" The ranch hand.

I stepped out of the car. "That's right. Nick Ewing." I put out a hand. Well, I'd told the truth. At least some of it.

He broke into a grin. "Fenn Willny. We don't get many come through here anymore, the word's got out the boss doesn't like it. He's soft on joeykids, though. Hasn't got any of his own." He gestured to the mansion. "We tore down the guest house last spring. Travelers stay upstairs. You eat in the kitchen. Come on, I'll take you to the boss."

We followed him inside. The mansion was built on the grand scale. Polished hardwoods with intricate carving decorated the doorways, bespeaking intensive labor at huge cost. The furniture in the hallway was elegant, expensive, and tasteful. Fenn Willny led us to a large office on a corridor between a dining room and a sitting room furnished with "Swedish Modern" terrestrial antiques that must have cost a fortune.

The manager's eyes were cold and appraising. He made no move to welcome us. I glanced at Derek, my stomach churning. What if the manager asked some question I couldn't answer? Why had I ever agreed Derek was a cousin?

"Mr. Plumwell, these are the two travelers, Nick and . . ."

"My cousin Anthony." I grabbed Derek's arm and propelled him forward. "Say hello to Mr. Plumwell, Anthony." I jostled his arm.

Derek shot me a furious glance. "Hello, sir," he mumbled.

I leaned forward confidentially, speaking just loud enough for Derek to hear. "You'll have to pardon Anthony. He's a little slow. I look after him." Derek's biceps rippled.

The plantation manager nodded in understanding. "Welcome to Carr Plantation. You'll be leaving in the morning?" It was a clear suggestion.

"Yes, sir, I guess so." I looked disappointed. "Actually, I was hoping—well, I know it's foolish."

"What's that, young man?" He looked annoyed.

"We only have two days left of our vacation, Mr. Plumwell. I work, and Anthony's in a special school." From Derek, a strangled sound. I said, "We've never seen a big plantation before, and I was hoping somebody could show us around. Of course I could pay . . ."

I couldn't read Plumwell's expression, so I rushed on. "They said to see either Carr Plantation or Hopewell, because they were both special. But Hopewell's too far, and I don't know when we'll get out together again." I spoke loudly to Derek. "Anthony, maybe next year if I get a few more days vacation we'll go to Hopewell. That's the bigger one."

Derek's color rose. He breathed through gritted teeth.

Plumwell frowned. "I suppose you're city boys and don't

know. It's an insult to offer money for hospitality on a plantation; that comes with the territory. Anyway, Hopewell is nothing special. We're the innovative ones."

He paused, looking us over. "We're not in the tour business, but I guess I could spare a hand for a few hours, seeing your brother's retarded. But don't let it get around back in Centraltown or we'll be flooded with freeloaders."

"Zarky!" I nudged Derek. "Did you hear? He's going to show us a real plantation, Anthony." Derek's lips moved, but he turned away and I couldn't see what he said. "He's real happy, sir. It's all he's talked about since Centraltown." I rolled my eyes.

Plumwell winked in understanding. "Why don't you boys stow your gear in your room. I'll have Fenn take you around the center complex before dinner."

"Great, sir!" I shook hands. "Shake hands with Mr. Plumwell." Derek fixed me with a peculiar stare. I pushed him forward. "Anthony, remember your manners, like we taught you!" Livid, Derek offered his hand to the manager, who gave it a condescending squeeze. "Good boy." I patted Derek on the back.

Fenn led us up a grand staircase to the second floor, and continued on a smaller staircase to the third. The rooms were clean and adequate, but less ornate than in the lower part of the house. "I'll wait for you in the front hall." He loped downstairs two steps at a time.

I closed the door behind us, dumped my duffel on the bunk. White-faced, Derek glared lasers across the room.

"Something wrong?" I sorted through my belongings.

Without warning he launched himself across the bed, clawing at my neck. I caught his wrists as I fell backward. He dove on top of me, seeking my throat.

"Listen!" It had no effect. He strained to break from my grasp. "Derek!" He thrashed wildly until his wrists broke free. "Stop and listen!" At last, he got his hands on my windpipe.

Unable to breathe, I twisted and heaved, throwing my hips and bouncing him up and down. When he bounced high enough I thrust my knee upward with all my strength. That stopped him. With a yawp of pain he rolled to the side, clutching his testicles. I rolled on top of him. Sitting on his back I forced his arm up between his shoulder blades, and waited.

He grunted between his teeth, "Get off! I'll kill you!" I slapped him sharply alongside the ear. He struggled harder. Each time he heaved I pulled his arm higher behind his back. Finally he lay still. "Get off!" A string of curses.

"When you're ready to listen."

"Off, you shit!"

I slapped him harder. I liked him, but there were limits. Finally he lay still. "All right. I'll listen when you get off."

I let go and sat on my bed. "You have a complaint, Derek?"

He bounded to his feet, sputtering. "Your retarded cousin Anthony? You say that *in my own house*?"

"Do they want company, Derek?"

My calm question gave him pause. "No, not much. Why?"

"What did I get us?" He was silent. "A guided tour," I answered myself. "A tour of the whole place. Anyway, you said I should call you my cous—"

"I'm a little slow? A SPECIAL SCHOOL? How DARE you!"

I let my voice sharpen. "Think! You can ask anything you want and they won't take offense. They won't even know why you're asking." As the realization sunk in he sank slowly onto his bed. "I got you in, when you didn't have the guts to come. I arranged a guided tour. I heard Vax call you retarded, and you took it. What in God's own hell is the matter with you?"

"That was the wardroom," he muttered. "Not my own house."

"What difference does that make?"

"You'd have to be one of us to understand. In your home you have respect. Dignity."

I shrugged. "You're just a middy. You don't get dignity until you make lieutenant."

I think at that moment he'd forgotten entirely about the Navy. He looked at the marks on his Captain's neck and gulped. "I'm sorry, sir." His voice was small.

"I have a right to dignity too," I told him. "Look what you've done to mine."

"I shouldn't have touched you." His gaze was on the floor.

Well, I'd told him to treat me as senior midshipman rather than Captain. Look where it got me. "You'll be sorrier. Seven demerits, when we get back to the ship." Oddly, it made him feel better. It made me feel better too. My throat hurt. I giggled. "I admit, though, you had provocation." I snickered, recalling his fury in Plumwell's office. The more I thought about it, the funnier it seemed.

Watching me roll helplessly on my bed in silent mirth Derek glowered anew, but after a while he couldn't help himself and began to laugh with me. After a few moments we stopped. I wiped my eyes.

"I'm sorry, sir, but you're a peasant," Derek told me. "You don't understand dignity." It started us going again. This time when we stopped all was well between us.

"Come on, aristocrat, let's inspect your estate." We left the room and hurried down the stairs. "Just remember to play along," I whispered at the last moment. Daringly, he punched me in the arm before we reached the main floor.

# 24

The helicopter swooped along the dense hedgerow marking the plantation border, while sprinklers made mist in the early-morning light. We were exploring the more distant sections of the estate, having toured the main compound the evening before.

"How much wheat do you grow?" Derek had to shout above the noise of the motor.

"A lot."

"No, how much?" Derek insisted. Fenn, in the pilot's seat, pursed his lips.

I leaned across from the back seat. "Just say anything. He won't know the difference."

Fenn frowned at my insensitivity. "No, I'll tell him. One point two million bushels, same as it's been for years."

Derek furrowed his brow. "Is that a lot?" Since dinner the previous night he had burrowed deep into his role.

Fenn smiled. "Enough. And then there's six hundred thousand bushels of corn. And sorghum."

"I like corn!" Derek said happily. I nudged him, afraid he would overdo it. "Nicky, why'd you poke me?" His tone was anxious. "Am I bothering him too much?" Nicky? I'd kill him.

"You ask too many questions, Anthony."

"He's no trouble," Fenn said.

Derek's look was triumphant. "See, Nicky?" He turned to Fenn. "Is this all yours and Mr. Plumwell's?"

"Don't I wish!" Fenn brought us down on a concrete pad outside a large metal-roofed building. "I work for Mr. Plumwell, and he's just the manager." His tone changed. "Course, he's been here most of his life."

"Doesn't the owner live here?" I asked.

"Old Winston died six years ago, but he was sick long before that. This place was started way back, by the first Randolph Carr. He left it to Winston."

"I take it he had no children."

"Are you kidding? Five." Fenn opened the gate. "They say his oldest boy was a heller. Randolph II. He gave the old man so much trouble Winston sent him all the way to Earth to college. He never came home while Winston was alive."

Derek was attentive.

"Will he ever?" I asked.

"Randy was supposed to be on the ship that docked this week, and we expected we'd find ourselves working for him. But he died on the trip, so it's all up in the air."

"What will happen?"

Fenn gestured toward the building we were about to enter. "This is the second-largest feed mill on the planet. It's entirely automated. Takes only three men to run it." We looked in. "Randy had a son, some snot born in Upper New York. They say he's on the ship. The joeyboy's never even been here, so he doesn't know squat about planting. I guess he'll be sent back to Earth for schooling. I don't know; Mr. Plumwell's made the arrangements. The joeykid won't have any say until he's twenty-two."

"Then what?" A new tension was in Derek's voice.

Fenn grinned. "Between you and me, boys, I wouldn't be surprised if by that time Carr Plantation's books were in such a state he'd need Mr. Plumwell more than ever."

I grinned. "The Carrs should have stayed if they wanted to run the place."

Fenn looked serious. "You're righter than you know. Someday we'll have a law about absentee owners. Sure, they're entitled to profits, but a resident manager who stays all his life and runs things, he should have rights too. The management should pass down in his family, not the owner's. If—"

"Now wait a min—" Derek broke in.

I overrode him fast. "Anthony, don't interrupt!"

"But he—"

"Haven't you learned your manners?" I shoved Derek with force. "Apologize!" He looked surly. I squeezed his arm. "Go on!" Derek mumbled an apology, and I breathed easier. Perhaps when he calmed, he'd realize he'd nearly blown our cover.

Fenn asked, "Aren't you a bit rough on the joey?"

"Sometimes he needs sitting on." My tone was cross. "His father let him believe he was too good for discipline." Derek shot me a deadly glance but kept quiet.

"You see how it is," Fenn said. "Mr. Plumwell's been here thirty years, and he knows every inch of this plantation. Last year we cleared thirty million unibucks, even after the new acreage. Carr Plantation has to be run by a professional."

"Where do you keep all the cash?" Derek was back in character.

Fenn smiled mirthlessly. "Some of it goes to the Carr accounts at Branstead Bank and Trust. The rest goes for salaries and expenses."

"So the Carr boy gets to play with the money even if he can't boss the plantation," I said.

"Not quite. The account is in the Carr name but Mr. Plumwell has control until a Carr shows up who has the right to run the estate. Mr. Plumwell makes sure the right people are on our side, that sort of thing. That money pool helps protect our way of life." He looked at me closely. "How did we get on this subject?"

"I'm not sure." My tone was bright and innocent. "What's this conveyor belt do?"

That night we were invited to dine with Plumwell and his staff. I made a show of nagging Derek about his table manners; he retaliated by calling me "Nicky". All the while Derek's penetrating glance was taking in the oil paintings hanging above the huge stone fireplace, the fine china, the crystal glassware, the succulent foods and drink. He eyed Mr. Plumwell's place at the head of the table with something less than delight.

In our room, after dinner, he moped on his bed while I got ready to turn out the light.

"What's bothering you, Anthony?"

His voice was quiet. "Please belay that, Mr. Seafort."

"What's wrong, Derek?"

"This is my house. I should be at the head of the table."

"Someday."

"But in the meantime . . ." He brooded. "Fenn mentioned one point two million bushels of wheat. The reports they sent my father listed seven hundred thousand. Someone's been skimming. Who knows what else Plumwell's stolen? I've got to do something."

"Why?"

He was surprised. "It's my money."

I had no sympathy. "You have your pay billet. Are you hurting?"

"That's not the point," he said with disdain. "Should this—this thief get away with what's not rightfully his?"

"Yes, if he's improving your estate." He was shocked into silence. "You're out of the picture, Derek. You're so wealthy you won't even miss what he steals. In the meantime, he's opening up new acreage that permanently benefits your plantation. He's doing a good job, stealing or not."

"That's easy for you to say," Derek said bitterly. "You never had anything, and you never will!"

I snapped off the light, determined not to speak to him before morning. I yearned for the isolation of the Captain's cabin.

Presently he said, "I'm sorry." I ignored him, cherishing my hurt.

After a while he cleared his throat. "I apologize, Mr. Seafort." I made no answer. He snapped on the light. "Am I talking to the Captain now, or Mr. Seafort the ex-midshipman?"

A good question. In fairness to him, I wasn't Captain at the moment. "The ex-midshipman."

"Then I won't stand at attention. I didn't mean what I just said. I was angry and wanted to hurt you. Please don't make me grovel."

I relented. "All right. But I repeat what I told you. He's doing a good job building Carr Plantation even if he does skim the profits."

"What if I tell him who I am, just before we leave. That'll show him he can't—"

I felt a sudden chill. "Don't even think about it, Derek." Thousands of uncleared acres adjoined the cultivated fields. Some of them had hardly been explored.

He shivered. "Well, maybe not while we're still here. But when I get back to town I'll file suit."

"No."

"He can't be allowed to get away with it. If I move fast I'll save—"

"No, I said."

"Why not?"

I was nettled. "Do you plan to stay on Hope Nation to fight a lawsuit?"

"I guess I can't, unless you let me resign, but—"

"Get this straight, Mr. Carr! For the next four years you're a midshipman in the United Nations Naval Service! You go where the Navy sends you. Understand? You took an oath, and a gentleman shouldn't need reminding. The life you see here—it doesn't exist yet."

"But—"

"This is a form of time travel. Perhaps someday you'll live here and worry about your riches, but not now. I took you on a visit to the future. You can't touch anything and nobody can hear you!" There was silence. "Understand?"

He didn't answer. I rolled over and snapped off the light. Presently I heard Derek Anthony Carr, scion of the Hope Nation Carrs, cry himself to sleep after his Captain's tongue-lashing.

* * *

In the morning I felt guilty for having spoken so sharply. We brought our duffels down to breakfast. I had Anthony thank everyone in sight. Even Plumwell smiled as we tooled down the drive in our electricar.

"Now what?" I asked when we were out of sight.

Derek's tone was petulant. "I've seen enough plantations, if I won't be—" His fingers drummed on the armrest; when he spoke again his voice was subdued. "Sorry, sir. Do you still want to take me to the Venturas?"

"Yes."

"I think I'd like that."

We headed back to Centraltown, camping once along the way. By the time we were back Derek was in good spirits, and I found to my surprise I'd begun to miss the organized bustle of shipboard life.

I decided to shuttle up to *Hibernia* for a couple of days before leaving for the Ventura Mountains; Derek opted to stay in Centraltown. The peasant and the aristocrat parted company with awkward shyness.

I changed back into Navy blues and tried to tame my wild hair before checking in at Admiralty House. Forbee confirmed that there was still no interstellar Captain in the Hope Nation system. Unless *Telstar* unexpectedly appeared, none was scheduled to arrive for another five months. In the meantime they'd radioed all local vessels to ask for lieutenants and midshipmen. If none volunteered, Forbee would simply assign me the necessary officers, and leave the local fleet short-handed.

After boarding, I took a luxurious hot shower in my cabin, ran all my clothes through the sonic cleaner, and hunted up a barber on Orbit Station. Hair trimmed back to my normal Navy length, I felt a new man. I roamed my empty ship as if looking for something, but I knew not what. Vax, when I stumbled over him, greeted me like a long-lost brother. He too found the ship's silence eerie and disturbing. I even unbent so far as to try a game of chess with him, to his delight. He was no match.

Vax had learned through the grapevine that I would remain with *Hibernia*. To my astonishment he was pleased rather than apprehensive. I'd have thought he had more sense than to look forward to a cruise with an unqualified Captain who had my peculiar emotional disabilities. I didn't remind him that depending on what officers were reassigned to *Hibernia*, he might be transferred out as a replacement. Time enough for that if it happened.

Depressed and not knowing why, I took the next scheduled shuttle back down to Centraltown. Customs and quarantine waved me through; by now I'd become a regular. Small-town life was amazingly relaxed compared, say, to Lunapolis.

I still had two days before I was to meet Derek for our trip to the mountains. I toured downtown Centraltown, explored the local museum, and ate in two of the recommended restaurants, occasionally encountering crewmen and former passengers. I stayed overnight in a prefab inn with the usual plastic furniture and decor. I bought a newschip and stuck it in my holovid; on page three was an announcement of an Anabaptist revival meeting in Newtown Hall. Mrs. Donhauser wasted no time. I thought of attending, but decided I didn't care to meet her in her professional capacity.

Thoughts of our passengers reminded me I'd promised to look up Amanda Frowel. I immediately decided against it. Then I spent the best part of an afternoon wandering aimlessly up and down the streets, arguing with myself. Sheepishly, I dug her address out of my duffel. After dinner I strolled across town to the address she had given.

"Nicky!" An apron around her waist, she smiled happily through her screen door, old-fashioned and domestic, inflicting a pang of regret that I soon had to leave the colony. "Come in!" Her home was the back half of a comfortable wood house on a quiet side street on the edge of town. She rented, so help me, from a widow trying to make ends meet.

"I was just passing by," I mumbled, sounding an idiot.

"But I was hoping you'd come. Look, my books are all over the place!" She brushed aside a pile of holovid chips scattered on a table. "I started work three days ago. Know what? They don't want me just to teach natural science; I'm supposed to set up the whole science curriculum! They've never had one, isn't that ridiculous?"

"Hasn't anybody been teaching geology and biology?"

"Sure, but not in any organized way. They just got people

who knew their subjects to come in and talk about them. Isn't it quaint?"

"Very." My tone was sour. Our world aboard *Hibernia* seemed light-years away.

"Would you like to take a walk? I'll show you the school." She was so enthused I agreed to go, wishing I hadn't come to visit. She threw on a light jacket against the evening cool, and we set out for the school, about a mile away. She chattered with animation at first, but after a while she sensed my mood and grew quieter. We walked, hand in hand, under two moons. Their crossed shadows began to make me dizzy.

The public school was a one-story building encased in sheet metal, apparently a popular local building material. Amanda unlocked the door and took me inside. "This is where I work." She showed me a classroom. The consoles at the student desks struck no chord of recognition, as my own schooling was at home with Father. Amanda's desk and master console were to one side, where she could watch both the large screen and the students.

"The new term starts in three weeks. Nicky, it's so exciting! The joeys will be so different from northamericans."

"You think so?"

"Wouldn't they, growing up in such a wild, free place?"

"I suppose." I was feeling more and more depressed. "Amanda, I have to go. I have an appointment."

"You couldn't stay awhile?" Her voice was wistful. My chest ached.

"Come, I'll walk you home." I wanted to leave and stay at the same time. On ship I'd never felt so bumbling and awkward with her. We walked mostly in silence through the darkened streets; Major had set and only Minor remained to guide us.

She hesitated, in front of her rustic home. "Will I see you again before you leave?"

"I don't think so. I'm taking Derek to the Venturas tomorrow, then I'll have to go back aboard." I hadn't mentioned I was still in command.

"Lieutenant Malstrom promised to take you there, didn't he?"

"Yes." I was grateful she remembered.

"Oh, Nicky." Gently, she kissed the back of my hand. "Life isn't the way we plan it."

"No," I said miserably. I forced myself to smile. "Goodbye, Amanda."

"Good-bye, Nicky." We looked into each other's eyes before she turned to go. As if in astonishment, she said, "We'll never see each other again."

"No." I couldn't stop looking at her.

"Well . . . good-bye, then." She crossed her yard.

"Amanda?"

She stopped. "What is it?"

"Nothing. I—nothing." As she opened her door I blurted, "Would you like to go with me?"

"To the mountains? I can't, Nicky. I have a job."

"I know. I thought maybe somehow—"

"School starts in three weeks. If I don't have my curriculum ready . . ."

"They'll fire you?"

She giggled. They'd waited three years for her; it would take three more to send for a replacement. "They won't be very happy." She frowned. "But I don't care. I want to see the Ventura Mountains."

"Really?" I said stupidly.

"With you. I want to see them with you."

My eyes stung. I felt light-headed and miserable all at once. I ran to her and we embraced. "You'll really go? God, can we start now?"

"Give me the night to get ready. And I have to explain to Mrs. Potter." After a while she managed to get me to leave.

Derek didn't seem put out when I told him I'd invited Amanda. He helped me buy a second pup tent and load the extra food and other supplies in the jet heli we'd rented. I had to promise the heli service three times not to tamper with the transponder; Captain Grone's disappearance must have made them skittish.

We took off for the Western Continent shortly after breakfast. I was the only licensed driver; they'd taught us helipiloting at Academy but Derek and Amanda had never learned.

The permabatteries had ample charge for months. From time to time I turned on the autopilot to lean back and rest my eyes. The craft was roomy enough for Derek and Amanda to switch seats; they did so several times before settling down.

At four hundred fifty kilometers per hour it took us more than eight hours to reach the western shore. The huge submarine trees growing from the bottom of Farreach Ocean sent probing tentacles to the surface to absorb light. Plants somewhat like water lilies floated on the surface, rising and falling with the swells. The ocean was a vast liquid field of competing vegetable organisms.

The jagged spires of the Western Mountains loomed on the horizon long before we reached the continent; their raw power was breathtaking. The low hills and gently sculpted valleys of the Eastern Continent were tame compared to the vigor of these much younger peaks.

Derek pored over the map. "Do you want an established campsite or should we find a place of our own?"

"Let's find someplace," I said. Amanda nodded agreement. The cleared campsites would be remote enough, but we had no need to settle for them. Even after a hundred years, there were places in the continent no foot had trod.

Western Continent had settlements, far to the south, but here in the northern reaches virgin forests covered the sprawling land. At the coast, phalanxes of hills plunged to the sea to bury themselves in the swirling foam. Farther inland, great chasms cowered beneath the bristling peaks of the Venturas. The heli service had marked some of the more spectacular sights on our map. Taking bearings from nav satellites I headed west over dense foliage.

As dusk neared I set us down on a grassy plain high in the hills. To one side was deep forest; a hundred feet beyond, the plain gave way to steep hills running down to a green and yellow valley. Across the vale a peak thrust upward so steeply that little grew on it. Waterfalls tumbled from the creases in the hill.

We got out the three-mil poly tents and their collapsible poles. I helped Derek pound stakes into the soft earth. We clipped the thin, tough material across the poles, and the tents were ready. Amanda began trundling in our gear.

Derek brought the micro and the battery cooler from the heli. He delved into the cooler and emerged with softies. While I downed mine in two long swallows, he kicked at the grass. "How about going really primitive?"

I asked, "How?"

"A bonfire." A heady thought. In Cardiff, as in most regions of home, wood was scarce and pollution so great that hardly anyone could get a permit to burn outdoors. Even the flue over Father's hearth had its dampers and scrubbers.

Here, we need have no such concerns, as long as we were careful. I began clearing space for a fire.

The tough native grasses didn't pull out easily; it took a shovel to dig them out. Their shallow intertwined root system ran just below the surface, and I had to spade to break the roots free.

Derek and Amanda returned from time to time with armfuls of firewood. I wondered if they intended our blaze to be seen from Centraltown. Our work kept us warm in the chill of the upland evening, but when we finished we immediately built up the fire.

I fed the flames from my cushion near the pit, while Derek and Amanda consulted on dinner like two master chefs sharing a kitchen. It pleased me that they liked each other.

We ate at fireside under the gleam of two benevolent moons. In the dark of the night, the crackling of the fire and the muted splashing of the waterfall across the valley were our only sounds. Knowing there were none, still I listened for insects and birds calling in the night.

Hope Nation seemed too silent. I knew our ecologists were preparing to introduce a few bird species and selected terrestrial insects. Bees to pollinate crops the old-fashioned way, for instance.

"It's beautiful, Nicky." Amanda sat between us. We'd devoured our dinner and were lazing around the campfire. Our once mighty stacks of wood were fast diminishing, but they'd last until bed.

I tossed twigs into the flames. "What will people make of it when they settle here?"

"They wouldn't ruin a place like this."

I snorted. "You should see Cardiff." I'd seen photos of home in the old days, before the disposal dumps and treatment plants and the litter of modern civilization had improved the terrain. Still, the picturesque old smelters remained, some of them, as ruins.

I moved closer to the fire, watching my handsome midshipman's face as he chatted with Amanda. Odd feelings stirred, recalling Jason, eons past. I shivered, wrenched myself back to reality. "Have you camped out with a friend before, Derek?"

He laughed. "On the rooftops of Upper New York?"

We stared into the firelight.

After a time he said to the flames, "I've never had a friend before, Mr. Seafort."

I didn't know how to answer. In Cardiff I had companions my own age. Together, we ran in the streets and got into mischief. Father, vigilant about my own behavior, grudgingly accepted my choice of associates. Jason and I were especially close, until the football riot of '90.

The silence stretched.

"Mr. Seafort, I want you to know." Derek's voice was shy. "This was the best day of my whole life."

I could think of nothing to say. Not knowing what else to do, I reached out and patted his shoulder.

After a while Amanda yawned, and I found myself doing the same. "A long flight. I'm ready for bed." I stood, and Amanda gathered her blanket.

An awkward moment. Amanda and I took a step toward the larger tent but stopped, embarrassed. Derek pretended not to notice. Hunching closer to the fire he peeled off his shirt in its warmth. I tugged Amanda's hand, gesturing toward our tent. On impulse, she let go my fingers, crossed to Derek. She leaned over him and kissed him on the cheek. In the flickering light I saw him blush right up to the roots of his hair. "G'night." He fled to his tent.

Smiling, I followed Amanda into our own shelter. We began taking off our clothes, poking and jostling each other in the closeness. I shivered when my skin touched the cold foam mattress. Amanda crawled in beside me.

Perhaps it was the first night in the exotic wildness of Western Continent. Aroused as never before, I tried to possess Amanda absolutely. My fingers and tongue roamed, caressing, probing, stroking, taking her warmth and making it mine. I sucked greedily at her juices, her feverish hands guiding me gently. When at last I entered her it was as if I had become whole, our bodies thrusting desperately for fulfillment in simultaneous passion.

When it was over I lay drained of everything, feeling her heartbeat subside slowly against my ear. We rested, but again and again in the night we were like wild animals, coming alive to the frenzy of youth and desire. When morning came at last I slept in Amanda's arms, peaceful, comforted, sated. Whole.

It was never so fine again. Perhaps the newness was gone; perhaps some subtle tides failed to mesh. In the stillness of the nights we came together, loving, tender, eager to satisfy. What we gave each other was good, and pleasing. But the first night remained a loving memory, never equaled.

Derek surely knew what we were experiencing. At least he must have heard Amanda cry out. But during the daytime we were a warm and friendly threesome, enjoying each other's company, relaxing together. Only when dark fell did the two of us shyly retreat to our haven while Derek crawled into his solitary cot.

A dawn came when, Amanda's head resting lightly on my shoulder, I woke with sadness, knowing our togetherness was drawing to a close. Amanda stirred in her sleep. As quietly as I could I slipped out of bed, gathered my clothes and crept out of the tent.

It was bitter cold; I threw some sticks on the embers and was at last rewarded with a sputtering flame. I fed it until it provided some warmth. I put a cup of coffee in the micro and when it heated, I held it between my two hands inhaling its vapor.

Restless, I wandered beyond the edge of the campsite toward the lightening sky, found a place to sit at the crest of a hill looking down into the valley below. Sipping my blessedly hot coffee I watched a moody yellow sun hoist itself over the peaks opposite, casting roseate hues on the bleak gray of dawn. The fog in the valley below began to lift. Across the glen, an eleven-hundred-foot waterfall threw itself endlessly over the cliff into the waiting valley.

Never had I seen a place so magnificent. Dawn brightened into day. Below, a smaller falls became visible as the night mists evaporated. The greens, yellows, and blues of the foliage brightened into their daytime splendor.

I had to leave this peaceful planet, and with it, Amanda. I must sail on to Detour, return briefly to Hope Nation to board passengers, then endure the long dreary voyage home to face an unforgiving Admiralty at Lunapolis. I knew they'd never give me command again. I knew I would never again come to this place. I knew I would lose Amanda to light-years of forgetfulness.

It was my lot to be banished from paradise.

Overwhelmed by despair amid the stark beauty of the Venturas, I mourned for Sandy Wilsky, for Mr. Tuak, for Captain Malstrom, for Father lost forever in his dour hardness. For the beauty I hadn't known and would never know again. I cursed my weakness, my pettiness, the lack of wisdom that made tragedy of my attempt to captain *Hibernia*. Then Amanda, sweet Amanda, came from the glade and enveloped me in her arms, caressing, hugging, rocking, lending me solace only she could give.

After a while we walked together back to the campsite, my soul clinging to the gentle warmth of her touch. Derek, wearing short pants, shirtless, was just starting off to the stream with a bar of soap. Seeing us, he went on his way, mercifully silent.

"Nicky, those terrible events on *Hibernia* weren't your fault."

I sat brooding near the firepit, waiting for the micro to heat my coffee. "No? My talent is to hurt people. I killed Tuak and Rogoff; you know it wasn't necessary. At Miningcamp I killed the rebel Kerwin Jones and his men, yet made a deal to spare his cohorts on the station. What was the difference?"

"You're too harsh on your—"

"I was cruel to Vax for months. I sent poor Derek to the Chief to be caned for nothing at all. Even Alexi—if I'd been a better leader I wouldn't have had to send him to the barrel. The way I treated the Pilot I can't even discuss. I think of them all the time, Amanda. Lord God, how I hate being clumsy and incompetent!"

"You're not, Nicky."

"Tell that to Sandy Wilsky." My tone was searing.

She was silent for a time. "Must you always do everything right?"

"Not always. But I'm talking about losing my ship and killing my midshipmen and brutalizing the crew!" Again the miasma of despair closed about me.

Amanda sat near, her arm thrown across my shoulders. "You've done your best. Give yourself peace."

"I don't know how." I lapsed silent until Derek returned, his skin pink and briskly scrubbed.

"Man, that's cold!" He plunged into the firesite and stood warming himself by the flames. He glanced at me with concern. "Are you all right, Mr. Seafort?"

"Fine." With an effort I lightened my tone. "What would you people like to do today?" It was to be our last full day in Western Continent.

Over breakfast, we decided we'd hike across the valley to the waterfall. I packed my backpack and set out with the others, hoping physical exertion would help banish my melancholy.

It took only a couple of hours to descend our side of the slope. But the valley was wider than it had appeared from the heights, and we had to pick our way among fallen trunks and viny growths that fastened to every crack. At last, weary, we reached the far side of the glen. A short hike brought us to the base of the waterfall where, to our delight, a pool was hidden in the dense undergrowth. Hot and sweating I began to strip off my clothes. After a moment Amanda did likewise. Derek hesitated, ill at ease.

"Come on, middy! It's no different from the wardroom!" My annoyance was evident. His shyness was from his aristocratic past, not his Navy present. Perhaps, groundside for three weeks, he'd forgotten he shared a bunkroom, head, and shower with Paula Treadwell and the other middies. Blushing, he took off his clothes and waded in.

I'd forgotten how wonderful were simple pleasures. A cold swim after our long hot exertion had a marvelous restorative effect. We cavorted and splashed like small children until our energy was spent. Finally we dressed, had a snack from our packs, and prepared to go back.

"Hey!" Derek pointed to the ground at the pool's edge, where a sandaled footprint was outlined in the mud.

"We're not alone." Amanda was crestfallen.

I said, "Just some other tourists." They'd come to see the spectacular waterfall, as we had.

"We didn't see anyone."

"They're not here now," I said impatiently. "Who knows how long ago they left that footprint?"

Derek stared at the mud. His voice was quiet. "It rained hard two nights ago." The hairs rose on the back of my neck as my imagination brought forth an alien creature sipping water from this very pool. Then I laughed at my foolishness. Aliens wouldn't wear sandals like our own.

"So, someone else is around," I said. It didn't matter.

Derek jumped up with enthusiasm. "I'll bet they're down there!" He pointed to a wooded area past an open field farther down the valley. "Let's find them!"

I didn't want to disturb the other group's privacy, but I had little choice but to follow unless I asserted my authority and demanded that we turn back. My sour mood returned. We scrambled across rocks and through broad-leaved vines until we reached the thicket. We walked along the edge of the field toward the woods.

"Good heavens, that's corn!" Amanda stopped to examine it. Several rows of stalks stood above low-lying vegetation that covered the meadow.

"It can't be; there's no native corn."

"Don't tell me about corn, Nicky."

Ignoring our conversation, Derek ran ahead, out of sight. "Wait," I called, to no avail. Uneasy, I hurried after him. "Let's go, Amanda."

I stopped so suddenly she caromed into me. Derek, his hands raised, backed slowly away from a ragged man waving a laser. "All of you! Stay right there!" The scarecrow waved his arm back and forth between Derek and the two of us. Casually, I stepped between Amanda and the laser. The man's eyes darted among us. Deeply tanned, he wore cutoff pants with ragged edges.

I cleared my throat. "Good afternoon, Captain Grone."

The gun wavered. "Who told you my name?"

"How many other settlers are hiding in the Venturas?"

"There could be more. How did you know my name?"

"The heli service told us about you." Not exactly a lie. They'd mentioned him in passing.

He waved the laser, sounding glum. "I can't let you go knowing where to find me."

Time to gamble. "Did you bring a recharger for that pistol, when you fled Centraltown?"

He glared, then dropped his eyes and lowered the gun. "It's been out for months," he admitted. "Damn the thing."

"It's all right, Derek," I said. "Put your hands down." Sheepishly, the middy let his hands fall. I stepped forward. "Nick Seafort of U.N.S. *Hibernia.*" I offered my hand. After a moment the ex-Captain took it. "May I present Miss Frowel, and Midshipman Derek Carr. Midshipman, you salute a Captain!" Derek snapped his fanciest salute, which after a moment the fugitive sailor in his ragged shorts and torn shirt returned.

"Honey, come out!" he called over his shoulder. In a moment a lithe, well-tanned young woman emerged. Amanda quietly looked her over, with a glance my way; I pretended not to notice.

"This is my wife Jana. Jana, this is Mr. Seafort and his friends Derek and Amanda."

"Hi, everyone!" Jana Grone seemed pleased at our company. "Come join us for coffee." As if it were an everyday occurrence, she turned and led us into the woods. We came to a simple hut, hidden under the leafy canopy. A precarious mud-bricked chimney rose from one side. She took a kettle from an iron grate and poured coffee into several glass jars. Ceremoniously, she handed them around.

"To our first guests," she said.

"And our last." Her husband was morose. "He'll report us and they'll come for me."

"As far as I'm concerned," I blurted, surprising myself, "you're a deranged joe who thinks he's the missing Captain Grone. Until I see proof, I've got nothing to tell Admiralty."

Hope flashed in his eyes. "You'd really do that?"

I thought briefly of impressing Grone back into the service to sail *Hibernia*, and decided the ship was safer even with me. "You're a local problem. I have nothing to do with it."

"You mean that?" He probed my expression. "Then we have another chance! Still, I suppose we'll have to move inland. You're the second group to camp within sight of the falls."

"We can move next spring," Jana told him. "Plant a new

field farther away." She added wistfully, "We could still hike to the pool sometimes."

Amanda inspected her glass. "Two questions. Where do you get coffee?"

"We plant a little of everything," Grone said, as if proud to show off his accomplishments. "We, uh, borrowed a couple of coffee plants from Hopewell, along with the other vegetables. They grow quite well here. See? They're in the seventh row over." I peered. It all looked the same to me.

"And your other question?" Jana.

"What are you people doing here?"

The two exchanged glances. Jana said, "Tell her."

He glanced about with caution and dropped his voice. "The meteors."

"What meteors?" Derek and Amanda, as one.

Grone spoke in a whisper. "It was night. I was piloting the ten-seater shuttle, helping out a friend. I was almost through the ionosphere when they came. Dozens of them."

"Meteorites," I said. He needed hormone rebalancing. A case for the psych wards.

"Yeah, meteorites. Some real ones, but others too. The ones that sprayed."

"What in hell are you talking about?" My shoulder blades twitched with the same eerie feeling as when I'd confronted Darla's glitch.

"My trajectory almost matched the meteorites. I rode with them a long while. I saw them spray something."

"Oh, come on!" For a moment I'd actually considered putting him on *Hibernia*'s bridge. I shuddered.

"No, they did! Long trails of vapor. You know what it reminded me of? Insecticide."

"So you jumped ship and came here?" My tone was wondering.

"I got out as fast as I could. After I landed I got Jana and we took a heli and a whole bunch of supplies and stopped at Hopewell and got some plants and we took off." His words tumbled. "I smashed the transponder so they couldn't track us."

"But why?"

"If you'd seen the spray you'd know!"

He was starting to bore me. "Know what?"

"They were spraying us, I told you. And you know what happened right after? The epidemic. Some bug nobody's ever seen, that breaks down cell walls and kills whoever it hits. We listened on our radio before it went."

"Who sprayed you?" Amanda was tense now.

"They were," he said darkly.

"Water vapor." My voice was reassuring. "Ice in the meteorites boiled into steam and vaporized. That's all." She studied my face, relaxed a trifle.

Vehemently, Grone shook his head. "Don't give me that goofjuice; you think I'm some groundsider doesn't know the difference? I've been around! I went interstellar three times and ran interplanetary for five years before. How old are you, sixteen? You joeykids think you know everything!" He subsided, grumbling to himself. His wife gave him an encouraging pat. After a moment he smiled at her.

"We're safer out here," Grone said softly, his voice calmer. He looked up to the sky as if for more meteorites. "If they think they've got everybody, they'll stop spraying."

I shook my head. "You've gone around the bend."

"Think so?" He looked cunning. "Then there's no point in reporting us, is there?"

Jana clasped his arm. "Peter took the time to save me before he ran for safety. That's how much he loves me." She squeezed his biceps and he rewarded her with an approving smile.

"The epidemic is over," I said. "Didn't you hear? We have a vaccine."

"They miscalculated this time. Next time will be worse."

I realized logic couldn't reach him, and changed the topic. How did they manage to survive in the wilderness? That set them both off. With pride, they took turns describing their inventions and accommodations. After a while I thought it safe to suggest leaving.

"I promise I won't mention you," I told him. "Good luck. I hope you make it through the winters." On the Western Continent, winter brought frigid winds and heavy snows.

"Oh, we have to," Jana said. "We have a baby coming." On that forlorn note we parted.

Climbing back to our campsite took most of our breath.

When we finally dropped our backpacks near the firepit it was almost dark. Derek and Amanda consulted on a farewell dinner and broke out a bottle of wine they'd saved. We dined on steak and potatoes, hot bread, coffee and wine. A lovely meal.

In our tent, knowing it was our final night together, Amanda and I were tender and solicitous, but our passion was muted. A bittersweet moment, but I cherished it nonetheless.

In the morning we packed our tents and equipment into the heli, carefully doused the remains of our fire, and lifted off for the long flight home. Once again I was the only pilot. From time to time I let Derek handle the controls and he was as pleased as a child.

Near home our conversation turned to Captain Grone and his pathetic state of mind. Amanda said, "Imagine the two of them trying to nurse a baby through a mountain winter."

"They'll be all right." I shrugged. "They've already been through it once."

"You seem pretty callous about it."

"Am I? Maybe it comes from being in the Navy. People make their own beds, then have to lie in them." I recalled saying the same to Pilot Haynes, and quickly changed the subject. "It's what can happen to a Captain under too much stress. Sitting alone in his cabin brooding, imagining everyone is out to get him . . ." Derek shot me a thoughtful glance, and I hurried on. "Having no one to talk to is the worst of it. That's probably why Grone snapped."

"Poor man."

"That's why I'm so worried about going on."

"About what?"

I should have been more cautious. Instead, I said with disgust, "Didn't I tell you? They can't find a Captain to replace me. I'm still senior. I'll have to sail to Detour and home again."

"You can't!"

"I have to," I said. "It's my job."

Her voice was ominous. "How long have you known about this, Nicky?"

"Since I reported to Admiralty." I made a helpless gesture. "There's no way out."

"You could resign!" With an effort, she took the edge

from her tone. "I know you tried your best, Nicky. But you were very lucky; you know that. You could have lost the ship."

"More than once."

"But you'll still go? Is glory so important to you?"

"Not glory," I said shortly. "You know I can't break my oath."

It seemed to anger her more. "All this time you knew you would go again as Captain, and didn't tell me?"

"That's why I was so upset all week!"

"I'm the one who has a right to be upset. I hate dishonesty!"

"Dishon—Amanda, I'd have told you if I thought about it. I figured everyone in Centraltown knew. And what choice did I have? I—"

"You have one honorable choice! Resign!"

"He's senior officer," Derek said. "It's his respon—"

"Midshipman, stay out of this! Amanda, that's not fair."

"I hate having gone with you under false pretenses." Amanda's tone was harsh. "And I hate you more for tricking me. I won't discuss it further!"

Enraged, I throttled as high as the motor would allow, indifferent to engine wear. After an hour of mutual sullen silence I spotted the coastline and followed it north to Centraltown.

Amanda, still refusing to speak to me, stalked off with her gear to find a taxi. I remained with Derek to return the heli and sort out our belongings. Late in the evening I saw Derek to the shuttle and thumbed a ride to Amanda's house on the edge of town.

The lights were out but I knocked nonetheless. After several raps she came to the door wearing a night robe. "What is it?" She spoke through the glass door.

I took a deep breath. She deserved honesty, no matter the cost. "Amanda, I love you. I'll never see you again and I want a better memory to carry home. I'm sorry for my faults. I'm sorry for not telling you. Please, forgive me."

She sighed. "Oh, Nicky. Why does it have to be this way?" She came out onto the tiny porch.

"I'm sorry," I said dumbly. "I wanted you to be happy. You made me feel so good."

Her eyes glistened. "I'll miss you, Nick. I'll always think of you."

"I wish I could stay, but I can't. I don't think I'll ever be able to come back."

"I know." She tried to smile and couldn't. She kissed me gently on the forehead. "Good-bye, Nicky. Good luck, whatever you do. Lord God be with you."

"I don't know how I'll get through this without you." I felt tears coming. "Lord God be with you always." I quickly turned away. I left without looking back, afraid if I faced her I could not let her go.

# 25

In the morning, the sun beat down on the sturdy grasses as I left Admiralty House and crossed the yard to the shuttle pad. I squinted, my head throbbing from the several drinks I'd downed after leaving Amanda. An electrolytic balancer would right me in a hurry, but I wasn't in the habit of carrying hangover pills and I'd had too much pride to ask for one at Admiralty.

Forbee had mixed news: only one lieutenant had volunteered for *Hibernia*, but they'd conscripted another from the Bauxite run. Bauxite, the third planet in Hope Nation system, was serviced by intrasteller Naval vessels without fusion drives. We would rendezvous with the officer's ship to pick him up.

Thus I would sail with three lieutenants including Vax Holser. I also had four midshipmen and cadets, but among them, only Alexi was experienced. If I chose to promote Alexi I'd have to leave Derek senior, and he wasn't ready to command the wardroom. I ordered Forbee to acquire an experienced midshipman however necessary. And quickly: we were to sail in three days.

As I walked toward the departing shuttle a *Hibernia* seaman crossed the tarmac from the shade of the terminal building. He saluted as I reached the shuttle steps. My nod was curt.

"Seaman Porfirio, sir. Uh, could I talk to you a moment, please?" He licked his lips.

"I suppose. Come aboard."

"Aye aye, sir." He didn't move. "Down here, please? It's important, sir." The shuttle pilot waited, ready to close the hatch.

I sighed. "Make it fast, sailor."

Porfirio looked about as if for assistance. "Would you come with me?"

Probably it had to do with a girl. Our petty officers were expected to handle these shoreside problems, but none was in sight. I was the last person the unnerved sailor should ask for advice, but for some reason he had fastened on me. I stepped away from the shuttle hatch. "All right, what is it?"

He backed farther from the shuttle hatch. "This way, Captain. It'll only take a moment."

His manner began to remind me of Captain Grone's. "Get on with it, sailor. No one can hear us."

"I want to show you something, sir." He backed away another few steps. "By the terminal."

Enough was enough. "What is this nonsense, Porfirio?" I stood my ground.

He made shushing gestures. "Please, Captain. There's someone I want you to meet." So, it was a girl. If he thought he could get my permission to bring her aboard, he would by Lord God learn otherwise. The fastest way to put a stop to this foolishness was to confront it right now. I stalked after him to the terminal.

To my surprise Porfirio led me through the building and out the other side. In another minute I'd miss my bloody shuttle, and Lord God knew when there'd be another. The sailor scuttled across the service road. I followed as far as the Centraltown welcome sign, but he showed no sign of stopping. I used my coldest voice. "Where do you think you're taking me, sailor?"

"We're almost there, sir. Honest." He pointed past the far curb to a wooded hillside.

"Of all the insolent, insubordinate monkeyshines!" I was

beside myself. "Is that where you've hidden her? In the woods?"

He looked astonished. "You know about her, sir?"

"You think I'm an idiot? How dare you haul me across town for your fun and games?"

His face mirrored his anxiety and confusion. "Please, Captain. You shouldn't talk about her in the open!" The man was demented. It must be something in the air.

Fuming, I followed him down the street. Just beyond the airport perimeter the undergrowth came almost to the road, completely obscuring the woods behind. Porfirio darted along a narrow path through the brush.

I hesitated. I could be mugged, even killed. No one would ever find my body. I almost turned back, but with a muttered curse I plunged in after him. I might as well see it through. I'd already missed my shuttle.

By the time I'd gone a hundred feet, the road behind had completely disappeared. We pushed past low-hanging leafy branches under a dense canopy. Porfirio stopped, put his hands to his mouth, and let out a shrill whistle. I whirled, crouching into karate stance, knowing I'd been lured into a trap.

The bushes rustled. Out stepped Alexi, dirty and unkempt. Behind him came the two cadets, Paula Treadwell and Ricky Fuentes, their uniforms wrinkled and stained. My fury battled with a sense of relief. I bellowed, "Why in God's own hell are you skulking in the woods?" I gave Alexi no time to answer. "Leading me on a wild-goose chase, making me miss my shuttle! I'll have you over the barrel the minute we're aboard, Mr. Tamarov! Ten demerits! A dozen!"

Alexi held out an appeasing hand. "I had to see you alone, sir. This was the only way."

I shrieked, "Alone? Have you lost your mind?"

He unfolded a crumpled paper from the pocket of his soiled jacket. "Please, sir. Read it."

I snatched the paper. "What is this nonsense?"

"A court order, sir. Jared and Irene Treadwell have petitioned for a custody hearing for Cadet Treadwell. They say you enlisted Paula against her will. They say they've changed their minds about going on to Detour and want to stay here.

The court issued a temporary order returning her to them until the hearing. It's set for two weeks from now. Sir.''

I scanned the legal paper Alexi had summarized, while Seaman Porfirio shifted nervously from foot to foot. Ricky watched, fascinated. Paula looked sheepish. Alexi added, ''Every shuttle pilot has been served with a copy, sir. So have all our officers groundside.''

''But—it's—I mean—'' I stumbled to a halt.

''Yes, sir. You ordered me to keep an eye on the cadets and to bring them back to the ship unharmed. I was lucky when they handed me the order, sir. Ricky and Paula—I mean, Cadet Fuentes and Cadet Treadwell—were sightseeing in town when I was served at the shuttleport. I rounded them up and hid them here. We've slept out every night and I've been sneaking into town for food.''

My head was spinning. ''And Mr. Porfirio—''

''I've had about a dozen of the crew keeping watch for you, sir. They're all under oath not to say a word.''

I was stunned by Alexi's good sense and leadership. It wasn't for him to question his orders; he knew that it was for me to decide whether to release Cadet Treadwell to the court. His instructions were to guard them.

Once the girl was back in her parents' custody we'd never see her again; scheduling the hearing ten days after we were to leave made that clear enough.

Alexi had preserved my options admirably.

I turned to our sailor. ''You're commended, Mr. Porfirio. I'll consider how to reward you when we're under weigh.'' I would give him a promotion and a bonus for his courage in decoying his Captain. The seaman grinned at my words.

''Mr. Tamarov, the demerits I spoke of are canceled. You've done a fine job. Outstanding. I'll mention your exploit in the Log.'' He broke into a slow smile of delight. ''As for you two . . .'' With a scowl I rounded on the cadets, who suddenly looked apprehensive. ''I'll deal with you after we get back to the ship!'' If they were silly enough to worry about it, that was their problem.

I took a moment to organize my thoughts. ''All right, I know how we'll handle this. Everybody stay put until I get back.''

A few minutes later I was at Admiralty House, in Forbee's

office, explaining the situation. "What's your opinion, Mr. Forbee?"

He seemed intrigued by the possibilities. "Well, sir, the United Nations Circuit Court represents the U.N. Government on Hope Nation. Because we're so far from home the only appeal is directly to the Governor, who's also a civilian appointee. He has plenipotentiary powers and he's a representative of the U.N. Government. While under weigh, you, as commander of the vessel, also have plenipotentiary powers. But groundside, a captain is subject to the civilian courts."

I objected. "They're challenging an appointment I made under weigh. Its validity isn't for them to decide."

"No, sir. But they may think differently."

I paused to think it through. "Admiral Johanson had full authority over Naval affairs even though he was based planetside. His orders weren't subject to the court, were they?"

"No, sir." Forbee blinked.

"I'm senior Naval officer and in charge of Admiralty House. I don't have Johanson's rank, but his duties and responsibilities devolve on me so long as I'm in Hope Nation system. So I have full authority over Naval matters as senior representative of Admiralty."

He considered it. "It's a sustainable position, sir."

"Sustai—" I came out of my chair wth a roar. "Don't give me that goofjuice! Paula Treadwell is validly enlisted under Naval authority. Maintain and support that position as vigorously as may be required. Do I make myself clear?"

"Aye aye, sir!"

With an effort, I made my voice calm. "Very well. Prepare a general order for me to sign. As senior officer in the Hope Nation system I endorse and ratify the enlistment of Cadet Paula Treadwell by Captain Nicholas Seafort of *Hibernia* and I order all personnel to defend and support that appointment."

Forbee typed into his holovid.

The next sentence was the one that could see me hanged. "I further order all personnel to defend and protect Ms. Treadwell from any civilian authority, including representatives of U.N. Circuit Court, who attempt to interfere with the performance of her duties."

I leaned back in my chair. "Now, Mr. Forbee, round up every local system officer who has children. If he or she is out of port, round up their spouse. All children of local officers are invited to a tour of *Hibernia* tomorrow forenoon. See to it that they accept the invitation. Order a shuttle for the tour. This evening you will pick up some friends of mine in your electricar—you have a car, yes?—and take them home with you for the night. In the morning they will join the tour in clean civilian clothes. Did you get that?''

He said faintly, ''Aye aye, sir.''

I straightened my tie in my cabin mirror. My hair was brushed neatly, my shoes gleamed, the pants of my dress whites were crisply creased, the length of service medals pinned to my jacket. I thumbed my caller. ''Lieutenant Holser to the aft lock, please.''

I strode down the Level 2 corridor to the airlock. Vax Holser was waiting when I got there.

It had been two days since I'd left an anxious Captain Forbee at Admiralty House; *Hibernia* was due to depart tomorrow. About half our crew had returned from shore leave and the rest were trickling in hour by hour. Passengers for Detour were being ferried up by shuttle. Paula and Ricky, safely aboard, were confined by my orders to Level 1 until embarkation. Paula apologized to me for the trouble her family made; I accepted her apology and ignored her breach of custom in daring to speak to me directly. The circumstances were unusual.

The officers' children had a jolly tour of the ship. The moment they filed out the airlock to Orbit Station, Mr. Vishinsky and his detail sealed both locks and posted armed sentries. Their orders were to allow no one aboard except crewmen and passengers for Detour. Passengers' belongings were searched for weapons before they were permitted aboard, and their papers scrutinized. As a final precaution I had sentries posted at the ladders to Level 1.

General Tho was of the U.N. Armed Forces, not the Navy. As soon as his shuttle pilot reported that two more children had taken the shuttle to Orbit Station than were waiting to go back, he knew what I had done. He demanded I return young Ms. Treadwell. I refused. Tension abounded, until I announced I would go planetside the next day—today—to appear in Circuit Court regarding Cadet Treadwell.

Now the time had come. I wondered whether I would see *Hibernia* again. I might well spend the next half year in a local jail waiting for a ship to take me back to Lunapolis in irons. Well, if so, Amanda would visit me in my cell.

"Mr. Holser, I order you to defend the ship against unauthorized entry. By that I mean entry by any person except crew or passengers. If I'm not back within twenty-four hours you are to assume I'm held under duress, and that I will not return. You are then to declare yourself Captain and proceed to Detour. Acknowledge your orders."

"Aye aye, sir. Acknowledged and understood. May I go groundside with you?"

"Of course not. Open the hatch, please." I waited in our airlock, our inner hatch sealed behind me, until Orbit Station's hatch opened. I strode into the station and turned toward the shuttle bay.

A U.N.A.F. soldier intercepted me. "General Tho requests you to come with me, Captain." Was I already under arrest? Uneasy but powerless, I followed him to the General's office.

I returned General Tho's formal salute. He waited until the aide had left, his fingers nervously twisting his tiny mustache. When the hatch had shut, he leaned close. "About time someone gave it to Judge Chesley." His voice was low. "Man's been too big for his jumpsuit for years. Good luck!"

Heartened, I shook his hand. The shuttle was the largest one I'd seen yet. Its many rows of seats were empty; only the pilot, a flight attendant, and I were aboard. General Tho was showing his sympathies the only way open to him.

Feeling a regal envoy, I sat in the center of the shuttle amid empty acceleration seats while the solidly built craft whisked me toward the surface. Because of the shuttle's great size reentry was barely noticeable. The pilot glided us toward the runway, brought us down gently, and touched the ground as light as a feather just as he killed the engines. A fine performance.

The flight attendant opened the hatch and I stepped out.

"Attention!" Lined up on the tarmac were Captain Forbee and a gathering of officers and seamen, uniforms clean and crisp as if for inspection. I halted, surprised, my hand on the hatch. I hadn't ordered this show. Apparently Forbee had arranged it to demonstrate the Navy's support, and to underline my status as senior officer.

"Carry on, gentlemen." I strode to the terminal, my manner more confident than I felt. Forbee hurried to catch up.

"This way to the car, sir." He gestured to a luxurious late-model electricar.

I smiled in appreciation of his efforts. "Very good, Mr. Forbee."

"With your permission, nine of our officers have asked to be in court with you, sir."

"How many officers do you have groundside at present, Captain Forbee?"

"Nine."

"Very well." Only Forbee climbed into the car with me. The rest piled into two older cars. Our convoy proceeded into town. The U.N. Building was an old-fashioned glass and steel edifice, intended to suggest power and authority.

The parade came to a halt. Accompanied by all our officers in their Navy blues, I marched into the building.

It was to be a special session. Already seated in the court-room, the judge impatiently tapped his fingers on the gleaming hardwood bar. Though aged, he was imposing in his flaring red robes and white wig. Behind him was displayed our blue and white U.N. flag. Jared and Irene Treadwell sat with their lawyer at one of the counsel tables.

The Naval officers filed into the spectators' benches and mixed with the already sizable crowd. Ignoring the bailiff and court officers, I strode past the polished wooden rail to the unoccupied table.

"You are Captain Seafort of *Hibernia*?" demanded the judge.

"No, sir, I am not," I said firmly. He looked up in astonishment. "I am Nicholas Ewing Seafort, senior Naval officer on Hope Nation and commander of Admiralty House. I am also in command of U.N.S. *Hibernia*."

His smile was not friendly. "Let the record show the defendant has identified himself."

I abandoned thoughts of being conciliatory; my voice rang through the courtroom. "I am no defendant, Judge Chesley. I have come to warn you, in my official capacity, that you have exceeded your authority."

There were gasps from the visitors' benches. The judge slammed his gavel. "How dare you, Captain? Any more such talk and I'll hold you in contempt of court, which you're already in anyway by your continued imprisonment of the Treadwell girl!"

I shot back, "Any more such talk, sir, and I will declare a state of insurrection and assume military government of Hope Nation until civil order is restored!"

It had popped out of my mouth, before I had time to think. Now my bridges were well and truly burned.

Pandemonium broke out in the courtroom. The judge was apoplectic. I let my voice ring out. "You know perfectly well, as does everyone in this room, that I am lawful Captain of U.N.S. *Hibernia*, that while under weigh I enlisted Paula Treadwell into the United Nations Naval Service, and that her enlistment may not be challenged in civil court. This piece of paper that purports to be an order"—I pulled out the crumpled paper Alexi had given me—"argues that Paula's enlistment was not voluntary and that therefore she should return to the Treadwells' custody. Is that your assertion?" I turned to the Treadwells and their advocate.

The lawyer jumped up. "It certainly is, Your Honor," she said. "The evidence is clear that the minor child was not in full possession of the facts which—"

"Thank you," I cut in coldly. "This court may take judicial notice of Naval regulations. Involuntary enlistment is permitted when in the Captain's judgment the safety of the ship so demands. Cadet Treadwell was so enlisted. She will remain in the Service for the full period of her enlistment. You, sir, have no authority whatsoever over my actions as Captain of *Hibernia* or as senior Naval officer in Hope Nation. I'm surprised you didn't know that or, worse, that you chose to ignore it. I shall suggest to the Government that they recommend your immediate replacement on those grounds." I turned to go. When I was two steps past the bar the judge's strangled voice broke the silence.

"Arrest that man!"

The court officers moved forward. I pointed to the judge, snapped to Captain Forbee, "Arrest that man!"

It stopped them in their tracks. The livid judge and I exchanged glares. After a moment of ominous silence I said calmly, "Would you care to retire with me to your chambers to resolve this matter?"

He glanced back and forth between my unarmed officers and his court officials. With a sharp nod he lunged off the bench to the doorway at his side. He slammed the door behind him.

I paused at the entryway. "Carry on," I said into the stunned silence. I followed into his chambers.

The judge, trembling with rage, faced me from behind his desk.

"Would you like a way out of this?" I made my tone as reasonable as I could manage. At first he was too furious to respond. After a moment he nodded. Apparently he knew the law as well as I did.

"Very well. One, I apologize publicly to the court for my lack of respect and manners. Two, the hearing never took place. The record of it is destroyed. Or gets lost. Three, you dismiss the case for lack of merit, which you discover immediately upon reading the filings today."

It was the Naval solution, of course. A confrontation like ours was intolerable, so we wouldn't allow it to happen. We wouldn't recognize its existence, just as a Captain would be blind to a midshipman's black eye. My apology would satisfy his pride, but would have no other effect; I'd be putting it on a record that was to be destroyed.

He glowered. "You goddamn wiseass."

I ignored the blasphemy. "You tried a fancy move and it didn't work," I said. "If I'd handed her over, you'd have kept her past the time I sailed and the issue would be moot. As it is, I win. Why'd you go out on a limb for the Treadwells? They're not even locals."

The Judge pulled out his chair and slumped into it. "Their lawyer," he muttered. "Miss Kazai. She's helped me out."

"Well, she'll know you tried." Having won, I could afford to be conciliatory.

He gave me a small, grim smile. "Never come back to Hope Nation as a civilian. Not while I live."

My triumph vanished. I thought of Amanda. "No," I said. "I won't be back."

We returned to the courtroom and went through our charade. I apologized humbly for my unmannerly remarks. The judge erased the record. He then looked through the file and dismissed the Treadwells' petition for lack of jurisdiction.

Mrs. Treadwell jumped to her feet as I passed her on the way out. "You won't get away with it!" she shouted. "The courts in Detour will help us! We'll see you there!"

I shrugged. Perhaps.

# 26

Though the hearing was officially suppressed, the story made its way through the ship. Vax wore a foolish grin for the rest of the day, even during his watch. Alexi went so far as to congratulate me openly; I bit back a sharp reproof.

The rest of our crew straggled back from shore leave. Our final passengers were ferried up to the ship and settled in their cabins. Among the last to board were the Treadwells. I had them escorted directly to the bridge.

"I thought of refusing you passage," I told them. "But I don't want to separate Rafe and Paula sooner than necessary. I let you aboard, but one more protest, one petition, a single interference with the operation of my ship—and that includes harassing Paula—and you'll spend the entire trip in the brig. Is that understood?"

It wasn't that easy. I had to threaten to have them expelled to the station before they finally gave me their agreement.

The purser's last-minute stores were boarded. A new ship's launch, replacing the ill-fated one on which our officers perished, was safely berthed by Lieutenant Holser under my anxious scrutiny. Darla recalculated her base mass without comment.

To my relief all our crew members returned from shore leave; we had no deserters, no AWOLs. Seventeen passengers for Detour chose not to continue their trip; that didn't bother me. Others took their places. On this leg, we would carry ninety-five passengers.

Derek paged me from his duty station at the aft airlock. "The new midshipman is at the lock, reporting for duty, sir."

"Very well. Send him to the bridge." Suddenly I was back at Earthport Station, smoothing my hair, nervously clutching my duffel, anxious to make a good first impression when I reported to Captain Haag. Now I was at the other end of the interview.

"Permission to enter bridge, sir." An unfamiliar voice.

"Granted," I said without turning.

"Midshipman Philip Tyre reporting, sir." He came to attention smartly, his duffel at his feet.

I turned to him and fell silent. He wasn't handsome—he was beautiful. Smooth unblemished skin, wavy blond hair, blue eyes, a finely chiseled intelligent face. He could have been lifted from a recruiting poster.

I took his papers, letting him wait at attention while I looked them over. He'd joined at thirteen and now had three years service. That put him senior not only to Derek, but to Alexi as well. A disappointment for Alexi, but that couldn't be helped. I had plans for Alexi soon enough.

"Stand easy, Mr. Tyre."

"Thank you, sir." His voice was steady and vibrant.

"Welcome to *Hibernia*." I stopped myself from offering my hand. The Captain must keep his distance. "You've been on interplanetary service for the past year?"

The boy flashed a charming smile. "Yes, sir."

"And you've been to Detour."

"Yes, sir. On *Hindenberg*, before I was transferred out." Tyre had seen a lot of service, more than I had when I'd been posted in *Hibernia*.

"It seems you're to be senior middy."

"That's what I understood from Captain Forbee, sir." His smile was pleasant. "I think I can handle it."

"Good. Mr. Tamarov was senior for a while, but I doubt he'll give you any trouble."

"I'm sure he won't, sir." Was there more emphasis in his tone than necessary?

"Very well, Mr. Tyre. Get yourself settled in the wardroom, and have a look around the ship."

"Aye aye, sir." He saluted and picked up his duffel with graceful ease. "Thank you, sir." He turned and marched out.

I made a note to reassure Alexi that he hadn't been intentionally demoted.

I sat back, comparing the new middy's entry to Mr. Chantir's. Our new lieutenant had come aboard the evening before. He'd reported to the bridge, saluting easily. He responded to my welcome with a warm, friendly grin. "Thank you, sir. It's good to be aboard."

"It says here you have special talent in navigation."

"I wouldn't say special, sir," he said modestly. "But I enjoy solving plotting problems."

"Then I'll put you in charge of the midshipmen's drills."

He smiled again. "Good. I love to teach." I knew immediately that I would like him. I thought of embittered, tyrannical Lieutenant Cousins and how I'd dreaded our lessons.

We were ready to depart. The Pilot at the conn, we cast off, maneuvered a safe distance from the station, and Fused almost at once. I was so busy I forgot to watch Hope Nation dwindle on the screens before they blanked.

It wouldn't be long before the stars reappeared; we were on a short run to Bauxite to pick up our third lieutenant. A voyage of five weeks by conventional power, in Fusion we could make the hop in less than a day. We'd take longer to maneuver the ship for mating with U.N.S. *Brezia* than to travel the interplanetary distance in Fusion.

*Brezia* was a small cruiser that shuttled back and forth among the planets of Hope Nation system, available for orbital rescues or other needs of the civilian mining fleet and the area's commercial craft. Lacking fusion engines, *Brezia* cruised at subluminous speeds. Unfortunately, her Captain was only rated interplanetary or I would have shanghaied him as well as his lieutenant.

Pilot Haynes and Lars Chantir worked together during the docking. The Pilot, true to his word, gave no trouble. As he'd said, he was good at his job. After we located *Brezia* he deftly maneuvered us into matching velocity. To avoid the cumbersome chore of mating airlocks, we drifted to within a hundred meters of *Brezia* and I had a T-suited sailor carry a flexible line to their lock. Shortly after, our new officer came across the line, hand over hand, his duffel tied behind his suit.

Having little else to do, I went to the lock to meet him.

Correctly, he stripped off his suit before coming to attention. "Lieutenant Ardwell C. Crossburn reporting, sir." A short, round-figured man in his late thirties.

"Stand easy, Lieutenant. Welcome aboard."

"Thank you, sir." He looked around at his new ship. "As soon as I get my gear stowed I can take up my duties, sir. I'll try to be of assistance."

"No hurry, Mr. Crossburn," I said in good humor. "You can wait until after dinner."

"Very well, sir. If you insist." An odd way to speak, but the man had a peculiar manner about him. Well, his record showed him to be a competent and experienced officer. I returned to the bridge and waited impatiently while Mr. Haynes and Lieutenant Chantir plotted Fusion coordinates and rechecked them together. Laboriously I went through the calculations myself and found no error. We Fused.

In seven weeks we would reach Detour, a younger colony than Hope Nation, and one whose environment was less hospitable to humankind. Its air held less nitrogen and slightly more oxygen, but it was breathable. They'd had to do a lot of terraforming to bring down the sulphuric compounds in the atmosphere before Detour could be developed. Now the planet was open for colonization and some sixty thousand settlers had already arrived.

Lars Chantir was my senior lieutenant. Mr. Crossburn, with six years experience, was second. Vax was last in line, but that mattered less among lieutenants than midshipmen, unless the Captain died. The barrel was duly moved to First Lieutenant Chantir's quarters; it was a traditional duty of the senior lieutenant.

I had time on my hands, time to miss Amanda. Our nights in the hills of Western Continent had provided the first sustained intimacy I'd ever known. Knowing how incapable I was, Amanda had still cared for me. I yearned for her presence.

We settled down to shipboard routine. I missed the familiar passengers: Mrs. Donhauser, Mr. Ibn Saud, and, of course, Amanda. Few of our original group were continuing with us; unfortunately the Treadwells were among them.

One day Vax came to me on the bridge, troubled. "Sir, there's something I think you should know."

"What's that?"

He hesitated, on difficult ground. "Lieutenant Crossburn, sir. He's been questioning the crew about the attack at Miningcamp. At first I thought he was just making conversation, but he's seeking out the men who were most involved."

I chose the easy way out. "You know better than to complain about a superior officer."

"Yes, sir. It wasn't a complaint. I was informing you."

"Drop it. I don't care what he asks." I had nothing to hide from my new lieutenant. My conduct would be subject to Admiralty's unblinking scrutiny as soon as we reached home, and I knew I had no chance of emerging without substantial demotion, if not worse. Mr. Crossburn's inquiry could do no harm to my shattered career, though it was unusual.

More disturbing was Lieutenant Chantir's casual comment while I perused a chess manual on a quiet watch. "I'm surprised your midshipmen don't make more effort to work off demerits, sir."

"What do you mean?"

"Yesterday I caned one of them for reaching ten. You'd think he'd take the trouble to exercise them off. They're only two hours apiece."

"Which midshipman?" I asked, my mind on the queen's gambit.

"Mr. Carr. I rather let him have it, for his laziness. What is your policy, Captain? Should I go hard or easy?"

"Neither," I said, disturbed. "Use your judgment." I had issued Derek seven demerits for trying to choke me—and I hadn't forgotten to log them when we got back—but he would have been too well trained by now to blunder into more. "How many did he have?"

"Eleven." Very odd. I didn't think Derek would step that far out of line.

"Let's look them up." I turned on the Log, suspecting I knew the answer. If a lieutenant wanted Derek caned he didn't have to trouble giving him demerits, he would merely send him to Mr. Chantir with orders to be put over the barrel. A first midshipman, on the other hand, couldn't issue such an order. He could only assign demerits, which if given fast enough would have the same effect.

I flipped through the daily notations made by each watch

officer. *"Mr. Carr, improper storage of gear, one demerit, by Mr. Tyre. . . . Mr. Carr, insubordination, two demerits, by Mr. Tyre."* Why hadn't Derek worked them off? I turned the pages. *"Mr. Carr, improper uniform, two demerits, by Mr. Tyre. . . . Mr. Carr, inattention to duty, two demerits, by Mr. Tyre."*

There it was. Tyre was piling demerits on Derek faster than he could exercise them off.

I decided I couldn't interfere. It was Derek's bad luck Tyre had made an example of him; the new first middy was asserting his authority. But though I put the incident out of my mind, I had been a midshipman too recently to miss the other signs of trouble. When I saw Alexi on watch he seemed more hesitant, more preoccupied. More significant, I never saw him off watch except at dinner. I realized all my midshipmen seemed to have dropped out of sight. I hoped Alexi would give me a hint, but he was too Navy to do that. Wardroom affairs were settled in the wardroom.

It was not a busy time for me. In Fusion, we had no need for navigation checks, no data on the screens, nothing to do except keep an eye on the environmental systems: recycling, hydroponics, power. Brooding about the wardroom situation, I began watching for new Log entries.

Derek, Alexi, and both cadets were fast accumulating demerits. Seven for Alexi in three days, two more for Derek. Sixteen between Paula and Ricky.

I bent the rules to ask Philip Tyre outright. "Everything going well in the wardroom, Mr. Tyre?"

He smiled easily. "Yes, sir. I have it under control." As always, he was immaculate. Slim and slight, his face was faintly disturbing in its perfection.

"You're working with a good group of officers, Mr. Tyre."

"Yes, sir. They need reminding who's in charge, but I'm on top of that." His innocent blue eyes questioned me. "Is anything wrong, sir?"

"No, nothing," I said quickly, knowing I had strayed across the unwritten line that kept the Captain out of the wardroom's business.

Dr. Uburu came to me next, catching me outside the dining

hall on the way back from dinner. "Did you know," she asked gravely, "that I treated Paula Treadwell this week?"

"No, I didn't."

"I thought not." She paused as we reached the top of the ladder.

"What for, Doctor? If I'm not violating your professional ethics?"

"Hysteria." She met my eye.

"Good Lord." I waited for her to continue. She said nothing.

"What was the cause?"

"I swore an oath not to tell you," she said. "My patient insisted, before she'd talk about it."

My hand clenched the rail. "I could order you," I said.

"Yes, but I wouldn't obey." Her voice was calm. She smiled, her dark face lighting with warmth. "I don't mean to make problems, Captain. Just keeping you advised."

"Thank you." I went to my cabin and lay on my bunk, wishing the Chief still visited for evening conversations. Since I'd broken off our sessions after Sandy's death he had been friendly and helpful, but had kept his distance.

My next watch was shared with Lieutenant Crossburn. After a long period of silence he made efforts to start a conversation. I let him lead it, my mind elsewhere. He soon brought up the attack at Miningcamp. "When the rebels forced their way on board," he asked, "who was most helpful in repelling them?"

"Mr. Vishinsky was invaluable," I said, not wanting to be bothered. "And Vax Holser."

His next question snapped me awake. "What made you decide to let a dozen suited men on board in the first place?"

My tone was sharp. "Are you interrogating me, Lieutenant?"

"Not at all. But it was an amazing incident, Captain. I write a diary. I try to include important things that happen near me. I'll change the subject if you'd rather."

"No," I said grudgingly. "It was a mistake, letting them on board. I very much regret it."

He seemed pleased at my confidence. "It must have been a terrible day."

"Yes."

"I write every evening," he confided. "I pour my thoughts and feelings into my diary."

"It must be a great solace," I said, disliking him.

"I never show it to anybody, of course, even though it reads quite well. I'm the only one who's seen it, other than my uncle."

It seemed polite to prompt him. "He's a literary critic?"

"No, but he understands Naval matters. Perhaps you've heard of him. Admiral Brentley."

Heard of him? Admiral Brentley ran Fleet Ops at Lunapolis, and this man had his ear! My heart sank.

"You've written about Miningcamp in that little diary, Lieutenant?"

"Oh, yes." His manner was modest. "It's very dramatic. Uncle will be intrigued, I'm sure."

I let the conversation lapse, fretting. After a while I shrugged. Admiralty didn't need Mr. Crossburn's little book to know how badly I'd managed.

But three weeks into the cruise I knew I would have to take action. Mr. Crossburn had left the subject of Miningcamp and was asking about the execution of sailors Tuak and Rogoff. At the same time, the morale of my midshipmen and cadets was plummeting. Alexi stalked the ship in a cold fury, civil to me but otherwise seething with unexpressed rage. Derek appeared depressed and tired.

"I've had Mr. Tamarov up twice," Lieutenant Chantir told me. "I went fairly easy on him, but I had to give him something." I was already aware; I was watching the Log carefully now. I began checking the exercise room, realizing that one of the reasons I rarely saw the middies and cadets was that they were usually working off demerits.

Perplexed, I took my problems to Chief McAndrews. At this point I didn't hesitate to display my ignorance. He already knew my limitations.

"What did you expect?" he asked bluntly. "You asked the Naval station to supply you officers. Where did you think they'd get them?"

"I don't understand." I shuffled, feeling young and foolish, but I needed to know.

He sighed. "Captain, Mr. Chantir volunteered, yes? The

other two officers were requisitioned. If Admiralty told you to supply a lieutenant for an incoming ship, whom would you pick?"

"Mr. Crossburn." I spoke without hesitation.

"And which midshipman?"

I swore slowly and with feeling.

"You gave the joeys in the interplanetary fleet a chance to get rid of their worst headaches."

I damned my stupidity, my blindness. "How could I have been so dumb? I asked for officers and didn't even check their files to see who I was getting!" A real Captain would have known to watch for that trick.

"Easy, sir. What do you think the files would have shown?"

I paused. A good question. The notation "tyrant" or "sadist" was unlikely to appear in Mr. Tyre's personnel file. As for Lieutenant Crossburn's diary, what the man wrote in his cabin during his free time wasn't subject to Naval regulations. Even if his officious private inquiries stirred up trouble, that was hard to prove, and moreover it would be foolhardy to rebuke a man who had the ear of the fleet commander. No wonder his Captain was delighted to get rid of him.

I went back to my cabin to think. I had no sympathy for those who misused our Naval traditions for their own ends, but I didn't know how to stop Mr. Tyre without violating tradition myself. As for Mr. Crossburn, how could I order him not to keep a diary? I found no solution.

In the meantime, I ordered Alexi to advanced navigational training, followed by a tour in the engine room under Mr. McAndrews. That should give him some respite from Mr. Tyre.

It didn't. Alexi continued to accumulate demerits. Again he reached ten and was sent to Lieutenant Chantir's cabin.

Two days later we shared a watch. He eased himself into his chair, wincing. I blurted, "Be patient, Alexi."

"About what, sir?" His voice was unsteady. Seventeen now, nearly eighteen, he could expect better treatment than he was getting. Yet his Academy training held firm. He would not complain to the Captain about his superior.

I deliberately stepped over the line. "Be patient. I know what's going on."

He looked at me, his usual friendliness replaced by indifference. "Sometimes I hate the Navy, sir."

"And me too?"

After a moment his face softened. "No, sir. Not you." He added quietly, "A lot of people are being hurt." It was as close as he would come to discussing the wardroom.

Meanwhile Mr. Crossburn continued his scribbling. On watch he would flip idly through the Log, scrutinizing entries made prior to his arrival. He was delving into Alexi's defense of the unfortunate seamen at their court-martial. He asked me how well I thought Alexi had performed.

"Lieutenant, your questions and the reports you write are damaging the morale of the ship. I wish you'd stop."

"Is that an order, sir?" His tone was polite.

"A request."

"With all due respect, sir, I don't think my diary is under Naval jurisdiction. I'll ask Uncle Ted about that when I see him. As for asking questions, of course I'll stop if you order it."

"Very well, then, I so order."

"Aye aye, sir. Since your order is so unusual I request that you put it in writing."

I considered a moment. "Never mind. You're free to carry on." A written order, viewed without knowledge of his constant prying, would appear paranoid and dictatorial. Anyone who hadn't experienced Lieutenant Crossburn firsthand wouldn't understand, and I was in enough trouble with Admiralty as it was.

I had little better luck with Philip Tyre. I called him to my cabin, where our discussion could be less formal than on the bridge.

"I've been reviewing the Log, Mr. Tyre. Why do you find it necessary to hand out so many demerits?"

He sat at my long table, his arm resting on the tabletop much as the Chief's had before I'd isolated myself. His innocent blue eyes questioned me. "I'll obey your orders, sir. Are you telling me to ignore obvious infractions?"

"No, I'm not. But are you finding infractions, or searching for them?"

"Captain, I'm doing the best I know how. I thought my job was to keep wardroom affairs from coming to your attention, and I've been trying to do that. As I certainly haven't called any problems to your notice, someone else must have." It was said so reasonably, so openly, that I could have no complaint.

"No one's complained," I growled. "But you're handing out demerits faster than they can work them off."

"Yes, sir, I've noticed that. I encouraged Mr. Carr and Mr. Fuentes to spend more time in the exercise room. I've even gone myself to help them with their exercises. A better solution would be for them to stop earning demerits." His untroubled eyes met mine.

"How do you propose that they do that?"

"By following regulations, sir. My predecessor must have been terribly lax. I observe a lack of standards in his own behavior, sir. It's no wonder he couldn't teach the others. I'm trying to deal with it."

I sighed. The boy was unreachable. "I won't tell you how to run the wardroom. I will tell you that I'm displeased about the effects on morale."

Tyre's voice was earnest. "Thank you for bringing it to my attention, sir. I'll make sure their morale problems don't bother you further."

"I want them eliminated, not hidden! That's all!"

The midshipman saluted smartly and left. I paced the cabin, bile in my throat. Very well; he'd been warned. I would give him until we left Detour. If he didn't improve, Mr. Tyre had made his bed; he'd have to sleep in it.

On my next visit to the exercise room I found Derek and Ricky working, Derek on the bars, the cadet struggling at push-ups and leg lifts on the mat. Alexi was absent. The two perspiring boys waited silently for me to leave.

I didn't come across Alexi for three days, until we next shared a watch. "You haven't been in the exercise room of late, Mr. Tamarov."

He glanced at me without expression. "No, sir. I've been confined to quarters except to stand watch and go to the dining hall."

"Good Lord! For how long?"

"Until my attitude improves, sir." His gaze revealed nothing, but his cheeks reddened.

"Will it improve, Alexi?"

"Unlikely, sir. I'm told I'm not suitable material for the Navy. I'm beginning to believe it."

"You're suitable." I tried to cheer him up. "This will pass. On my first posting my senior middy was very difficult to deal with, but we got to be friends." I realized how fatuous I sounded. Jethro Hager was nothing like the vicious boy fate had put in charge of my midshipmen.

"Yes, sir. I don't mind so much, except when Ricky cries himself to sleep."

I was alarmed. "Ricky, crying?"

"Only two or three times, sir. When Mr. Tyre isn't around." That was bad. Ricky Fuentes was a cheerful, good-natured boy; if he was in tears something was very wrong. I thought briefly of the lesson I had given Vax Holser when I succeeded to Captain, an approach I'd decided against with our new midshipman. In Vax's case I'd recently been a member of the wardroom and had personal knowledge of his behavior. Also, Vax was a good officer who was making a sincere effort to combat a personal problem. Philip Tyre was not.

In three weeks we would Defuse for a nav check, and then we'd have only a few more days to Detour. I could wait.

But a few days later Mr. Chantir raised the subject openly. "Sir, something's gone wrong in the wardroom. I've had Mr. Carr and Mr. Fuentes up again. The Log is littered with demerits."

"I know."

"Is there anything you could do?"

"What do you suggest, Mr. Chantir?"

"Remove the first midshipman, or distract him. Lord, I'd enjoy having him sent to me with demerits after what he's done to the others."

"He'll make sadists of us all, Mr. Chantir. No, I won't remove him. I have witnessed no objectionable behavior. He's scrupulously polite, he obeys my orders to the letter, he's excellent at navigation drills and in his other studies. I can't beach him simply because I don't like him."

"That wouldn't be the reason, Captain."

"No, but that's what it would look like to Admiralty. They don't know that Derek and Alexi aren't giving him a hard time."

"What do you expect of me when these joeys are sent to the barrel, then?"

"I expect you to do your duty, Mr. Chantir." He quickly dropped the subject.

As time passed Mr. Crossburn threw caution to the winds. Twice he mentioned how eagerly he was looking forward to seeing his uncle Admiral Brentley and talking over old times. I ignored him, but my uneasiness grew.

For a diversion I called drills. The crew practiced Battle Stations, General Quarters, Fire in the Forward Hold at unexpected intervals. The sudden action seemed a relief.

At last came the day Pilot Haynes took his place on the bridge, along with Alexi and Lieutenant Chantir. I brought the ship out of Fusion, and stars leaped onto the simulscreens with breathtaking clarity. The swollen sun of Detour system glowed in the distance. We would Fuse for four more days and emerge, hopefully, just outside the planet's orbit.

I waited impatiently for the navigation checks to be done. With Pilot Haynes, Mr. Chantir, and Alexi all computing our course there was no need for me to recheck their calculations, but still I did. Finally satisfied, I ordered the engine room to Fuse.

That evening, I had a knock on my cabin hatch. Philip Tyre stood easily at attention, his soft lips turned upward in a pleasant expression. "Sir, excuse me for intruding, but a passenger wishes to speak to you. Mr. Treadwell." A passenger couldn't approach officers' country; he needed an escort to arrange contact with me unless he found me in the dining hall.

"Tell him to write—oh, very well." Though I could refuse to see him, another tirade from Jared Treadwell about his daughter was no more than I deserved for rashly enlisting her. "Bring him." The middy saluted, spun on his heel, and marched off. I paced in growing irritation, dreading the interview.

Again, a knock. "Come in," I snapped. Mr. Tyre stepped aside. Rafe Treadwell came hesitantly into my cabin. I blurted, "Oh, you. I was expecting . . ." I waved Philip his dismissal.

The lanky thirteen-year-old smiled politely. "Thank you for seeing me, sir."

"You're welcome. Is this about your sister?"

"No, sir."

I waited. He stood formally, arms at his sides. "I'm hoping, Captain Seafort, that you'd allow me to enlist too."

For a moment I was speechless. "What?" I managed. "Do what?"

"Enlist, sir. As a cadet." Seeing my expression he hurried on. "I thought I wanted to stay with my parents, but things have changed. I don't know if you need more midshipmen but I'd like to volunteer. I'd like to be with my sister for a while longer, and I just can't believe how much the Navy has done for her."

I shot him a suspicious look. If the boy was twitting me I'd stretch him over the barrel, civilian or no.

"I mean it, sir. She always used to ask me for help. Now she doesn't even have time for me and when I do see her, it's like talking to a grown-up. She's about three years older than me now." He shook his head in wonderment.

"What about your parents?"

"Paula and I were creche-raised, sir. Community creche, back in Arkansas. I knew our parents but we didn't spend much time with them. They took us out of creche when they decided to emigrate. They can survive without us."

"They don't act like it."

He grinned. "They think togetherness is something they can proclaim. They don't realize you have to grow up with it. They'll get used to being without us."

"And the discipline? You'd enjoy that?"

"No, I'll probably hate it. But it might be good for me." He sounded nonchalant, but, at his side, his hand beat a tattoo against his leg.

I paced anew. Another midshipman would be useful, though hardly necessary. Having Rafe in the wardroom would certainly help Paula's morale. But taking both Treadwell children without their parents' consent wouldn't be appreciated by Admiralty at home, to say nothing of the Treadwells. Well, I was already in so much hot water that one more mistake didn't matter.

"I'll let you know." I opened the hatch.

"But I've only got—"

"Dismissed!" I waited.

"Yes, sir." His tone was meek, passing my first test.

That night Mr. Tuak came, for the first time in months. He peered at me through the cabin bulkhead, making no effort to grab me, until at last I woke. I was disturbed, uneasy, but barely sweating. I showered and went back to sleep, unafraid.

Three days later we Defused for the last time on our outward journey. We powered our auxiliary engines for our approach to Detour. Pilot Haynes, Mr. Tyre, and Alexi had the watch; of course I was also on the bridge.

Philip Tyre sat stiffly at a console checking for encroachments. I noticed he kept Alexi on a very short leash, ordering him to sit straight when he relaxed in his seat and observing Alexi's work closely. Tyre never raised his voice, never asked anything unreasonable, and never missed a thing.

Detour Station drifted larger in the simulscreens as the Pilot maneuvered us ever closer. Finally the rubber seals on the locks mated. We had arrived.

I thumbed the caller. "Mr. Holser, arrange a shuttle. I'll be going planetside."

"Aye aye, sir."

I turned to Philip Tyre. "Where's Mr. Carr?"

"In the wardroom, sir. I believe he's sleeping."

"In the middle of the day?"

"Yes, sir. I had him standing regs last night. Then he did some exercises." His wide blue eyes regarded me without guile. "Shall I wake him?"

"I was going to take him groundside."

"Yes, sir. I'd told him he was confined to ship during the layover for his insubordination, but of course your wishes prevail."

"I'll take Mr. Tamarov, then."

"Him too, sir. Unless you countermand my orders." As he'd spoken in front of Alexi, it was impossible for me to countermand him. Discipline had to be maintained.

I turned to Alexi. "What did you do, Mr. Tamarov?"

"I was insolent, sir," he said without inflection. "So I was informed."

A cruel punishment. The midshipmen had long leave in Hope Nation so they weren't entitled to go shoreside as a matter of right, but to travel so far and be denied what could be their only chance to see the colony was harsh indeed.

"Very well. I'm sorry, Mr. Tamarov. You'll stay aboard; I'll go alone." As I left the bridge the rank injustice helped steady my resolve. I saw Lieutenant Crossburn coming up the ladder from Level 2.

"Mr. Crossburn, find young Mr. Treadwell—Rafe Treadwell—and take him to your cabin. Keep him there until I order otherwise." I would keep the Treadwell twins together. Their parents be damned. Injustice was the way of the world.

Crossburn gaped. "Aye aye, sir. Don't the passengers disembark today?"

"They'll start later this afternoon. Do as you're told." I went on to my cabin.

A few minutes later I was climbing into a shuttle in the station's launch berth. Everything about Detour Station was smaller than at Hope Nation: far fewer personnel, smaller corridors, lower ceilings. Even a smaller shuttle. This one held only twelve passengers and looked well used.

"I've radioed down to tell them we're coming, Captain," the shuttle pilot said as we drifted clear off the station.

"Thank you."

"A ship from outside is a major event. You're the first since *Telstar*, half a year ago."

"*Telstar* made it, then?"

"Of course." He waited for me to explain.

"She didn't reach Miningcamp."

"Where is she?"

"No one knows." I stared bleakly at his console.

The pilot shrugged. "She'll turn up. Anyway, have you brought us the polyester synthesizer?"

I tried to remember my cargo manifest. "I think so. Why, are you short of clothing?"

"Somewhat. We've made do with cottons over the years, but all the fashions are in polyester and the ladies are restless. Hang on, atmosphere is building." In a moment the buffeting from pockets of denser atmosphere occupied his full attention.

Detour was considerably smaller than Hope Nation, smaller in fact than Earth, but its greater density made for near-terrestrial gravity. I peered through the porthole. Much of the planet was still barren, with patches of lichen and moss taking hold on the outcrops of bare rock. If I could see the patches from our height they must be huge, evidence of massive terraforming.

We swooped lower into a horizontal flight pattern. Now I could spot patches of greenery, and soon, checkerboard fields dotting the landscape. Tall trees grew in random patterns. I found a road, then another. We were approaching what habitation we'd find on this recently barren planet.

The pilot powered back for touchdown. We glided over the runway, wings in VTOL position, and hovered before drifting to a landing. Silence assaulted my ears. The Pilot grinned. "Welcome to the center of civilization, Captain."

I smiled back. "Thanks. It's good to be here." The hatch opened and I took a deep breath. A distinctly sulphurous smell. My eyes watered. "Gecch. Do you get used to this?"

He looked surprised. "Used to what? Oh, the air? Sure, just takes a week or so. Don't worry about it."

I climbed out of the shuttle. About twenty men and women were gathered beyond the wingtip, waiting. One of them came forward, a tall, graying man with an air of authority.

"Captain Seafort? Welcome to Detour." He held out his hand. Around his shoulders hung a blue and white ribbon from which was suspended the bronze plaque of office.

I shook his hand, then saluted. "Governor Fantwell? I'm honored."

The colonial Governor smiled. "Let me introduce you around. Mayor Reuben Trake, of Nova City. Walter Du Bahn, president of the Bank of Detour." I began shaking hands. "City Council President Ellie Bayes, Jock Vigerua, who owns the mines nearby. You don't realize, Captain, what an event it is for a ship to come in; we only get two a year. Miss Preakes, editor of the *Detour Sun* . . ."

The introductions were finally completed. He guided me to an electribus; we all clambered in and found seats. "We've put on a lunch at City Hall." The Governor was genial. "Then we'll show you the town."

"I don't suppose you have any Naval personnel about?"

"Not a one," Governor Fantwell said cheerfully. "Nary a seaman. Are you shorthanded?"

"There's a billet I wanted filled." My own. But I'd known there was no Naval station on Detour and wasn't surprised.

City Hall was a plain, metal-sided building in the center of town. I could tell immediately it was City Hall; a large sign hanging over the door said so. In other respects it was exactly like all the surrounding structures.

Seated at a table draped with a fancy cloth and festooned with bright silverware I said quietly to the Governor, "Actually, I came to talk to you before dumping a problem in your lap. Yours and the judge's."

"Oh?" He raised an eyebrow. I wondered if any problem I brought could faze him. "Just a sec. Let me get Carnova." He beckoned across the hall to a rugged man who promptly joined our table. "What do you propose to dump on us?"

I told them briefly about the Treadwell situation. "I've decided to let the boy enlist, and the parents will explode when they hear. They raised quite a ruckus on Hope Nation."

"This isn't Hope," Judge Carnova said bluntly. "We do things differently. The Navy isn't under my jurisdiction. I won't even give them a hearing."

"I'll back you up," the Governor told him. He turned to me with an easy smile. "You see? Your problem is solved."

I fiddled with a fresh fruit cup. Oranges and grapes, kiwi, bananas, and other fruits I couldn't identify. "I wish everything were that easy."

"Tell me," said the Governor. "Is it that I'm getting older, or are you rather young for a Captain?"

I sighed and launched into the familiar explanation.

# 27

After returning to my ship I summoned Rafe Treadwell to the bridge. He entered hesitantly, his apparent calm betrayed by the fingers twisting at his shirt.

"I'm prepared to enlist you."

"Thank you." His shoulders slumped. "I was afraid you'd change your mind at the last minute."

"Sit at the console. Write a note to your parents telling

them you've enlisted voluntarily. Give them your reasons. As soon as you're done I'll give you the oath.''

"Yes, sir.''

"Before you do, I have to warn you. Conditions are, uh, rather strained at the moment. You'll be subjected to unusually intense hazing, even for a cadet.''

He swallowed. "Yes, I've heard.'' Of course, his sister would have told him. He bent to the console and typed his note.

After I administered the oath I thumbed my caller. "Mr. Tyre, bring Mr. Tamarov to the bridge.''

A few moments later they appeared. Alexi was heavily flushed and breathing hard; I must have interrupted a session in the exercise room.

"Mr. Tyre, I'm seconding Mr. Tamarov for special duties for two days. He'll guard our new cadet until we leave port. Kindly release him from his other requirements.''

"Of course, sir.'' Tyre smiled pleasantly. "Will they stay in the wardroom?''

"Not until we leave Detour.'' Knowing the Treadwells, I would take no chances, even in orbit far above the planet. I ordered Alexi and Rafe Treadwell bunked in the crew's privacy chamber on Level 3. Alexi couldn't conceal his relief at escaping Mr. Tyre, however briefly.

Tyre appeared not to notice. "I'll help them move, sir,'' he said. "Can I do anything else to be useful?''

I sent them away, reflecting on the irony. Other than an insane desire to destroy his subordinates, Philip Tyre was an excellent midshipman, eager, helpful, diligent at his studies. I was sure he felt no guilt for the torture he inflicted.

I made a gesture of disgust. Imagine Derek standing regs, at his age. Ridiculous. I wondered how Philip had passed the psych interviews, and how he'd been dealt with as a cadet. Had he been brutalized? Not that it would be the slightest excuse for his own behavior. Still, I wondered.

At dinner Lieutenant Crossburn asked, "You're keeping the Treadwell boy on board?'' I braced; obviously his question was but a preliminary.

"Yes.'' Another affair for him to probe.

"I could be of assistance with the senior Treadwells, sir. That is, when they find out their son isn't going ashore.''

I could imagine Crossburn helping with the Treadwells. Asking how they felt, for instance, to record their reactions in his little diary.

"No thank you. I'll attend to it."

"How many enlistments without parental consent do you think the Navy's seen, sir?" His eyes were guileless.

"That's quite enough, Mr. Crossburn." My rebuke, too, would find its way into his record. I didn't care. I was tired, lonely, perturbed by the effect my new officers had on the crew. I missed Amanda, and in a few weeks I'd pass tantalizingly close to her one last time. That would be almost too much to bear.

I thought of home. Perhaps Father would take me back, after I was forced to resign. He would say nothing, of course. That was his way.

As my watch ended, our first departing passengers were crowding into the small shuttles that serviced Detour Station. Several trips would be required to accommodate them. The Treadwells were due to leave in the morning; tonight they would surely notice their son's absence. I went to bed wishing I knew how to avoid the forthcoming row.

I woke to a commotion in the corridor. I thrust on my pants and flung open the hatch, peered to the east. Irene Treadwell, trying unsuccessfully to twist free from Vax Holser's firm grip.

She caught sight of me. "Tell this brute to let me go!"

"You aren't allowed up here, ma'am," Vax said. He flashed me a glance of apology. "She was trying to get into the wardroom, sir."

"Where's my son?" Ms. Treadwell's voice rose. "What have you done to Rafe? I went looking for him and he's nowhere to be found! Are you stealing my other child?"

"We're not steal—"

"Are all of you people crazy?" At last she freed herself and rubbed her reddened wrist. "I tried the purser but he wouldn't tell me anything. I went to the lounge and Rafe wasn't there. I tried the wardroom—yes, I know I'm not supposed to—and a big boy was on a chair in his undershorts reciting a book! He didn't even stop; they just closed the door on me! What have you done with my Rafe?"

I thought of sending for Lieutenant Crossburn. I took my

holovid, slipped Rafe's chip into it. "Go back to your cabin and read this."

"Does it say you've taken Rafe? You monster!" Her scream echoed down the corridor. "Not my boy! You can't!"

"Lieutenant, take her away!" I tried to close my hatch but she blocked it with her foot. Vax hauled her into the corridor. I closed the hatch quickly, leaned against it until the shouting died away. My limbs felt weak. I climbed into bed, lay wide awake.

How often were similar scenes played out, back on Earth? When the origins of melanoma T were understood and the Navy lowered cadet enlistment age to thirteen, did parents face the loss of their children without qualms? How many mothers reacted with hysteria like Irene Treadwell? The Navy required consent from but one parent. I thought of my own host mother, in Devon, whom I'd never seen. What did she look like? Would she have cared?

I tossed fitfully until early morning, then dressed and went to the officers' mess for breakfast. I sat at the long table, alone except for Lieutenant Chantir, and sipped coffee while waiting for my scrambled eggs and toast. Other officers drifted in, found places. I picked at my food.

"I hear there was a ruckus outside your hatch last night." Lieutenant Crossburn took a seat alongside me.

"Um."

"Mrs. Treadwell was on the first shuttle down this morning." A pause. "They say when she went to court in Hope Nation you tried to throw the judge in jail." Crossburn took a forkful of his eggs.

My tone was acid. "I told you not to talk to her."

"Oh, we spoke several days ago, before your order. I merely listened."

"More grist for your mill, Mr. Crossburn?"

"Sir, I fail to understand your objections to my diary. Frankly, I intend to bring the matter up with my uncle when we get home."

I stared. No lieutenant could speak so to his Captain.

Mr. Chantir intervened. "Ardwell, I order you to be silent. Leave the Captain alone!"

"Aye aye, sir." Crossburn pursed his lips. After a moment's thought he pulled a piece of paper from his pocket and made a note. I considered hurling my coffee at his face, decided against it.

"Pardon, sir, may I join you?" Philip Tyre. My nod was curt, but he sat anyway. "Good morning."

I responded with a grunt.

"Sir, do you think I might go groundside tonight? It's been a year since I've seen Detour." A shy grin. "I met a girl there last winter, but I suppose she's forgotten me." Your typical lighthearted youngster. I thought of Derek, humiliated, made to stand regs when Mrs. Treadwell barged into the wardroom the night before. About to refuse, I thought better of it. I would play out my hand. "Permission granted, Mr. Tyre. But a word with you first."

For privacy I took him to the nearby passengers' lounge. "Mr. Tyre, I think you're too hard on the midshipmen."

He reflected. "I'll obey every order you give, sir. Please tell me exactly what you want me to do."

"Ease up on them."

He wrinkled his brow. "I'm afraid I don't understand. Should I ignore their violations?"

I lost patience. "No, just ease up. Consider this a warning. Keep riding them and you'll get a surprise you won't like."

His face clouded with dismay. "I'm terribly sorry I've offended you, sir." Agitated, he ran his hand through his hair. "I try so hard," he muttered, half to himself. "I really do, but people misunderstand . . . I wish I could figure . . ."

Abruptly his gaze returned to the present. He stiffened, almost coming to attention. "I didn't think I was riding them hard, but I'll try my best to do what you ask. I'm truly sorry, sir." He seemed near tears.

I left him for the bridge.

All that day we disembarked passengers and unloaded cargo. I checked the manifest: a poly synthesizer was indeed on our cargo manifest and would be off-loaded with the next shipment. I stayed on the bridge, not sure why. I was free to leave the ship. Should I remain aboard, considering the wardroom tension and my problems with Ardwell Crossburn?

No, we were docked at a distant port. I'd be blessed if I'd let those two joeys ruin my leave. I put on a fresh uniform to go shoreside. Too bad Derek couldn't accompany me. Or Alexi.

Waiting for the aft lock to cycle I abruptly turned away, leaving the startled rating to gape at my retreating back.

I stalked down to Level 3, to the crew privacy room, where Alexi opened at my knock. He seemed fresh and rested. Cadet Rafe Treadwell stood proudly at attention in his new gray uniform.

"As you were, cadet. Mr. Tamarov, come with me. Mr. Treadwell, do you think you can you obey orders exactly?"

"Aye aye, sir."

"That's 'yes, sir'." Alexi, with disgust.

Rafe looked abashed. "Yes, sir, I mean."

"These are your instructions. Lock the hatch when we leave and open it only when you hear my voice or Mr. Tamarov's. Understand?"

"Yes, I—which do I say?" he asked Alexi.

"Aye aye, sir!"

"Aye aye, sir." Rafe's anxious glance darted between us.

I couldn't help smiling. "Very well." I went back to the ladder. Alexi followed, worried. At the airlock I keyed the caller. "Bridge, this is the Captain. I'm going groundside, alone."

"Very well, sir." Lieutenant Chantir would log me out.

"Come along," I snapped at Alexi. The sentry gaped. I glared. "You have a problem, sailor?"

"No, sir!"

"I'm going groundside, alone. Note it in your report."

He was a slow thinker. "But the midshipman—?"

I fixed him with a cold glare. "What midshipman?" Eventually the man smiled weakly. We cycled through the lock.

We boarded the waiting shuttle. As we sat I said to Alexi, "Detour is quite interesting. If you weren't confined to ship, I'd show you the town." Comprehending at last, his face lit with pleasure.

For the rest of the day we wandered Nova City. Detour, with a population of only sixty thousand, was far less developed than Hope Nation, though it was growing fast.

The countryside bore the fresh scars of construction I'd expected to find in Centraltown. Trees and bushes grew in profusion, planted in their thousands by the terraformers, who'd brought insects and worms to aerate the soil, nitrates to fertilize it, and seeds to sow our crops. After seventy-six years of their labor, the terrain surrounding Nova City had at last begun to resemble home.

I wondered how much of the food chain they'd managed to introduce. Did Nova have rats, or mice? Cockroaches? I never did find out, but I did notice a few flocks of birds overhead. We also saw grain scattered in oversize bird feeders, among the fields.

Alexi relaxed further as the day wore on, grateful both for my company and the respite from his nightmare aboard ship. "It's beautiful, sir. If only the air were easier to breathe."

"They're working on it." Huge skimmers sucked air into the desulphurization works, which removed sulphur oxides from the air. The plants had been operating for decades, and Detour's sulphur level was measurably reduced.

After several false starts, not knowing how to begin, I blurted, "I'm sorry for what you're going through."

He stiffened. "I'm under orders not to discuss it, sir. I'm told it's bad for morale."

"They're countermanded."

"Aye aye, sir. I hate his guts! I want to kill him!"

I glanced at him, shocked. He meant it. "Don't, Alexi."

"He's a monster! You don't know the half of it, and I won't tell you."

"Can you hang on?"

His smile was bleak. "I'm like Derek, sir. I can take anything."

"I'm hoping he'll reform. If not, then we'll see." It wouldn't be fair to Philip to tell his subordinate about my deadline.

"I'll call him to challenge, when we get home."

I sucked in my breath. Alexi truly intended to kill Philip Tyre. "Why not challenge him in the wardroom, then?"

He shot me a look of reproach. "I believe in law and order like you do, sir. It's the first middy's place to run the wardroom. I owe the ship loyalty, I owe the same to you. Even to him."

My fists bunched. Philip had three times sent this youngster to the barrel. "Still, tradition allows wardroom challenges."

"I've always thought that's for younger joeys. A way for them to let off steam if they can't take it. I believe in the Navy and its rules. The regs can't permit this to go on. If I thought that, I'd have to quit the Service. Either he'll step over the line and be brought up on charges, or there'll be some other solution. I'm not going to fight the system."

I said quietly, "Alexi, you're the finest officer I've ever known." He was startled. "You've been my friend since I first came aboard. You have such decency. I've never known you to be mean-spirited or spiteful."

He shook his head. "Just watch if I ever get a chance with him!"

"Still. I respect you enormously. I love you as a friend and comrade." He turned away, but not before I saw his eyes glisten. I rested my hand on his shoulder. "Let's have something to eat before we go back." After a moment he nodded. We found a restaurant. After the meal Alexi insisted on paying for us both.

Two hours later we were back aboard. Alexi resumed his babysitting duties, while I went to the bridge.

I shared a watch with Vax when the ship's caller buzzed. "Captain, you'd better—Midshipman Tyre reporting. We have a, um, situation here, and—"

I snarled, "Report by the book, middy. Two demerits!" If the boy thought he could niggle over every petty infraction by his charges, then himself get away with—

"Aye aye, sir! Midshipman Philip Tyre reporting, from the Level 2 lounge. Ricky Fuentes is—that is, Jared Treadwell has a knife; he's taken Cadet Fuentes hostage and says unless he gets his children back he'll—"

I was halfway to the hatch. "Vax, page Mr. Vishinsky to the lounge! Three seamen with stunners. Flank!" I dashed out.

I don't remember using the ladder but I must have plunged down at least three steps at a time. I fetched up panting against the Level 2 corridor bulkhead, outside the lounge.

Philip Tyre poked out his head, saw me, slipped into the corridor, saluting. "They're inside, sir. The far end. I tried talking to him but he—"

I brushed the middy aside, strode in. Behind me, the hatch slid shut.

Ricky's right arm dangled as if useless. Jared Treadwell, Rafe's father, had an elbow wrapped around the boy's throat, holding him nearly off the floor. Ricky's head was pressed tight into Treadwell's chest. The cadet's good hand pawed at the throat hold, seeking air.

The knife was poised a millimeter from Ricky's eye.

Treadwell's voice was a snarl. "Want to bet I c'n take an eye before you stun me?" His swarthy face glistened with a sheen of sweat.

"Easy, Mr. Treadwell. Just put—"

"You think this is how I wanted it, Seafort?"

"No, of course not—"

"Give me my son! And Paula!" The knife flickered. Ricky's breath hissed in terror.

From the corridor, pounding feet.

"Mr. Treadwell, Ricky Fuentes has nothing to do with—"

"We tried petitions. We tried going through the courts. No matter what, you had to have your way!" A wrench of his elbow; Ricky squealed. "Call Rafe in here, or so help me, I'll blind him."

The hatch burst open. I whirled. "Out, until I call!"

"But—" The master-at-arms.

"Out!"

Vishinsky backed through the hatch. I spun back to Jared Treadwell. "Listen, sir, I know you're upset—"

"No more talk! I'll do the first eye to show you I mean it!"

I roared, "By Lord God, you'll let me finish a sentence!"

It was so ludicrous he was stunned. So was I, but I knew for Ricky's sake I had to keep the initiative. I flung off my jacket. "You don't need the cadet. You have me."

"Get away!" The knife flicked; Ricky moaned.

"I'm your hostage." I moved closer.

"Don't, sir!" Philip Tyre, behind me. I hadn't seen him enter.

"This was my doing," I said. Fitting that I pay the consequences.

"Sir, you mustn't!"

"Another word, Mr. Tyre—just one—and you're dismissed from the Service." My tone was ice. "Now, Mr. Treadwell . . ."

"Here goes the eye."

"Do it and I'll kill you. With my bare hands." Something in my inflection gave him pause. I took another step.

His manner became almost conversational. "Irene went groundside this morning. Three lawyers she called, all she could reach. The first told her nothing could be done; you'd already ordered the judge not to hear the case. The others wouldn't even talk."

Another step. "You'll let the boy go. I'll take his place." Now I was quite near.

"You leave us nothing, see. No law, no court, no appeal." Suddenly his voice was a shout of torment. "Who appointed you Lord God?"

I swallowed. Who, indeed?

Mrs. Donhauser had warned me, months back, of the hazard I'd blundered into. Protecting children was a basic human urge. And I'd set it against me.

"Mr. Treadwell." My tone was more gentle. "First, let the boy go. I'll take his place. Then we'll call Rafe and Paula. If they want to leave with you, I'll allow it. Else, they stay."

"What good's that, after you've brainwashed them?"

"Would you keep them by force?"

"No. Yes. I don't know what—Lord, help me!" A rasping breath, akin to a sob.

I gave the terrified cadet what I hoped was a reassuring smile. "Ricky, in a moment Mr. Treadwell will set you free. Mr. Tyre, when I sit down in that chair, take Cadet Fuentes out to the corridor and explain to Mr. Vishinsky. Then bring Cadets Paula and Rafe Treadwell to the lounge."

"Sir, if he takes you host—"

"*AYE AYE, SIR! SAY IT AT ONCE!*"

"Aye aye, sir!"

I sat, kicked my chair to within Jared Treadwell's reach. For a moment we were frozen in anguished tableau.

With a cry of hurt, Ricky tumbled free to the deck. Treadwell wrenched back my hair, caught my chin, yanked upward. His knife dug at my throat. It took all my strength not to move. Please, Lord. Keep the children safe from harm.

In the edge of my vision I caught sight of Ricky's face. It was unharmed. "Philip, take him—"

"Shut up, Captain!" The knife pressed.

"—out to the corridor. Flank."

"Aye aye, sir." Tyre darted forward, helped Ricky to his feet. The two of them stumbled out.

Silence. Then Treadwell's voice came in a hiss. "I hate you. I hate your arrogance, your certainty that you're doing right no matter how much you hurt others. If it weren't for my children, I'd slit your filthy throat and have done with it!"

I made a sound.

"What?"

"I said, do it."

"Jesus, you're crazed."

I could think of nothing to say.

A knock on the hatch. "Are you all right, sir?"

The knife tightened. "No tricks!"

"Fine, Mr. Vishinsky. Remain outside."

Now that the die was cast, I felt more peace than I had in months. I waited, watching the hatch. "They'll be here in a moment, I think. If I might suggest . . ."

"Hah. As if I care what you—"

"Do you want your children to see you with the knife?"

"There's no way I'm letting you—"

"I give you my word I'll sit still." My chin ached. It was hard to talk, with his fingers grinding into me. "Do you want their sympathy or their horror?" Nothing. "Mr. Treadwell, you haven't a chance to persuade them if they see you hurting me."

"Are you insane? Why would you help me?"

I thought a long while. "So the test will be fair."

His hand wavered. "Shut up. I want to despise you."

A knock. A tremulous voice, from outside. "Cadet Rafe Treadwell reporting, sir."

I said quietly, "Put the knife away, Mr. Treadwell. I'll stay seated where you can reach me."

His moment of decision. Slowly, the knife lowered, disappeared. "Go ahead. Betray me." Vast bitterness.

"Come in, Cadet."

Rafe entered, snapped a rough salute. He hadn't had much time to practice. "Sir, I heard—what's . . ." He gave up, came to a ragged version of attention.

"As you were, Rafe. It seems your father wants you to go ashore. To resign. I'm willing to let you."

"No!"

Behind me, a hiss of breath.

The boy cocked his head, looked at his father strangely. "Jared, why are you doing this? I'm a cadet now. I'm where I want to be."

"You can't just walk away from your family." Treadwell's voice was hoarse. "You're barely thirteen."

"Old enough to enlist."

"And you left us nothing but a note. You didn't have the guts, the courtesy to tell me to my face!"

The boy's eyes teared. "Would you have listened?"

I said, "Rafe, it may have been a mistake. You decided so fast. Wouldn't it be best if—"

"You said it was for five years, and I couldn't change my mind!"

I nodded.

Rafe cried, "That's what I want, not a chance to back out! You think it was easy, signing up?" His jaw jutted. "See what you've done, Jared? Now he'll have me whipped for insolence. Can't you leave things alone?"

At the hatch, a knock.

"Son, I . . ." Mr. Treadwell sounded uncertain. "Your mother and I, we thought—" His voice broke. "Rafe, why do you run from us?"

"Because I'm not your son!" Rafe's face twisted. "I'm a creche boy. Sheila was my nurse, and Martine. I had forty brothers and sisters. God, how I miss them!" He ran fingers through his short-cropped hair. "It was your choice to creche us as babies. When you took us out, Paula and I warned you: we weren't really a family. Irene paid no attention, and neither did you."

"She's your mother!"

From the hatchway, a quiet voice. "She was once." Paula. Her eyes roved among us. "Are you all right, Jared?"

"I—yes, I think so." Her father seemed uncertain.

"Captain, sir?"

"I'm not hurt."

She took two steps in, halted. The rebuke in her face pinned Jared to the bulkhead. "Why did you break Ricky's arm?"

"He tried to get away, and I needed—"

"The poor joey is hunched in the corridor, crying. He

won't go to the Doc until Mr. Seafort is safe. Nobody wants to hurt Ricky. He's too good-natured. How could you?"

"I—" No words came.

She faced me, came to attention. "Sir, Mr. Tyre said you had a question for me?"

"Do you want me to annul your enlistment?"

"No, sir."

Her gaze, when it met her father's, held pity, and something more stern. "I'm sorry, Jared, really I am. But it isn't the way you thought it was."

My mouth was dry. They wouldn't be leaving *Hibernia* with their father. That meant his attention would be turned to me. So be it. "Cadets, you're dismissed."

Paula saluted, turned to the hatch. Rafe clumsily imitated her motions. Seated, I couldn't return salute; instead, I nodded.

"Before you go . . ." I was proud of them, and probably wouldn't have another chance. "You've done well. This isn't your fault. No matter what happens—" It was the wrong line. I cleared my throat, and tried again. "The Navy will take care of you. That's all."

"Yes, sir." Paula hesitated. "May I?" I nodded. "Jared, I'm sorry. For hurting you, for Irene, for all of us. Please don't make it worse." Another salute, and she was gone. Her brother followed.

A hand, on the back of my neck. I flinched, steeled myself.

"There's nothing left. Except you." Treadwell's voice was ragged. "At least I can see that you don't ruin any more lives."

"Yes." I raised my head, exposing my throat. "If I . . ."

After a moment, he said, "Well?"

My voice was unsteady. "If I come for you, afterward. It's just a dream. Sooner or later, I'll go away."

"Lord God." A whisper.

Then a sob.

Eventually I lowered my head. It was beginning to cramp.

Vax smoldered; I did my best to ignore him. After a while I gave up. "Get it said, Lieutenant."

"How could you let him go!"

"You'd rather I hanged him? And then ate at mess with his children?"

"He threatened you with a knife!"

"I'm unhurt. He's groundside, so's Irene, and the matter is closed."

Vax shook his head with stubborn negation. "If I may say so, you—"

"No, that's enough. I understand you disapprove."

Vax subsided, muttering.

Earlier, in the quiet of the lounge, I'd picked up the knife Jared Treadwell had let fall, tossed it aside. Half a dozen steps saw me to the hatch. "It's all right, Mr. Vishinsky. Dismiss your detail."

"Sir, is he—"

"Help him remove his things from his cabin, and escort him to the lock." I turned to Ricky. "You'll be all right, boy. To the sickbay. Now."

"Aye aye, sir. Did he hurt—Captain, I'm sor—"

Philip Tyre snapped, "Cadet, two demerits. About-face, march! When the Captain gives an order, jump. I'll deal with you in the wardroom!"

I managed to hold my tongue until Ricky was out of sight. Then, "Mr. Tyre, you argued with your Captain, twice!" I shook with fury. "My compliments to Lieutenant Chantir, and tell him I'm displeased—no, tell him I'm thoroughly disgusted—with your conduct, and he's to correct it forthwith!"

Philip blanched. "I didn't mean—aye aye, sir!"

"Go!"

After, I leaned against the bulkhead. Rafe and Paula were in quarters, the master-at-arms with Jared Treadwell, Ricky having his arm attended. Philip had gone to his chastisement.

I stopped at my cabin, changed my shirt, sat awhile on my starched blanket.

My life had been at risk, and I felt nothing. Well, perhaps not quite that. When the knife had fallen, I'd felt relief. But not much.

I'd think about that later. Time to return to the bridge.

From my seat beneath the blank screens, I reviewed the Log. Mr. Chantir had recorded a caning. Philip Tyre was banished to the wardroom. I sighed. Now more than ever, the boy would lash out at his juniors. And of all of them, Derek had been pressed the hardest.

I thumbed the caller. "Mr. Carr to the bridge."

A few moments later Derek appeared, his uniform immaculate, hair brushed neatly. "Yes, sir?"

I indicated the chair next to Vax. "I need you tonight, Mr. Carr. Assist Mr. Holser. A double watch." Absolutely unnecessary, docked at an orbiting station.

"Aye aye, sir." Derek knew better than to question orders. I could say nothing to explain. Abruptly his eyes flooded with gratitude, as he realized I was keeping him out of Philip Tyre's reach.

"Mr. Carr has had a hard day, Lieutenant. If he dozes, let him be."

"Aye aye, sir." Vax's face lit. "We'll manage."

Satisfied, I went to bed.

The next day we began taking on passengers for Hope Nation and Earth, as well as cargo of metals and manufactured goods. I noticed from the manifest that we would carry the Detour Olympic team home to Earth for the decennial interplanetary Olympics. I suspected the exercise rooms would be well used.

"Aft line secured, sir." Lieutenant Holser, at the aft airlock.

"Forward line secured, sir," Lieutenant Crossburn, at the forward lock.

I tapped my fingers, waiting for the routine to play itself out.

"Forward lock ready for breakaway, sir."

"Aft lock ready for breakaway, sir."

"Very well." I blew the ship's whistle three times. "Cast off! Take her, Pilot Haynes."

In response to the Pilot's sure touch, our side thrusters released jets of propellant, rocking us from side to side. We broke free.

Lieutenant Crossburn, on the caller. "Forward airlock hatch secured, sir."

"Secured, very well." I paced the bridge while the Pilot

held our thrusters at full acceleration, speeding us ever farther from the station and Detour's field of gravity. In two hours, we'd be clear enough to Fuse.

Our return voyage had begun. Seven weeks to Hope Nation, then the long grim journey home. I would endure it. I must. I settled into my chair to prepare coordinates.

At last, all was ready. "Engine room prepared for Fusion, sir."

I looked to the Pilot, raising my eyebrows. He nodded.

"Fuse the ship." I ran my finger down the screen and the drive kicked in. The stars faded from the simulscreen. We entered the subetheral realm of nonspace, sailing from Detour on the crest of the N wave we generated.

That evening at dinner I played host to several young members of the Olympic team. Though sociable and friendly, they seemed unimpressed by the honor of the Captain's table. They talked animatedly among themselves, including me on occasion merely out of courtesy. After months among passengers who'd taken seating at the Captain's table so seriously, I found their attitude refreshing.

Later, restless, I wandered the ship, where excited passengers explored corridors, lounges, and exercise rooms they'd soon find all too familiar. I wandered back to Level 1. Outside the wardroom Rafe Treadwell stood at attention, his nose to the bulkhead. Well, he'd asked for it. Enlistment was his own choice.

I slept badly, still keyed up from the bustle of departure. I knew it would take days to settle back into the dreary routine of Fusion. Nonetheless, I haunted the bridge, with nothing to do.

"Have you noticed the Log, sir?" Lieutenant Chantir pointed to the past two days' entries. *"Mr. Tamarov, slothfulness, three demerits, by Mr. Tyre. Mr. Tamarov, uncleanliness, two demerits."*

So it had started again. I snapped off the Log without comment, leaned back.

"How long will it go on, sir?"

I opened one eye. "Until I say otherwise, First Lieutenant Chantir."

He flushed. "Sorry, sir."

"You're a good officer," I said. "But don't nag."

His smile was weak. "Aye aye, sir." He changed the subject. "Have you ever played chess, sir?"

I came awake. "Yes, why?"

"I'm not very good, but I like to play. I'll bet your puter plays a mean game, though."

"Thank you." Darla, in a dignified tone.

"I can't play on the bridge, Lars. You know that."

"Really? Captain Halstead played all the time. I loved to watch. Once he actually beat the puter."

The speaker said, "She must have had an off day."

"Butt out, Darla," I growled. Then, "He actually played on watch?" Hope stirred.

Chantir said, "Sure, when we were Fused. What else is there to do?"

"Isn't it against regs?"

"I read them again, sir, before bringing it up. They say you must stay alert. They don't say you can't read or play a game. All the alarms have audible signals, anyway."

"I'll warn you if we have a problem," the puter said helpfully.

"Is this a conspiracy? Darla, did you ever play with an officer on watch?"

"Lots of us do. Janet said she sometimes let Halstead win just to keep his spirits up."

" 'Captain Halstead' to you. Janet is their puter, I suppose? When did you talk to her?"

"When her ship docked at Hope Nation to bring you your only intelligent officer, Midshi—I mean, Captain Seafort. I tightbeamed with her as a matter of routine."

"Who did you play chess with, Darla?"

"Captain Haag, of course. He wasn't much of a match." She sounded disconsolate.

I was flabbergasted. Justin Haag, whiling away the hours playing chess with his puter? I debated. "All right, set them up."

She won in thirty-seven moves.

It relaxed me so much that I stood double watches just to be near her. After a week I rationed myself to one game a day; any more and I'd become addicted. When a game was over I busied myself studying my moves.

One happy day I forced a draw. A few hours later Alexi reported for duty, relieving Lieutenant Crossburn, who had radiated his silent disapproval during my game.

I was still jovial. "Take your seat, Mr. Tamarov."

He gripped the back of his chair. "I'm sorry, sir, I can't sit." A vein throbbed in his forehead.

My contentment vanished. "Have you been to Mr. Chantir?"

"I just came from his cabin." He stared straight ahead at the darkened screen.

"What for?"

"Nothing, sir. Absolutely nothing." A long moment passed. "Sir, I want to resign from the Navy."

"Permission refused," I said instantly. I hesitated. "I'm sorry, Alexi." I didn't know what else to offer.

"Yes, sir." His voice was flat. He added, "Do you have a reason?"

"For what?"

"Waiting. Not doing anything about him."

"You're out of line, Mr. Tamarov."

"I don't think I care anymore, sir."

I cast aside my rebuke. "Yes. There's a reason." I nodded to the hatch. "You're relieved, Alexi. Lie down for a while."

"If you don't mind, sir, I'd rather stay here." I understood. On the bridge he was safe from the first middy.

"Very well." I let him wait out the watch. Afterwards I ordered him to Dr. Uburu for healing ointment. He had no choice but to go. I think he was grateful.

I played no more chess for several days.

Mr. Crossburn performed his duties satisfactorily, as always. On his free time he roamed about the ship, asking questions. He finally exhausted the matter of the Treadwells.

Mr. Vishinsky brought me the news first. "Captain, I've been interrogated by one of our officers." He stood at attention beside my chair.

"What about, Mr. Vishinsky?" No need to ask by whom.

"About Captain Haag's death, sir. About how the launch happened to explode, and how the puter came to be glitched. An implication was made that it was no accident."

My heart pounded. "You know better than to tell tales on a superior officer, Mr. Vishinsky. You're rebuked."

"Yes, sir." He appeared undisturbed. "What should I do when he questions me, sir?"

"If he orders you to answer, do so. Obey all orders else place yourself on report."

"Aye aye, sir. May I go?"

"Yes." I watched him leave. "Thank you," I added, as the hatch closed behind him. I willed my heart to stop slamming against my ribs. Crossburn was a lunatic. He was only a step from endangering the ship.

As soon as my watch was done I went to my cabin. I stared into my mirror. "You're the Captain," I told my image. It gave no response. "You have the authority. Remember Vax's story about his uncle, the lawyer? He had to remind himself that his clients weren't in trouble because he'd failed them, but because they had fouled up in the first place."

I scowled at myself in the mirror. "So why do you feel guilty?"

A rhetorical question; I already knew the answer. If I were competent, I'd have found a way to avoid this mess.

"But don't they have it coming, nonetheless?"

I started at myself for a long while, then sighed. I still felt guilty.

At lunch I chose to sit next to Mr. Crossburn instead of at the small table where I would be undisturbed.

He started almost immediately. "What kind of man was Captain Haag, sir?"

"Well, I was just a middy. To me he seemed remote and stern. They say he was an excellent navigator and pilot." I took a bite out of my sandwich, decided to give Mr. Crossburn more rope. "His death was a tragic loss."

He seized the opportunity. "How could a puter glitch have gone undiscovered so long, before it destroyed the launch? If you're sure it wasn't known earlier, that is."

I spoke very quietly. "I can't tell you now. See me after lunch; we'll talk then. I have a job for you."

"Aye aye, sir." We ate in silence. I pretended not to notice his speculative glance.

I waited for him in my cabin. When the knock came I went out, shutting my hatch behind me. "Come with me,

Lieutenant.'' I took him down to Level 2, through the lock into the launch berth, where our new launch waited in its gantry. "This is where it was," I said. He looked puzzled. Of course this was where it was. Where else would you stow a ship's launch?

"I need someone I can trust." Galvanized, he leaned forward with excitement. "It might have been sabotage," I said with care. "A bomb hidden in one of the seats. It could happen again. I need you to check the seats."

"You mean take the seats apart? Unbolt them all and remove them?"

"That's right." I waited while he thought it over. "I know I can trust you, Lieutenant Crossburn. With your Admiralty connections you're invaluable."

A look of satisfaction crossed his face. "I'll get a work party on it right away."

"Oh, no." I looked alarmed. "Nobody must know. If it really is sabotage, we can't tip them off. Do it yourself."

"Alone?" He seemed disconcerted. "It'll take all day, sir."

"I know. It can't be helped. Unbolt all the seats, take them out, open them for inspection. I'll come back later to see how you're doing. We won't put the seats back until we're sure they're all right."

"Aye aye, sir." His tone was doubtful. "If you're sure that's what you want."

"Oh, yes," I said. "Very sure." I left him.

I posted orders at the launch berth hatch that no one was to enter, and went about my business. An hour before dinner I went to check on him.

About half of the fourteen seats had been removed, their components spread about the bay. Crossburn had draped his jacket over one of them and pulled off his tie. I found him in the launch, on his back under one of the seats, struggling to work loose the bolts.

"Good work, Lieutenant. Find anything yet?"

"No, sir. Everything's normal." He wriggled out from underneath the seat.

"No, stay where you are. I'll be back later." I went to dinner. I ate well.

It was past midnight before he finished reassembling the launch. I met him coming out of the berth, face smeared with grease, jacket slung over his arm.

I whispered, "You're sure there was nothing, Lieutenant?"

"Absolutely sure, sir." He seemed anxious to get to his cabin. I could imagine how the night's diary entry would read.

"I knew I could count on you." I walked him through the lock. "Now we know the launch is safe, for the moment. I want you to check it again tomorrow."

He went pale.

"Is something the matter?"

"But, sir," he stammered. "We just disassembled all the seats. We know there's no bomb there."

I leaned close. "There isn't now. During the night they might try to put one in."

"Sir, that's not—"

"We have to know for sure." My voice grew cold. "Unbolt and disassemble all the seats again first thing tomorrow. That's an order."

"But, sir—"

I was icy. "What does an officer say when he hears an order, Mr. Crossburn? Or didn't your uncle tell you that?"

"Aye aye, sir! I'll start again in the morning, sir!" He knew enough to retreat.

I returned to my cabin.

The next day I checked him at lunchtime. Again, seats were strewn all over the bay. I went to lunch, fueled by a grim satisfaction. I timed him; it took Lieutenant Crossburn just over twelve hours to tear down and reassemble all the launch seats. Having started just after breakfast, he was done by ten in the evening.

The next morning I was on the watch roster. Mr. Crossburn arrived, scheduled to share the watch. "Lieutenant, you're relieved from watch. I have a more important job for you. Tear down and recheck the launch seats."

He stood slowly. "Captain, are you sure you're all right?"

"I feel fine." I stretched luxuriously. "Why do you ask?"

"You can't want me to tear the launch apart three days in a row, sir."

"Can't I? Acknowledge your orders, Lieutenant."

Stubbornly, he shook his head. "Sir, I insist that you put them in writing." He spoke with confidence, knowing I would do no such thing.

"Certainly." I snapped on the Log and took a laserpencil. "I order Lieutenant Ardwell Crossburn to remove and disassemble all the seats on the ship's launch and check them for hidden explosives before reinstalling them, as he has done each of the past two days. Signed, Nicholas Seafort, Captain." I showed it to him. "Is that in proper form, Lieutenant?"

He was trapped. "Aye aye, sir. I have no choice."

"True. You have no choice. Dismissed."

Alone on the bridge I played chess with Darla. I was ahead on the fourteenth move when the caller buzzed.

"Sir, Lieutenant Chantir." He sounded grim. "I have Mr. Tamarov in my cabin with eleven demerits. I'm sorry, but I will need your written order before I proceed." He was a decent man, and he'd had enough.

The moment was approaching. "Certainly, Lieutenant. Come to the bridge at once." When he arrived I handed him a paper. He glanced at it. "I protest your order, sir."

"I understand. Carry it out anyway."

"May I ask why, sir?"

"Tomorrow at dinner, if you still want to." That puzzled him; he saluted and left the bridge. I lost my game to Darla.

That night before going to bed I stood again in front of my mirror. I didn't like the face I saw. I told myself what I was doing was necessary, and didn't believe a word of it.

Restless and uneasy, I left my cabin again. I passed Lieutenant Crossburn's cabin, once Mr. Malstrom's. On the spur of the moment I went to the infirmary. Dr. Uburu was there, reading a holovid.

"Good evening, Captain." She saw my face. "What's troubling you?" Only the Ship's Doctor could ask the Captain such a question. Perhaps it was the reason I'd gone to her.

I slumped in a chair. "I've used a friend, manipulated him, and I'm disgusted with myself."

"Yours is a lonely job," she said. "Sometimes one can't do directly what must be done. Is it for the good of the ship?"

'I think so," I said. "I'm not sure."

"We're seldom sure, Nic—Captain. If you believe it's for the good of the ship, isn't that enough?"

"Then why am I miserable?"

"You tell me." It was a challenge, in its calm, quiet style. I avoided it. "Because of my weakness, I guess. I wish I were wise enough to find another way."

"I absolve you." She smiled at me. "Sleep well tonight."

"I don't want a pill."

"I didn't offer one." I started for the corridor. "I wish I could help you, Captain," she said. "But you have to help yourself." Puzzled, I went back to my cabin. I went to bed and slept peacefully.

In the morning I met Alexi and Derek at breakfast. Both studiously avoided my eye. At noon I took my place on the bridge. Vax Holser and I sat in silence. When the watch was done I thumbed the caller. "Mr. Tyre, bring Mr. Tamarov to the bridge." Vax looked at me curiously.

The midshipmen arrived. "Permission to enter bridge, sir." Philip Tyre's voice was firm and vibrant. He snapped a smart salute.

"Granted." They came to attention. "Darla, please record these proceedings. I, Captain Nicholas Seafort, do commission Midshipman Alexi Tamarov to the Naval Service of the Government of the United Nations and do appoint him Lieutenant, by the Grace of God." Alexi was stunned.

Philip Tyre swallowed, his face ashen.

"Mr. Tyre, you are dismissed. Lieutenant Tamarov, you will remain." With jerky motions Philip Tyre saluted, turned, and left the bridge. As soon as the hatch closed Vax leaped up with a whoop. He pounded Alexi on the back.

"Easy, Mr. Holser, you'll kill him!" Vax's brotherly blows could break ribs.

"Congratulations, Alexi!" Vax turned to me with a wide grin. "It's wonderful news, sir." Alexi didn't move.

"You're free, Alexi," I told him quietly. "Free of him."

"Am I?" Alexi spoke without inflection. "Will I ever be?" Unbidden, he sank into a chair, wincing. He began to sob.

Shocked, Vax withdrew a step. I motioned him to wait in the corridor.

After a time Alexi gained control of himself. "Why did you leave me there so long?"

"So you'd be sure." I despised myself.

"Of what?"

"I already have three lieutenants; you won't be overwhelmed with duties. I'm putting you in charge of the midshipmen. Put things back in order."

He thought about it. Silence stretched for over a minute. "Don't," he said in a small voice. "I beg you; don't put me in charge of him."

"It's done. Those are your orders."

"I swore an oath to myself, Mr. Seafort. I won't be able to stop."

"I wanted you to be certain whom you were dealing with." I stood. "So I waited until it was absolutely clear. Perhaps too long. I'm sorry, if that's any use." I was too ashamed to meet his eye, so I paced, my eye traversing the bulkheads. "It's a long cruise home. I have the welfare of the other midshipmen to consider. Keep them safe, Alexi. Do what you must."

He put his head in his hands, then rubbed his face. He offered a tentative smile. "Sorry, sir. I've been a bit . . . emotional lately. It's like waking from a nightmare."

"I know what that's like," I said. "Believe me."

# 28

The next day I called the engine room to give Chief McAndrews private instructions. Then I summoned Mr. Crossburn and handed him a written standing order to disassemble and inspect the launch seats every day until further notice.

He looked around wildly, as if for escape. "Captain, I can't do that. Not all day, every day!"

I was inflexible. "You can and you will."

"I protest, Captain!"

"Noted. Begin your work."

"No, that's crazy!"

"What did you say?"

"I said no! You can't mean it."

"Mr. Crossburn, come with me." I led him, protesting, down the ladder to the engine room, to the lower level at the fusion drive shaft. The plank I had ordered the Chief to make ready was set across it; Mr. McAndrews stood by, his face a grim mask.

"Stand at attention and look at the shaft." Crossburn did so.

"This is where I hanged Mr. Tuak and Mr. Rogoff. And the rebels who tried to take over the ship. It's been a rough voyage and we're on the way back to Miningcamp, where we were attacked once before. *Hibernia* is in an emergency zone, Mr. Crossburn, and war rules apply. I tell you now, if you refuse to obey an order, I will hang you. Be silent and think about it."

I gave him ten minutes. Then I released him. "Go to the launch berth."

Shaken, he complied. "Aye aye, sir." Then he added angrily, "You can be sure my uncle will hear of this!"

"Two months pay, Mr. Crossburn, for insolence and insubordination. Anything else?"

"No, sir!" He fled.

I looked at the Chief, let out my breath.

He asked, "What if he'd refused, sir?"

"I'd have had to proceed." A sudden thought. "Would you have let me?"

"By the regs, I couldn't stop you."

"That was no answer." I decided not to press. I'd made enemies of them all, abovedecks. Why alienate the Chief as well?

Several days later I shared a watch with Philip Tyre. He looked pale and shaken. I said nothing.

Vax chose to keep me informed. "Alexi's all over him, sir. Demerits for attitude, for sloppiness, for inattention. Twice he's sent him to the barrel outright, in addition to the demerits."

"I know. I can read the Log."

"Yes, sir. Philip is going to have an interesting cruise."

He would indeed. Alexi was slow to anger and I doubted

he would be faster to forgive. I shrugged. Tyre had made his bed.

"When are you going to let him off, sir?"

"I'm not."

Vax looked awed. "All the way home? Eighteen months?"

"Seventeen and a half." I wondered how soon I could start counting the days.

The Olympians had taken over Level 2, jogging endlessly in the circumference corridor, swinging from the bars in the exercise room, doing push-ups on the mats. From time to time Philip Tyre joined them, sweating profusely in strenuous effort, supervised by a stern and watchful lieutenant.

Soon we would Defuse for a navigation check. Then a few more days to Hope Nation, and our mooring. We'd remain there only two days, just enough to take on passengers for the trip home. Somewhere below me would be Amanda, but I wouldn't see her again.

Dr. Uburu came to the bridge to speak to me. "Captain, Lieutenant Crossburn has been questioning your sanity. He wants me to join him in removing you."

"Is he correct?"

She looked at me thoughtfully. "I don't think so. You might be vindictive, but not insane."

"Thanks so much."

She smiled. "Captain, do you recall when the Chief, the Pilot, and I met to find a way to stop your taking command?"

"Yes."

"I can't believe how wrong we were. This is a jinxed voyage, Captain. *Hibernia* will go down in Navy legends. There's nothing that hasn't gone wrong for us. And you've coped with it all. You've done better than anyone had a right to expect."

I looked at her to see if she was serious, angry at her blind stupidity. "Leave the bridge at once, Doctor. That's an order!"

"Aye aye, sir." She saluted and left, unfazed by my anger. She thought well of me, perhaps, like the foolish seamen in the Hope Nation bar. But I knew better. I had Philip Tyre and Ardwell Crossburn to add to my long list of failures.

Days later, Lieutenant Chantir told me Philip had been sent to him again. Lars was obviously unhappy.

"I don't need daily reports, Lieutenant. Just do your duty."

"I will, sir. It's not a pleasurable one."

"Even with Mr. Tyre?"

"Even with him, whether he earned it or not."

"It's the first lieutenant's job, Mr. Chantir." I brightened. "However, if your arm bothers you I will excuse you for medical reasons."

He considered it. "My arm is troubling me somewhat, Captain. Not enough to see the Doctor, but it's noticeable."

"Very well." I summoned Alexi. "Mr. Tamarov, the first lieutenant has a sore arm. Move the barrel to your cabin. That duty is yours until further notice." Ruefully, Mr. Chantir shook his head. Alexi, expressionless, saluted and left.

I went to the launch berth every day at random hours. I always found Lieutenant Crossburn at work.

I shared a watch with Philip Tyre. He walked carefully onto the bridge and eased himself into his chair. "Good morning, sir." His tone was meek, his eyes riveted on his console.

"Good morning. I'd like you to run docking drill today, Mr. Tyre."

"Aye aye, sir." I called up the exercise and he began his calculations. Halfway through, he stopped and looked up. "It isn't fair, sir."

"What isn't?"

"What he's doing to me. I can't stand it. Please."

"What are you talking about, Mr. Tyre?"

"Mr. Tamarov. He's after me all the time!"

"Are you complaining about your superior, Philip?"

He didn't have the sense to deny it. "Not exactly complaining, sir. I'm just telling you."

"Oh, no, Mr. Tyre. That won't do. My compliments to Mr. Tamarov. Please tell him I'm annoyed with your conduct. Right now."

"I've just been there," he wailed. "He'll cane me again! Please, sir. Please!"

I raised my voice a notch. "And six demerits for disobedience, Mr. Tyre. Another word and it's six more." He fled the bridge to meet his fate. Never again did I hear a word of complaint from Philip. On the few occasions that I saw him he appeared miserable. It bothered me not at all.

* * *

At last it was time for our nav check, before a final jump to Hope Nation. "Bridge to engine room, prepare to Defuse."

"Prepare to Defuse, aye aye, sir."

I waited.

"Engine room ready for Defuse, sir. Control passed to bridge." The Chief's familiar voice came steady over the caller.

"Passed to bridge, aye aye." I set my finger at the top of the drive screen while Derek watched. "Let's see where we are." I traced a line from "Full" to "Off".

"Confirm clear of encroachments, Derek." A normal check, hardly necessary but part of the routine. He checked his instruments.

"Hey! An encroachment, sir, course two hundred ten, distance fifty-two thousand kilometers!"

I gaped. "What?"

"Encroachment, sir. There's something out there."

"It can't be. We're interstellar." I puzzled. "A stray asteroid, perhaps. How big is it?"

"I read two hundred sixteen meters, sir." Darla.

"Small for a planetoid. What's it made of?"

"Metal," Darla said. "Too far away to see, but it's radiating on the metallic bands."

I thumbed the caller. "Mr. Haynes to the bridge. And Mr. Chantir." No, Lars Chantir had a fever and was in sickbay. "Belay that summons, Mr. Chantir. Mr. Holser to the bridge."

Vax came bounding in. He stopped to take in the situation. A few moments later Mr. Haynes arrived, breathing hard. The Pilot slipped into his customary seat. "Morning, sir." He glanced at the sensors. "Want to go take a look?"

"Good morning, Pilot. I think so."

Vax nodded. "If we're this close, we might as well check it out." I hadn't asked his opinion, but he didn't seem to notice. "It's probably just a hunk of ore skewing Darla's calculations."

"Button it, joey!" Darla flared. "I remember the last time you insulted me!"

"Cool it, Darla. He meant no harm. Pilot, put us on an intersecting course."

"Aye aye, sir. Just a moment." Pilot Haynes was carefully affable. I felt a twinge of guilt. He thumbed his caller. "Engine room, auxiliary power."

"Auxiliary power on standby."

"On standby, aye aye. All ahead one-half. Steer two ten, declination twenty degrees."

"All ahead one-half, aye aye. Two ten at twenty degrees."

After two hours, the Pilot at last began braking maneuvers.

I cleared my throat. "Mr. Holser, start calculating Fusion coordinates for our jump, please. No need to waste time."

"Aye aye, Captain." Vax reluctantly tore his eyes from the simulscreen and tapped figures into his console.

We were closing fast. "Maximum magnification, Darla."

"Whatever you say, boss." The screen flickered.

The unmistakable outline of a ship.

"Holy God!" The Pilot was on his feet.

Vax looked up from his calculation and froze.

The Pilot whispered, "One of ours!"

I swallowed. Not again. All those people. "Focus on the disk, Darla." Pointless; we were already at maximum magnification.

The image expanded slowly as we neared. Darla obediently narrowed her view to the ship's disk.

A gash ran across all three levels, right down to the engine room, as if parts of the hull had melted. The entire disk was open to vacuum.

The name stood out against the gray metal of the hull.

"*Telstar*!" Vax whispered. "Gone, like *Celestina*. No lights, no power. No signals."

There might somehow be survivors. "Pilot, bring us alongside. Mr. Holser, organize a boarding party. Three seamen. We'll take the gig."

"Aye aye, sir. Shall I go with them?"

"No."

"Lieutenant Tamarov, then?"

"No. Me." I saw Vax's expression and added, "I need to know firsthand what happened." For a brief moment I recalled Captain Van Walther, and the crowds of travelers who visited the memorial he'd left on *Celestina*. With shame I suppressed the comparison.

Vax was stubborn. "It could be dangerous, sir. Don't leave the ship."

"This time it's in good hands. Mr. Chantir, Alexi, you. I'm going across; don't argue."

I'd left him no choice. "Aye aye, sir."

I made it even clearer. "Lieutenant Holser, you will remain aboard under all circumstances."

"Aye aye, sir." His tone was glum.

I smiled. "Besides, I'll be all right. I'll carry a rad meter and stay away from jagged metal. Don't be my nanny." That produced a reluctant smile.

The Pilot carefully maneuvered us to within two hundred meters of U.N.S. *Telstar*. With gentle applications of the thrusters he brought us to rest relative to the stricken vessel.

"Vax, be prepared to Fuse as soon as I'm back. Derek, come help me with my suit."

We went down to Level 2. I took my regular suit from its bin in the launch berth lock and began to struggle into it. Then I stopped; I might want to clamber around the outside of *Telstar*'s hull. "Get me a T-suit, Derek."

A thrustersuit was cumbersome but had the advantage of greater mobility. In my own suit I could walk, step by magnetized step, across the surface of *Telstar*'s outer hull, but in a T-suit I could lift off from the hull and skim over for a better look. At Academy I hated regular suit drills but loved the T-suit instruction.

I stepped into the semirigid, alumalloy reinforced suitframe. Derek handed me the helmet; I slipped it into the slots and gave it a half turn. Derek locked the stays into place; I double-checked them all. I had no intention of accidentally breathing vacuum.

With a grunt Derek lifted the heavy tank assembly and clipped it to the alumalloy supports on the back of my suit. We strapped the propellant tanks into place. My helmet's sensor lights flashed green; I was ready to go. Derek's hand fell on my arm and lingered. "Be careful, sir," he said softly. "Please."

I shook loose my arm. "Remember you're a Naval officer, Mr. Carr." He meant well, but a midshipman must know better than to touch his Captain, no matter how many vacations they'd taken together. Sometimes Derek had no sense of propriety.

The three sailors were suited and waiting. We cycled through the lock and clambered into the gig. "Open the hatch, Vax," I said into my suit radio.

"Right, sir." I jumped; his voice was loud in the speaker.

All seamen were given a modicum of training on small boats; I gestured to a sailor I knew had additional experience. "Go ahead, Mr. Howard. Take us across."

A couple of squirts sent us gently out the hatch. We glided across the void. From *Hibernia*'s bridge, the distance to *Telstar* seemed small, but from the tiny gig it was immense. We neared the silent ship.

"Steer past the disk, Mr. Howard." At negligible speed we drifted past the rent in the fabric of *Telstar*'s hull. The edges of the tear appeared to have melted and run. What could have generated so much heat?

"What's the radiation reading, Mr. Brant?"

The sailor held the rad meter steady. "None, sir. Nothing at all." Odd. If *Telstar*'s drive had blown, we'd find substantial emissions.

When the trouble arose, *Telstar*'s drive couldn't have been ignited, or we'd never have found her in normal space. *Telstar* had Defused at the usual checkpoint, as we ourselves had, to plot position before proceeding past Hope Nation to Miningcamp. With a six percent variation for error, that meant she could have Defused anywhere within eight million miles of where we'd emerged. Pure luck that we'd stumbled upon her.

If *Telstar*'s drive was turned off, what could have vaporized her hull? I had no answer. Whatever it was, we had to know, lest the same happen to us or other vessels in the fleet. I remembered Darla's glitch and shivered. "Mr. Howard, take us to within a meter of the hull. Mr. Brant, open the hatch and get another reading up close."

A moment later Brant put down the rad meter. "Still nothing, sir. The hull isn't hot."

"It could have been hull stress, sir."

I jumped. "Damn it, Vax, lower your voice before you give me a heart attack. And that's no stress fracture. We'll see what we find inside."

I had Mr. Brant transfer to *Telstar*'s hull. He planted a magnetic buoy from our gig at his feet, activated it, hooked our mooring line to it. Now, if one of us pushed against the boat as he stepped off, the gig couldn't drift away and leave us stranded.

We climbed out onto *Telstar*'s hull. Her locks were sealed from within; the simplest way to board was to drop through the gaping hole into one of the cabins. The edges of the tear were rounded and smooth, minimizing the risk of ripping our tough-skinned suits.

"You first, Mr. Ulak. Take a light with you." The seaman jumped down through the hole, into *Telstar*. "What do you see?"

"Just a mess." He opened the cabin hatch, peered into the corridor. "Come on down, sir. We can walk around easy enough."

"Be careful, sir." Vax sounded anxious.

I climbed into the opening in the hull and jumped down.

I was in a passenger cabin.

Everything loose had been swept out in the decompression. A bed remained, bolted to the deck. A sheet drooped forlornly from one corner. I swallowed.

"Vax, we're on Level 2. The corridors are dark, but we all have lights. Mr. Brant, explore Level 2. Mr. Howard, Mr. Ulak, go down to the engine room; see if you can figure out what caused the damage. Vax, it doesn't look like any of the disk sections are sealed. I'll go up to Level 1 and try to get onto the bridge."

"Take one of the men with you, sir."

"Don't nag, Mother."

I clambered along the debris-strewn corridor. Flotsam flung about by the decompression had settled everywhere, making the ship seem grossly untidy. I walked slowly, checking hatches as I went. Many were closed, but none were sealed from inside. I climbed the ladder to Level 1.

I passed the wardroom, then the lieutenants' common room. The hatch was slightly ajar. I opened it, stuck my head in.

"Oh, Lord God!" My scream echoed in my suit. I flung out my arms, stumbled back in terror.

"Captain! What is it?" Vax was frantic.

I gagged, swallowing in a frantic effort to hold down my gorge. "Unh! God. I'm all right, Vax. A corpse. Somebody in a suit, with a smashed helmet. The head is damaged, like it was eaten away. Something must have penetrated the helmet." It had been inches from my nose.

I breathed deeply over and again, in an effort to slow my pounding heart. The adrenaline had left me trembling. I sagged against the bulkhead, steadying myself. "Sorry."

"Let me come across, sir!"

"Denied. Stay on the bridge. I'm all right; I just got a fright." I headed for *Telstar*'s bridge. "I'm trying to figure out what happened here. Right now I'm about ninety degrees along the disk from the damage." If I kept talking, I wouldn't have to think about what I'd seen. "The cabin where I found the corpse had no hull damage. I guess something ricocheted down the corridor and hit him just as he opened the hatch. Okay, I'm at the bridge now."

I slapped the hatch control, to no effect. "The bridge is sealed; I'll never be able to get in without tools. I'll check the remaining cabins past the corridor bend." A figure moved in the dim standby light. "Mr. Ulak, is that you?" I hurried toward him. "What did you find belo—"

I froze.

"Captain?" Vax.

My mouth worked. No sound came.

"Sir, are you all right?"

I produced a small whimper, like a child in a nightmare. Urine trickled down my leg.

"Say what's wrong!" Vax bellowed.

I whispered, "Ulak. Brant. Howard. Back to the gig, flank! Mr. Holser, sound General Quarters! Battle Stations!"

I tried to back away. My feet seemed glued to the deck. The figure in the corridor quivered. It wore a kind of translucent suit that sat legless on the deck, flowing from an irregular base to near my own height.

Globs of matter seemed to flow along the skin of the suit. A jagged patch on the suit, a meter above the deck, contracted and expanded again. Colors flowed.

I willed myself to step backward. "There's something here! It's alive and it's not human." Why did I whisper when nothing could hear through vacuum? I took another step. "Lord God . . ." *We ask thy mercy, in this our final hour*.

"General Quarters! Man your Battle Stations!" Vax bellowed orders into the caller. "Mr. Carr, seal the bridge!"

The creature moved. I couldn't see how. It . . . flowed toward me. I took another step back, then another.

It moved again. It changed shape as it flowed, then regained height. It seemed subtly changed.

Suddenly I understood.

"Oh, Lord God, it isn't in a suit! That's its own skin; it can live in vacuum! Vax, it's changing shapes!" A surge of adrenaline freed me to move. The creature darted away, heading the opposite direction along the corridor. It moved with breathtaking speed.

I turned and ran. "Ulak, Brant! Where are you?"

"Back at the gig, sir! Hurry!"

I stumbled down the ladder, the steps pulling at my magnetized feet.

"Howard reporting. I'm in the gig. Where is it, sir?"

"I don't know!" Panting, I pounded down the corridor. I risked a glance backward. Nothing.

"Oh, Jesus Lord! It's coming out of the hull!" A shriek.

"Launch the gig!" I shouted. "Back to the ship! Don't wait!"

Vax roared, "Belay that! Pick up the Captain first!"

"Go!" I gasped for breath, racing to the cabin I'd first entered. Wait. I skidded to a stop. If one of the beings was emerging from a tear in the hull, it must be in one of these cabins. I couldn't get out the way I'd come.

"We're clear of the hull! Captain, come on out, we'll try to reach you!"

Vax. "Man the lasers! Seal all compartments!"

I keyed my caller. "Mr. Howard, back to the ship!" I raced to the ladder to Level 3. "I'll come out below!"

"We're thirty meters distant, sir! Where are you?"

"Engine room!" I swung my light wildly around the darkened compartment. Stars glinted through a breach in the hull. I clambered toward it, squeezed myself through. In a moment I stood on the hull, trying to spot the gig against the black of interstellar space.

There, about fifty meters aft.

"Here!" I waved my light.

"Right, sir." Seaman Brant maneuvered the gig closer. "That . . . thing is halfway out of the hull, behind you." I spun around; an alien form quivered in a gap in *Telstar*'s hull, over one of the cabins. My skin crawled.

I remembered my jets, touched the nozzle control at my side. I lifted off. Clear of the infested ship, separated from whatever scampered in its corridors, I felt weak with relief. Still, I floated alone in space, with no protection but a suit. I hadn't even thought to go into *Telstar* armed.

*Hibernia* shrank perceptibly. I shuddered. Vax was moving the ship clear to Fuse. To abandon us. Helpless, I calculated distances. My panic ebbed. He was only turning the ship to bring her lasers to bear. "Darla, record!" I shouted. "Full visuals!"

"I have been, sir." Her voice was calm. "Ever since you took the gig."

I keyed my thrusters, propelled myself toward the gig's silhouette.

Someone moaned.

A voice; a sailor in the gig. "Our Father who art in heaven, hallowed be thy name; thy kingdom come, thy will be done, on Earth as it is in heaven . . ."

With a squirt of my side jets, I rotated to face *Telstar*.

A plump oval shape drifted from behind the dead ship. It looked, Lord God help me, like a huge goldfish with a stubby tail. It was almost half as large as *Telstar*.

It pulsed. A mist spurted from an opening near the tail. It glided past the hull toward us. Colors flowed on its surface. Rough-surfaced globs projected from its sides.

I found my voice. "Gig, back to *Hibernia*! Flank!" I slammed on my thrusters, veered away from the gig, spun toward my ship.

The creature I'd found within *Telstar* recoiled against the hull, launched itself at the fish as it floated by. It touched the being's side and clung there for a moment, growing smaller.

The surface of the huge creature seemed to flow. The being outside of it disappeared, absorbed within.

One of the rough globs on the goldfish lengthened, began

to spin in a slow, widening circle. It gained momentum. Abruptly it detached and flew directly at the gig.

"Look out!" My cry came too late. The projectile splattered on the gig's hull, oozed along its side. The gig's alumalloy frame sputtered and melted beneath the glob.

A choked scream, suddenly cut off. The gig's engine flared and died. The glob ate away at the gig's hull. Frantic motion, in the cockpit. Metal dripped onto a suit and pierced it. There was a visible rush of air. Blood, a wild kick, then nothing.

I looked back at the goldfish. Another, much larger projectile began to wave.

"Vax!"

"Yessir, I'm coming!"

"Fuse the ship!"

"Jet this way, sir! Hurry!"

"Fuse! Go to Hope Nation! Save the ship!"

"You're almost aboard, Captain!" *Hibernia*'s bow drifted around.

An icy calm slowed my slamming heart. "Mr. Holser, Fuse the ship at once! Acknowledge my order!"

"Captain, move! Jet over here!"

The fishlike being released its projectile. The mass whipped toward *Hibernia*. It struck the gossamer laser shields protruding from the nose ports. They disintegrated in rivulets of metal.

Vax shouted, "Fire!" The tracking beam of *Hibernia*'s laser centered on the goldfish, just now drifting clear of *Telstar*. A spot in its side glowed red. The skin colors swirled. The goldfish jerked as if in convulsion.

The creature's skin swirled and opened to form half a dozen tiny holes. Droplets of fluid burst from them. The goldfish slid away toward the protection of *Telstar*'s hull. The laser followed, centered again on the side of the fish. More holes spouted protoplasm. Abruptly, it was behind *Telstar*.

In slow motion I drifted across the void. *Hibernia* had to be saved, regardless of my fate. "Fuse! For God's sake, Vax! Obey orders!" I was frantic.

"Hurry, sir! Use the forward airlock! Alexi, cycle the lock!"

I was too far from the ship. The enemy might come out

at any moment. I sobbed with rage and frustration. "Vax, Fuse!"

"Hurry, Captain!"

I was beside myself. *"VAX, FUSE THE FUCKING SHIP!"*

His soft response came clear in my speaker. "No, sir. Not until I have you aboard."

Cursing, I accelerated until I was almost upon the ship, then flipped over and decelerated full blast as Sarge had taught us years before, at Academy.

I'd waited too long. I sailed into the airlock feet first, still decelerating. My feet smashed into the inner hatch just as I snapped off my jets. I crashed to the deck.

The outer hatch slid closed. I scrambled to my feet, in a frenzy for the chamber to pressurize. Alexi's anxious face stared through the transplex. The hatch slid open. I stumbled aboard.

"Captain's on board!" Alexi slammed shut the hatch.

Vax roared, "Engine room, Fuse!" I felt the engines whine. Alexi lifted the jets from my back while I unsnapped my helmet stays. Rafe Treadwell, white-faced, helped a sailor pull me out of my suit.

My wet pants clung to my legs. "Are we Fused?"

Alexi grabbed the caller. "Mr. Holser, Captain asks if we're Fused."

"Yes, sir. Energy readings are normal. Fusion is ignited."

I trembled with rage. "All officers to the bridge. Everyone! I'll be along in a minute." Yanking my other arm free of the T-suit I pushed past Rafe and half ran up the ladder to my cabin.

Inside, I stripped off my pants and shorts with mindless haste and threw on a dry pair of slacks. I stumbled out of the cabin, buttoning my pants as I ran toward the bridge. I slapped the control; the bridge hatch slid open.

Derek, Alexi, Vax, and the Pilot stood by the console. Behind them were the Chief and Mr. Crossburn. Philip Tyre waited uncertainly by the hatch.

I crossed to my chair. For a moment I stood holding to the back of it. Mr. Chantir came in, pale, breathing hard. Dr. Uburu followed.

Vax came close. "Are you all right, sir?"

"Get away from me!" I shoved him.

"Lord God." We all turned to Dr. Uburu. She bowed her head. "Almighty Lord God, we thank you for our deliverance from evil. We ask you to bless us, to bless our voyage, and to bring health and well-being to all aboard."

"Amen." I murmured the soothing word with the others, feeling the Doctor's calm and strength flow into me. "Good heavens." My voice was quieter. I sank into my chair. "Darla, did you get that?"

"Every bit of it." Her tone was grim.

"Play it back."

"Aye aye, sir." Thank Lord God she knew not to be flippant.

Her screen flickered. Mesmerized, we watched her recording of *Telstar*'s torn hull while our past conversation flowed from the speaker. "I'll go up to Level 1 and try to get onto the bridge."

A long pause. My bloodcurdling scream, and Vax's shout. "Captain, what is it?"

I spoke over my recorded reply. "It must have been one of those—things that smashed his suit visor. Then it did something to his head." I tried not to retch.

On the speaker, I whimpered. Then, "Battle Stations!" Vax's shouted commands. For a moment nothing changed on the screen. A spacesuited man appeared, scrambling into the gig. Then another. After a moment the third.

The speaker said, "Oh, Jesus Lord! It's coming out—"

"Freeze!" The image hung frozen, in response to my order. "Maximum magnification." The screen swooped in on the amorphous shape halfway out of the hole in *Telstar*'s hull. Blobs of color set almost at random in the outer skin.

"Christ, it looks like an amoeba!" said Lieutenant Chantir.

"Don't blaspheme!" I studied the screen. "It can't be single-celled. Not if it's that large."

"I don't ever want to know," Alexi muttered. I glared him into silence.

"Go on, Darla." The image began to move. The gig pulled clear in response to my order, drifted alongside the dead ship, waiting for me to emerge. I jetted toward the gig, tiny against the bulk of the dead ship's hull. The bizarre goldfish floated from behind the hull. In space, I twisted to look at it. Sickened, I watched the destruction of the gig amid my own frantic shouts to Vax. "Fuse! Go to Hope Nation! Save the ship!"

The commotion blared from the speakers. "Fuse! For God's sake, Vax! Obey orders!" I listened, unwilling, to my desperate pleas and Vax's repeated demands that I hurry. Then Vax Holser's soft voice said the irretrievable, damning words. "No, sir. Not until I have you aboard."

I put my head in my hands. "Turn it off." My words hung flat in the sudden silence. A long moment passed. I got heavily to my feet. "Darla, please record." Her cameras lit.

I faced Vax. "Lieutenant Holser, you deliberately disobeyed your Captain's orders to Fuse, not once but five times. Without question you are unfit to serve in the United Nations Naval Service. I suspend your commission for the remainder of our voyage. I will not try you, as I am not capable of judging you fairly. I have already concluded you should be hanged." Dr. Uburu gasped; the Chief closed his eyes, shook his head.

"I will, however, recommend a court-martial on our return, and I will testify against you. For the remainder of our voyage you are forbidden to wear the Naval uniform or to associate with me or any officer. You will be moved to a passenger cabin at once. Get off my bridge!"

Vax's face crumpled. He tried to speak, couldn't, tried again. His huge, beefy fist pounded the side of his leg once, twice, three times as he fought for control. Then he took a deep breath. "Aye aye, sir," he whispered. His face was ashen. He turned, marched to the hatch. Alexi slapped it open, and he was gone.

No one spoke or moved. "I am Captain here," I grated. "No one, not one of you, will ever disobey my order again. Not now, not ever!" I studied their faces. "I should have hanged him for mutiny." I walked among them, stopping in front of each. "I didn't hang you either, Mr. Crossburn, for your refusal to do your duty. I won't make the mistake again, with any of you. I warn you all."

The silence was absolute. "We will maintain a three-officer watch at all times until our arrival home. You will all participate. Not you, Doctor, but everyone else. We are at war. There will be no inattention to duty, no idle talk." My lip curled. "No chess." I studied them again. "Pilot, Mr. Chantir, Mr. Tamarov, you have the watch. The rest of you are dismissed."

I took their murmured "Aye aye, sir" in silence. The four off-duty officers filed out. I watched the Pilot and Lieutenant Chantir at their consoles for several minutes, before leaving the bridge.

I went to my cabin, sealed the hatch. Mechanically I took off my jacket, my shirt. I stripped off my pants. I stepped into the shower, stood under its hot spray for a quarter of an hour. After, I dried myself and sat on my bunk. I waited for the inevitable reaction.

My stomach churned. I ran to the head, reached it just in time. I vomited helplessly, again and again, heaving against nothing. I shuffled back to my bunk clutching my aching midriff.

When the alien had appeared in *Telstar*'s corridor I was utterly terrified. But whatever it might have done, facing it would have been easier than going on with my life.

# 29

I stayed in my cabin all that evening and into the next day. I sent for my meals. When I ventured into the corridor it was only to stalk to the bridge. I stood my watch in absolute silence, then returned to my cabin.

On the second day I went with reluctance to the dining hall, because it was my duty. There was little conversation at my table; my haggard face discouraged anyone who might have tried to speak.

After dinner I walked the ship, past the wardroom, the lieutenants' cabins, the bridge. I took the ladder down to Level 2. I strode with unvaried pace and frozen expression. I passed the cabin to which Vax had been exiled. Passengers I met in the corridor stood aside.

I went down to Level 3, past the crew berths. Knots of crewmen were gathered in the corridors, talking softly. I ignored them. I went into their berths, looked about. I checked the crew exercise room, their lounge. In the engine room, the Chief stood stolidly at attention with his watch while I glanced around, then left.

I climbed up to Level 2. In the corridor young Cadet Fuentes came to attention. "Are we all right, sir? Did anything follow us?"

"Cadet, go to Lieutenant Tamarov for discipline." My tone was harsh. "Don't speak to the Captain unless he speaks to you!"

I knocked on the wardroom hatch. Derek opened. Paula Treadwell was lying in bed in her shorts, half asleep. Philip Tyre looked up from his bunk. Printouts of regulations were stacked on his blanket. I turned to leave and collided with Rafe Treadwell, just coming in. He jumped to attention. I ignored him.

I went back to Level 2, through the lock to the launch berth. Lieutenant Crossburn was carrying a seat onto the launch. He said nothing, his face grim. I turned on my heel and left.

I went to the infirmary. "I won't be able to sleep tonight, Doctor. What will you give me?" I was brusque.

She looked at me a moment. "I'd prefer you tried to sleep first."

"I don't care what you'd prefer. Give me something."

Still she hesitated. "Why can't you sleep, Captain Seafort?"

"Because I'll think."

"About what?"

"You said this was a jinxed ship, Doctor. I'm the jinx. I didn't make the revolt on Miningcamp, or create the life-form out there, but when things go wrong I ruin people. If I'd been a leader, Vax would have obeyed orders and he'd still have a career. Now I've destroyed him. And Philip, and Mr. Crossburn, and Alexi. And others. Give me the pill."

She hesitated, then got it from the cabinet. She held it out. "Don't take it until you're in your bed. And not before midnight."

"All right."

"Do you promise?"

I smiled sourly. "I promise." I thrust the pill in my pocket and went back to my cabin.

I took off my jacket and tie and sat in my chair to wait out the evening. Below, Vax would be alone in his cabin; I closed my eyes and waited for the pain to abate. After a time I eyed my spacious quarters.

I hated this cabin. I hated the ship.

I wondered why the creature on *Telstar* hadn't hurled one of its globs at me. Certainly *Hibernia* would have been better served. I no longer had a reason to live. My career was shattered. I'd be separated by light-years from the woman I cherished. I had no friends. And, worst of all, I'd done it all to myself.

A knock. Annoyed at the interruption, I flung open the hatch. Chief McAndrews stood waiting. "What is it, Chief?"

"I need to talk to you privately, sir."

"Not now. I don't want to be bothered."

"It's important."

The gall of the man. I was Captain. "Another time. Go below."

"No." He pushed past and shut the hatch behind him. I was stunned. He said quietly, "You can't go on like this, Nick."

Hope stirred. "You've come to relieve me?"

He raised his eyebrows. "No. I've come to talk sense into you."

"This is mutiny! I'll have you hanged!"

"You'll do as you see fit." His voice was stony. "When I'm done." He shoved out a chair. "Sit."

Numb, I sat. He pulled up another chair.

"You're walking the ship like death warmed over, and it gives everyone the willies. Why?"

I looked to the deck. "Because I can't stand how badly I do my job. Because I hate myself."

"Why is that?"

"I've done my best and failed. I was friends with you, once. I ended that. I brutalized Alexi, the cadets, even Derek. Instead of inspiring the men, I threaten to hang them. Sometimes I do it. I caused Sandy's death along with all the others. I savaged the Pilot and I destroyed Vax. Do you need more?

I'm ruining Philip Tyre and Ardwell Crossburn. I broke up the Treadwell family for my own amusement. I killed three men in the gig because I was too stupid to circle *Telstar* before mooring to her hull. And the worst is, it will go on. Either I fail my oath to Lord God, or I continue making things worse!'' My eyes stung.

He asked, as if puzzled, "Why must you do that to yourself?"

"Do what?"

"Cast everything you do in the worst possible light. Why do you never give yourself credit?"

I waved it away, with contempt. "For what?"

"You intuited a glitch in Darla and saved us from catastrophe. You took us to Hope Nation on course and on schedule without commissioned officers. You had the guts to carry out Captain Malstrom's executions, and steadied the crew for the long haul. You saved us all at Miningcamp. Can't you see it?"

"I killed Sandy! I killed Mr. Howard and the others! Can't you see that?"

He shouted, "No! No one can, except you!"

I recoiled in shocked silence.

"God damn it, Nicky, you're as good a Captain as *Hibernia* ever had! What in the bloody hell is the matter with you?"

"I'm not! A Captain leads! Look at Justin Haag—no one would dream of questioning him. I have to bully everyone! That's why they dislike me so."

"Who?"

"Vax, for one. Ever since I brutalized him in the wardroom!"

"Vax would die for you," he said quietly.

"He can't feel that way!" A tear found its way down my cheek.

"They all do. Derek—you made a man out of him and he reveres you. You can't imagine how strongly he feels. Alexi idolizes you. He'd follow you anywhere."

"But look what I did to him!"

"You didn't do that!" the Chief thundered. "Philip Tyre did!"

I recoiled from his anger. "Philip, then. I set him up, and delivered him into Alexi's hands."

"He deserves it. Alexi's taking revenge. So?"

"I could have stopped Philip, won him over."

His meaty fist slammed the table. "Nobody could stop him! That's why he was sent to you!"

I stopped cold, realizing the truth of that. Doubt began to eat at the edges of my disgust.

"Ricky Fuentes," the Chief said. "He talks of you with stars in his eyes. Paula and Rafe. What made them want to leave their parents to sign up, you idiot? Not the Navy. You!" His vehemence took away my breath. I swallowed.

"Why must you be perfect, Nicky?"

"That's why we're here!" I saw our drab, worn kitchen, Bible open on the rickety table, while Father waited.

"Can you be perfect?" the Chief demanded, as if from a distance.

"No, but we have to try!"

"Is trying ever good enough?"

His voice faded. Father glowered. Sullenly, I glared back. No matter how hard I tried, I could never please him, because I wasn't perfect. Only Lord God could be perfect; only Lord God could be good enough. No matter what I did I couldn't win his approval. Yes, I could be good. I could be excellent.

I could never be perfect.

"It's not fair!" I cried in anguish to Father. He slapped me; my head snapped to the side. But it wasn't fair. Lord God couldn't expect perfection, no matter what Father sought of me. My chest tightened in helpless frustration. If God couldn't expect it, why must I?

Father's visage glimmered; I began at long last to comprehend. I demanded perfection because Father would accept no less. I sought proofs of my own imperfection, as Father must.

My eyes opened. I was in my cabin, with Chief McAndrews. Father wasn't aboard. Unless I brought him with me.

I looked at the Chief. "But I can't lead. Take Vax. He refused to obey a lawful order. I had to destroy him."

"Why did he disobey?"

"Because he was foolish. He wanted to get us back aboard. He risked everyone to save a few."

"Why?"

"I don't know!" I said, tormented. "If I knew I could have stopped him!"

"Because he loves you."

My breath caught in a sob.

"He knew what he was doing." The Chief was remorseless. "He was willing to give up his career for you. Perhaps his life as well."

"But why, after all I did to him?" The rag and polish in the launch berth; before that, the brutal icy showers.

"You saved him from being a Philip Tyre. You were the only one who could do that. He loves you for it."

My hateful words on the bridge echoed. "Oh, God."

"Stop torturing yourself, Nick."

"I've fouled up so badly!"

"Because you weren't perfect." His words hung in the air.

After a long while I forced my gaze to meet his. I took a long breath. "Yes. Because I wasn't perfect."

"But you're a good Captain."

I tried a smile. It wavered. "Am I?"

I could banish Father. I had banished Mr. Tuak, hadn't I?

"Yes, you're a good Captain."

I would miss Father. Perhaps I could learn to live without him.

"I shoved a man out the airlock once," I said.

"I gutted a man once," he answered.

"My God, what for?"

"I won't tell you."

We were silent. Finally I asked, "What do I do about Vax?"

"Decide that yourself."

I sighed. "It's lonely. It's always been so lonely."

He stood, took a step forward. His hands darted toward me, then drew back hesitantly. "I'm going to touch you," he said, for the first time unsure.

I nodded dumbly. He rested his big, powerful hands on my shoulders. He squeezed. I began to cry. After a while I stopped. He sat back in his chair.

"Do you think," I said after a time, afraid of his response, "do you think perhaps, sometimes, you might want to sit with me again? With your smoking pipe?"

"If you wish, sir." His voice was quiet.

"I would like that."

\* \* \*

"We're mated, sir," Alexi reported.

"Very well." I swiveled my chair. "When do they come up?"

"I'd expect them anytime, sir," Mr. Chantir said. "We called last night, if you remember." Now that we were in Hope Station system, I had radioed ahead to Orbit Station, requesting an emergency conference aboard ship with General Tho, Governor Williams, and Captain Forbee.

"Mr. Tyre."

The boy leaped from his seat, stood at parade-ground attention. "Yessir." His blond hair was trimmed shorter than before. His hands and face were scrubbed pink.

"Go to the Commandant's office and find out when they'll arrive."

"Aye aye, sir!" He spun about and marched out. I glanced at Alexi. He returned my gaze, impassive.

I leaned back. "So. One more port safely arrived at. Pilot, an excellent job, as usual."

Surprised, he flushed with pleasure. "Thanks very much, sir."

"Alexi, you're in charge of arrangements here. We leave in twenty-four hours. Make sure the oncoming passengers are told we'll sail two days early. See that our supplies are boarded on time." None of that should be a problem; we'd already radioed instructions.

"Aye aye, sir. If you'll excuse me please, I'll get started now."

I nodded permission. "Lieutenant Crossburn."

"Yes, sir?" Subdued and chastened, he seemed much relieved to be freed from his punishment detail. Defused, we couldn't have our launch out of commission.

"Go below and bring Vax Holser to the bridge."

"Aye aye, sir."

I thumbed the caller. "Chief McAndrews to the bridge." I waited with the Pilot and Lieutenant Chantir.

Philip reported, breathless. "Sir, pardon, please. The Governor is on the station. General Tho is with him. Captain Forbee's shuttle is just docking."

"I'll be with them in a moment. When I call, escort them to the bridge."

"Aye aye, sir." Tyre hurried off. Before, his manner

had been cooperative. Now it was something more intense. Alexi's doing, perhaps.

Vax Holser and Lieutenant Crossburn appeared at the hatchway. Vax seemed ill at ease in borrowed civilian clothes that didn't quite fit.

"Bring him in, Mr. Crossburn."

Vax, expressionless, followed onto the bridge. I stood waiting. The Chief hurried in, stopping short when he saw Vax.

I paced. "You all know I suspended Lieutenant Holser's commission because of his actions the day we found *Telstar*. I have reviewed the matter and I conclude that I made a mistake."

I glanced at the Chief, felt my face redden. "True, Mr. Holser's actions could be construed as mutinous. But I failed to take into account certain mitigating evidence. First, the Captain had left the ship, and because of the emergency, Mr. Holser had no time to summon a superior. For the moment, he was in charge. He chose not to Fuse. It could be argued that as the senior officer present, the choice was his. I don't take that view, but I can't conclude beyond doubt that his action was mutinous, despite my utter disapproval."

The other officers listened, absorbed. Vax, of course, hung on my every word. "Mr. Holser knew Admiralty would take a dim view of abandoning a Captain in interstellar space, and I must take that into account as well." I couldn't mention Vax's true motive, but I knew it now. "Therefore, I revoke my suspension of Mr. Holser's commission and I restore him to active duty. Darla, can you erase a recording I ordered you to make?"

"Yes, Captain. You have to order me to erase it and copy your order into the Log. Then the recording is irretrievably wiped."

I opened the Log and wrote. "Darla, erase my suspension of Mr. Holser from your records."

"Aye aye, sir."

I turned to Vax. "You're reinstated. I still consider your actions reprehensible. They indicate an appalling lack of concern for the safety of the ship. I therefore fine you three months pay and deprive you of three months seniority. I rebuke you."

He stood at attention, his eyes glistening. "Aye aye, sir."

"Put on your uniform and report for duty."

"Aye aye, sir!" A grin broke through his solemnity. With a crisp salute, he turned and strode off the bridge. He broke into a run before he reached the hatch.

"Clear the bridge, please." I thumbed the caller. "Mr. Tyre, escort our guests on board."

Three hours later the shaken Governor walked slowly down the corridor with General Tho, Captain Forbee, and myself.

"You can't stay to defend us, of course," Governor Williams said.

"No, sir. Above all else I have to warn Admiralty."

"Some of our local vessels have lasers, Governor." General Tho. "If we can organize a unified command—"

"You have it," I assured him. "Captain Forbee, put yourself under General Tho's command regarding the defense of Hope Nation."

"Aye aye, sir."

The General looked relieved.

"I can't believe you really found Grone," Captain Forbee said. "That story of his . . ."

"It would explain the epidemic," said the Governor.

"But why an epidemic? Why not bombs?"

I said, "If they're unicellular organisms they certainly understand viruses." We walked in chilled silence.

The General muttered, "If I hadn't seen your holos I'd try to have you committed."

"Judge Chesley would be happy to oblige." They smiled. "Gentlemen, you'll be on your own. I'll warn Miningcamp and shoot straight for Earth. You know you won't have help for three years at least." No radionics could outrun a fusion drive. We'd be seventeen months each way, and Admiralty would need time to mount a response.

"Right." We paused at the airlock. The Governor glanced around uneasily. "I'll feel better back on the surface. Lord God help us all."

The next day was a blur of activity. Supplies, cargo, and passengers were loaded in record time. Later, I'd get a chance to meet our new passengers; for now I was so busy I hadn't even checked the manifest. I remained on the bridge, answering questions and directing the harried crew, breaking only for meals.

The planet rotated below, visible in our screens. Amanda was somewhere below; if I looked carefully I could probably spot Centraltown. I sighed. I would learn to live without her.

At last we were ready to leave. I gave the Pilot the conn. As soon as we cast off the lines he rocked us free.

We drifted ever faster from the station. In an hour we were far enough to Fuse; with deference he returned the conn to me. I fed our calculations to the puter.

"Coordinates received and understood." Darla.

"Chief Engineer, Fuse, please." I burned Hope Nation into my memory before it faded from the simulscreens.

We Fused.

Saddened, I left the bridge to Vax and Lieutenant Chantir's watch, and went below for something to eat.

Passengers milled excitedly in the corridor, exploring the ship. I spotted Derek, grinning foolishly. "Well, Mr. Carr." I fell in alongside him. "You'll be back someday."

"Perhaps, sir." He didn't seem much concerned.

"Why so happy, Mr. Carr?"

"I met the new education director, sir. I think we're going to be friends."

I didn't need a reminder of Amanda. "That's nice," I said, glum. I grimaced at the sealed airlock. "It's going to be a long trip home."

A familiar voice, behind me. "Think so?"

I whirled. Amanda waited, hands on hips.

"Hi, Nicky." She smiled. Her eyes danced as she came into my arms.

# EPILOGUE

"Are you all right, sir?"

I blinked as I emerged into the bright sunlight. My head ached miserably. I swallowed my nausea. Vax hovered; Alexi waited by the car.

"I'm fine." Despite my claim I felt awful from the P and D I'd voluntarily undergone. For three days they'd pumped me full of drugs, questioned me without end. I remembered little of it. Ever-changing faces, persistent demands that I explain in detail each decision I'd made. They'd stripped me of reasons, facts, motives, and exposed my foolish mistakes to the merciless light. I wanted nothing more than to curl up in bed beside my wife.

"What happened, sir?"

"I passed, Mr. Tamarov." I swallowed again.

Alexi guided me to an electricar. "What next, sir?"

"They'll decide whether to court-martial me."

"They wouldn't dare!"

"Watch your tongue, Mr. Holser." Even among comrades I wouldn't allow that.

"Aye aye, sir. Do you want to go back to quarters?" The entire crew had been shuttled from Lunapolis to Houston Naval Base as soon as my report was read, and we were still there.

"Admiral Brentley wants to see me before the Board of Inquiry makes its report. His office is that way." I pointed toward Houston.

"You drive, Alexi." Vax got in the back seat next to me and closed his eyes.

"How do you feel, Vax?" I could guess; he'd had the same drugs as I.

"I've been better. It's all right."

"What will they do with you?"

"They offered me a posting. I'll tell you later, if you don't mind."

I drew back, a little hurt. "As you wish."

We pulled up before the Admiral's sunbaked residence, its yard surrounded by tall, unkempt bushes. A sentry saluted. I paused. "Get some sleep, you two."

Alexi shook his head. "I'm going to round up the others. We'll be back to pick you up when you're done."

I was too weary to argue. "Whatever you say."

The Admiral's entryway was dark and cool. An orderly took me through a sitting room into a sunny first-floor office. I came to attention.

"Carry on." Admiral Brentley's gruff voice suited him. Sixtyish, graying, his athletic body had thickened into the heavy muscle of an athlete's later years. He studied me without expression.

"Aye aye, sir." I chose the at-ease position.

The Admiral Commanding, Fleet Operations, sat himself on the edge of his desk. "Well, Seafort. What do you have to say for yourself?"

With a pang I realized that he knew it all, had seen the reports, heard my testimony, spoken to his nephew whom I had sentenced to the launch berth for most of the return voyage. Our interview was a formality. Court-martial or not, I would never again see command.

"I've nothing to say for myself, sir."

"No excuses, no defenses?"

"No, sir." My voice was firm. "I did the best I could with what knowledge I had."

He regarded me quizzically. "What am I supposed to do with you?"

"Am I to be court-martialed, sir?"

"That's up to the review board." His tone was brusque. "I'm not a member." He walked around the side of the desk and stood looking out the window behind him. "However, they'll damn well do what I tell them to do. It's my fleet.''

I was shocked by his confidence. It meant either that I wasn't in as much trouble as I thought, or I was in so much trouble that what he said didn't matter at all. "Yes, sir."

"I'm not happy with some of your decisions." He tapped a sheaf of papers on his desk. "Pardoning Mr. Herney, for example. And your commutations for the mutineers on Miningcamp."

"I'm sorry you feel that way, sir." I spoke quietly.

"You don't care, do you?" The accusation surprised me. I didn't think it showed.

I wouldn't lie to a superior. "No, sir, not really. I've had months and months to go over it. I did the best I could given who I am and my lack of abilities. I don't expect you to see it that way, sir, but I've learned to live with it." With Amanda, in the long, loving nights in our cabin. With the fumes of the Chief's smoke, across my companionable cabin table.

He growled, "Well, I asked for it. I won't penalize you for the truth." He came around the desk, faced me with arms folded. "I can't court-martial you. The public wouldn't stand for it."

"The public?" What on earth was he talking about?

"Court-martial the hero of Miningcamp? The Captain who saved his ship with pistols blazing?"

"That's utter nonsense!" I said, forgetting myself.

"The crew swears to it." He paused, and added, "Court-martial the first man to make contact with another species? No. I won't do that."

I closed my eyes. My stomach hurt anew. I just wanted it over. "Very well, sir."

"Still, I can see to it that you never board a ship again."

I was only mildly interested. "Is that what you intend?"

He came closer. "There are some things I can't overlook. That business with the circuit judge. It indicates a lack of respect for civilian authority. Couldn't you have handled him more diplomatically?"

I raised an eyebrow. "What business, sir? I don't recall any mention in the Log or Governor Williams's dispatches."

After a moment the corners of his mouth turned up. "Yes.

Well. You covered that nicely. It only came out in the interrogation." He brushed it aside. "The worst of it was leaving your ship to visit *Telstar*. Absolutely inexcusable."

I no longer had anything to lose. I said, in a tone for which I'd have caned a midshipman, "Tell me you wouldn't have gone across to look, in my place."

Admiral Brentley, taken aback by my disregard of rank, seemed to swell. He strode back to his desk, threw himself in his chair. He glowered; I stared back with indifference.

Slowly, his shoulders relaxed. "I would have done exactly as you did, Nick," he said. "I'd have gone over to take a look for myself. I'd want to know what happened to their ship: it was identical to my own."

"Yes, sir. But I still should have circled the ship first."

"Why? To check for aliens? In two hundred years we've never found anything but a few boneless fish on one watery planet. Why should you be on guard?"

I considered. "I wasn't sure, thinking about it. It just seemed I should have been more wary. As I should on Miningcamp. I just opened the locks and stood aside."

"Since when has the Navy gone to Battle Stations to dock at a U.N. orbiting station?" he demanded. "That one, you're clear on. We've already decided. If every Captain has to ready a defense party before opening locks at a station, we'll all go glitched. No, it's the U.N.A.F. Commandant who'll pay for that."

He tapped the reports. "I can go along with most of it, even when your decisions differed from mine. Hell, that's why we send a Captain, to make decisions. We back him up with total authority. Hope Nation is three years out; we can't pull strings from home port." He stopped. "But there's one matter you've forgotten. Lieutenant Ardwell Crossburn. My nephew."

"Yes, sir." I sagged. He would stand by his family; he had to. Blood was stronger than regs. Anyway, my treatment of Crossburn was further proof of my disrespect for authority. What Captain in his right mind would abuse the nephew of his Commanding Admiral?

"He's come to see me several times, Seafort. Some of his reports are shocking. Did you actually make him take the launch apart every day for eighteen months?"

"Almost every day, sir. Not while we were Defused."

"And you thought you could get away with it?" Brentley's tone was menacing.

"I didn't care, sir." I spoke with civility, but I'd had enough.

"He says you're a lunatic. That you're paranoid, you were suspicious of bombs."

"It kept him in the launch berth, sir."

He glared at me. I stared back.

In his eye, an odd twinkle. "You really did that?"

"Yes, sir. I did."

"What do you think of him, Mr. Seafort?"

I could be insolent to him, but I wouldn't lie, though my answer would cost me my career. "He's dangerous, sir. He never should have made lieutenant. He throws his family connections in the face of his seniors, and takes it upon himself to investigate us. I wasn't going to put up with that. I'd do exactly the same again. Or maybe I'd brig him. I don't know."

Brentley shook his head. "Do you know what trouble I went to, getting him out of the Solar System? The wires I pulled so his orders would come from someone else? And you, you ungrateful whelp, you bring him back and dump him in my lap again!"

I snorted. "He was dumped on me, sir. I had no choice. I was under weigh when I found out about him."

He turned away disgusted. "I know. It's not your fault. I never thought it was." He looked up. "You know how he made lieutenant? Some toadying Captain thought I'd be pleased. He did it for me. For me!" The Admiral turned back to me, shaking his head. "By the way, don't worry about challenging that pair of Dosmen who glitched your puter. It won't be necessary; they've been dealt with."

"Good." My tone was dull. What did any of it matter?

"Seafort, I can't give you *Hibernia*. You're too young yet. It wouldn't sit well, even if you are a hero. And your rank as Captain, I can't confirm it."

"I understand, sir. Will I go back to midshipman?"

"No."

A lieutenant, then. It would be hard for me to adjust, but I could do it.

"Actually, I was thinking of Commander," Admiral Brentley said. "I've got a sloop coming in, *Challenger*. Crew of forty-two, two lieutenants, three middies. She takes seventy passengers. I can put you back to Captain after your first trip out, when your youth won't be so offensive to us oldsters. You're only twenty; hardly any of your classmates have made lieutenant yet."

Commander? But that was the same as Captain; the title differed only by a technicality. And a sloop was a full command, with—I forced my attention back to his words.

"She's got a new drive unit, supposed to cut a month off the run to Hope Nation. And she's bristling with lasers. She'll be part of the squadron we're sending. Will you take her?"

I was speechless. Confirmed as Commander, with my own vessel? My mouth dry, I nodded.

"Good. Your wife?"

"Amanda will ship with me." Despite the risk of melanoma T, we'd already decided that, at her insistence. It was unusual, but permitted.

He grimaced. "I don't like that. I'm old-fashioned. But I suppose it's your choice." He went on to another subject. "Oh, I had a visit from your Midshipman Tyre. He begged me to let him resign from the service."

"For what reason?" I remembered Tyre on watch, one long, dreary day halfway home. Unexpectedly he'd put his head on the console and began to weep, in long, desolate sobs.

"Now what, Mr. Tyre?"

"Please, let me out. I want to resign. I can't take any more, sir. Oh, I beg you!"

"Steady, Mr. Tyre."

"They're torturing me! I get caned every week. It hurts so much! I have eight demerits right now, and I've already worked off six since Monday! They're on me every waking minute, both of them." He raised his tear-stained face. "I don't understand, sir. What have I done? Why is this happening to me?"

"You were rather cruel, Mr. Tyre. They haven't forgotten."

"Cruel? How could I have been? I was just doing my

job, sir. I tried to help them!'' I sighed. He would never understand.

"I'll make you an offer, Mr. Tyre. You're a fine midshipman when you're dealing with your superiors. You're competent, courteous, friendly on watch, eager to help. It's your juniors you can't handle. Forget about that part of your job, just ignore them, and I'll pass the word to go easier on you.''

"You mean it would stop?'' He looked beyond me, as if toward heaven.

"I don't think it will ever stop, Mr. Tyre. You've seen to that. It might lighten a bit, though.''

"Yes, sir. Very well, sir. I accept. Please!''

I nodded. I would have a word with Alexi. I couldn't know that a smoldering Derek Carr would choose that very night to challenge his senior middy, to follow him to the exercise room, to beat him coolly into a bloody unresisting pulp, afterward kicking his bruised rump along the circumference corridor back to the wardroom. Derek was effectively in charge of the juniors for the rest of the voyage home.

"The boy wouldn't complain about any of you, not a word,'' the Admiral was saying. "I couldn't get any reasons out of him. I suppose I should let him go, if he's such a weakling.''

It was my fault, in a way. If I had been able to get through to him . . . I sighed. "He still might make a good officer,'' I said. "I can keep him with me awhile.''

Brentley looked relieved. "Another problem settled, then. I can't give you full shore leave, not with an interstellar war on our hands. If I hadn't seen those recordings . . .''

"I know, sir.''

"Who do you want with you?''

"Mr. Carr as a midshipman. Lieutenant Tamarov,'' I said instantly.

"You need one more middy and a lieutenant. Let me know or I'll assign them to you.''

"Aye aye, sir.''

"It's a hell of a thing.'' He stood next to me for a moment, in silence. He held out his hand. "Good luck, Commander.''

I shook his hand soberly. "I'll need it, sir.''

Outside, the sun had lowered toward the horizon; the evening cool was settling on the scrub trees and the fields. Alexi waited on the sidewalk with Vax, the Treadwell twins, Derek, and Ricky. They all stared at me, anxiety, worry, concern reflected in their young faces.

I grinned. "Commander. U.N.S. *Challenger*. I leave in a week."

Alexi whooped, dancing around the car. Vax broke into a grin. "Who do you take, sir?"

"Alexi goes with me. If you don't mind, Mr. Tamarov." He was beside himself, grinning idiotically. "You too, Derek. We're going back to Hope Nation." Carr said nothing, but his eyes closed with relief. "I need another middy."

Midshipman Paula Treadwell would be going to navigation training school on Luna. Ricky was slated for Academy. I had recommended it in the Log; I wanted him to have the best.

"Me, sir?" Rafe looked hopeful.

"Speak when you're spoken to, Cadet," I snapped. Then, "Still, I suppose you'd do. I'd have to promote you to midshipman. Are you sure you're ready for Last Night?"

The fourteen-year-old grinned at Derek Carr. "I can take anything, sir." It had become a wardroom byword, since our aristocratic cadet had made his stubborn vow.

"Very well." I looked at my lieutenant. "What's your posting, Vax?"

"They offered me *Caledonia*, on the Ganymede run. I turned it down."

"Command of your own sloop? Why?"

"I want to sail with you, sir. I told Admiral Brentley if he gave you a ship I wanted to go along."

"You're ready for command, Vax."

"No, sir. Not yet."

"Why not?"

He faced me. "You've taught me a lot. I'm not convinced you don't have anything more to teach. Sir."

My eyes misted. We hung, all of us, in that uncomfortable moment before parting. Ricky Fuentes, gangly and awkward in his early adolescence, came to me hesitantly. We looked at each other. Suddenly he flung himself on me, burying his head in my chest, hugging me fiercely. I gave him a squeeze. "Good-bye, boy. I'll see you again."

"Will you?" His eyes were red.

"Yes. I promise." I regarded our onetime ship's boy with affection. "I have some advice. At Academy, don't hug your drill sergeant, no matter how much you like him. It's bad for your health."

"Aye aye, sir!" He grinned like a foolish puppy.

I eased into the car. "Take me home, people. I'll see you later at the party." I closed my eyes, feeling the car jounce over the potholes. I was going home. To Amanda. To my crew. To my ship.

**David Feintuch** worked as an antiques dealer, photographer, real-estate investor and attorney before becoming a full-time writer. His lifelong interest in the British Navy and the Napoleonic era provided background material for his five-book Seafort Saga, for which he won the John W. Campbell Award as best new writer for 1996.

Raised in New York, schooled in Indiana and Boston, David Feintuch now lives in a small Michigan town. His home is a stately Victorian mansion furnished entirely with antiques, except for his writing room, which has every electronic toy he can find. An inveterate traveller, his other interests include sociology, politics and medieval European history.

# THE SEAFORT SAGA

Look out for these magnificent adventures:

## Challenger's HOPE

An alien attack and an admiral's betrayal leave a wounded
Commander Nicholas Seafort stranded aboard a doomed ship
of arrogant colonists and violent street children . . .

## Prisoner's HOPE

To save the world, Nicholas Seafort must forsake his vows –
and commit an unthinkable, suicidal act of high treason . . .

## Fisherman's HOPE

Alone at the centre of a cosmic apocalypse,
Nick Seafort faces his final battle . . .

## Voices of HOPE

For Nicholas Seafort, the race to save mankind from
destroying itself has become personal – for to save his son,
he must save the world . . .

### THE SEAFORT SAGA

The science fiction adventure of a lifetime.

Published by Orbit

ORBIT

**Orbit titles available by post:**

| | | |
|---|---|---|
| ☐ Challenger's Hope | David Feintuch | £5.99 |
| ☐ Prisoner's Hope | David Feintuch | £5.99 |
| ☐ Fisherman's Hope | David Feintuch | £5.99 |
| ☐ Voices of Hope | David Feintuch | £6.99 |
| ☐ The Still | David Feintuch | £6.99 |

*The prices shown above are correct at time of going to press. However, the publishers reserve the right to increase prices on covers from those previously advertised without prior notice.*

ORBIT

**ORBIT BOOKS**
Cash Sales Department, P.O. Box 11, Falmouth, Cornwall, TR10 9EN
Tel: +44 (0) 1326 372400, Fax: +44 (0) 1326 374888
Email: books@barni.avel.co.uk.

**POST AND PACKING:**
Payments can be made as follows: cheque, postal order (payable to Orbit Books)
or by credit cards. Do not send cash or currency.
U.K. Orders under £10   £1.50
U.K. Orders over £10    **FREE OF CHARGE**
E.E.C. & Overseas       25% of order value

Name (Block Letters) _____

Address_____

_____

Post/zip code:_____

☐ Please keep me in touch with future Orbit publications

☐ I enclose my remittance £_____

☐ I wish to pay by Visa/Access/Mastercard/Eurocard

Card Expiry Date

_____